THOSE WHO
ARE LEFT

THOSE WHO ARE LEFT

JOSH STRICKLIN

ISBN: 0692415335
ISBN 13: 9780692415337

All you could hear was complete silence, and I think I'll never, ever in my life forget that moment.
—Ray Lewis

PROLOGUE
THE BARN

Setting sail.

The walls are going up today. That really puts a sense of finality on the whole thing. It started over with a flood. I don't know what they'll call this exactly. I guess for the most part it's over. There's just this one last thing to do. Something so those who are left can move on. A favor for a friend. I really believe that everyone, at least once in his or her life, wants to do something the entire world cares about. Something that matters. I think this is probably my turn to take a swing at that. No one is ever really ready for what they're forced to do. But we make it. That's what I think is most important to remember when flipping through these pages. We make it. I was told that when this was completed, I would be finished. I don't know why, but that makes me nervous.

If another survivor walked into this nearly empty room, that person might see a man sitting on a stool in the white glow of an LED electric lantern as it casts panels of light along the walls, banishing the darkness to oblivion. The visitor would maybe notice the blue-and-red-patterned carpet and the two full-sized beds against the wall. The visitor would see the woman lying on the bed across the room, attached to an IV drip. What that person wouldn't see is the story of the past week. Sure, the visitor would see the bruises and wounds, but that would only be the moment right before the credits roll in the movie—the part when everything has already happened. The visitor would ask what happened to her, but I would just shut the door with him or her on the other side. Before that, though, the visitor would undoubtedly notice a rusty typewriter sitting on the middle of the table, one of the heavy black ones with the circle buttons. The visitor may even make a comment saying he or she didn't think they made those anymore. This visitor would see the little black circles and the metal L-shaped pieces that rise up and slam a letter onto the paper. There's a chance the visitor would notice the reams of paper sitting at the foot of the stool, but he or she wouldn't be looking that hard. The visitor would only see the constructed metal instrument sitting plainly on the table. But where our visitor sees a square foot of antique keyboard, I only see a minefield of letters. I remember hearing of Al Davis once, that playing with a clenched fist was encouraged, and at this point that idea is the only thing I can think about.

Chapter 1

I always felt safe in the barn. Maybe it was the gun cabinet or the assortment of blunt instruments—shovels, posthole diggers, and, my current favorite, the pickax—that could be used to make quick work of what Mark would undoubtedly call marauders. He has a way with words. Occasionally, we'd get a violent wild animal or a wanderer from town holing up in the field, eating the vegetables. It's pretty surprising which of the two we had to threaten with the branch cutters more often. Before all this happened, I owned a considerably large farm. I inherited the place, but in time it became mine just as it was anyone else's. I employed a number of people. Their families counted on our work to survive. I say that more for me than anyone else. Now no one counts on what I used to do. They only count on what I do now—this. I assume one of the little bald doctors with the clipboards will come wanting to know what I was up to, but then I'll have more important things to worry about than my profession—like this. For all anyone else here knows, I was a carpenter or accountant. Although I could have just as easily been a murderer.

The barn was sort of my home away from home. About one hundred yards away. I always went there to unwind. When the barn was rebuilt, I had a small office put in one of the far corners. It was soundproof, smell-proof, windowless, and air-conditioned. A lot happened for me in the barn. When Sarah and I were on the verge of divorce, I used the futon multiple nights of the week. I lost the tip of my finger fixing a combine harvester not long after things between us smoothed over, and right there in the office, she cleaned me and sewed me up. After she kissed it all better, we shared the bottle of scotch in the minifridge, and she kissed me even better. Hundreds of great moments in my life happened in that barn. When the new barn went up in place of the old one, I felt like I had taken all my childhood memories from the first barn and moved them into the new one. Including the memory of when I found out something had happened. Here in New Orleans, we call that instant when we found out something happened the "how I lost my virginity" story. We call it "the moment." I've told mine so many times, and I've seen so many of them—the screamers, we call them—that I've stopped thinking of Tony as a person.

I was sitting in the office. The wall unit moaned and groaned, no doubt in pain from the dirty filter destroying its life expectancy. I had done so much paper work that morning that my fingers smelled like pencil shavings. Cleaning up the office didn't do anything to abate the smell. I don't remember exactly what I was doing at the time—maybe looking for an air conditioner repairman in the phone book—but suddenly I heard a muffled crash on the other side of the wall. I remember standing up, outraged, and ripping the door open. Before I could say anything, I was met with a cacophony of banging metal and wood. I saw Tony, like a wild animal, tossing random tools around the barn. His short, muscular stature jerked back and forth, his sweaty black hair flinging side to side with every yank of his head. He furiously grunted. He was looking for something. Not just looking for something but tearing his way through my barn to find it.

"Tony, what the hell are you doing, buddy?" I asked the thing wearing Tony's body. He ignored me completely.

A feral cat ran from beneath a counter top coming out from one of the nearby walls. Tony snatched a pickax that rested on two hooks on the wall just over his head. I walked toward him, hands up and trying to stop his rage. He swung the ax at the cat, missing. A hole blew out of the wall at the sharp impact.

"Shit, Tony. Stop! What the hell happened?"

The cat made for the opening at the opposite end of the barn. Tony dove, grabbing the cat's hind legs. Tony squealed with what I now understand was delight. What it sounded like then was a woman screaming in terror. The cat bit and scraped at his dirty, sunburned hands. Tony stood up and slammed the cat into the wall.

"What the fuck, Tony?"

I grabbed a shovel from the wall. He slammed the cat another time. And another. I slammed the shovel into his head. He really saw me then. His eyes were bloodshot and filled with a homicidal rage I've always associated with video-game characters. His dark, stubbly face was an orgy of fury, surprise, confusion, and fear. He shook as he heaved air. His shoulders rose up and down, up and down.

Tony charged at me, dropping the cat on the ground. *Fomp*. I jammed the end of the wooden handle into his nose. Blood popped out like a tiny water balloon busted on his face. He shrieked again.

Tony swung the pickax. His movements were clumsy. He lost his balance and tipped over onto one knee. I hit him in the face. His blood coated my fist. He fell back onto the ground.

"Knock it off. Have you lost your goddamned mind?" I screamed at him.

From where he lay on the ground, Tony clumsily swung the ax again. It stuck in my leg about an inch deep. I looked at the pickax hanging from my leg, not believing it. I screamed. Then I was on the ground. I remember having time to groan once before I was fighting Tony off. He was screaming and slobbering. He bit my forearm hard enough to draw blood. I called for help between gasping breaths. Tony moved closer and closer. I could smell his dirty breath. He bit at my cheek, barely missing. I could hear his teeth clamping to-gether. He jerked and flailed. His knee connected with my crotch. His fingernails raked my face.

Then there was a loud, hollow bang. And Tony went limp. Blood dripped in my face from the top of his head.

I came out from beneath him. A hand dropped. I looked up. Mark stood looking down. He bent lower, his six-foot-seven-inch frame towering over me. His scared eyes peeked out above a scraggly beard. They were so dark, I thought they were black. For a second it spooked me.

"I think we gotta go, bro. There are more of them."

He helped me to my feet, and we ran out of the barn.

Chapter 2

I had been in my office all morning. I usually only spend about an hour a day in the office, but that morning I came in at eight for my monthly cleanup—the paper work, empty bottles of scotch, muddy rug—and when I heard Tony's meltdown, it was after lunch. It's weird to think that when I started the whole routine, Mark was twenty miles away in Mobile.

"What was that? And what do you mean *more of them*?" I asked him.

"I'm Mark." He threw the Wrangler into reverse.

I waited. When he said nothing, I answered, "Derrick. Derrick Martin."

"By the way," he said, "I haven't driven a stick in a while, so I'm sorry if I fuck something up."

"That's fine. Just drive."

He floored the accelerator in reverse just as someone ran up behind the car, shrieking like a maniac. His face busted on the back windshield.

"Shit!" I screamed, jerking my head around. The back tires missed the bump, but the front tires didn't. "What are you doing?"

"Calm down. Plug up your leg."

I pulled a rag out of the glove compartment. I managed to keep most of my blood out of the seat. When I got the rag over the hole, I reached under the seat for the duct tape and wrapped it around my leg. "So what do you mean *them*?" I asked again.

"I don't know what I mean. I thought it was some virus or something. You know, like the movies? Like biowarfare gone totally fucked, but thank God, right?" He lifted his hand wrapped in a makeshift bandage covered in red blots. "Then I thought maybe they were just crackers, you know? Like crazy. Maybe a cell-phone signal malfunctioned. Like that movie by the *Pet Sematary* guy. Still a no-go. The first guy I ran into just outside Mobile was on his phone. Hung up just to point a shotgun at my dick and balls. Told that fucker I got the picture. Luckily, before he hung up the phone, I had heard him say, 'You wanna meet in NOLA or Indianapolis?' I think that means people who aren't all nuts are meeting in the bigger cities."

"What?"

"How long have you been in that barn, bro?"

"I don't know. Four...five hours?"

"How far do you live from the rest of the world? People started tearing each other apart last night."

"I guess I didn't notice. My wife is out of town. Oh, God. Sarah." I felt like I was being shocked from inside my chest. I yanked my cell phone out of my jeans.

"Won't help."

"Why?" I asked, not stopping.

"Towers went down this morning. I guess with most of the people losing their minds, something had to go down eventually. Looks like computers have a long time to go before they rule the world."

I tried dialing. The phone didn't even try to connect. I immediately flipped over to a screen that displayed "Call could not be made," but it offered to try again.

"Seriously, it's not going to work."

I turned the screen away from him and touched "Call Back," again to no avail. "What are they?"

"It's like they're just mindless, pissed-off shells of people. They just über-rage and kill."

"My wife," I said to him.

"Is that Sarah?" he said. His smile was huge and white, and with the dirty, black Miami Dolphins baseball cap he had kept in his back pocket now on his head, he looked even younger than I originally thought.

I looked out the window. Usually my part of the world is fairly empty of foot traffic. Scattered around the fields and homes we passed, there were people everywhere. A group of about six or seven pulled a cow apart, and then they just...walked away. Like the old days, only instead of four horses dismembering a person, it was people dismembering a cow.

"Is everyone like that?"

"Well, I know at least two people aren't," Mark said.

"How many people have you seen?"

"Since I left my apartment? Hundreds. Very few were real people. Most of the real people were scared. It's weird. When I was just like everyone else, I never had a gun pointed at me. Then when most everyone else turns into a weirdo, I get one pointed at me by a real person probably once an hour. Got the one in the backseat from a guy being pulled apart like that cow back there. Only takes two of them to do a person."

"Where did you come from?"

"Mobile. I heard a riot start last night and assumed it had something to do with the national championship. People around here get a little too excited about that stuff. I mean, come on, guys. It's not the pros, for Christ's sake." He tapped the bill of his hat. "Fins up, motherfucker."

"You walked here from Mobile? That's like twenty minutes away."

"Yeah, by car. Much longer run. Especially with lunatics sprinkled along the way."

"Why did you come here?"

"Well," he began, shifting the Jeep to its highest gear, "I got up, completely late for work, so I scrambled to get some clothes on and make my way out when I heard something going down outside the door. I figured, *Oh, it's just some marauder getting away,* but he was being loud as hell, so I didn't know how professional he was. I decided I better take it slow because he was no doubt on his guard. When I got to the hallway, there were three of them beating the brakes off this guy. Holding him down. I yelled at them to leave him alone. They didn't say anything. Didn't even look. They were little guys, so I figured I got at least two, and if the third one jumped in, worse to worst they'd run into each other in the skinny hallway.

"So I brain the closest one to me, and he ripped off this death yell, like the guy who ran into the back of the car here, and your boyfriend from the barn. Never heard anything like it in my life. It slowed me down, for real. The other two started yanking on the guy's legs. I mean, you know, giving him the business something fierce." He mimicked a violent yanking motion. "You could hear his joints give up. He tossed me his pistol. He was trying to tell me to shoot them when the one closest to me—on the guy's head—kind of stepped a little hard, if you know what I mean. I've seen some things in my field, but that's going to stay with me for a while. Then the other two kind of joined with the first—screaming, I mean. I took off back to my bedroom. I had a gun in my closet just in case something like this happened. Dammit. I should've grabbed it. It didn't cross my mind. I just left it there. That sucks. Anyway, I made for the window and Indiana Jonesed down the window ledges to the first floor and then dropped. Not what they did. They just took all the floors at once." He dropped one flat hand onto the other. "Splat. I rarely hear broken bones…just study the aftermath. And that's on very rare occasions. I'm in med school. That's when I realized they were the guys I had hung out with a few nights earlier, and I knew something was wrong."

"Really?" I said.

"Yeah. And the thing is, they look normal, you know? No missing skin. No eat your brains. Just beat ass and move on. Don't even take names."

"Where are we going?"

"Jackson."

"Why Jackson?"

"My sister Jackie. She's a police officer there."

"That's like the Chrysler of police jobs."

"No joke. She's been shot. I figure we can swing by and make sure she's fine, at least. We should get Sarah first, though. Where does she work?"

"She's in New Orleans."

"Why?"

"She's a nurse. She was there for a special training."

"Cancer?"

"Yeah. How'd you know?"

"Just a guess. They have a good facility there."

"It was there or Wisconsin. She wanted to fly, but her parents live in Baton Rouge, and she wanted to spend time with them on her off days. Have you talked to Jack—" Another screamer ran at the Jeep. Mark jerked the wheel to miss her. Still not used to what was happening, I jumped. I caught my breath. "Have you talked to your sister since all of this?"

"Not directly. She left a voice mail last night. Like I said, I was in no hurry to get on the phone after the hallway incident. So I took off to this part of the world thinking surely I'd find someone normal. When the shotgun guy showed me the door, I immediately checked the message. I got that she was OK and would be held up at the station. She told me how to get there, but midway through, the phone just went down. There was no signal, so I just left it behind, too. Shouldn't be too much of a hassle to find her, though. I've been there a few times. But I mean, what's in Jackson? Probably won't be too difficult to talk her into coming. Everyone's sort of working pro bono now."

"You seem pretty calm about this whole thing."

"Is pouting going to make the situation better?"

I said it probably wouldn't. I waited another minute or two nursing my bruised hand before I asked what he planned to do.

"Well, I'm going to find a gas station first. Then we'll go from there."

"Why didn't you drive from Mobile?"

"Some of the people who got pissed were driving. Some of those people were driving in the same parking lot my car was in. Just a Leaning Tower of Twisted Metal."

"So you just decided to walk to the country because you thought we wouldn't have cell phones?"

"No," he said, a little defensive. "I was chased. The good thing is, though they're fast, it's like they go at one hundred percent until they give out. Really, as long as you can stay ahead of them for about a minute or so, they'll wipe themselves out."

"How far does this go?" I asked.

"All I know is Mobile and Jackson. From what I put together from the guy on the cell phone, I assume at least Louisiana and Indiana."

"I guess that's all you know. No information on what happened to the people in New Orleans?"

"I have no clue," he said.

Mark pulled into the Valero station just before the exit ramp. "But assuming this and any other gas stations still have the power to fill the tank, we're going to find out by the end of the day."

Mark and I both got out of the car. We watched the price tick up to around fifteen dollars before the machine stopped. The old Jeep always overflowed a little when the tank was full, so I tried to keep the flow of gasoline going, but nothing happened. The digital display on the machine went blank, although the lights on the inside of the building remained working. There were no discernible signs of chaos behind the glass entrance. So we made our way inside.

To get to the front door, we passed a red Corolla and a beat-up white truck. There was a ladder hanging on a rail above the cab and bed of the truck. All the compartments on the sides of the truck were open. Tools covered the ground around the truck as if on show for a garage sale. I watched Mark bend over and pick up a one-handed sledgehammer as he passed. I chose a large red monkey wrench and followed him inside.

The glass doors were in pristine condition, but the rest of the store really drove down the resale value. My eyes immediately went to the opposite wall, where a massive hole at least fifteen feet wide circled around a Coke truck. Flotsam piled up around the grille and tires. Shelves of candy were tipped, and the products were strewn everywhere. The freezer doors were open, and water leaked onto the floor.

"I think this one's on the house," I told Mark.

"We may as well get something to eat, right?"

I actually agreed with him on that score. I had completely forgotten about lunch. I grabbed the biggest bottle of water I could find. Luckily, it was the middle of winter; otherwise, everything in the place would have been cooked rather than a couple degrees below room temperature. I snagged a big bag of chips and made my way to the exit. Mark was right behind when a screamer fell through the hole in the wall, calling out to someone in the next county.

I would have taken off if he had stayed where he was, but instead the former gas station attendant ran at Mark. I flung the wrench. It clipped the old Indian man square in the temple. He went to the ground, convulsing violently.

"Jesus," Mark said, staring down at the old man.

Chunks of building fell from the sides of the hole in the wall. People moved on the other side of the truck. There was another scream from behind the truck. Then two more chimed in. Mark and I bolted. There was a girl between the store and the white truck. Rage filled her face, and as we came closer to her, she started running toward us. There was a crunch when the sledgehammer caved in her forehead.

I picked up a ball peen hammer en route to our escape vehicle. No one else was in the parking lot. I took over the reins in the Jeep. When I saw five once-people filtering out of the store, I panicked to get the car started. I turned the ignition. The dashboard just buzzed at me. I made eye contact with one of them, and the screamers started running. I yanked on the ignition again.

"The clutch, bro," Mark said as calm as ever.

I mashed the clutch into the floor, and the Jeep roared to life. The crowd of screamers pressed their faces against the windows and punched at the side of the car. Luckily, they managed to avoid busting out any windows.

"Derrick! Punch it!"

I did.

"You know how to get to Jackson, right?" he asked.

I did.

The Jeep shivered as it pushed to reach its maximum speed. The wobble became a shake. The shake became a vibration.

"He was going to kill you, you know." Mark sounded like he just lost a puppy.

"Who?"

"Tony," he said. He was looking down at the food in his hand. The foil bag wrinkled noisily. In that moment he was barely a decade old. He looked like a kid pleading with a sibling not to tell Mom about the stolen candy bar or Dad would get the belt. "That was his name, right?"

"I know he was."

"He was one of the different ones. I'm sorry. It wasn't to hurt him. It was to save you."

"Hey, nah, you saved me. I don't know what has happened, but you did me a real solid." I hoped I sounded sincere because I genuinely was. "You did what you had to."

"I won't do that to you."

"I believe you."

"Because you are normal."

"And I plan to stay that way."

"If you turn, though," he said, "I'm-a bust you open with a hammer."

I don't know why, but that made me laugh. It was the first in a long line of laughs. That one though is the one I remember better than any. The first cut is the deepest, or whatever.

"No kidding. I will fuck up your face," Mark said, opening a bag of chips. He passed it to me.

We didn't talk for a while as we ate.

Chapter 3

I think we were an hour out before I had to either stop or piss myself. I took the exit to Jackson. I waited for a remotely empty area. We passed the university from which Sarah got her undergrad, and that sent a surprise pang of worry through me. Then we passed a strip of abandoned places—restaurants, apartments, and motels. I figured it best to avoid the potentially heavily populated areas. A "don't bother the wildlife in their natural habitat" kind of strategy. I mean, no one would kick down the doors to Africa and slap a lion in the face. Probably not, anyway.

The Jeep had been sputtering off and on for nearly a mile. It finally came to a stop at the bottom of a long hill in the middle of an intersection, and we got out. On one side of us, there was a Valero next to a Krystal, both empty, and across from that there was a huge purple-and-gray convention center that looked like a small coliseum. The lights inside the store were dim as if powered by a generator, but the ones outside—the ones we needed—were out.

"Well, shit," I said.

"What do you want to do?"

"Do you know how to hot-wire a car?"

"I know how to *drive* a car," he said sarcastically.

"I can probably figure it out."

We left the Jeep in the middle of the road and made our way to the pumps at the Valero. Most of the car doors were open, and all of the cars had keys either inside or nearby on the ground. When I thought about it, I guessed if people were here when it happened, they were probably going to or coming from their cars. Then, when the change took over, if the keys weren't in the car, they probably wound up on the ground. No need to keep them when there was beating and ripping to do. And with so little time.

The only locked car of the six had a trash bag for a window. None of the others had more than a quarter of a tank, so I ripped a hole in the plastic bag and made my way inside. The keys were in the cup holder, so I tried it. Still not much use, even less gas than the others.

"OK, so we have a couple of choices. We could walk, or we could use one of these with a little bit of gas. Then we take it to Southern Miss and get one with a full tank."

"How far?" Mark asked.

"From here? If we go back that way"—I pointed to the road leading behind the gas station, in the direction of an old movie theater and a Cracker Barrel—"maybe three miles. This road is basically a straight shot. The only thing is, we'd pass three or four apartment complexes."

"Why don't we just wire a car at the apartments?" he asked.

"That's where people lived. Probably more likely that people were home last night. They probably walked or carpooled from Southern. If not, the people who are still actually people will no doubt show us the same courtesy as your boyfriend with the shotgun."

"Nice," he said, smiling.

"Well?"

"Well, I don't want to walk to Jackson."

"I don't either." I unlocked the passenger door for Mark, and we crept up the road toward the campus.

I didn't realize how long three miles was, especially at ten miles per hour. Blood-smeared cars lined the streets. I slalomed between debris and wreckage. I drove past a house with a car half in and half out of the side of the garage. Because someone had busted out the driver's side window of our stolen car, I didn't have any problem hearing the screamer that had been sandwiched between the wall and the hood of the car. Blood covered the hood of the car. There were about fifteen cars on this half-mile stretch of patchy back road—more than the total number of cars I had ever seen on this street.

We came to the stop sign at the entrance of the first apartment complex. As we passed, I could see almost nothing wrong. There were a few windows that had been boarded up and broken back into, but other than that, it was the closest image of normalcy I had seen since I left the barn. I gassed the little white Honda closer to the campus. There were a couple narrow hills and curves before the heavily wooded road opened to a park on the left and the apartments up ahead on the right. There was a black Escalade teetering over the edge of a stream in the middle of the park. Skid marks ruined the surface of the sod. Divots from the tires had ripped open the perfectly flat green surface of the ground. That was as far as we could go, though. Just before we reached the next two apartment complexes, a smoking pile of cars blocked the rest of the street, rendering our stolen car useless to us.

"How far is it now?" he asked.

"Little less than a mile."

"Hoof it?"

"Got your piece?"

Mark tapped the sledgehammer on the dashboard in front of him. The airbag exploded in his face. He bounced from the airbag and hit the seat. I jumped. As the airbag deflated, it was obvious he was OK, so I laughed. Very, very hard.

"Dude, fuck this," he said, exhausted. He slapped at the deflating bag.

There were tears on my cheeks when I finally stopped laughing.

"Seriously, it's not that funny," he said, trying not to laugh. "Shut up. They're going to hear you."

"All right, all right. Let's—" I started to laugh again but stifled it. "Let's go."

We were parked at the top of a hill. Before he got out of the car, Mark released the parking brake, repurposing the vehicle as an unmanned kamikaze missile.

"Couldn't hurt," he said nonchalantly as the white car slowly descended in reverse.

We took off for the end of the street without looking back at the car. We weren't running, but we certainly weren't giving anything behind us the chance to catch up. We crouched behind a line of cars. There were screams coming from deep into the cemetery on our left, but the more troubling screams came from the apartments across the street. The screamers were in the cemetery, and that's all we heard from there. It was something we had almost gotten used to by then. Enough of them had run at the Jeep or stood in the middle of the road along its way that we expected their shrieks of fury, and they were far enough away on the opposite side of a rusty chain-linked fence that we didn't have much to worry about.

The problem came from the apartments. From the time we left the car, rolling back to infinity, to the time we reached the second complex's entrance, I heard two separate cries of agony cut short. We quietly decided that we couldn't go through each home to make sure no one needed help, but I have no doubt the looks on our faces said we regretted it.

We maneuvered between pileups as quietly as church mice. I stopped to check for anyone, quiet or screaming. Mark kneeled down beside me. The sledgehammer he carried hit the wound in my leg. It felt like someone was opening it up fresh. I jumped, both scared and in pain.

"Shit, my bad, bro. You good?"

"Just scared me is all."

There was a shriek from the graveyard, much closer than before, and Mark jerked. Immediately I flushed with relief that he was just as on edge as I was.

"It looks clear. If we can get to the intersection and cross the street, there's a bike trail straight to one of the biggest parking lots on campus. Should be simple."

It was supposed to be—until we heard the cries for help coming from behind us.

Chapter 4

We almost didn't hear the cries at all. We had made it to the intersection and were standing in the middle of the road. My first instinct was to look from where we had just come to the line of cars. The sound of her screaming through a closed window sounded like a death-metal remix of a cry for help, but then I heard an apartment window go up. At first I thought the screamers were learning words. The building was about a hundred yards away.

"Help me, please," she cried out. Tears caught her by the throat. "Please, I'm trapped. Help me!"

I looked around wildly in search of an open window. My eyes wandered over numerous buildings on the opposite side of the tall, barbed-wire-lined fence separating the complex from the rest of the town. Then I saw it, a single pale arm waving in wide strokes in front of a red-brick background. She was in the middle window on the second floor, only a building farther than the one on the exact corner. I think even then I could see the bright-red fingernail polish.

"OK, do we go back, or do we jump the fence?" I asked.

"What?"

"Help!" the woman screamed again.

"We have to get her," I explained. "Do we go back to the entrance, or do we hop the fence?"

"We *have* to get her?"

"Yes."

"Yeah, I know, dammit," Mark said, defeated.

"Up or around?"

"Help!"

"OK!" Mark screamed. "We're coming! Be quiet so they don't hear you!" Then to me he said, "Shit."

"Well done. Probably shitting herself. Let's hurry. What's the plan? Up or around?"

"We could use those." He pointed up to a bar that divided the wire into sections of the fence. "And it would probably be a little nicer on our manhood. I don't like the idea of going back with them running around in that cemetery. I'm currently blown the fuck away that none of those crazies saw us."

"They could see us climbing."

"By the time they get to us, we'll have a fence between us and them."

"Yeah. Did you see any running around inside the fence?"

"No. Just heard them in the buildings. I'm not totally certain they know how to use doorknobs actually."

"OK," I said. "What are we waiting for?"

He folded at the waist, his hands on his knees. "I have to get over a few internal hills to make myself go back."

"Take your time."

He let out a painful groan.

"You good?"

He paused. "Yeah." When he straightened his back, his face was blood red. He let out a deep breath, and we made for the fence.

He boosted me up the fence. I held onto the divider and awkwardly made it over the barbed wire. By then Mark was laughing quietly at my lame maneuvering. As I dropped to the ground, my jeans ripped up the side. Mark nearly lost his quiet, blowing that weird raspberry we all blow when something hilarious suddenly overtakes us.

"Shut up. Hurry up and get over."

He stopped laughing. His eyes were locked on something on the ground. He started laughing again. "Hold this up for me." He pushed the uprooted bottom of the fence.

"Shit," I said, feeling very silly. I held the fence up and allowed him to come to my side.

"Please, hurry," we heard from behind us. Her voice was a very loud whisper. I could make out her reddish-brown hair and very white skin.

Mark and I fled for the window. "What number are you?" I called to her.

"No, you can't," she said in a panic. "They're in my house."

"OK, what the fuck are we supposed to do?" Mark said. He said it so fast it was all one word.

"Calm down," I said to him. Then to her, "Do you know where a ladder is?"

"I have one in my storage shed." She pointed to the row of sheds across the parking lot. "Mine is number—"

There was a loud bang from her apartment.

"What was that?"

"I think they're coming in," she said, starting to panic.

"OK, I need you to climb out. We're going to catch you."

"OK," Mark said to me. "We've only seen her face. We can't promise we'll catch her."

"I'm scared," she told me.

"Don't panic. We're going to help. Just take it one step at a time, OK?"

"What do I do?" she said.

"Just climb out slowly. One leg at a time," I told her.

She started out the window. As she made her way over the edge, I noticed a blue tattoo on her shoulder to one side of the strap on her tank top. It was of a palm tree, and a piece of something peeked out from a stray white bra strap. I heard another bang from inside the building. She let out a small cry.

"Just ignore that, sweetie. You're doing great. You're right there. Now just hang onto the ledge and let your weight fall over."

She did just that, and as she hung from the window ledge by her fingers, the door in her room broke and flew open. Screams came through the window. At the same time, a single screamer appeared from behind the corner of the building.

The woman cried out, "What do I do?"

Mark used the hammer to halt the screamer in its tracks.

"Just drop. Put your feet against the wall and fall back. That's all you have to do."

"You'll catch me."

"I'm going to catch you," I said, just as much for myself as for her. "Just drop." I watched hands from inside the window grab her wrists. Two hands for each of her wrists.

She let go of the ledge, but she stayed where she was. Panic overcame her, and she screamed. The arms pulled her back into the window. I jumped onto the windowsill below hers and leapt up to her, grabbing her by the waist. The weight from the two of us slid her out of her two roommates' hands. We fell onto Mark, and he toppled to the ground.

"Come on. Come on. Come on," Mark said. All one word again.

We ran to the place in the fence that had been uprooted. Mark yanked it up. I slid under and waited for our new companion and then Mark.

The fence snapped back down, and we were left on the corner of the street. We were breathing hard. Mark was holding his side, but we were all in one piece.

"I'm Derrick Martin," I said between gasps. "This is Mark."

"Katy Hughes." Her low feminine voice had a touch of rasp to it.

She was wearing red lipstick that seemed to be much brighter with her white skin and perfectly white teeth. Her face was thin, her lips full, and her body trim. Her dark-red hair was messy, but I somehow could tell that typically it was well styled. I bet to myself that her bangs were usually perfectly level above her big green eyes. Even in her black tank top and denim pants, she was beauty stuck out of time. I knew that if anything happened to her, it would break my heart. And when something eventually did, my heart absolutely shattered.

"Come on," I said and pointed to the entrance of a bike trail.

I meant to use the path as a straight shot for the university. When the two of them turned, I saw Katy's tattoo again. The palm tree was still there, and then I realized the piece of the tattoo beneath the strap was a comically curved quarter moon. I had seen the picture before. I thought maybe it was a college team logo or something, but I couldn't put my finger on it. Trees and a downward slope from the road hid the entrance to the bike trail. Woods flanked both sides of it, so I thought if it didn't hide us, the crackling leaves would at least tell us from which direction those things were coming.

"This bike trail goes straight to the place we want to be. It's not even a mile from here," I said.

We crossed the street. There was a corrugated wooden sign that said we could find the Longleaf Trace down and just to the left. We found it. Right there at the end of the sidewalk entrance. Across from where we had entered stood another apartment building. It was a small two-story building that housed maybe eight different families. From the second-floor walkway, a screamer noticed us. It looked like a small Mexican woman. When she noticed us, she immediately ran and leaped over the railing. There was a muffled pop when she hit. Then everything was quiet again. It was then that I saw my first flashes since the world had turned.

Chapter 5

Since I can remember, I've always had these sorts of images come to me. They're not anything psychokinetic or telepathic or whatever you call it. They're just little clips of Sarah in the present. I had them even before I knew her. When we met I told her she was the woman I had always pictured dating. It wasn't lying. I always wondered if she had them, too, and maybe that was why the line worked.

When I saw a flash, I always caught a glimpse of what she was doing or where she was. I've never told her about them out of fear that she'd think I was crazy on the off chance she didn't also get them about me. When I see her though, it's usually her walking down a hospital corridor or in the backyard feeding the cats. Never anything totally coherent.

This time she was standing next to her bed in a hotel. The bulb from the bathroom and the sun pouring through the gap in the curtains gave light to the whole room. She had pulled her shoulder-length brown hair into a short ponytail, which is something she rarely did anymore because it made her look like a picture I found of her once when she babysat her Indian neighbors' kids. I saw every detail of her face because this time we were standing so close I could've felt her breath. The joy I felt in seeing her allowed me to take in everything about her. The freckles on her cheeks stood out more than ever. Bright-red lipstick covered the scar dividing her bottom lip in two. She earned the scar at cheerleader practice when the squad practiced stunts a little too close to the basketball goal one rainy day after school. Sarah's clothes, tons of them, were strewn all over the floor as if when she opened her suitcase everything shot up and spread out.

Near the door the clothes and the carpet were wet. I couldn't hear it or see it, but I knew the sink was not only running but somehow overflowing. Like I said, these things were never totally accurate, and that's what I attributed this to. I couldn't tell if she wore sleeping clothes or scrubs, but I saw her, and that was enough to gather hope. Sometimes hope is the only thing we need.

Chapter 6

"**D**o y'all have a plan?" Katy asked.

"Yes, we both have family out of town," Mark said. "First Jackson then New Orleans."

"What about you?" I asked. "Where can we take you?"

"I don't know," she said quietly. "Everyone I know is like that. My stepdad attacked a reporter on the news this morning. He and my mom were inseparable. I sort of hope she's one of them."

It sounded strange to hear someone actually say that. But when she did, I immediately wondered if I would rather that Sarah be pulled apart by strangers in a hospital or be the one pulling.

"Well, you're welcome to come with us," Mark said.

We started walking toward the bike trail that led to the university.

"You're planning on walking all the way to New Orleans?"

"No." I pointed toward the school. "We're going to walk to one of the parking lots on campus and wire a car with enough gas to get us to Jackson, then pretty much go from there."

"The parking garage would be the best place to check, then."

"There's a parking garage now?"

"Yeah, a couple years ago when I was still an undergrad they put it in. There was nowhere to park. I had to ride my bike to school. If we get off the trail at the overpass up there, we'll just cross Fourth Street and be there."

The overpass was only about half a mile away, but it looked about 150 miles down the paved trail. We walked three abreast with Katy in the middle, our hammers wielded. Only one screamer came out of the thinning woods around us. I swung at it, but it ran faster than I expected. The mallet missed, but the handle connected with its shoulder. The screamer's momentum carried it forward, knocking me down. It latched onto my leg as if it knew I was injured. Katy screamed and slapped at the thing. It squeezed hard onto the damp hand towel around my leg. Mark took it down with the tool he held before I could do much to help. When our labored breathing calmed, the woods fell silent again.

I never realized how many apartment buildings there were along the trail until I was actively trying to avoid them. By the time we left the trail, we had passed three more complexes.

"This is where we go," Katy said as we approached the overpass.

The place where we left the path was just a sidewalk, not a road, for students who lived along the trace and walked or biked to school from the apartment buildings. The sidewalk led to an empty parking lot and what I assumed was Fourth Street. On the other side, instead of the parking lot I remembered, there was a five-floor parking garage. I couldn't hear any screams right away, and I saw no movement yet.

"Let's pick up the pace," I said.

"Hang on," Mark whispered. "Look at that."

There were screamers on the top floor of the garage, pacing back and forth. It seemed as though they had no real agenda—they were just roaming around, shrieking.

"I think it'd be wise, you know, to just ease in there."

"Yeah," I said. "Just make sure you're out of plain sight."

They followed me. We crossed the empty parking lot undetected and used the ticket office to peer around for any lower-level stragglers. The garage was so close I could almost hear the screamers on the top floor moving around.

"I can't see anything," I said. "I say we sprint inside. I can see a walkway entrance directly ahead. Go in and find the first car that's unlocked and get in it. Lock the doors and wait for me. I'll come to you if mine has no gas. OK?"

"Yes," Katy said plainly. Behind her Mark was psyching himself up.

"Mark, you good?"

He pumped out three deep breaths and took off.

"Shit," I said to myself. "Katy, go." I let her go between us.

Crossing the street, I noticed that with the exception of one small car, the street was clear. I tripped over the curb before I looked back. I hit the ground, rolled, and sprang back up. Mark had the first car. Katy the next, but it was locked. I gave her the third and took the fourth. The fourth car was a black Pathfinder, and it was unlocked. I got in and shut the door. I wondered how many people were going to their cars when it—whatever *it* was—happened. I couldn't imagine that out of four cars in a row in a university parking garage, three would be unlocked and left there. Maybe one, but certainly not three.

Junk littered the inside of the SUV—golf clubs in the passenger seat, a pretty large chunk of hose, a car seat in the back littered with papers and crumbs. I went to work pulling the starter wires. When the car rumbled to life, the needle barely scraped past the quarter-of-a-tank mark. I separated the wires and went to the next car. It was a small, light-blue hybrid. I knocked on the window, and Katy jumped. I asked her to let me in, and when she reached over the seat to unlock the door, her eyes were still closed. The backseat was tiny, so whoever sat back there would have to lie across the seat.

"OK, uh," I said, "either climb over or move your legs a little."

There was no room to climb over, so she pressed herself against the door. I reached over and felt around for the compartment under the wheel. I got it down and went to work, doing my best to work around Katy's lower half. I could tell she was uncomfortable with my pocketknife so close to her. I stripped the wires and connected them. If the Pathfinder roared to life, this kitten purred at best. I leaned up to check the needle and fell onto the floorboard, catching myself on Katy's thigh.

"We have about three-quarters," she said, her voice filled with excitement.

"Really?" I asked, avoiding the awkward positioning of my hand. I leaned up in the seat, and sure enough, the needle sat at three-quarters of a tank. "Yep," I said, repositioning myself in the seat. I grabbed the hook meant for clothes, and it broke off in my hand. "OK, that's enough of that."

I looked around in the tiny cab. There was nothing of any use. "I want to see what Mark found. I think we'll need something a little less fragile than this one." I opened the door. Immediately, there was a blood-curdling shriek from one of the higher levels. I slowly left the car.

"What are you doing?" Katy asked in a panic. "Don't leave me."

I sat back down and closed the door as quietly as I could. "I'm just going a few cars over. If there's nothing in it, I'll be back in less than a minute. I don't think this car will actually make it to Jackson. Those things will run into the car. Moving or not. I don't think this thing could handle running into a person. Or a teddy bear. I just don't want to be stranded along the way."

"Please, don't leave." She grabbed my arm. Her eyes started watering.

"OK, I won't leave. Can you drive?"

She nodded. Her hair flew in her face. Her hands shook as she reached for the wheel.

"Just back the car up, and get as close as you can to the red truck over there. That's where Mark is. Luckily, I don't think we're actually making any noise."

She backed up.

"That's it. Just ease over there." Riding in the car, it felt like it took a full ten minutes for Katy to move the little hybrid over four places to the handicap space next to the towering truck.

"OK," I said. "I'm just going to tell Mark to get in the backseat, and then you climb over this seat and into the truck."

"I can do that." Her eyes were dry now but still a little puffy.

I put everything into action. Mark fell into the backseat. The suspension creaked. I motioned for Katy to move. She froze. I heard the screamers running down from the next floor up. Katy screamed. I shut the door to the truck and jumped back into the hybrid.

"Katy, I need you to move. They're coming. I don't want you to be in here when they get down. Please."

"OK." She started tearing up again.

"Can you move?"

She nodded.

"Good. Climb over the seat and jump in the truck. Are you ready?" I caught a glimpse of the side rearview mirror. Three of the crazies ran full speed past the car and out the entrance to the garage.

"I'm OK," she said, trying to calm down. "I'm fine."

I checked behind the car. They were no slowpokes coming down the lane, so I moved. I opened the truck door. Before I could move, Katy was inside and in the passenger seat. She flattened against the door. I got in after and went to work on the wires. "Great job, Katy. Thank you."

Katy didn't say anything. The corners of her mouth slightly turned up, though. That's all I needed.

"What about me?" Mark said.

The truck was a little bigger than the other two vehicles, so I had plenty of room to work around. The cab was extended, so the backseat had a door that could be opened when the front door didn't block it. The electronics took a lot longer to figure out because I hadn't worked on many cars from whatever year this one was. Once

I stopped overthinking the task at hand, I was able to work without a problem.

This one's engine made the Pathfinder's sound like waves on the ocean. The gas level was much lower, though. Not even half of a tank. *Shit.* I took in a breath, dropping my head on the steering wheel, and then exhaled. Then I remembered the hose in the Pathfinder. I opened the door. The gas tank was on my side of the truck. The hybrid's was not, though. I couldn't hear its engine, but I could see the lights from the dash through the window. "Guys, I'm going to be right back. Mark, make sure nothing happens. We're taking this one, so don't move."

"Fuckin' done," Mark said. An extended thumb shot up from behind the bench seat.

Katy reached over and grabbed my forearm.

"Why are you leaving?" There was panic in her voice.

"There's a hose in the first car I tried. I'm going to try siphoning the gas from the wagon to this one. We'll have gas in this one, and it's durable. We'll be fine. Just stay down so they can't see you if they run by."

"You're coming right back?" The floor of the truck was so big that Katy easily fit her entire body below the dashboard with room to move around.

"Right back. Am I clear?"

Katy turned to the window. "Yes," she said quietly.

"Be careful, bro."

I went around the back of the hybrid. The tank was on the back fender on the driver's side. I would have to back it in when I came back. I climbed into the tiny car, sucking in to fit behind the steering wheel. I drove the wannabe go-kart to the Pathfinder. Leaving the door open, I stumbled out. I creep-walked to the SUV's open door. I climbed to my knees onto the seat, looking wildly around the backseat for the hose I knew I had seen. I checked the floorboard; the glove compartment, even though I knew I hadn't opened it; and amid the papers and discarded diaper-bag contents in the backseat. I started to panic. I took one last look between the door and passenger seat. Pay dirt. Apparently I'd knocked it off the seat while trying to find it. I scrambled for the hybrid again.

I stopped. A screamer with its back to me examined the little car. It was a mere six or seven inches from my door. I climbed over the passenger seat as quietly as I could, thanking the heavens for illegally tinted windows. I eased the passenger door open, dropped to the ground, and slid beneath the Pathfinder. I couldn't tell what the screamer saw or heard. I kept my eyes fixed on its feet between the ground and the SUV's undercarriage. The feet moved along the side of the car but didn't move all the way around. The dirty high-tops turned, pointed at me, and stopped. They turned back around and stopped. Then it slowly walked to the open car door above me.

I was aware that I was terrified. Because when you're scared, your senses intensify, and you become more acutely aware of every shaky, angry breath echoing all around you and the vibrations from the footsteps on the concrete and the minuscule cracks in the asphalt at the tip of your nose. And you become increasingly aware that there are two people locked in a truck only a few feet away, waiting for you not to die. I inched toward the back of the car as quietly as I could. The screamer got into the Pathfinder. I climbed out from beneath the SUV and ran around to the front. I slammed the locking bolt down and closed the door behind the screamer. It noticed what had happened. It screamed and beat its head against the window. My head hurt for the thing. When the glass cracked, spider-webbing between us, the screamer maximized its efforts, slamming again and again. Pieces of the window fell onto the ground each time the screamer thrust forward. Then in some jarring twist of fate, the thing in the Pathfinder smashed its head into the metal doorframe. It lay across the console totally limp.

I didn't want to, but I laughed as I climbed behind the wheel of the hybrid, simultaneously feeling horrible for the poor, dumb thing. There's just something funny about someone bound and determined to do something and right at the last moment, it goes hilariously awry.

I drove the dinky car across the space and lined up its gas tank with the gas tank on the truck, which was nearly twice the car's size. I got out and went to sucking the gas from the hybrid. At first the gas wasn't coming. I dismissed the idea of the inevitable rush of gas forcing its way into my mouth and doubled my efforts. The taste made me gag when it hit the back of my throat. I jammed the spewing hose into the truck and got inside. After ten minutes the needle in the truck jumped past the halfway point.

"Probably as good as it's going to get," Mark said from the back. He fell back into the bench seat. "Hi-ho, Silver! Away!"

"Good enough for me."

Katy looked over. "We'll make it to Jackson?"

"Unless there's a block in the road."

"OK," she said quietly. "Away."

I put the cap back on the tank, leaving the hose dangling from the dinky hybrid. When I put the truck in gear, Katy put her hand on mine.

"Thank you, Derrick," she said. "Y'all saved my life."

The truck was loud in the confines of the garage. In the open street, I barely noticed it at all. I swerved around the one car on Fourth and got back on the highway that brought us to this town.

Chapter 7

If we were in the truck for twenty minutes, Mark had been asleep with his dirty Dolphins cap over his face for nineteen of them. I don't know for sure how long it was; the dashboard in the cab didn't light up for whatever reason, but twenty minutes is about how long it felt as I tried not to let on that I could hear Katy crying on the other side of the bench seat. She was doing her best to hide her face, but the flickering reflection in the widow as the sun peeked through spaces between the trees gave her away. I looked out my own window. A busted-up barrier lay mangled up ahead in the median. There were no cars around, so I was certain it was the result of some drunk who was "good to drive" or a group of teenagers laughing their asses right off. That kind of thing happens a lot in the South. I remember thinking that some mother somewhere probably teared up every time she drove past that mangled break in the metal. That made me depressed. I turned back to Katy. I considered putting my hand on top of hers the way she had done but decided against it.

"You OK?"

"It's—how are *you* OK? It's so much to deal with, you know? Everything is screwed up to space and back. My parents are gone, and everyone is trying to kill us."

I realized then that everything had happened too fast to give any of us a chance to deal with what was going on. For someone who had lost her parents and potentially everyone she knew, Katy held it together pretty well. I, on the other hand, hadn't had anything to cope with just yet. I had no kids, and my parents died a while back. So far as I knew, Tony was the only person I lost. I didn't mean to be insensitive, but I didn't even know him very well. He was a new hire and barely spoke English. From the woods lining the highway, another screamer ran at the truck. I swerved to miss it.

Katy jumped. "Why do they do that?" A tear rolled down her cheek.

"I don't know." I suddenly was overcome with a need to know her story. "What happened in your apartment today?"

"What do you mean?"

"What made you stay in your place, screaming out the window, instead of running outside to find help? Clearly you knew something happened."

"I was leaving for my morning class with my roommate."

"You're in school?"

"I'm a doctorate student."

"That's pretty awesome."

"Not always. I forgot the papers I had graded, so I went back to my room to get them. We had heard the screams earlier, but we thought it was something we could avoid. When I turned, she opened the door and someone grabbed her. They pulled her into the hall, and the door slammed closed. She was screaming. I cried out and ran after her. Then all of a sudden she wasn't screaming anymore. They were. Instead of leaving, I locked the door, deadbolt, and chain. I tried to call the police, but all I got was a busy signal. I dragged the couch in front of the door and locked myself in my room. I could hear them screaming all around me. Above me and below. There was banging all over the place. Like a riot was going on. I looked out the window, and there were people running around in the parking lot.

It looked like a huge fight, so I thought it was some kind of a gang thing. But these were the nice apartments. Police lived there, so I didn't think that was possible.

"I turned on the TV. All the channels were the same. They switched to a number of different cities around the country. After about ten minutes, a reporter in Charleston, South Carolina, of all the places in the world to be, came on. That's where I saw my stepdad. It took a while for the station to cut to a different feed while he beat the reporter. I only kind of recognized him, but I have a DVR, so I rewound and played it a couple times before I was certain it was him. I watched from the window for however long it took for the power to go out. Those things started beating on the living room door. I want to say an hour had passed between seeing my dad and calling out the window. Long enough for the parking lot to empty. That's when I saw y'all sneaking down the street like cops. I don't assume that's the case."

"Farmer..." I pointed to the backseat. "And I don't know what he does other than med school."

"Well, I knew they didn't walk that way. They're always straight up or on all fours, swinging. I called out. Then I heard the door breaking open. Not off the hinges—from the middle inward. I dragged my bed in front of the door and went back to screaming. There were some in the next apartment. They started beating on the wall. You know the rest."

She waited for a second, turning toward the view of the woods. I didn't know if it was because she was waiting for me to say something or hiding her tears or whatever. Hopefully not the former, because I had nothing to say. Nothing appropriate, of course. *I don't think your complex understands room service* came to mind, but I clamped shut. When she started talking again, she sounded sleepy.

"And I know it sounds crazy, but they didn't have anything. No hammers or axes or whatever you use to knock down doors and walls. But they got in," she said, still looking out the window. "Bare hands."

I was looking at her, honestly feeling sad for her, thinking *those sad eyes*, when a screamer ran out into the street. I jerked the wheel, but the yell was cut short by the thump of headlight and grille against torso.

"Shit!" It was the only that came to mind, honestly.

Mark yanked himself up on his elbows. I thought that with the red surrounding the near black in his eyes, and the fact that he had fallen asleep so quickly earlier, he would soon lie back down. I was wrong, though. He was up for good.

"Quad...the fuck was that?" Mark asked, exhausted.

"One just ran at the car," I said. We didn't know them as screamers just yet, and when I tried to think of what to call them, *one* was the only word I could come up with. "We're good. You can lie back down."

"I'm fine, Coach," he said, slowly pulling himself to a seated position with the back of the bench seat. "Has it been like that the entire time?"

We topped a hill, and at the bottom lay a scattered pile of cars for as far as I could see, which was only until the next hill. Cars were toppled and flipped like the dip between the two hills was the exact epicenter of some devastating California tremor. One this size would have definitely been on the news. The mangled Freightliner on the opposite end of the rubble looked like a cat's eye in a gigantic game of marbles. I slowed the truck to a crawl, praying to myself that we wouldn't have to ditch it for one on the other side.

"Actually, no," I said. "I forgot anything was different for a while there."

I inched the car into the wreckage, my eyes wide in search of screamers. That heightened awareness washed over me again. I weaved the truck between cars, shrapnel, and debris, arbitrarily taking note of every leaking engine, every unmoving body part jutting from beneath an overturned car, every still-smoking motor. The truck's cab was eerily silent. The three of us stopped breathing as if we might hear even a twig snapping outside of our mobile fortress. There was nothing for a while. Then we saw one crawling with its arms. It lay between two overturned cars. It was dirty and scrawny, making it difficult to define the gender. This really hammered in the "it" status of whatever they had become. Bones stuck out of its legs, at the end of which there were no feet. It saw the truck and hopped up from its elbows to its hands. It charged the best it could toward the truck. The image of the sexless screamer vanished below the view from the door and was followed by a loud thump on the door, which was then followed by a short, female scream from inside the cab. Fingernails scraped and fists pounded down the side of the truck as we slowly moved past. Not for the last time, part of me wanted to go back for the person that thing used to be. I was struggling to get used to the fact that they weren't people anymore.

After a few minutes, the eighteen-wheeler lay directly ahead. The brakes screeched as we came to a halt before the obstacle course of broken pottery pouring out of the trailer. Before the truck had lain down for a nap, I image it was a Hobby Lobby nightmare. Afterward it was a wave of broken ceramic, shattered glass, and splintered wooden pallets. There were nails like teeth jagging out of the busted-up wood. There was black liquid dripping off most of the sharp debris, as if the pieces of metal and wood salivated at the sight of fully inflated tires. Oil from the leaking engine had spread everywhere. The only way around was the median, and the only way through was undoubtedly with flat tires.

"Do we risk it and go through, or do we risk it and go around?"

"What are we risking going around?" Katy asked.

"Getting stuck in the ditch," Mark said. "I don't know about here, but where I'm from it's been a very wet winter. And that one's deep. We'll get stuck for sure. But there's another option."

"I don't think we will fit the other way," I said. The eighteen-wheeler stretched as close to the woods as possible.

"What if we clear a path?" Mark suggested.

"I don't think that would be smart. Besides, what would we use to clear it?"

"We got two hands each."

"Wouldn't that take a while?" Katy said.

"Not if we hurry. Regardless, we're going to be risking something. At least this way, we can get back in the truck to work out a plan B."

"What if they come from behind us?" Katy asked.

"Well, you could stand in the bed or even on the roof so you can see in time to warn us. We'll leave the doors open so we won't have to fuck around with the handles. I mean, it's just a plan A."

"Wow." I turned around to face Mark. Then I stopped before saying anything else. The redness in his eyes had dissipated, as had the deep black brown. At first I didn't believe it, thinking it was a trick of the light. There was a green, about the color of the logo on Mark's hat, around his pupil. It evanesced to olive then back to the nightshade brown.

He looked at me confused.

I began slowly again. "That sounds pretty solid. Very low risk given the situation. You OK with that, Katy?"

"If I see something, you'll come back to the truck immediately?"

"Yeah," Mark said.

"The doors open?"

"Yeah."

She scanned the area through the windows of the cab and then opened the door. I swung mine open until it bounced back, and then I opened the latch to the back of the cab. We piled out. Mark jumped into the bed of the truck and helped Katy onto the roof. The metal mimicked thunder as it bent under her feet.

"Let us know if you see anything at all," I told her.

Mark jumped down, and we picked up the larger chunks of pottery and glass and tossed them into the median and the grass on the side of the road. Only a minute had passed by the time we finished with the bigger pieces, and we started kicking the smaller pieces out of the way with the sides of our shoes.

Mark stopped, looking pensively at the siding hanging from the trailer's frame.

"What is it?" I asked.

"Why don't we just lay that over the glass?" He pointed at the serrated side panels, which had collapsed into the storage space. "I can't imagine it would be as much trouble as cleaning this shit out of the way."

I didn't have time to say anything before he was on his way, hands out like a kid reaching for candy. I heard a crash coming from the opposite side of the truck. Something large and metal. I took off after Mark. I looked wildly for anything to defend against. There was nothing of any significance other than the door to the cab of the eighteen-wheeler had bent at a ninety-degree angle and was now tepeed on the side of the truck.

"Mark, be careful," I said, jogging up behind him.

There was a commotion coming from the cab.

"It's stuck in there, I think," Mark said cautiously. "Just leave it."

I looked to the open hole in the side of the truck, which looked more and more like road kill lying on the side of the road the longer we stayed there.

"Guys," Katy called. "I think I see someone coming. Please hurry."

"Shit, help me with this," Mark said, yanking on a large mass of metal siding. It had jammed between the ground and the underside of the trailer.

"Guys, did you hear me?"

I jogged back to where she could see me and scream-whispered, "We heard you. Get back in the truck. We're coming."

I helped Mark pull the siding out. We had freed all but a corner when Mark slid in the glass and sliced his hand on the metal as he fell to his back. The blood formed a perfect hand shape on the gravel.

He groaned in a painful effort to not scream. We yanked and yanked and yanked, and inch by inch, the final corner of the siding crept out from under the overturned trailer. We flipped it over and laid the side with no glass facing the sky. We dragged the metal siding an inch or two before the nails-on-chalkboard sound accompanying the grinding crunch of gravel berated our ears.

"OK, stop. Stop. Stop. I..." Mark said, pausing to breathe, "hate that. I don't care if they hear it. I do."

"Can you pick it up?" I asked.

He worked his gashed hand beneath the metal and lifted. "I can prop it up on my arm and carry it this way. You get the other side. I'll go backward."

Katy groaned, scared, from the back bench of the cab. She was just loud enough to be heard. I looked in that direction. Three screamers strolled up from behind as if not knowing we were even there—as if shopping through the aisles of a grocery store.

"You there, bro?"

"Yeah." I ran around the slab of metal and lifted it to my waist. Like two medics carrying a heavy person on a stretcher, we scurried back to the truck. The screamers were closer, inspecting the bed of the truck. We dropped the siding on top of the remaining debris, not gaining any more attention than before.

Mark crouched as he ran to the passenger side, which left me the only visible target. As I made for the driver's side door, they lined up one by one alongside the truck. They advanced in my direction. The first stared daggers into me as the ones behind it reached for the opening in the cab. Its skin was painted in thousands of coats of red hate. Its patchwork beard was only half shaved, and torn pajamas hung loosely around its waist as if this happened in the middle of someone's nightly routine.

Katy screamed.

I kicked the door closed, slamming two sets of fingers in the door. The first screamer stumbled back and roared. I bolted around the grille as Mark moved across the bench to hammer the lock down with a hand clad in a makeshift bandage of some kind of cloth. Screamers leaped into the bed of the truck in an attempt to cut me off before I reached the door. I flung the passenger door open into the screamer who moments ago was burning holes through me with its raging eyes. It stumbled back again and watched, shaking with rage as Mark floored the truck past it. The two screamers with their fingers in the door ran alongside the truck's path until they tripped over one another. Their fingers made low popping sounds as they ripped from the door.

One of our two tagalong passengers toppled over the tailgate when Mark floored the pedal. It happened in a way that would have made me laugh to the point of tears if I'd seen it in a movie. The other rolled around on its fat back like a pale turtle. Its pigtails and bloodshot eyes were the same color. It got on all fours and then stood erect. The thing that had once been a teenage girl pounded on the roof. Katy ducked onto the floor. Mark jerked the wheel. The screamer stumbled to one side, rebounded, and punched a web into the back window. Mark yanked the wheel again, sending it tumbling over the side of the bed and onto the shoulder of the highway. The truck's engine revved louder, taking over any sound in the cab.

Chapter 8

"So what's y'all's story?" Katy asked once the truck was firmly back on the road.

I looked to Mark and nodded for him to go first. I thought if anyone could use a good laugh, it was undoubtedly Katy. If anyone could make her laugh, it was probably him. We began the first of many tag-teamed deliveries of our story.

"Well," Mark began, "it started last night. I heard people going nuts in the parking lots and streets around my apartment. I didn't hear anything other than that. No explosion. No electric energy. Just like someone flipped a lunatic switch somewhere. Like I told Derrick, I thought it was a national-championship riot. And I'm still not totally convinced that's not what is going on. Those fans are too much. It happens in Mobile when Bama wins *or* loses. Even in the cold, like last night. I didn't think anything of it. I just went to sleep. I guess me being quiet all night kind of hid me. They don't seem to be overly skilled at hunting or using doors. Just grabbing and pulling apart."

Katy winced.

"Yep," I said, hoping to move the conversation past this little roadblock.

"When I got up late for work this morning," Mark continued, "I made for the door like Usain Bolt, looking back at my furniture and laughing as I left it in the dust. I opened the door and immediately returned to the comfort of my own home. A couple of them came after me. So obviously I Jackie Channed it out the window, and they followed face first to the ground floor."

"I thought you Indiana Jonesed it out the window," I said.

"Nah, I feel like Jackie's better. Plus he's real, so he wins out."

"Right," Katy said.

"Long story short, I decided to hoof it to Jackson to meet up with my sister. Our dad and stepmom live in Arkansas last I heard. I figured the best thing to do would be find her and then make our way to the bigger cities."

"What happens in the bigger cities?" Katy asked.

I could feel her mood change from one of fright to one of discovery. At that moment it really hit me that she had been in shock this whole time. Her parents were gone. Made the news even. Now we were getting glimpses into the real Katy.

"Not sure what exactly," Mark said. "Just that they are somehow making the bigger cities safe havens. Maybe in the big cities, they're outnumbered enough to smoke 'em out."

"That sounds awful," Katy said.

"That's not even the worst part."

"What is?" I asked.

"I hated that job. Retail itself is a drag. On top of that, my manager just shit in my heart daily. Just a mom-and-pop appliance store in the mall, so I understand not caring, but that motherfucker could delegate like a master. Ninety percent of his actual job consisted of masturbating over his rare-coin collection that he literally brought to work every day. Not kept at work. *Brought* to work. I longed for the day I would kick open his office door, knock those dickhead coins on the floor, give him the only finger that matters, and invite him to spin widdershins on it. It sucks that I was so good at that job.

I can sell you actual shit and customer-service you so hard you'd be walking bowlegged to your car. I really hated working there. Any job dealing with the public sucks. The good thing about the medical field is that they need you, so they're a lot easier to deal with. Money was good, though. Not as good as what I was going to college for, but good.

"I tried to get my car, but it was about six cars deep in a pile. The longer I looked around the more I realized I had to just take off. Hot-wiring or even stealing a car never crossed my mind. I assumed someone would pick me up. I saw a house outside of town and found out the big-city info. Three hours later I was pulling a bitchy Mexican off this guy and dealing with him. We broke down about a mile from your place, and you know the rest."

"I was in my barn all morning. I live in the middle of nowhere. I had no idea anything had happened until Mark showed up."

Mark grabbed my hand. "And here we are," he said in a theatrical, crying voice.

"OK," I said, pulling my hand back, laughing.

Katy laughed, too. She was coming around. Or at least adjusting, which in the long run was something we all had to do to make it. She just got it over with first.

"How about we do this," Mark said. "Let's forget this is happening. Let's not worry about how long this is going to last. What were you doing this time yesterday?"

"Actually"—I looked at my watch—"this time yesterday I was changing the blades on a combine."

"What kind of farm is it?" Katy asked.

"Wheat, mainly."

"Was that what you were after?" Mark asked. "I can't imagine you majoring in farm inheritance."

"Nah," I said. "I wanted to be a writer."

"Much different."

"Yeah. I just kept letting things get in the way."

"Maybe now's your chance," Katy said from behind me.

I laughed. "What better time, right?"

"Sure," she said, enthusiastically. "Why not?"

"I was an advertising major in college," I said. "That never actually turned into anything. Looks good on a resume, though. So basically it was a waste of time."

"What about you?" Mark asked.

"I was in the polymer-science doctoral program."

"Wow, so science?" Mark said, and the three of us laughed.

"Yeah." Katy laughed.

"You married?" he asked. "You do have the adorable features of someone who takes orders from a jacked-up mouth breather with hairy arms and a wife-beater."

"Whoa, now," I said. "Play nice."

"I'm just saying…in my experience attractive—and smart as we now know—women who can choose from anyone typically shove the ones they claim to be looking for in the friend zone with a fervor usually reserved for drowning the toilet baby—"

Katy and I busted out laughing.

"—who was humped into their loins by Jonny Caveman. Am I wrong?"

He looked at her in the rearview mirror and grinned as smug as I had ever seen anyone. I turned back to her with a question mark on my face.

"To answer your question," she said, putting on the best straight face she could muster, "I am single."

"That's really all I was asking."

"What about you guys? Any special ladies?"

"Nope," Mark said. "I'm testing a cunning dating program I call the Med-School-Get-Rich-Trophy-Wife Initiative."

"So you're like a douche?" Katy said. She leaned up and matched his smug grin pound for pound.

"Well, I have a very scattered personality. My plan is really more like learn everything I can in college so I don't have to learn in real life then get a girl when I know what I'm doing. I just don't want to be stuck with my hand up some patient and only be able to think of a Jell-O shot I sucked out of someone's naval."

"Now that's actually not douchey at all," I said.

"What kind of doctor?"

"Oncologist."

"Seriously?" I asked. "Cancer?"

"Yeah. Fuck that shit. It's a personal thing. Took both my grandfathers and the grandmother I like. Myeloma was her sentence. No one should have to lose a limb and still not make it. No one should have to lose a limb ever. If no one else is going to find an ironclad cure, I'm going to. It doesn't matter if I can only help a few people. If I can help them, that will make their day pretty fuckin' awesome."

Then the engine was the only sound in the truck. I looked out the window. The sky had burned into orange, and the sun had begun its descent, peeking out from the cracks in the tree line. The short hand on my watch pointed just beyond four, and the long hand hovered firmly above the eight. We were driving sixty-five miles an hour, and for the first time, the three of us had a moment of normalcy. A perfect run-of-the-mill awkward silence. Nothing ran out into the road. Nothing pierced the silence with a blood-curdling shriek. Three people just sat in a dirty pickup during the end of days.

"Sorry, guys," Mark said. "I didn't mean to bring down the vibe."

I started laughing. "Way to go, bro."

"Yeah," Katy said. "The world has pretty much gone to shit, and you somehow manage to bum everyone out."

Even Mark laughed then. "Yeah, I guess I forgot why we know each other."

"I guess that's one good thing about all this," I said.

"OK," Mark said. "Don't make the apocalypse lame. Tell me more. It seems like we're going to be in this one together. Let's settle in."

"OK," I said. "Where do we go?"

"I don't know," he said as he adjusted the makeshift bandage on his hand. "What's your favorite band?"

"Foo Fighters," I said.

"I tell people OK Go," Katy said.

"The treadmill band?" I asked.

"Yep," she answered.

"What do you mean you tell people OK Go?" our inquisitor asked.

"Well, my actual favorite band is They Might Be Giants, but I can't say that."

"Why not?" I asked.

"Because then people will want to listen to them."

"Isn't that a good thing?" I asked. "I've never heard of them. Shouldn't you want to spread the word?"

"Of course, but they've been kickin' it as a band for more years than I've been kickin' it as a person. And they're still kickin' it. They don't need my help. Plus, they're...different."

"How's that?" Mark asked.

"It's hard to say exactly. If I knew it'd come up, I'd-a brung my CD collection," she said, grinning. "It's like someone asking you to tell a Louis C. K. joke. It's hard to do, and you can't really tell them why."

"I tell you what," Mark said. "When we get to Jackson, we'll loot the mall. I can't imagine security coming in today."

"That's the thing, though. If you hear it and think it's weird, you'll think I'm weird. Regardless, you won't like them the way I do. And that'll bum me out."

"Have they done anything we'd know?" I asked.

"Ever watch *Malcolm in the Middle*?"

Mark and I said yes, and she said they did the theme song.

"Really?" Mark said. "I didn't realize a band did that song."

"I've never really thought about it," I said.

"They won a Grammy for it. But when people actually listen, they do it with an uncomfortable there's-crap-in-my-mouth face. It's basically to a point where I don't even like telling people what my favorites are. I usually skip down to number three or four."

"I get that," I said. "I mean, *Forrest Gump* is pretty widely beloved, so you say that, because *Shawshank Redemption* is a little more violent and uncomfortable. I mean, *Shawshank* is a pretty widely beloved movie too, but the argument's there."

"Not everyone is into forced guy-on-guy action, even if it is implied," Mark said. "It's a very niche market."

"And it's a very intimate thing—your favorite band or movie or whatever," Katy said. "They're our favorites for a reason. We spent the time and, most of the time, money to inadvertently memorize the lines—to quote the scenes word for word—so it becomes important to us. I get offended when other people act like their interests are better than mine."

"Some people's interests just don't mash up," I said.

"I love a good mash-up," Mark said. "I'm a huge fan of Me First and the Gimme Gimmes. A punk cover band? Man, that's where it's at. I want to see more of stuff like that. Movies, music, sports, all of it."

"They are starting to make horror-comedies now," Katy said. "That's a roller-coaster ride for sure."

"I want a horror sport," Mark said.

"Football can be violent—why not make it nightmare inducing," I said.

"Exactly. Come along with me on this journey. I want a wide receiver going deep and being gunned down at the one. You can't hit 'em anymore; how else you gonna stop 'em? All I know is if you're gonna talk that much, you better not fumble when the away team's jerseys are painted red."

"Why stop there?" Katy said. "Get the cheerleaders involved. Knives and pom-poms."

"Exactly, bro!" Mark said. "Give me a *G*, goddamn it!"

As the laughter subsided, we topped another hill, and Mark eased on the brakes. Just below was another crash site—the second of the four we would encounter between Mobile and Jackson. This one was barely crowded enough to slow down below thirty miles per hour. Hardly a blip on the radar, but it was enough to slow us down. I've thought about that a lot since we ran into the flashlight people. What would've happened if we hadn't had to slow down at all, if that gas station in Hattiesburg had been powered enough to steal some gas, where Katy would be. If she would even *be* at all. A lot of things had to break just the right way for it to turn out the way it did. Some things turned out for the best, some for the worse, and the flashlight people absolutely turned out for the worse. But that's coming. What I really want you to know is that before we made it to Jackson, we were a group of friends on a road trip. Just like anyone else. I hope you keep that in mind. We were just normal people.

Mark weaved through the cars strewn along the road. On the other side of the mayhem, relief washed out the anxiety of having to clear a path for the truck again. The noise from under the hood grew louder and fell as we settled back into the idiosyncrasies of everyday human interaction. The truck continued on toward the inner city of Jackson. The sun continued on its path below the tree line.

PART 1
JACKSON

We are sailors, uprooting our lives in favor of a lonely, moving horizon. We search for treasure.

Chapter 9

We made it through the fourth pileup with Mark's hand and my thigh being the only damaged goods for the day. Luckily there wasn't a need to ditch the truck for a new one. There was still a quarter of a tank when Mark hit the headlights a few miles from where we were headed.

After what felt like light-years of sparsely placed RV parks and infiltrated gas stations, we finally came upon some signs of civilization, beginning with an Ace Hardware with a massive metal paint can spilling fake green paint out into the grass between the parking lot and the highway. Beyond that, cell-phone stores, every fast-food restaurant in the book, and a few mom-and-pops were clustered in a wide spot in the road. Then the buildings thinned out along the road, and forest reconquered the landscape.

Just before the highway became a complicated web of ramps and overpasses, there was a wooden A-frame sign. Three simultaneous messages had been painted across its facade. The first and original message read HE1P AT M0V1E TH3TER, and it was spelled out in what looked like gas-station letters affixed to the wood with packing tape. Sprayed below that, blue paint declared Jesus Christ Saves! to the world. And above that was the word *Fuck* in bright red, which seemed like a juvenile way to vandalize the makeshift billboard. Then I recognized the red scribble over Saves! for what it was. We were on our first ramp when Katy's voice spoke up from the backseat.

"What do you think they are doing?"

"Who?" I looked first out my window and then the driver's side window. Jackson lay just beyond the interweaving streets and one-way lanes below the ramp. The power was out, and the city stood black. The lack of a glow in the sky made me think we were still hundreds of miles away. I wondered how long it had been since someone had seen this city lit by nothing but stars. Then something changed that. A light. To my left there was a collection of five glowing dots blinking in and out of view on the streets below the overpass.

"Them," she said.

"I don't know," I said.

"Are they people?" Mark said as he snatched glances out the window.

"Don't know," I said. "Looks like they're using flashlights."

"Yeah," Katy said, consumed with what she was seeing. "Did y'all see any of them using tools?"

"Yeah," I said. It was Tony I pictured. I saw him swinging the pickax with both hands over his head, missing and swinging until the tip of the pick drove into my leg. "But it was daytime, so I don't know if they use flashlights."

"Why would people be out there right now?" Mark asked. "Wouldn't the lights give them away?"

"I don't know," Katy said.

We watched the five pale-yellow dots disappear simultaneously.

I wondered which would be worse—if the bodies holding the flashlights were people or screamers; I felt a wave of cold. After a second or two, a red 1980s Mustang came into view on the side of the road. Its license plate read 1COBRA1.

Mark pointed at the license plate and said, "Because that guy is a fuckin' badass."

I smiled at that and watched the tag and car pass from windshield to side window to rearview mirror. I also watched the car's headlights power on from behind us. The bright-yellow dots shrunk as we pulled away and then grew as the car sped up behind us. Then it hit me that this was the first moving car we had seen for nearly two hundred miles. I hadn't noticed so much as a bird flying overhead.

"Finally," Katy said. "Someone else."

"What? We're not good enough company?" Mark asked, sneaking glances into the rearview. "I don't think that's a good thing, anyway. You see how he was waiting for us? Kinda sketchy, you think?"

"You're right. I don't really like that," I said.

"Should we see what he wants?" Katy said.

"I don't think that's going to be our choice to make," I said as the lights grew larger and more defined.

"Getting a little close don't you think, asshole?" Mark said and glared at the headlights through the rearview mirror. He put on the blinker and switched lanes, giving the car plenty of space to pass us. He slowed a little to make the pass as quick and painless as possible.

The old Mustang rammed into the tailgate of the truck. It hit so hard I came out of the seat, and my head grazed the sun visor.

"What do you think he wants?" Katy asked, starting to panic.

"Should I pull over?"

"I don't know," I said. "Any way you can lose 'em?"

"I can—"

The car slammed into us again. The back wheels lifted off the ground and screeched when they came back down.

Katy groaned.

"OK, you shit." Mark stomped on the accelerator.

The truck hitched and surged forward. We pulled ahead thirty or forty feet. Mark told us to hang on and stood on the brakes. The Mustang slammed into us a third time, sending the truck into a violent fishtail. Before Mark could gain control over the skid, the car rammed us again, and the truck slowly started to spin. Steering into the skid did Mark no good. The Mustang caught the corner of the truck. The truck slammed into a barrier, knocking my head hard into the side window. Tinnitus rang loud in my ears for a second.

The front of the truck ground against the barrier for what felt like miles before coming to a stop. There were pieces of the passenger-side headlight on the hood. Mark twisted the ignition. The engine chugged once and then clicked a couple times before dying completely, never actually turning over.

"Stay here," Mark said as he flung the door open. When he was out of the car, he said, "Well, I hope you have your insurance card, bro. Bit of fucked-up driving back there, wouldn't you say?"

I searched through the cab for a flashlight. The best I could do was a dead laser pen, which I threw back into the glove compartment. The sound of a large gun being cocked broke through the air. When I looked out the window, I saw the headlight from the Mustang spotlighting two men, both wearing plaid button-up shirts—one wore khaki pants, the other jeans. Both were thin. Both pointed rifles at Mark.

"All right, I tell you what," Mark said. "We'll just call it square and walk away now. I promise that's for the best."

"Whoa," I said, hurrying across the bench seat. I used the door as leverage to pull myself through the cab. It dropped off the hinges, and I fell out of the truck. I got up and hobbled toward the newly formed trio. "There's no problem here. We're all cool."

"Get on over here," the one wearing khakis said and then spat a wad of chewing tobacco onto the street.

In the Mustang's crooked headlights, it looked like a massive, wet sack of spider eggs. Other than a grotesquely fat lip, he looked like a normal enough high school kid. His dark-brown hair fell over his eyes, and patches of beard grew in no specific order on his otherwise smooth face.

"No deal, Mr. Khakis," Mark said. "Get back in the truck, buddy. I'm just dealing with something."

I slowed, leaving the door hanging open on one bolt at the bottom. I had my hands up, which I'm certain looked silly in conjunction with Mark's bowed chest and spread shoulders. With his thin legs, he looked like a cobra ready to strike.

The truck door closed, and both men pointed their guns past us to the truck.

"Who else is with you?" Khakis said, overcompensating for his lack of mass. He was thin and about my own height, but his voice demanded attention.

"Don't worry about who is in there," Mark said. "Because we're either going to walk away from here or run away. No one's going to make friends. No one is going to get shot. Simple as that."

"Get on out the car," Khakis hollered at the truck.

"Yeah, come on, sweetheart," Mark said. "We need to leave."

"You ain't going nowhere," the equally thin kid wearing jeans said.

"Oh, Blue Jeans has some shit to say?"

"Mark, shut up," I said.

"Come on out, Katy," Mark called. "We have to walk the rest of the way."

"Boy, you better shut up," Khakis said. "That mouth is going to get you and your friends hurt."

"Is it, Khakis?" Mark yelled. "Katy, come on. We're leaving."

The truck's back door opened.

"Where you headed?" Khakis asked and spit again.

"That's a beautiful thing," Mark said. "You don't have to worry about it."

"Yeah, come on, guys," I interjected before Mark could say anything else. "We're just trying to find the police."

The plaid-shirt boys looked at each other. Then Khakis spoke up. "You cops?"

"Why?" Mark spat.

"Because the ones at the station are on the other side. The theater cops are the real cops. They're *with* the flashlight people."

"The fuck you mean, flashlight people?" Mark asked.

"They're the ones getting rid of the crazy people."

"Get rid of how?" I asked.

"Whatever it takes," Khakis said.

"You're telling me," Mark started, talking a little louder than his usual voice, "if I find the police station downtown, there will be people against getting rid of these pricks ripping people apart?"

"Yeah," Blue Jeans said.

Mark pointed to an exit ramp about two hundred feet away. "You're saying if we take this exit right there onto West and go up to Pascagoula then take a left toward Congress, we'll find a police station where the cops aren't trying to help put a stop to this."

"Yeah," Blue Jeans repeated.

"I like you, Blue Jeans. You got nothin' to say. You're not like this guy." He thumbed toward Khakis. "Look at him. Pointing the gun, scowling. He's doing everything right." Then Mark turned to me. "You hear that shit? If you take West to Pascagoula to Congress, you'll find police who don't wanna help the people who pay their salary."

"OK," I said, completely out of the loop.

"Hey, shut up," Khakis interrupted.

"Hey, fuck off," Mark mocked.

Khakis stepped forward, slapped Mark, and repositioned his rifle, locking it onto Mark's forehead.

"You little *fuck*."

"Slowly, girl," Khakis said, pointing the gun between Mark and me to Katy.

I stepped in front of his barrel.

"Slowly, *woman*," Mark said matter-of-factly.

"Mark. Dude," I said, doing my best to project exhaustion. Because in my head the only way we would get out of the situation was to play nice.

Katy was between us now. She wasn't scared. She only glared at both our new acquaintances with her stony emerald eyes.

"Is it just the three of you?" Khakis said.

"I don't want to talk to you. I want to talk to Blue Jeans."

"It's just us," Katy said as neutral as I'd ever heard anyone, let alone her.

"Blue Jeans, I don't know what's happening, but what we're going to do is wipe our hands of this whole misunderstanding," Mark said as he mimed dusting off his hands. "We're going to walk away, and we didn't even see you or your charming little girlfriend."

"No, you're not," Khakis said.

"Talking to Blue Jeans, sweetie," Mark said.

"What's going to happen then?" I asked. I felt more confident with me, Mark, and Katy together. Even the twenty or so feet we had been separated by made me uneasy. "You going to shoot us in the face? Just listen to him. We're going to leave."

"No. You're going to get in the car with us."

"First of all," Mark began again, "there's no way we're going to fit in there. Second, you're going to get in your car, and you're going to drive to I don't give a shit where."

"No, we're not," Khakis said, putting his arm out to grab Mark.

Katy ignited the flare she was hiding and threw the flaming stick into Khakis's face. He flinched back, and Mark grabbed the barrel of Khakis's gun. The gun went off, barely missing Mark. Mark jerked again, bringing Khakis with the gun, and Mark struck him square in the nose. At the same time, Blue Jeans jerked his gun in their direction. He was struggling to get a clean shot on Mark, so I punched him in the gut and wrestled him to the ground. Katy pried the gun out of Blue Jeans's hands, managing to avoid a second shot that might give away our location to anyone willing to rip us apart without hesitation.

I got to my knees, still holding Blues Jeans down. He pushed me off, but Katy met him with the barrel of his own gun before he could get higher than to his elbows. I rose to my feet as quickly as I could. By then Mark had wrestled the rifle free from Khakis's grip. Mark punched Khakis in the gut and pushed him to the ground. Mark stood over him, looking down at a face of embarrassment painted on Khakis's thin skeleton. Fog came from Mark's mouth like an active volcano. He flung the gun over the barrier, to the streets below. There was a weak splash as though the gun landed like a long stick on the surface of the river.

"Get to the police station," Mark said, taking the gun from Katy. "Run!"

"Come on, Katy."

"I'll meet you guys there."

Katy and I ran.

Before we got too far down the exit ramp to see, I turned back to them. Mark was putting Blue Jeans and Khakis into a car. I could hear him talking to them, commanding them. That's the first time the thought came to me: *We're just normal people. What's happening?*

We continued down the ramp to the bottom. We saw the headlights pass by and waited long enough for Mark to run down to us. Then long enough for him to walk to us. Then long enough for him to crawl.

"What do we do?" Katy asked when it was obvious we were wasting our time waiting for him.

I looked up at a sign that said S West ST.

"We go to the police station."

Chapter 10

"That was brilliant," I told Katy.

The cold air came out in walls of fog as we made our way down the sidewalks toward Pascagoula. Katy warmed her arms, sliding her hands up and down from shoulder to elbow and back. Her sleeveless shirt didn't do much in the way of warmth. If mine had long sleeves, we'd have switched. There's something so weird about winters in the South. Nights are always cold, but days are the wild card.

"You just had a flare on you?"

"I found it under the seat. That's why it took so long to get out of the truck."

"Thank God," I said.

"Do you think he is coming for us?"

"I think he's going to beat us there, honestly. I haven't known him very long, but one thing I know is he gets shit done."

"Do you know where we're going?"

"Not really. I think so. Mark was being pretty blatant about the directions. How are you doing over there?"

"Good," Katy said. "I think I'll be fine now. Just had to work out the initial jitters. The shaking is more adrenaline than shivers. What did I miss, by the way? I heard y'all talking awhile before I got out of the truck."

"First off, just in case something happens and you and I get separated, too, we're looking for Pascagoula then Congress, for the police station."

"Hopefully that won't happen," she said quietly.

Moonlight can be surprisingly bright. We squeezed close to buildings, hoping to blend in or find a shadow to hide in—maybe even to feel normal and be out of the street. That part of town had been kind of a slum even before everything happened. Even then I wouldn't have felt comfortable walking down this part of town this time of night. Blobs of asphalt and holes covered the street. There were surprisingly few cars on this service-like street. I guess that makes sense. No one hangs out near the police station. There were footsteps down the alleyways, and off in the distance, a scream ripped through the blanket of silence.

"Hopefully, Mark will run up behind us in the next couple seconds. He said his sister is there."

"How does he know?"

"Actually, I don't know. Now that I think about it, he never actually said anything to *me*. He really seemed to be sure about it, though. It's hard to explain, but I'm pretty certain that if we head over to the police station, he will probably already be there."

There was a glass bottle in the street. I didn't see it. I never saw it. I just hit it with the side of my foot—not even a kick. It left my foot and went immediately into Katy's path, pinging and rattling all the way. It spun off the sidewalk and got lost in the grass between the sidewalk and brick wall. Katy and I froze. The fog from our breath floated up and dissipated in the moonlight. Everything stilled. Perfect silence filled the open city like a flood. Then, like a hot blade, a scream tore through the city of Jackson.

The woman was big. Even staring back at the foot of the exit ramp, I could see that. My first thought was of a softball catcher.

Maybe a famous one. I don't know if there were professional leagues or not. Probably should have asked for her autograph just in case. Her clothes were ripped along the edges, and her hair stood out wildly from her head. She was a black silhouette, but I imagined that when the second shriek scraped out of her throat, her face was blood red.

Katy and I stood immobilized by the monster. Katy's face scrunched up as her jaw dropped. I imagine I looked the same way. When the thing started running, we were still frozen. Luckily, we had enough space between us and it to be safe. I think Katy and I both knew that even one of those things would probably be too much for us. We turned and ran.

The screams that followed grew closer quickly—almost as though Katy and I weren't running at all, but standing back by the broken bottle. When I looked back, the black figure had gotten to that bottle. It was fast. Watching a person use 100 percent of her potential was unnerving. This woman could single-handedly crush a team of NFL players giving that "110 percent" they mumble so much about.

Our run escalated from just that to a full-on sprint. I looked back, and the screamer was less than twenty feet away. I faced forward just in time to see the Pascagoula sign overhead. I ran into Katy trying to turn. I thought the screamer would be on us by then, but when I looked back, the once-woman was falling back a little. I slowed my pace and got Katy's attention. The thing's screams were weaker, as if dealing with some inner confusion. Her legs shook with violent tremors. The spasms stopped her cold in her tracks. Her hands searched wildly for some kind of cause of the problem, pulling at the muscles in some haphazard attempt at teaching its legs how to operate again. Writhing and moaning in anger, it hunched over, retching and ready to evacuate its stomach. It was like the body was shutting down without its brain's permission. Then it actually picked its leg up and tried to make it move toward Katy and me. It collapsed to its knees under the shifting weight.

I stood there like a caveman when a chain-link-fence post swung into view and crushed the thing's face. Mark hobbled past Katy and me.

"Good. You guys made it," he said, limping past us. The crooked fence post clanged on the street and echoed. "It's right up here. Let's go."

Chapter 11

The second vision of Sarah came. She was still in the hotel, star-ing into either a dirty or a foggy mirror hanging on the wall beside the television. The mirror was huge. It stretched from the floor all the way to the ceiling, and if Sarah stretched both of her arms to the side, she would probably be able to reach both sides of the thick wooden frame surrounding it. She didn't do that, though. She stood facing it. I could almost make out her features in what I'm now convinced was fog. Then she was sitting at the foot of the bed in her scrubs, a pile of papers strewn around her. She kept switching between her scrubs, everyday clothes, and nothing. As I said, they come in flashes.

The light from the television fell over her face. The television displayed a white bold-print number shown on a navy-blue back-ground: 410. The numbers lit the entire room.

My view was cut off as Sarah stood at the mirror again, *glitching* between outfits. That's the only way that I can describe it, *glitch-ing*. One moment she'd be standing at the mirror wearing a robe, and then she'd jerk the way the old movie film projectors would jerk when the film wasn't put together just right, and then she'd be in her scrubs. It wasn't the entire room that would jerk, just her standing at the mirror or sitting on the bed.

I wanted to say something to her. I wanted to make sure she was OK. I never can in these strange scenes. It never works. She walked backward to the bed, and when she sat down at the foot, I could see someone standing in the corner. A shadow covered most of the figure, but I could tell enough to know it was a person—or what once was a person. I wanted to turn toward the person in the corner. The thing about the visions is that they controlled themselves. Looking around did no good. I always saw what came. I was just a passive receiver.

I took two things from that vision. The obvious question of "Who was in the corner?" stuck with me the rest of the night. But the number on the television started showing up everywhere. I would have worried about her, but in the space between the bed and the wall, her purse sat nearly empty. It sagged and leaned over on the ground. Jutting out of the opening was a corner of a picture frame, striped red and white like a candy cane. I knew that frame. It was a picture of us from our long weekend away at Niagara Falls. She takes it to work or anytime she leaves overnight. In the picture we stood on a wooden deck, water falling on us. A photographer took it, and I paid him twenty bucks to e-mail it to me. We were soaking wet, and even I sometimes had trouble making out the faces behind the falling water.

Sarah always loved the picture, but the picture wasn't the important thing to her. She said powering our way through Niagara Falls in two days was the most fun she had ever had. For most of the two days, we didn't leave the hotel room. But really, after the first few hours to a couple madly in love, a big waterfall is still just a big waterfall.

Chapter 12

"You all right?" Katy whispered.

"Girl, you know it," Mark said. "It's the building right up here. The one with the flagpoles out front. That's where we're going."

"And you know your sister will be there?" I asked.

"Oh, she's there."

"How do you know?" Katy said.

We were taking turns staring down at his leg. No blood, but I still worried.

"Because she's a police officer," he said, laughing.

A light came on in an upstairs room of the building with the flagpole out front. A shadow fell over the window. Mark raised a hand in a small wave, and the upstairs window snapped back to black. We didn't make a sound after that.

We continued toward the police station, pacing between a walk and a jog. The city was eerily quiet. No cars. No stray cats darting through alleyways via the tops of garbage cans. Not even the distant cries of a screamer. I remember thinking about that. In the cold, chilling silence, I felt shipwrecked or, better yet, lost at sea in the dark. The wind served as the lightly rising waves against our tiny paddleboat. It is so strange the stupid things we think about just before the mood changes. *Steeeroke!* I remember thinking as we moved through the calm, cool waters of Jackson's inner city— the syllables changing as each foot went forward. Right, left, right, left—*Steeeroke! Steeeroke!* I continued to think as the audible wall of cocking shotguns and military-grade rifles filled the air around the police station. We turned to statues in the still-dark street.

"Stop right there," a strong female voice commanded from some-where around the center of the still-clicking safety buttons. "Show me your hands."

We showed the seemingly empty stoop our palms. I noticed the thin black barrel in the moonlight, protruding from the window just to the left of the entrance. Then I saw the rest of them almost all at once. From the bushes, the windows, behind both leafless trees up front—one even in plain sight hiding in the shadow of the doorway. The only positive feeling I had was the knowledge that Mark's hands were also facing out.

"What are your names?" the voice asked, still stern, but coming down with our obvious cooperation.

Mark's head jerked toward the voice. He took a step forward.

"Mark, what are you doing?" I whispered. "I'm pretty confident that they'll shoot you."

"Stop where you are."

"Bitch," Mark said, sharp and high-pitched. "Get out of the bushes."

"Mark!" Katy snapped.

A pistol shot boomed in the small entry courtyard. A cloud of concrete dust puffed about eight inches above Mark's toes. He stopped where he was. "The fucking hell?"

"They're good. It's Mark," the voice said.

"Who?" a man yelled.

"My brother."

The barrels lowered, and I could breathe again. The thump in my chest began to slow.

"You shot at me, you jackass?" Mark said.

"No, I shot at an intruder," the officer said, walking toward Mark. "I just figured out it was you."

"You dick," he said.

They hugged. It was a really sweet moment. Jackie was obviously Mark's sister. Her face looked just like his, only with more experience and knowledge behind her eyes. She stood level with me and looked up to Mark, like most people, but for a woman I considered her tall. Her posture was strong, and she was very lean. Her hair was pulled tight in a black ponytail and lay flat on the back of her police uniform. She was the quintessential police figure. Mark turned to Katy and me with his arm still around his sister.

"Jackie, this is Derrick Martin and Katy Hughes. They helped me get here. They're cool."

I felt the air of it before I heard it—or before it registered at least. The bullet, I mean. It passed by my arm. Then from behind me there was a boom. I saw the small dot on the police uniform begin to spread into a large red inkblot as Jackie fell to her back. Mark caught her and eased her down. The police officers—a nearly cartoonish number of them—came from everywhere. Katy and I were statues again. Unable to move or think, I couldn't process what was happening. I saw the chaos in front of me, hearing none of it. I could only hear my heartbeat. A small man ran out of the entrance to the station surrounded by even more police officers. He was carrying rags and immediately started covering and working on the bullet wound. The other police officers pulled Mark away from her. I'd never seen someone get shot, especially not a police officer. Another thing I remember is thinking how much more serious this was because she was a cop. And how this inevitably would be on the news tomorrow. No reporters came to take down the story, though. Like I said, we think of silly things sometimes.

When Mark knew they were taking her inside to help her, he ripped away with fury in his eyes. He searched wildly across the rooftops until he saw Khakis standing on a nearby building. He was breathing so hard that his shoulders rose and fell. He was still then, watching as Khakis fumbled to reload the rifle. The officers behind me slowly became audible again, cocking their guns. Mark raised his hand toward Khakis and pointed a gun made from his thumb and forefinger. The roar of weaponry boomed through the air. I grabbed Katy, and we moved clear of the line of fire. Mark fired his hand. The thumb went down, and the recoil jerked his pointer finger up. He lowered his weapon, but the police officers ran toward the building. I never saw Khakis on the top of the building a few blocks away. The moonlight didn't reach to where he had gone by the time I looked in the direction from which the gunfire had come. I didn't know that Khakis had gotten away. I thought they got him and he fell off the building. I didn't ask. I just watched Mark as he stood in the street with his finger and thumb still in that position pointed toward the ground.

Chapter 13

Despite being on a backup generator, the fluorescents in the station were too bright.

Mark, Katy, and I sat in a room somewhere in the middle of the station. At one point the room had been some kind of conference room. Now it was just a lonely sea of open space where our rowboat barely lay above the surface. We sat in a small triangle, Katy and I between Mark and the door. We didn't speak—only looked at our feet. The muffled noise from somewhere deeper in the building stopped. Finally, Mark said something.

"She's OK."

"Of course she is," Katy said, sliding her small white hand across Mark's back.

"No, really, she's fine," Mark said. "I mean, she got shot, but she's fine."

I caught a glimpse at his eyes then. Again I saw a little flicker of green in that infinite black. A quiet rattle of the doorknob interrupted the conversation. A police officer entered the room. The sea poured out the door, and our little boat hit land. The cop's eyes were red, and wrinkling lids drooped in a failing attempt to hide them. He was a large, fit man. His white hair was full and neatly kept despite every other indication that exhaustion was taking over. From somewhere behind the white broom of a moustache came a rumbling voice.

"Hey, Mark, guys, she's fine. The bullet missed everything vital. They are patching her up now. Give her a few minutes." He nodded, and the door closed behind him.

"Thank you," Mark called back to him through the door.

"That's great," I said.

"Told you," Mark said.

"What happened to your leg?" Katy asked after a couple beats.

"Oh," Mark said, laughing to himself. "Nothing today."

"What do you mean?" I asked.

"About four years ago, I was hit by a car." He rolled up his pant leg to show a swollen and misshaped knee. Painted on the leg was a treasure map of scars. Just above his ankle, on the outside, was an inch-long incision mark with little dots lining both sides from top to bottom where five or six stitches had held the wound together to heal. On the inside were three filled-in holes, one on top of the other. Neither of these was of any significance and paled in comparison to the huge line leading from his shin up into his rolled-up pant leg. The scar was thick and lined with the same tiny dots from where the skin had been mended back together.

"*Holy* shit," Katy said after a long moment.

Mark and I accidentally blasted her with surprised looks. She didn't seem to notice. Her hand was already reaching toward the slab of once-shattered bone. Her fingertips came into contact with the holes at the bottom of Mark's leg, and he jerked in feigned anguish.

"I'm kidding," he said, smiling. "Happened years ago."

"What happened?" I asked.

"Well—and tell me if you want to stop," he warned.

At the time I thought it was because the story would be that gruesome. I think Katy did, too, because her face turned up on one side.

"I was coming home from work. I had a bike back then that I took everywhere—a brown Panama Jack beach number with a basket on the back and a cup holder on the front. Even had a bottle opener right there on the side of the bar that holds the wheel, whatever that's called. No gears, just hold on to the handlebars, let your head fall back, and breathe that smooth bike-riding air. You kidding me? I loved it.

"Back then I didn't have a car and had no plans to get one. I mean, I lived walking distance of school and T-Mobile. I worked at T-Mobile at the time—was only about four miles away. Gas was three-something, and I was fat as shit, so I decided, *Fuck it. I'm going to be a bike rider.* And that is exactly what I did, ladies and gentlemen. Eight miles a day, rain or shine, five days a week."

"Does that work?" Katy said.

"Dropped thirty pounds in a month. My mom thought I was sick. I get it. I went from a creepy guy with a neckbeard standing behind you in McDonald's, breathing hard, to a respectable defensive end who let himself go a little in the off-season. It wasn't until last year that I joined the gym and got down to this lovely Anthony Davis bod you see here.

"But that's not what you asked. Anyway, one night I was coming home from work. Bebop, bebop." Mark mimed riding a bike as if from an early 1920s cartoon. "Well, there were no sidewalks exactly, so I'm on the side of the road but out of the way enough. They may not see me from space, but they don't have to in order to miss me. I know what I'm doing. Even four years dumber than I am now, I knew what I was doing. So I turn onto a busier road, still with no sidewalks. As per usual it's too crowded to cross all three lanes—two normal ones and a turning one—all in one go. What I usually did was wait until this stretch of road where there is nowhere to turn for a few thousand feet and cross one lane and wait in the turning lane for the other side to clear. Boom. Easy peasy. Done it hundreds of times, and no one ever got hurt. Well, not until this fateful night when some fuckin' douche Nazi comes flooring it down a side street, attempting to pass people in the turning lane. Completely failing at maintaining safe-driver status. Succeeding at fuckin' my life up, though. I wasn't expecting it, and for good reason, I think. Repetition breeds comfort and expectation. Besides, no one ever thinks bad shit is going to happen to them. But when it does. It's a roller coaster."

"Jesus, man." I didn't mean to say it.

"Yes. Jesus Man, Jesus Woman, and Jesus Child," he said.

"Were you knocked out?"

"*Hell* no," he said, almost proudly. "I was conscious through every single flip, wishing to Jesus Man to just let me land. Just hit the ground. Just get out of the fuckin' air so I can check and make sure I can move my God Man damn feet. That's all I wanted. I was in the air for twenty minutes at least, just fuckin' flipping. Eyes wide open. I saw it all. I saw the streetlights spinning. Saw the ground come into view then abruptly leave. Even the white Lincoln's grille when it destroyed my favorite bike in the world, and then my leg. Yes, I do my own stunts."

"Was the driver drunk?" Katy asked.

"I don't know," Mark said.

"What did the driver do?" I asked, knowing the answer.

"I like to think he went home to kill himself. Or herself. Luckily, someone stopped because I remember getting her to call the police, my mom, and my girlfriend. When she was doing that, I heard— multiple times—tires screeching to avoid hitting me again. This guy who looked like Lenny Kravitz in a Starbucks commercial dropped a red blanket over me. I thought, *Well, this looks good.*

"Eventually, the ambulance came, and I saw my leg just hanging there as they picked me up onto their big, orange cutting board. Plop on the gurney. The ride was excruciating. Every bump was a leg full of hate. I didn't even realize my hand was fractured."

He held up his right hand. Looked normal enough until I saw the knuckle on the pinkie. The joint that connected the pinkie to the hand was about an inch lower than it should be. Mark balled his fist.

"See, the knuckle is supposed to be here." He pointed. "And it is. But since they just set the fracture, it looks like it fell about this far down. It's funny. This never even hurt. Not once. That's how bad this hurt." He slapped his leg.

"That night they put pins in my ankle and three in my thigh. That's what the holes are from. They connected them with these metal rods that basically kept the shattered bones away from each other for three weeks. I can tell you now there is nothing worse than having metal rods connected to the inside of you being on the outside of you. Not to mention I had baby foot something fierce."

"What's baby foot?" Katy asked.

"Chubby and swollen. Like a baby's foot. It was at least twice the size.

"My mom was frantic, apparently. I never saw it, but I was told she cried a lot. We got into a number of screaming matches just so I could drag her attention away from her phone. The nurses had to separate us. I really found out who loved me that year. Or half a year. I had six months of leave of absence, and I required every single day of it. It was funny. The doctor had to reminisce just to know what he was dealing with. That was the first time I ever heard the phrase *back in the nineties*. First time I ever felt old in my life.

"Anyway, about that time something happened with my family. Everyone just became unpleasant with each other. That's really all I want to say specifically, but the reason I tell you that is because she wasn't there for me then. Everyone else was. My girlfriend's family saw that I was watered daily and made sure the pins in my leg were taken care of properly.

"So I get the second surgery—the one to take the pins out and put the metal in me to hold my bones together. My mom made everyone go home. I assumed, and still do, that it's because she felt guilty for not being helpful while I was in the hospital bed or when my piss bottle was full and needed dumping during the weeks prior. And I get it—I was twenty-four. I was a grown-ass man who could help myself. But anyway, the entire time I was in the hospital, she was there. And she was on her phone. Eventually I snapped. Screaming at her between pain treatments. It left our relationship in shambles.

"After six months I was able to walk and get around on my own, which I was told I'd never be able to do again. I had to buy a car. I couldn't drive a stick while I relearned how to walk. I had to get to work somehow. The operating doctor gave up on me. After two months of rehab, I wasn't as far along with my recovery as the typical broken-tibia patient, which I wasn't, should be. He told me I didn't have to continue physical therapy and said I should get a cane. I think he was just bored. He got his money, so what did he need me for anymore? I shoved it up his ass, though. That happened at Christmas. I was on a bike by July. I never went back to him. Plus disdain for the city grew, as I hope you can understand. I'm not bitter.

"So I took off and decided to go back to school. I said, 'Good-bye, hometown. You were a dirty, stoned prostitute laying on the sidewalk, pulling on my pant leg and asking me for money.' I haven't been back. My family and I quit talking. My sister, who at that time was just entering training, was part of that group. Another year later I wasn't speaking to Jackie or my mom. Or my dad—who never did anything wrong. I always felt bad about that. Because my parents eventually divorced, and my mom died of an aneurism before a year passed.

"At the funeral Jackie told me not to be such a stranger. I promised her I wouldn't. But aside from the occasional text message, I totally was."

"That's awful," Katy said.

"Yeah," Mark said as he rubbed up and down the scar. "You said that. But that's what happened in a nutshell. There was a point when they were just gonna go Paul Bunyan and hack it off. Then they got a pulse in my foot, and that went out the window. Then they thought I'd never do a bunch of stuff. Ride a bike being one, funny enough. All that wound up happening is, when I run or walk too much in a day, it'll throb, and I'll need an aspirin. Nearly a full recovery. Can't bend it all the way back, but close."

"The driver didn't stop?" I asked.

"Didn't even stop," Mark said, rolling down his pant leg. "I think we're OK to go now. How's your bedside manner?"

Chapter 14

Police officers circled the wooden table that stood in the place of an operating table. Jackie sat up, weak and drugged up from whatever pain-killer they had on hand. The small man who had rushed out into the courtyard dumped blood-soaked gloves into a wastebasket. Then he washed his hands in one of the sinks lined against the wall, cleaning the little bits of red out of his salt-and-pepper beard and horseshoe haircut.

Mark walked to Jackie.

"Go easy on her," the doctor said. He was wiping his thin, gold-rimmed glasses clean. "She's going to be a little out of it for the next couple of hours. She felt most of that."

"How are you, Jack?" Mark said. His hands were on her knees, and he was in a classic pep-talk stance.

"*Nyerm fin*," she said. She lazily shook her head back and forth, her ponytail brushing both ears. She went to stand up and slid partially off the table. Mark caught her and put her back on the table.

"Nope. Park it, son," Mark said. Snapping his fingers in her face, he said, "Look at me. Up here."

When she did, Mark said she was going to be fine. Jackie laughed and put her finger between Mark's lips and teeth, pretending to brush them.

"*Bus, bus, bus,*" she said to the rhythm of her finger's swipes across Mark's mouth. "*Bus, bus, bus, for teef.*" She giggled like an eight-year-old and repeated, "*Nyerm fin.*" She wiped her finger on Mark's shirt, popped him in the face with her open hand, and went to sleep.

"Good," the doctor said. "She's going to be OK. She'll feel it when she gets up, but she's fine."

"She's a hoss," Mark said. "Who did this?"

"I don't know specifically," the doctor said as he held out his hand to each of us. "David Nipper. Typically orthopedics, but I've had something like this before. Luckily, it was a low-caliber gun. You can bet this was the handiwork of one of the theater people. No one else in town can work a rifle."

"What do you mean 'theater people'?" I asked. "We were stopped by two dickheads in plaid talking about theater cops and flashlight people."

"I don't assume theater people have theater cops *and* flashlight people for parents," Mark said.

"Zing," Katy lobbed his way.

"Come here. Let me see that leg." Dr. Nipper yanked my jeans to my knees and had me sit on the end of the table that Jackie was on. He removed my makeshift tourniquet and quickly went to work. "They are both. The flashlight people and the theater cops, I mean. The theater people are there because they are trying to kill the screamers. I assume you know what I'm talking about. Except they call them crazies. Well, at least you're starting to heal already. Not much use in stitching you up. Hand me that jar, could you?"

"Who are they exactly?" Katy asked, picking up a jar of some kind of ointment from behind her.

"They're just people. Can't really say there's a strategy to who went where. Just people who didn't"—he waved his hand as if to grab the word out of thin air—"change. Some people stayed here, waiting for family, friends, what have you, or just waiting to leave. I don't know if you heard, but the bigger cities are becoming a kind of haven. So if you know anyone near one of them, I suggest you find out how to get there. Anyway, most of the rest of us broke off, threatened to 'do something' about this. Trying to kill them. I guess they're after us now as well."

"What do you mean they're trying to kill them?" Katy asked.

Dr. Nipper covered the gash in my leg with the salve, and lightning went up my leg. I sucked air through my teeth.

"Yep, that'll happen." The good doctor moved to the shelves screwed into the locker-room wall and rifled through small empty boxes. "Most of them are under the impression that if the area can be cleared of them, then everything will go back to normal. So they started picking them off, one by one. Nice little mess they made. The problem is, when the world forces this drastic of a change, you can't stay normal. You have to move with it. What happens in a year when Jackson—if it's anything more than a paragraph in a history book—is cleaned of the screamers and one from the backwoods of Brandon kills its way here? You need walls to keep them out...and people to make the walls. That's why everyone is going to New Orleans and Dallas. I bet New York will have some great walls. Those people in the theater don't understand. There is no normal now. It just happened. Took most of the police staff with them, too. The higher-ups, I mean. Sergeants? Chiefs? I don't know what. We have these twelve folks and a number of 'civilians' in the offices upstairs."

Nipper found a large square bandage and pressed it onto my leg. I immediately stood up and reset my pants back where they were. I saw a smirk on Katy's face.

"Any cuts or breaks?" Nipper asked her.

"Totally fine." She held up her arms and modeled her legs as if they were a behind door number two on *The Price Is Right.*

"OK, big guy. You're up. Let me see that hand...The flashlight people are sort of a thrown-together hunting crew, honestly." Dr. Nipper laughed as he said it. "It started early into the night, from what I know."

He stopped, looking into Mark's palm. Then, baffled, the doctor asked, "When did this happen?"

"I don't know exactly. Recently," Mark answered.

"You can put some of this on it if you want. It's pretty well healed." He handed Mark the jar of ointment, and Mark applied it.

"What?" Mark asked.

"Yeah, I mean, it looks fine to me."

Then there was a pause where I convinced myself that the cut on his hand wasn't as bad as I originally thought.

"So why are they called flashlight people?" Katy asked.

"They use the flashlights as bait. It also blinds them temporarily. They flick them on and off until they hear a scream. Then they all go off until they find whoever made the sound. They surround the screamer. Then…you know. They do the same thing all day with mirrors and sunlight. You'd be amazed what these people can do with a little spray paint and debris in the ways of camouflage. We've been hearing gunshots in the distance all day."

"Why use the flashlights and mirrors? Why not a noise or food to lure them somewhere?" I asked.

"Because the screamers can only see," Dr. Nipper said. "No other senses that we can tell. See *and* kill, but I suppose that's not a sense."

"Seriously?" Mark said. "All our efforts to be quiet while traveling here were for nothing?"

"Wow," I said, feeling silly.

"It's almost as though they're some unevolved monster stuck in our bodies," the doctor said. "They aren't used to having a physical limitation or something. We think that's why they scream. Since they can't hear, they scream to overcompensate. You know how hard-of-hearing people are at the dinner table. They are trying to communicate, but in this case nothing actually gets through."

"That makes sense," I said. "The one chasing me and Katy through the street earlier, it was like she had no throttle. Then she just fell out. Her legs were spasming or whatever you call it. She still wanted to get at us even though her body couldn't."

"Who are they?" Mark said. He was suddenly in a fury again.

"Who?" Dr. Nipper asked.

"The theater people," Mark said. "Do you have names? Khakis—I know what he looks like. I saw him on the roof of a building. Hell if I know how he got here so damn fast, but he did. We had a run-in with him on the way here. Got his panties tied tight."

"Real young fella?" Nipper asked.

"Couldn't really tell," Mark said. "It was something like an hour ago. Not a lot of light. Sounded my age."

"Did he have a brother with him? Little slow?"

"Honestly," Mark said, "I'd-a told you they both were slow. What kind of shit is that? Pulling a gun on strangers just because the lights go out. Fuckin' lunatics."

"Yeah, I know him. Not who he is, but he was one of the young impressionable ones who decided those screamers out there were no longer human as soon as someone put a gun in his hand. That's how they got so much steam. Most of those people are younger than thirty. Too young to know any better. You said you saw him on the way in?"

"We did," I said.

"I guess they started a little welcoming committee. He say anything of interest?"

"That there are crazies running around, and that there are theater and police-station people," I said.

"Well," Nipper said, "that's really all there is to know. It all happened so fast. This barely started twenty-four hours ago. Everything has already gone to shit. Isn't that wild? How quickly the world falls into chaos?"

We didn't say anything to that.

"We'll be here for the next two days," the doctor said. "There are two school buses behind the station."

"Which theater is it?" Mark asked.

"Tinseltown, on the other side of the city." Dr. Nipper gestured to his left as if the theater were just beside us.

"Right on." Head down and determined, Mark left the room.

Chapter 15

"Where you going, bro?" Katy asked as she and I chased Mark out the door. She grimaced. Apparently it felt as weird to say it as it did to hear her say it.

"Gonna spill a little red in those khaki pants. I'm a new-age clothing designer. Taking risks. Pushing the boundaries and shit. I'm a regular Calvin Klein."

"Whoa, whoa," I said, grabbing his arm. "Can't do that. Those things will tear you apart."

"Like fun, they will."

"Yes, they will," Katy said. "It's one thing to drive across the state in a car, making jokes and carrying on, but when you're out there with a head full of steam, you could get careless and make a huge mistake."

"No. I'm actually very calm," Mark said. And he really was calm. He spoke confidently, as if he had thought everything out for hours. "Here's the situation. My older sister just got gut-shot by some child-diddlin' jerk-off who basically was told no probably for the first time in his life. Unless you know of a different reason." He paused. His eyebrows reached for the ceiling. "Great. I'm going to walk over to that theater, shove my foot through his sphincter, and walk right back with a human-shaped right shoe. I'll be back in a couple hours."

"What about the screamers?" Katy said. I only later realized that we had very quickly taken to calling them that.

"What about them?" he asked. "They can't hear or smell or taste or whatever else. All they can do is see. Nighttime is the best time for sneaking around them. I can duck off in the shadows and hide behind a tree and boom—done deal."

"How are you going to get there? Do you even know where it is?" Katy asked.

"Yeah, I used to live here. It's about five or six miles down the road. I can be there and back by midnight." He waited a minute with his hands out, beckoning for another excuse to stay. I believe he was ready to swat anything back down. Except for one thing.

"What about your knee?" I asked after he had turned toward the courtyard door again.

He put his hand on the bar to open the double doors and then turned back to us. "My knee is fine. I can walk, and that's all I need."

"Maybe to get around the screamers, yeah, but is that really going to be enough to put the red on the pleated tan pants, Mr. Klein?" I asked.

"Plenty," he said. "He wasn't aiming for her." He pressed the handle down, pushing the door with all his weight.

The heavy metal door didn't budge. Mark rammed his face into it, and the black Dolphins cap slid back and off his head. He reached around with one hand and snagged it before it fell to the ground.

"The blue hell is this about?" Mark asked the door. He shook the handle bar violently and pushed again to no avail.

"What's going on?" a deep voice called from down another hallway. We heard a chorus of gun clicks.

"Nothin', Officer," Mark said like a teenager who was clearly caught in the act. The three of us raised our hands in submission. "Just headed out to destructively violate a skinhead. Nothin' wrong with a little harmless revenge sodomy with a boot, right, fellas?"

"You can't go out there." A thin black man in jeans, a T-shirt, and a badge eased around the corner behind a gun. He wasn't scared, but forceful.

"Dude, I'll be fine. I just need to make it to the theater. I'll be right back."

"Why are you going to the theater?" the officer asked.

"I know who shot Officer Phillips. And will you *please* lower the peashooter?"

"Take your hand off the door." When Mark did, the officer lowered his weapon.

"He was part of the welcoming committee when we got here," Mark said.

"What's his name?"

"Khakis," Mark said.

"What?"

"We don't know his name," I said. "I just know his face for the most part. And what he was wearing. And what the guy he was with was wearing."

The officer considered this. "All right, but I can't just let you go out there. The screamers will kill you." He said that last part as if it was an everyday problem—with the same emotion he might have used to tell Mark not to go outside because the mosquitoes would bite him. He put the gun in his belt loop behind him, marking the first time I had ever seen that done in real life. "But I'll tell you what," the officer said. "I have a house about a mile from there. I can take you that far. We can rest for the night and go sometime tomorrow."

"By then they will have regrouped and planned for someone to come," Mark said.

"I really don't think so," the officer corrected. "If we go now, they will be on their guard. Probably even lined up on the roof waiting to pick you off. If we wait a day, they'll be a little more at ease, and we can still use the cover of night."

"Besides, Mark," I said, "we have two days. We may as well stake out somewhere and figure out anything we can about these things. It seems like we are going to be dealing with them a lot until we get where we are going."

Mark waited. "What's your name?" he asked the officer.

"Ted."

"Ted?"

"Yes, Ted."

"But you're black."

I've never heard a room go so silent so quickly.

Ted looked down at his hands. "No. No, this can't be. I woke up white and perfect. *Why?*" he screamed. "Why, God? Why did you do this to me?"

"OK, that's plenty. Don't make it a racist thing. I've just never heard of a black man named Ted. I'm sorry."

"What'd you think it was?" Ted asked.

"I don't know. Denzel? What's it short for?"

"Theodore."

"Oh, well, why don't you go by Theo?"

"Why would I?"

"Because…that's what Cosby's kid did, right?"

Everyone within earshot cried out laughing.

"Come on, man," Ted said. He calmed his laughter and put his arm around Mark.

Officer Ted led Mark down a dim hallway. Katy and I followed, trying to listen to what Ted was telling Mark. It didn't seem like much more than two frat guys hanging out.

Katy got my attention. "Should we let someone know where we're going?"

"I don't know," I said. "It seems like we're in capable hands. Besides, who would we tell?"

She shrugged.

"I guess we just keep up if we can."

The pace at which Ted and Mark walked was outstanding. For the first time, I was able to see how tall Ted was. He was only an inch or two shorter than Mark.

A chocolate-colored door stood at the end of the corridor. Ted depressed the lever door handle, and the door creaked open. The noise was loud, and I was grateful the screamers were deaf. Even after the door was open, the droning of a generator remained. Through the doorway there was a small carport. This part of the station wasn't much larger than the conference room where we'd waited to hear about Jackie. The carport opened straight ahead to a two-lane street. A single bulb that hung from the hood of one of the vehicles lit the carport. We had opened the door to the back bumpers of two red-white-and-blue Jeep Cherokees. The police stickers decorating the sides shone in the light. They looked like brand-new cars. A chain-link fence surrounded the two cars, and chains loosely hugged the gate closed. Just beyond the gate, two screamers, oblivious to the fluorescent light from the carport, ran back and forth with no obvious agenda and then disappeared down a dark alleyway.

"This is where we keep the cars." Ted made a wide sweeping gesture around the room with his arm. "I guess that's obvious." Then to an unrealistically big officer working under the hood of a car, he said, "Hey, Jacobson, when Phillips comes to, can you make sure she knows I have her brother and the people he was with?"

"That's us," I said, being generous with the sarcasm.

Jacobson, whose reddish stubble contradicted his black hair, wiped grease on his barrel chest. He angled the light hanging from the raised hood toward us and said, "I'll let her know." He sounded like a greaser straight out of the 1950s. He twitched his head to swing his wet-looking hair out of his eyes.

"*Noice*," Mark said, examining the Jeeps. That's what it sounded like, anyway. "All right, so I say we pony up and head to your place. Then, like SEAL Team Six we wait until sleepy time, convoy to Tinseltown, run one of these mad bastards into the building, hop back in this one, and head on back. Easy peasy."

"Well, not really," Ted said, gesturing toward where the two cars were facing. "One of them is being worked on. The engine is shot."

"Really?" Katy asked. "It seems a lot newer. What happened?"

"It's a repo. The engine is missing pieces and wires. The previous owner went in and ripped everything out before the collection agency got to it. We won it in an auction. We're going in this one. The backseat is pretty busted up, though."

"Didn't waste any time getting those stickers on them," Katy observed.

"Priorities, right?" Ted said. "We can take this one. I have a walkie, so we can check in with your sister. If there are no objections, you can pile in."

Mark waited for a nearly immeasurable moment with his hand on the door. I like to think he was debating on leaving his sister. Weighing the need for revenge against the need to reunite. But as I said, the moment passed quickly. He hopped in the shotgun seat like a little kid. The SUV teetered on the shocks. Katy and I followed suit in the backseat. Officer Ted tossed the chain on the gate to Jacobson.

The Cherokee roared to life and lurched forward with the headlights off. Ted stomped the brakes and didn't move until the chain lightly hugged the gate again. "Sorry, guys, the quicker we're still, the quicker we're unnoticeable."

Two screamers that crossed the street in the darkness, running like they were on fire, didn't even notice the big SUV in the street. After a few noiseless moments, Ted eased the Jeep onward toward his home a mile out from the theater.

"This is Officer Carter," Ted said on the walkie-talkie. "I'm taking the three members of the Phillips party to the house on the hill. We're going to hold up there for the night to see if anything can be found out on the developing situation. Also I'll be looking into a suspect for the attempted murder of a police officer. Over."

The walkie-talkie clicked. Then went silent. Then clicked again.

"Copy that. Fedora here. We'll keep the seat next to Phillips warm for you. Y'all be careful out there."

"Over and out."

The walkie clicked one last time. Mark gave a weird little salute to the empty streets of Jackson as Officer Ted dropped the walkie onto the floorboard.

Chapter 16

The large white house stood strong and tall behind a black steel gate. A perfectly manicured lawn came right up to the entrance from the gate. Three steps led up to a wide porch that stretched across the entire front of the house. Only one tree stood in the front yard. The leaves hadn't fallen off the evergreen. A tire swing dangled from a high branch. The tree looked like a bored kid on the front lawn playing with a yo-yo. The Jeep stayed parked on the outside, pointing at the dark property.

"Shit, bro," Mark guffawed. "How do you afford this place?"

"My wife was a surgeon," Ted said.

"What is she now?" I asked.

"One of them." Ted's voice dampened.

There was nothing to say to that. We all knew it.

"There a generator, or you think we should keep it dark?" Mark asked.

"I don't have one, but getting in will be easy." Ted pointed to the garage. "It's unlocked, and I can manually open the garage. We'll just go in there and shut the door behind us. I don't see any movement, so we should be OK on that front. I want to go in first, though. There's a gun under your seats and on the side of yours, Mark."

"Y'all keep these in the backseat, too?" Katy pulled a small hand-gun from the blackness beneath the driver's seat.

"This is a raid vehicle. No arrests." Ted opened the door when all seemed clear to get out and open the gate. "Mark, slide over to the driver's seat and pull forward for me."

The door closed slowly, locking in the silence.

"You think we're going to need these?" Katy asked, holding onto the handgun as if it were plastic explosives.

"I'd prefer not to." Mark cocked the handgun from the place in the door I always kept receipts. I thought that was probably a better use of the little cubbyhole. Then he climbed over the seat and inched the car forward.

After a few moments, Ted hopped in the shotgun seat. "Go ahead and pull into the garage. I'm going to go in first and make sure it's still empty. I want to go by myself so no one gets hurt. I'll come back when we're in the clear."

The Cherokee came to a stop in the nearly empty garage. Ted dropped the garage door. The cab of the SUV fell into a darker blackness. Ted stumbled around the car and entered the house.

"Would you rather?" Mark didn't allow the silence to take over again.

"Would I rather what?" I asked.

"No, the game." Mark poked his head through the space between the front seats.

"Sure, I'll play," Katy said.

"All right, go first," Mark said.

"OK, would you rather eat spoiled milk or starve?" Katy ventured. I was happy to see that she was loosening up.

"That's an interesting attempt at being gross," Mark said.

"I know it's not a great one," she said. "But it's a place to start."

"How spoiled is the milk?" I asked.

"I believe the question answers that." Katy crossed her arms in satisfaction.

"What conditions are we looking at?" Mark asked, sitting forward again.

"Lost at sea?" she said. "No, plane crash in Antarctica."

"Why would we be flying over Antarctica?" I asked.

"You were in Chile, and it's easier to get to South Africa that way," Katy said.

"Well, clearly not if we crashed. But I'll say eat it because it's been frozen since weeks before the expiration date, and the snow isn't doing it for me anymore." I leaned back, confident in my answer.

"Well, that's not gonna be fun," Mark corrected. "It'll be hard as a rock chewing on that thing. I say this. Day one: plane crash. I use the fiery engine to thaw the milk, maybe even spoiling it a little better. I'm not hungry enough to commandeer the flesh from the bone graveyard, so I'm going to use the spoiled milk to attract the attention of a would-be predator or penguin or whatever they keep down there. Then, *pow*, use the shrapnel to snag lunch from a safe distance."

"So I guess you survived the crash completely unscathed?" I asked.

"The cold air hardened my bones to adamantium strength."

It was too dark to see, but I imagined Mark looking pretty smug.

"OK." Katy was excited now. "Who's next?"

"Would you rather go to a strip club with your church group or have sex with someone you know has itchy-crotch syndrome?" Mark proposed.

"Jesus." Katy nearly screamed with laughter. "This game spun out of control very quickly."

I asked, "Do I have to sit with the church group?"

"Yep." Mark spoke like a 1920s radio broadcaster. "Genesis six through nine. That's right. It's Noah's night down at the ole Snatch and Grab—so you know this is low quality—and you've got a choice to make."

"Right." Katy was on the verge of laughter.

Mark employed a typical southern-belle accent. "Do you sweat it out with Marge and the girls?" He adopted a more modern-day radio announcer. "Or do you and Gina of Nazareth walk two by two to the Garden of Eden to commit the not-so-original sin?"

"Is the stripper hot, at least?" Katy asked.

"Derrick's is a six; yours is an eight."

"Why is mine a six?"

"Because you get a girl. You're fine with a six. Katy has to be penetrated, and let's face it, no one likes to be staring down the barrel of an unkempt cock-and-balls. Even if he's a ten. Gotta give her something for her trouble."

"OK," Katy started. "First of all, he's not a ten if he's unkempt—"

"Oh, he's unkempt," Mark cut in. "It's always unkempt in biblical references."

"Second—"

Katy was cut off by a roaring boom from upstairs in the house—then a series of thumps as if someone up there was running around. Katy's hand gripped my arm.

"Do we do something?" Katy asked.

"He said sit here," Mark reminded her. "Besides, I think if there was more than just the one shot, something would be up."

We waited a long time. An hour by the feel of it—three minutes by the hands on my watch. Mark turned the key enough to get the windows rolled down. He was about to call out when Ted opened the door to the garage, earning at least a small scream from the three of us.

"Christ!" Mark screamed.

"Everything is fine. Had one in the backyard after something—probably just its own shadow—but the house is clear. Just take off your shoes on the way in." Ted smiled and led us inside.

Chapter 17

The house was incredible. The doorway from the garage opened to a foyer that was about as big as my office back at the barn. An old, dim LED lantern placed in the middle of the bigger rooms, away from the windows—just enough to keep our little toes safe from table legs—spread orange light throughout the bottom floor. Pictures hung on the wall, although not enough light filled the room to tell who the people were in them. Fake plants sat on the ends of tables on every corner. Across the foyer from the door to the garage was an open half bath. There was no light coming into the room, but the sink—a large glass bowl with a pump-style well faucet—reflected what little light peeked around the doorframe. The foyer led to an open living room with black leather couches along the walls, aimed toward the television, which was a sixty-inch and dwarfed by the size of the room. At the opposite end of the living room, a swinging door led to an equally huge kitchen-and-dining-room combo. Everything but the counter tops, tables, and chairs was made of stainless steel. I noticed that Ted and I had the same microwave. We followed close behind Ted to avoid getting lost. We took the stairs next to the garage door to the second floor.

On the second floor, there were enough rooms for each of us to get a one with an adjoining bathroom. There were five bedrooms in all—three on one side and two on the other. We made our way to the middle room—it actually felt more like we were being pulled to it.

A balcony connected the three rooms as sort of an upstairs porch. A potted plant stood between each of the three doorways, and a five-piece, steel table-and-chair set took up the middle of the balcony. It was there that at 11:35, by my watch, Ted and I sat, looking into the thinly wooded area down the hill behind the house. Behind us, in the middle room, Mark and Katy had already clocked out for the day.

"Where you from?" Ted set two open bottles on the table and put his feet up into one of the empty chairs.

"Semmes." I took a drink of the still-cool beer. "Mark is from Mobile, I'm pretty sure. He said he lived here briefly, so I'm not positive. Katy's from South Carolina. She's down here for school. We picked her up along the way. You?"

"Jackson. Born and raised."

"Wow," I said. "Your whole life, and you've never lived anywhere else?"

"Never."

"You've left though, right? Like vacation and stuff?"

"Oh, of course." Ted drank from the other beer bottle. "New Orleans, Baton Rouge. The Delta. Been all over."

I couldn't tell if he was kidding. He moved around in his seat. I could tell he was searching through his pockets in the dim moonlight. Then a metallic scratch and a spark. One more time—it's never on the first try, after all—and the tiny flame came alive, lit the tiny homemade stick, and died. The ash brightened and dulled as Ted took a drag. For a second I was taken aback that a police officer would be smoking weed, but the smell not only assured me I was still dealing with a straight cop but also struck a deep chord of nostalgia. The smell of my father's pipe filled the balcony's air space, and the thought fled.

"Is that Tinder Box?" I took a deep breath.

"Yeah, it's technically pipe stuff, but I never liked how messy those are. It's easier for me to use the papers."

"My dad used the same stuff. In a pipe, though."

"Small world." Ted clinked his beer with mine. "So what's your story? What did you do twenty-four hours ago?"

"I had a farm. That dad I was talking about left it to me. I used to be a mechanic. I have a degree in advertising, but that never worked out for me."

"He left it to you?" Ted puffed again.

"Well, it went to me. He was killed."

"Shit, man, I'm sorry."

"It's no problem." I waved him off.

"What happened?" The embers of Ted's cigarette bounced up and down, and I thought of Samuel L. Jackson from *Jurassic Park*. "He a drug dealer on the side or something?"

"Who's a drug dealer on the side or something?" Katy said. She closed the French door and sat in one of the other patio chairs.

"Can't sleep?" I asked.

"Could you sleep in a sawmill?" She feigned snoring. "What are y'all talking about?"

"How Derrick came into his farm. I can get you a beer if you want."

Katy waved him off. "What happened?"

"Well," I said, debating whether or not to tell the truth. I still don't know why I told them what I did. "When you work on a farm, there's a lot of...I guess the word is...camaraderie between other farmers who don't grow whatever it is you grow—especially if what you do helps what they do. This is my experience in the field, anyway. For instance if you have the soil for tomatoes but not lettuce, you would more than likely partner with a farm that does have the soil for lettuce. Then the two farms send a joint representative to go to a grocery store or restaurant or whatever with more to offer, giving you a better chance to gain business than if you were doing everything on your own. When a business can go to one place to make an order or file complaint instead of two, they like that."

"That makes sense," Katy said, picking up the beer in front of me and taking a swig.

"Pretty easy concept. I mean, that's a very dumbed-down version of it, but you get it. You know Big Jim's, right?"

"The meat company?" Ted asked.

"The meat, produce, livestock, you-name-it company. At one point it was strictly meat. Sausage mainly. It was the nation's leading manufacturer of pork products. But after Big Jim went missing, the company had to scramble to stay afloat. This was years and years ago. Before our parents were even born. So it branched out. Started a chicken plant. Raised cattle for a dairy farm. I guess the plan was to corner the market on breakfast. Eventually, the company couldn't keep up with the expenses. Somewhere along the line, it made a business-model change. Now it is more of a property management company that knows how to operate a farm. I don't think it expands by building anymore. It just goes to farms and plants all over the country to buy the ones it sees as productive, slaps its logo on the front gate, and sells the farms' products. It doesn't even centralize its ingredients anymore. A Big Jim's chicken sandwich in Seattle probably tastes nothing like one here."

I could tell they were looking at me with bored expressions, even in the dark. I'm not one to make a history lesson exciting by any means.

"Anyway, so when you establish that sort of a relationship, you are opening not only a vendor partnership, but in a lot of cases, you also open a personnel relationship. Let's say, Ted, you have a chicken processing plant, and two of your workers win the lottery and move to Venezuela. Katy, you have a line of chicken houses, and you guys are partners. So what you do is send one or two of your guys who already know how to handle chickens to help him until the positions can be filled so production doesn't miss a beat."

"Still with you." Katy finished the bottle.

"Well, before Big Jim's business model spread to Semmes, my grandfather started this sort of arrangement with a neighboring breeding farm. Horses, donkeys, cows, dogs, whatever you want. Our farm also grew hay, and during the winter when the grass was dead, the neighboring farm would use our hay to feed their animals at a significantly discounted price while my grandfather would get his horses from that farm for next to nothing, and that partnership stayed through the generations. Even when my dad ran the farm, he still got his horses from that breeding farm, and they still got their hay from us. Eventually, the other farm started producing a large number of pigs. Getting the attention of Big Jim's. A few years back, Big Jim's bought that farm. Called it Big Jim's West Mobile. Because the farm wasn't prepared for the mandatory increase in production that Big Jim's called for, it had to hire a lot of people without running stringent background checks. Even if it had, it probably wouldn't have seen a drug dealer's client's mental history at all. Although I like to think the farm wouldn't have hired a recently convicted coke peddler if it did do a background check, but when you consider how cheap it could get the work, I can see how the farm managed to look the other way. So keep that in mind.

"His name was Jamie Cochran. Or it was supposed to be, anyway. From what I know, my dad's combine driver was arrested under the influence on the way home. Got thirty days. So one of the guys who collected the hay bales moved up to combine driver, and the neighbor farm sent Jamie. And if a month later the person had left quietly, I wouldn't be telling you guys this story. I probably wouldn't even be here, or know who Jamie Cochran is.

"But Jamie Cochran isn't the man who killed my parents."

Even the leaves on the tree branches stopped moving. Funny how quiet the world gets when you're used to the screams.

"The night before Jamie was supposed to show up at our farm, he was murdered by a man named Lee Reynolds. He was a cokehead who not only thought Jamie had sold him a bad batch but also got Lee's wife pregnant. Both were true of course. So Lee broke into Jamie's house and knifed him a few dozen times more than what was necessary to bring down a bear. They found Jamie with a butterfly knife sticking through bloody sheets and between two of his ribs.

"What they found out was that Lee suffered from bouts of homicidal rage and intense panic attacks. When he killed Jamie, he snapped. I guess 'he snapped again' would be a more appropriate way of saying that. Instead of heading for the border, or whatever he would have done, Lee just assumed Jamie's life and started working for my father. I don't know—maybe he was broke and couldn't leave. He apparently wasn't great, but he wasn't a fuckup either, so my father had no reason to bring him up to the other farm's owner.

"About two weeks into the thirty days, my dad got a call. Nothing serious. 'Hey, George, get Jamie to call me. Want to make sure he's handling the transition OK. Tell Carol her man is a lazy dog, ha-ha.' That's it. My dad relayed the message to both Lee and my mom, having no idea that was enough to have a visitor of his own later that night. My mother was on the phone with the police when he killed her. Lee didn't even leave. He lay in the bathtub when they came, talking to himself. Laughing."

"Oh, Derrick," Katy said softly.

"Man." Ted finally spoke up. "That's totally fucked."

A hand from Katy's direction slid over mine on the armrest of the metal chair. It lightly squeezed once, and then it was gone.

"Yeah." There was something in my throat. "So what exactly is going to happen tomorrow? It seems a little weird to just go face first into a building filled with idiots with shotguns and rifles, because someone shot his sister. I do get it, but that doesn't seem smart."

"No," Ted said, his voice low, almost soothing. "That's not what we're going to do. I don't know what exactly we're going to do yet, but we have to find out if there are any people in the theater who want to leave. Maybe figure out what they're doing, but the important thing is bringing anyone who wants to leave with us when we go. If you guys want to help, you can. I just thought since only two people know what you look like and that was in the dark, you'd be the best people to help. I have no idea what we are looking at as far as safety goes, so keep in mind, this is strictly voluntary."

"I mean, if it's safe, I don't see why we couldn't help," Katy said. "I can't say I'm OK with getting shot at over it."

"I'm not going to ask you to." Ted puffed on his cigarette and stamped it out.

"If none of them know what we look like," I offered, "why don't we just show up to the theater? I assume all of them aren't so dickish to newcomers. We could talk to people for a few hours. Be low key about everything. Find out if anyone wants to leave and bring them back here at night."

"You can change into some of the clothes we have here. Katy, you may have to look a little baggy, but we can pull it off. I think if we do this right and they don't recognize you, we'll be fine. The good news is, everyone over there chooses what they want to do as a way of helping out. Or at least that's the way we planned to do things before we split into two groups. Hopefully, Bo and Luke will still be ushers tomorrow, and we won't have to worry about them blowing the whistle. The only concern I have is that at least one of you will have to stay here. If they've heard of a group of three people driving through the city, they will be on the lookout for just that. I would say there's magic in numbers, but they would recognize anyone coming from the police station."

"That's fine. Mark and I can go," I said.

"Actually, because Mark is the one they came into contact with, I would strongly suggest he be the one to stay. Plus they'll be able to spot the six-foot-eight gorilla from here."

I would've protested, but I didn't have a very powerful argument. "We should try to sleep."

"Gonna be a long night," Katy said.

We walked back into the disheveled bedroom where Mark had buried his face into a stack of pillows and lay spread eagle on the one queen-sized bed. His muffled snoring emanated from the pillow.

"Should we try to move it?" Katy asked.

"Nah, let him sleep. You've got other bedrooms, right, Ted?"

"Yeah, but I think it'd be best if we all held up in the same room. Just in case one of them makes its way inside, it would be safer if we were all together."

"Makes sense," I said. "We can just make a pallet on the floor. Like the good ole days."

So we did. We pulled pillows and comforters from the other rooms and laid them on the floor between the bed and the door to the balcony. Ted was asleep within five minutes. Finding a safe place to lie down didn't come easily, but when we did, sleep came pretty much without asking. The only thing keeping me up that night was the thought of the *glitching*, shadowy hotel room. I knew she was alive—or at least not pulled apart. Part of me knew even then that if that were true, if she actually was dead, I wouldn't be seeing her at all. I couldn't get past the person in the corner. I didn't know if she knew anyone in New Orleans. I didn't know if they were hiding out together because of the screamers. It could've just been one of the maids getting out of the line of fire. I didn't know how many possibilities I would have to count to fall asleep, but I had burned through a good dozen before I felt a cold hand on my wrist.

"Are you awake?" Katy whispered.

"Always." I cleared my throat and whispered back. "You all right?"

"Yeah." She stopped.

"Yeah?"

"I'm just wondering if we should be killing them," she admitted.

"What do you mean?"

"Well, what if this is just temporary, you know? OK, of course I'm aware of what's happening, but what if in a year or a month or even tomorrow they come back online and everything becomes normal again?"

"You think that might happen?"

"I have no idea. I mean, this has never happened to me before. I just don't think we should be killing them is all. A day ago everything was normal, and now we're openly shooting at one another. That can't be right, you know?"

"I think you're right," I said.

I didn't know for sure if she was talking about the screamers or the flashlight people, but I took it to mean both. Because looking back, it's hard to tell which ones were "the crazies" in Jackson. I can't imagine what those people would be doing now if we never showed up. I think we were supposed to go there, though. From what I've pieced together, there was no way we wouldn't have wound up there.

"I don't know if there's any way to tell if everything will return to normal, but just in case, we won't kill anyone. Unless it is absolutely necessary to keep the three of us safe, we will not."

"The three of us will stick together?" she asked.

"That's correct. Well, four of us now. We have to circle back and get Jackie. I don't think Mark is going to leave without her."

There was a long pause.

"Hey, Derrick," Katy said. She was nodding off, and even though her lips were inches from my ear, I almost didn't hear her.

"Hey, Katy." I matched her volume.

"Why did Ted kill the one in the backyard?"

She didn't let me answer that. She just fell asleep. That may have been for the best because I didn't know how to answer that. I was certain there was a reason. The last thing I remember thinking that night was 410. I wondered what it meant.

Chapter 18

The sun warmed me awake. That's the thing about the South. You can shiver yourself to sleep, but you'll wind up kicking off the comforter to keep from sweating. It was a quarter to eleven in the morning.

Mark slouched in the metal chair on the patio. I climbed to my elbows to see if I could read his mood. When I did, the comforter pulled, and Katy groaned. It was small and pleading. I slid out from underneath the blanket and made sure she was fully covered before I went outside, closing the door behind me as though I was sneaking out after curfew.

"Have a seat, bro." Mark waved me toward him. "Ted's getting breakfast. Or whatever he has that isn't spoiled."

"How'd you sleep?" My feet slapped on the tile.

"Like a bear."

"Like a loud, growling bear."

I noticed that he had changed clothes. He wore clean, darker jeans and a white T-shirt instead of black.

"You changed clothes?" I asked.

"Yeah, figured I'd go incognito."

"As what?"

"A black guy."

"It's just a T-shirt."

"Black guy owns it. Oh, by the way, I snore. Additionally, all four of us snore. Good thing they can't hear, or we'd all be goners."

"Well, I'd feel bad, but—" I looked over the balcony railing.

There were dead people strewn not only across Ted's backyard but everywhere. In every yard. The hill Ted's house sat on top of was littered with people and pieces of people.

"Yeah," Mark said. "I guess we missed a couple things last night. Apparently, something atypical happened yesterday where people just started kicking the shit out of each other."

"Who the hell did this?"

"If I had to guess, most of it was done by the screamers. Come on, man. Sit down. Don't look at it."

I backed away from the handrail, my bottom jaw reaching for the ground.

"Here, boy," Mark called. "Seriously, shut that thing or a bird's going to nest in there."

"Holy shit," Katy said from behind me.

"It's a mess, right?" Mark said.

I turned around.

Katy looked like she was staring down a twister.

"Did they do this?" Katy started for the railing.

"Yeah," Mark said. "That's what it seems like, anyway."

Katy crossed her arms and ran her hands up from elbow to shoulder and back down. Her hair was in a ponytail, and despite just waking up, she was totally coherent. The image had shocked both of us into total awareness.

"Why doesn't everyone have a seat," Mark said. "It seems there is a lot we have to talk about."

We sat down at the table. I was still processing the sight, which was now at my back.

"Now," Mark began, "our friend Teddy, downstairs, has put a few of these things down, including the one last night. I'm a little ashamed to say that I've gotten rid of one of them myself. I don't know everything that's happened with you so far, but I'll put my money on you having to do the same thing before we settle in NOLA."

He stopped, looking at his hands.

Ted walked through the door to the bedroom and used his foot to close it. He had boxes of cereal, sticks of beef jerky, hamburger buns, and bags of chips dangling from his arms.

"But all the ones we've killed and will kill will only be dead because we had to do it to survive. I mean think about it. If there was a rattlesnake in your yard, you could see it slippin' and slidin' toward the woods or street, would you deliberately go outside and kill it just for fun? Probably not. But let's just say you have a sweet new French bulldog hanging out in your living room, sleeping on the couch while *SpongeBob* plays on the TV. Then the snake crawls out of a crack in the wall and makes for little Fifi. You'd shoot it in the face and drag it through nails. That's basically what we do when we stop one of those things from coming in the house or stabbing us to death with a pickax."

"Well said," I humored.

"But these people have not only shot and killed what we can basically assume are wild animals at this point and not only shot a police officer doing her job to protect people and get them to a safe place, but they've shot my sister. Now, I'm aware of the recon plan to infiltrate, learn, and rescue. It's shitty that I'm not going, but I admit I see the merit. I might as well be wearing a shirt that explains that I'm the big, lanky guy who jumped Blue Jeans and Khakis. And it's my own fault. I'm too big. I breastfed a little too long."

"All right," Katy said.

"You're right," I said.

"I'm sliding off the rails here," Mark said. "I just want you to keep in mind that we aren't dealing with normal people anymore. We wouldn't be dealing with normal people if they were only shooting the screamers. I think we can all agree that it takes a very specific kind of fucked up to hunt something just to kill it. So just keep that in mind if you find yourself in a spot like that when you're over there looking for people who want to leave. Because if I had to guess, I'd say those people over there wouldn't do either of you the courtesy of thinking twice before knocking your heads in. Maybe they'd get a little handsy with Katy first.

"Ew," she said.

Ted and I laughed.

The food had made its way to the center of the table. I thanked Ted for graciously giving us a bed—and floor—to sleep on and for the food we were about to make quick work of. I then reached for a vacuum-sealed stick of beef jerky.

"Hang on now," Mark said. He held out his hands to Ted and me, who were on either side of him. "Let's pray."

The three of us looked at each other totally dumbfounded. Then Mark exploded with laughter.

When we finished eating, even the crumbs were a memory.

Chapter 19

After lunch Ted showed Katy and me where we could find some new clothes. Then he went back to the porch to talk everything through with Mark.

The room was huge, just like everything in the house. A television set—at least as big as the one in the living room—hung on the wall. A king-sized bed stood against the center of the opposite wall. A black wooden nightstand sat on either side, both with magazines on them. On the left side of the bed was a window area with a daybed sitting beneath it. Outside the window was a view of the front yard and the road. I watched as two screamers ran full speed in one side and out the other. Katy stood across the room from me at a large chest of drawers to the left of the doorway. To the left of her was the door to a walk-in closet and bathroom.

"I'm beginning to think Ted might be a drug lord." I was only halfway sarcastic.

"Jesus Christ," Katy said, pulling a bra out of one of the drawers. "Look at this thing." It was a black-and-white lacy number, which in that moment sat on Katy's head like an oversized yarmulke. "Come here."

I stood up, and she wrapped the other cup around my head.

"Look at us." She stood on tiptoes to even out the picture in the mirror. "We make one great pair of breasts."

She tossed the bra back in the drawer as we shared a laugh. Seeing her ease a little further out of her shell made me smile.

"Can I ask you something?"

"Sure," she said.

"What do you think is happening? I know it seems like everything's gone to shit, but I'm trying to make sense of it. It feels like we're in this little paddle boat just inching forward into forever, you know?"

She sat down beside me on the daybed. "I don't mean to get into some weird philosophical debate with you or anything," she said sympathetically. "But I really don't think everything needs a meaning. I mean, did what happened with your family have a meaning? I guess you could talk yourself into anything. Like maybe that happened so you could make sure Mark and I get to where we're going safely. I just don't think that's the case every time. If everything has a meaning or can be explained because of something else, it takes away the chaotic nature of life. That would mean you could potentially map out everything that's going to happen ever. If I thought that everything meant something, I would have made myself crazy by now trying to figure out why everything bad happened to me growing up. But doing that would've made me neurotic and twitchy. Sometimes it's just as simple as bad shit happens to good people."

"Maybe you're right."

"Maybe." She stared off into space. "I could obviously be way off the mark on this one. Maybe it does. Maybe the plane crash that took my dad and brother twenty-something years ago has some meaning to it, but the way I see it is that it was a shitty thing that happened to good people."

"It just went down?" I asked.

"Yeah." Tears pooled in her eyes. She stood up from the bed, clearing her throat. "So have you picked what you want to wear? I think I can make this button-up work. It's massive, but I can tie it up at the bottom, and it'll look OK."

She pulled off the black tank top, and underneath was an even smaller, even tighter white shirt. I could almost make out the pink hearts or dots on the bra underneath. She pulled on the denim shirt she was holding and buttoned the middle buttons and tied the shirt up at the bottom. Then she walked into the bathroom, resetting her ponytail.

I stood up and traded my shirt for a gray T-shirt with a black pocket sewn on the front. I searched through Ted's pants drawer for any that weren't comically too long for me. There were basketball shorts, jeans, and even a few folded pairs of dress paints. One pair of men's yoga pants hid at the bottom of the drawer. I pulled them out and shook the fold out of the legs. I held them to my waist the way every person does before putting on new pants. They must have been high-waters on him because they were only kind of long on me. The waistband gave a little tug on the edge of the bandage on my thigh as I pulled them up my legs. I breathed through my teeth again.

"Oh, dammit," Katy said in the doorway. "I missed the show."

The bedhead had been combed from her hair, and as I knew they would be, her bangs were perfectly level over her eyes. She had found Ted's wife's stash of makeup supplies and had removed her lipstick and redone her mascara. The shirt sleeves were rolled to her elbows, and even though it was huge on her, she totally pulled it off. She looked like a 1950s girl clad in roller skates and a poodle skirt. Like I said, beauty stuck out of time.

"How long were you in there?"

"I'm a world-class makeup artist. I can have you Broadway-ready in five minutes."

"Good to know." I laughed. "How do I look?"

"Like you want to hold cash in your shirt while you work out."

"Perfect."

"What about me?"

"You look like the lady paleontologist from *Jurassic Park*."

"Really?" She sounded excited.

"Only with red hair. And you need a hat."

"Maybe she was trying to cover her hair with the hat." Katy was looking at herself in the mirror, adjusting the oversized shirt.

"Hey, what is that tattoo all about?"

"The one on my shoulder," she said, adjusting the clothes in the mirror, "or the one on my butt?"

"I've only seen the one."

"I'm only kidding. I just have the one. It's the flag of South Carolina. I always wanted something reminiscent of home because I knew I'd leave there. I didn't know what though, and the Hootie and the Blowfish logo was a bit gaudy. Or was it?"

"I think you made a bad call on this one."

We laughed. Then she stopped, looking hard at something in the mirror.

"Hmm..."

"What?"

"Is that Ted's wife?" She pointed to the mirror.

"That's you, I think."

"No." She turned and picked up a small, framed picture on one of the nightstands. "Look at this. I think that's his wife."

To be nice, the woman in the picture was ample. Her arm was around Ted's waist—I assumed because she couldn't reach his shoulders. Ted's armpit could be seen over her head. Her short blond hair sat in perfect order. She wore a gray suit and held in her hand a briefcase that rested against her considerable hip.

"I was not expecting that," I admitted.

"Seriously? Look at that booty. It literally doesn't quit."

"Hey, be nice." I laughed.

"Ever." She laughed.

"She'll sue you."

As we discussed the physics of their sex life, footsteps started down the hallway.

"OK," Mark said from the opposite side of the door. "I think we're ready to go. You guys have clothes on?"

"Come on in," Katy called.

Mark opened the door with one hand over his eyes.

"We're totally clothed," Katy said.

"Nice. How was it?" he asked me. I missed the meaning at first, but Katy got it.

"Ha-ha." She tossed him the picture. "We think this is Ted's wife."

"No way," he said, gawking at the picture. He looked serious all of a sudden.

"I think she's taken." Katy laughed.

"This woman is in the backyard," Mark said. "I mean, she's a little facedown, but I'm pretty sure that's her."

"What do you mean?"

"I think this is one of the people Ted had to, you know—" He mimed shooting a gun.

Another set of footsteps came down the hallway before any of us said anything. Mark tossed the picture frame under the bed before Ted came into the room.

"Why don't you guys come pick out what you want?" Ted led us downstairs to the living room.

Spread out on the couch was a number of different blunt instruments, from a meat tenderizer to an ominous lead pipe. The table held a number of handguns. Within five minutes we were out the door and on our way to the theater.

Chapter 20

The walk to the theater was excruciating, mainly because for near-ly all of it, we walked through the woods, complete with more thickets, sloppy wet ground, and briar patches than we could ever ask for. It was hell.

Seemingly for no reason, Ted told us to hide. We jumped behind fallen logs and dead trees. I landed awkwardly on the metal bat I carried, and the wind was temporarily knocked out of me. I couldn't tell if Mark was pretending or overly committed to the moment, but he looked like an actual war vet propped against the tree with his rifle at the ready. I thought again on what he said to reassure Ted that he was capable of using the gun. "Walk across the yard and hold out your hand."

I heard the flashlight people talking as they passed. We stayed hidden for nearly thirty minutes as they combed the area. One of them propped against the tree Mark was hidden behind. Always on cue, Mark turned to me and mouthed, *I'm gonna fuck him up.* I shook my head. *Please, bro.* I shook harder. He stifled laughter the best he could. There were six of them in all. They had calls for specific movements. One kept yelling, "Alpha, alpha!" and we'd hear crack-ling dead leaves. Another would yell, "Roo, roo!" and the footsteps would stop. I peeked out from the angle between the log and the ground to see what they did. After *roo* sounded, they held up their mirrors. I wondered why they didn't just talk. What they were hunting wasn't going to hear them. I guess playing army is just more fun.

Farther in the distance, I heard "Bravo, bravo!" The original six slumped down in defeat and then jogged out of view.

"OK, they met the other group," Ted whispered. "They're going to spread out and keep going—if it's anything like yesterday, that is. Let's go. Just be quiet."

The four of us crawled, snuck, and walked for another couple football fields before Ted stopped us.

"All right, guys, this is as close as we can get without being in the road. You see that?" He pointed to three towers that looked like they fell right out of a *Jetsons* cartoon and into the Jackson skyline. "That's the theater. There are buildings between here and there, so you'll be on your own for a while before their people start helping you out. I'll bet the closer you get the less likely you'll have to worry about that. This is probably the cleanest place for miles as far as screamers go. You can have a gun if you want one."

"I don't think that's necessary," Katy said.

"I'm actually a little worried they'll be more on edge if they see us with a gun," I said.

"OK, just do your best to blend in," Ted said. "If something happens—"

"Run for it?" Katy laughed.

Ted made a face that told her, *Basically, yeah.*

I said, "I feel like it's a little late in the game to ask this one, but why don't we just leave them there? If they don't want to leave, why don't we just go without them?"

"Because we don't know if they don't want to go," Ted explained. "We had signs posted telling people that the police would be at the theater, but that was when there was only one set of police officers. When we broke apart, the ones who wanted to move on to bigger cities were at an obvious disadvantage. We had more police, but they had more people. We don't know if anyone who went there even knows there is a plan to leave town. It's important for people to know that they have a choice to leave."

"I get it," Mark added. "You're just trying to help people. That's what I'm all about. If you can save even a couple, you should."

"You do know how to get back, right?" Ted asked.

"Yeah, we'll be able to find it."

"Derrick, do me a favor?" Mark said. It was the first genuinely serious thing he had said since I met him. "Map the place out for me, OK? See if you can find out where he stays. I'm coming for him."

"I will," I promised. "Try to rationalize it, though. Jackie *is* alive."

"And take care of him." He put his hands on Katy's shoulders and looked directly into her eyes. "You can handle this. I know you can. You are strong. Independent. Kind. But he absolutely can't. He's ugly. Fat. Probably into dudes. But we need his big arms to move things. Just keep an eye on him. That's all."

Katy pulled a cell phone out of her back pocket and wiped off the screen.

"You planning to make a call?" I asked her.

"You never know," she said. "We may need it for something."

"We'll see you two tonight," Ted said.

"Right on," Mark added. "Me and Theo will be at the house."

He put his arm around Ted and pulled him close like he was a frat brother.

Katy and I turned toward the theater. Everything slowed for a moment. There was no movement, no wind, not even a bird singing. The entire landscape was still. Everything was quiet. So quiet I wanted to scream.

Katy squeezed my arm.

We walked toward Tinseltown.

PART 2
THE FLASHLIGHT PEOPLE

Only in the moment of death, we rest. We cross the edge of dark water.

Chapter 21

The Tinseltown Theater sat in the center of a number of other buildings, all of which were boarded up. The facade was a circus of color and pattern almost to the point of nausea. The three towers that jutted out from the center of the building looked more like massive walkie-talkies sitting on a charging station. Each of them had what looked like an antenna sticking straight up out of the tubes striped white, pink, red, and green. They stood in front of the huge blue entranceway to the building and led down to three separate box offices. A thick platform painted red and silver acted as a veranda to cover the sidewalk and entrance area. We came up on the building from the side where a massive checkerboard-painted wall advertised "XD: Extreme Digital Cinema" for all the screamers to see. I searched for people in the box office because that's what I was used to doing. No one came to work that day. I didn't see anything except for three numbers stuck onto the middle office: 410.

"Why do you think they don't use the hotel over there?" Katy asked.

It hadn't clicked with me just yet, but it certainly would eventually. There was a much larger building just next door to the theater with enough rooms to give everyone in town a place to start life anew.

We had almost made it all the way inside before we noticed anyone. One thing I did notice, though, was that bodies didn't decorate the parking lot the way they did Ted's backyard.

Then we heard the second barrage of metallic clicks and cocks. A much smaller one, but as it turns out, size doesn't matter. The sound of the guns clicking into the locked-and-loaded position stopped us cold with our hands in the air. Nothing happened. No one spoke. No one came out to tell us what to do. We just stood there. I've always believed in a stalemate—the one who speaks first giving up the power—but after a while I got bored, and I felt stupid standing around with my hands to no one.

"Hey," I finally said. "We saw a sign. It said come to the theater."

Nothing.

"We saw a sign," I said much louder. "We're just looking for somewhere safe."

Still nothing.

"We can help," Katy matched my volume.

Movement from inside one of the huge metal tubes.

"You shitting me?" I said to Katy.

"It's a woman's touch," she said, biting her lip trying not to laugh. "You wouldn't get it."

The commotion on the inside lasted for a good minute or two before we saw two boot-clad feet dangle from the ceiling of the left box office. The feet slowly descended from the ceiling as if the person lowering them was suddenly hesitant about making the drop to the floor. We took a step toward him.

"Hang on, right there," a voice from the top of one of the *Jetsons* suites said.

Honestly, it was a kid's voice but with an affected deepness that was counterproductive because it told me two things. It told me he was a kid, of course, but also that he was either scared or had a chronic case of little-man syndrome. I figured in either case, it'd be smart to play ball.

"One of us is coming down."

The legs hanging from the box office dropped with the rest of the person behind them. I can't guarantee the person bit the dust on the floor of the little room, but I definitely heard someone hit the ground pretty hard. I heard a faint voice tell him to "use the ladder next time, dumbass. Now get out there." The person got up and unlocked the office with keys already in the door. He jogged our way, making a lot of noise. He wore huge black parachute pants, pockets everywhere; a bulletproof vest; a walkie-talkie on one side of his belt and a pistol on the other; and a Windbreaker jacket, which I didn't know they still made, and he carried a shotgun. He was probably half the size he looked while wearing all that nonsense. A greasy black mop of wildly made hair reached in all directions from the top of his head. He had the makings of a moustache sprinkled under his nose to go with a nice pair of thick muttonchops and a face full of acne. Aside from that he looked like a kid dressing as a cop for Halloween. There were a lot of those working their way through the ranks at the theater.

Once the child reached us outside the shade provided by the huge metal awning of the theater, he pulled a pair of aviators from some secret compartment behind him and dropped them over his eyes. He was already sweating.

"Wow, you're really playing the part," I said.

"Are either of y'all one of the crazies?"

"Do you usually get this close to them?" I asked.

"I've been face to face with plenty," he said, puffing his chest. I half expected him to climb up the side of one of the space-age pillars and beat on his undoubtedly hairless breast.

"Yeah? And how'd that go?" I asked.

"They'll kill you," he said. He had suddenly become a sixty-year-old war veteran. "They come at you full speed, hollerin' and rippin' atcha like the maniacs they are. They'll kick *your* ass and use *you* as a toothpick, ma'am. They just as soon pull your face off and shit on it than let you go on about your day." He stamped it all by hocking a mouthful of spit on the ground.

"Intense," I said.

"Yeah," Katy added, feigning amazement.

"Let me ask you something, man," I said.

"Wha'sat?" he said, gawking at Katy.

"Any of that happening now?"

"Nah," he said, tilting his head to me.

"Then I think we're good. You got a name, brother?" I asked, hoping to sound friendly.

"Officer Myrick."

"Your first name is Officer?" Katy asked, keeping a straight face.

"No, it's Danny. I mean, Daniel. I am an officer."

"Now, we're friends here, Dan," I said, trying to divert attention from Katy. "We're just trying to find a place to sleep for the night. We'd be more than happy to help with anything you need us to."

"That's fine. It's Officer Myrick, by the way. Names?"

"Peter," I said.

"Mary." She didn't miss a beat.

I don't know why we lied. It wasn't something we talked about, but Danny accepted it.

"Mary, huh?" He looked at her legs.

Katy shook her head and moved closer to me. Her fingers laced between mine.

"OK, Peter. Mary. We just have to make sure y'all aren't one of them."

He patted me down. Found nothing but the bat I carried and pulled it unnecessarily hard out of my hand. He poked at the bandage around my thigh. "What happened to your leg?" He took a deep breath and turned to feel Katy for potential weaponry.

"No," she said sternly.

"I have to, ma'am."

"I'm not letting someone half my age feel me up in a parking lot in the light of day."

"I'm eighteen."

"No, you're not," she corrected.

"I'm almost eighteen."

"In how many years?"

"Look, she's fine." I put my hand on Katy's arm. "Where is she going to hide something?"

"That's a big shirt," Danny said.

"Fine." She unbuttoned and untied the shirt then slid it off her shoulders and held it out to me. I handed it to him. He wadded it up, obviously a little hurt that he didn't get to cop a feel.

"OK, you're good." He handed the shirt back to Katy.

"Shoes, dummy," the voice from the pseudosuite called down.

"Oh, you have to take off your shoes."

"That's fine," I said.

We slipped off our shoes. He glanced into them, and passing inspection, we slipped them back on.

"Come on. Y'all're good."

Danny Boy turned to the door, fishing a key out of his back pocket. I could barely make out movement behind the tinted-glass doors, but I was relieved to see that someone else was there. The lock clacked, the door opened, and the sound of an entire city came pouring out.

For the first time, we entered the theater.

Chapter 22

Despite the circumstances, there was life inside that building—people making jokes, singing, and some created a prayer circle right in the center of the huge lobby. An energy ran through the lobby that could get the lights back on, at least for this part of town. There were movie posters decorating the walls, advertising anything from Disney to the newest installment of the demon-possession genre. There were benches placed around the lobby. Someone had even been nice enough to bring in a few bright-red Naugahyde couches. Kids ran in all directions like ants on a destroyed anthill. One little kid fell onto the multicolored-leaf-patterned carpet. I expected an oncoming tantrum, but the little blond guy just rolled to his back, inspected his knee for scrapes, pulled his pant leg back down, and returned to the game he was playing. The gaudy light fixtures displaying the myriad of snack and drink choices were dim, but in their reflective surface, the shapeless movement of the lobby danced.

A short, squat woman waddled up to us at the door where Katy and I were left to fend for ourselves. Her denim skirt was pulled tight around her hips. She had short reddish-brown hair, I think, and freckles. In the sweetest southern-belle voice I've ever heard, she welcomed us. "Y'all come in. Make yourself at home. We pretty much just do what we want while we're here, and y'all are part of *we* now. As you can tell, we have a lot squeezed into this room. We call the lobby the rec room. Oh, and my name is Peggy. Peggy Townsend."

From the center of the lobby where the prayer took up most of the room, I caught a few untrusting glances being sent our direction. Peggy led us through the crowds, around the once-thriving concession stand—it looked lonely that day with people only going behind the counter to get a broom and leave—to one of the corridors lined with doors to screening rooms.

"We've turned the theaters into sleeping areas," she said. "The bathrooms still work."

The noise from the lobby dissipated as we continued farther, toward the end of the hallway. Eventually, we found ourselves standing in front of a door with an *Office* plaque glued to the center of it.

"We'll just come in here and get a little info from you real quick." Peggy opened the door to the office.

Inside the room stood a tiny desk pushed against the wall. A small empty chair sat dully on one side of the desk, and two wooden stools faced it on the opposite side. Against the wall to our left were stacks and stacks of boxes packed to their brims with paper work. I assumed in the hustle to get a work space, the theater's paper work was literally pushed to the side.

"Have a seat," Peggy said and gestured toward the stools. She rifled through the drawers and came out with a yellow note pad. There was already a list of generic information made up doctor-office style.

"Y'all are making it pretty well here," Katy said, carefully watching Peggy's reaction. "You must be pretty set on sticking around."

"Oh, of course. Jackson is the best place to live."

"We heard that people were going to bigger cities," Katy said. "We were headed to New Orleans. I didn't know Jackson was one of those cities."

"I didn't know people were doing that," she said. There was a very brief moment when she stopped looking for a pen, and then she continued. I wondered what family member from what city went through her mind in that instant. "Like I said, Jackson should be where everyone is coming."

"Here you go." I handed Peggy the red pen that was wedged between the desktop and the wall.

"Thank you, darlin'. Now, what are y'all's names?"

"Derrick."

"Honey, don't mess with her." Katy playfully slapped my arm. "He's such a kidder. His name is Peter. I'm Mary."

"And your last names?" Peggy went to writing, not reacting to my obvious flub.

Katy grabbed my hand. "Grabowski."

"Oh, my goodness." Peggy gasped. She lowered her voice. "Are y'all Jewish? I've never met a Jew. I'm sorry, Jewish person. Jew is such a nasty word."

"No, we're protestant," Katy said, waving her off. "We are Polish. Well, he is. One hundred percent American here. All the way back to the settlers."

"Well, good for you," Peggy said with excitement in her voice.

"It's S-K-I," Katy said. She was slowly putting more and more southern in her accent as the conversation progressed.

Peggy looked up, confused.

"I'm so sorry. Our last name is spelled G-R-A-B-O-W-S-K-I. Not S-K-Y."

"Oh, dear. I'm sorry about that." Peggy went back to writing.

I looked at Katy with the best what-is-happening-right-now look I could make without cracking a smile. She grinned pretty hard.

"Where are y'all from?"

"Well, originally Tupelo, and Swieta Lipka for this one—that's Poland—but we live in Clinton now."

"Did you walk from there?"

"We had to. There were pileups trapping us on our street. People were everywhere. They were just hurting other people. We were so scared."

"Bless your hearts," Peggy said. I swear I saw her tear up. "You must have been so scared. We're going to get rid of those things."

"Yes, it's been a long day," Katy said. I could tell she was making an effort to not break character. "We tried getting to the police station."

"Well, good thing you didn't," she said. "We can do a lot more to help you get settled down. No one wants to be out and about with those things doing what they do. Besides, if y'all woulda went to the station, y'all'd found nothing but empty rooms."

"Empty rooms?" Katy asked.

"Oh, yes," she said with gusto. "No one is there anymore. Everyone came over here last night. Let's see. Married?"

"Six years this June." Katy laced her fingers in with mine.

By this point I was just along for the ride.

"Such beautiful, young people together. It's so good to see." Peggy wrote with glee.

"So the plan for everyone here is to stick around?" Katy asked.

"The plan is to clear the surrounding areas and expand until we get the entire city back." I could see her actually swelling with pride as she said, "We have a team of engineers and hunters making its way across town to the power plant tonight. We're all very excited. That's just one step closer to getting back to the way things were, you know?"

"I do," Katy sympathized. "So, basically, everyone here is pretty set on rebuilding right where they are?"

"Oh, yes," Peggy said as if there were no other option. "We love it here. OK, next question. What did you do before all this?"

"I was a software programmer," Katy said. "And he owned a Best Buy."

"Is anyone else traveling with y'all?" Peggy asked. She didn't bother to write the last answers. A big "E" sat behind the line designated "Careers," and we were on to the next thing.

"Nope," Katy said. "Honey? You OK?"

"Oh, no. All my family is in Poland." That was the first time—and certainly not the last—that I wondered if this was a nationwide pandemic or a worldwide one. "I'm so sorry. My throat is killing me. Is there any way I could get a glass of water or something?"

"Of course, darlin'," Peggy said.

"Could I bother you for one, too?"

"Two waters. Don'tcha go moving a muscle. I'll be right back." She hefted herself up from the straining chair and waddled her girth out of the small room.

"Who are you?" I asked.

"What do you mean?"

"You're not the same person we picked up yesterday. You were crying. Terrified. Now you're some espionage expert."

"I haven't seen one of those things running around all day. After we ate, everything kind of seemed normal. It's easy to be myself when nothing is trying to pull me apart. I can think now that I've had a break from it, and thinking's what I'm good at. These are just people. They can be reasoned with. Besides, I can't just be a baby. I have to help. Also, everything I've said is common sense."

"Well good on ya. Now fill me in on what just happened." I stood up and adjusted my spine.

"Fake names. That part's obvious." Katy put up her fists, ready for a punching bag. "What else you got? Give it to me."

"Grabowski, though?"

"How many Grabowskis do you know?"

"Literally none." I didn't even have to think about it.

"Right, so no one is going to be like, 'Oh, do you know Jane Grabowski?' because it's too weird a name. Also why I chose Grabowski. No one can remember that, so they're just going to think of us as Mary and Peter. Probably even Pete."

"Never Pete. I hate that." I was a little impressed with her quick thinking. "Why did you pick those jobs? Why would it matter?"

"Because both of those jobs revolve around technology, making us a little less useful given the situation. People are going to be a lot less likely to ask us to do something if we only know how to do things that are currently obsolete. That way we're a little more under the radar, and we won't be noticed if we leave. I mean, we'll be noticed, but it won't be a giant red flag. You're welcome, by the way. Nice little farm boy like you, they'd be glad to put you to work." She shot me a smile.

"Right. So why are we married?"

"So they won't separate us. This is still the South. Wouldn't look right for two people sleeping side by side in sin."

"I had never thought of any of that." I went from moderately impressed to totally blown away because the only thing I knew to do was use a fake name. And if that was all, what would it have mattered in the long run?

"I'm telling you," she said, "I'm a thinker. I should've went to grad school."

"Wh—"

Peggy came back into the office with two room-temperature bottles of water with the theater's logo on the labels. They were soaking wet. "Sorry about the mess."

She plopped back down in the chair across from us and took more information from us. Nothing we necessarily had to lie about, but I'm sure Katy did. Birthdays; anniversary; who, if anyone, we knew was still alive; whether or not we had any paper work, like birth certificates, driver's license; anything else we thought would be helpful to share. When it was over, Peggy stood up. We rose from our stools. She shook our hands. She smelled like potpourri. I half expected her to tell us that she would let us know when she had made a decision on whether we could be useful to them or not. But instead she put her fat arms around Katy and me.

"We're so glad to have you." Her voice was not quite a whisper. "You're going to love it here. Make yourself at home."

She opened the office door, and the sound from the lobby came to us from down the open hallway.

"I would go see Hank first. He's got black hair and a red beard. He keeps the sleeping bags and camping supplies. Hank'll help you find a space to lay your heads."

"Thank you, Mrs. Peggy," I said.

She slid her hands off our backs as we each walked out of the office.

"You're so very welcome, darlin'," she said, putting her stamp on one of the last pleasant things that happened to us in the theater.

Chapter 23

The commotion in the lobby hadn't lost energy in the time we had been down the hall a couple hundred feet away from it. The sound grew the way a train's will when it's coming through a tunnel. Instead of a single light at the end of the tunnel, there were a dozen gas lanterns hung on a wire just above eye level on both sides of the walkway. We only saw a couple of people going from room to room in the corridor. They carried damp towels and bandages from the center screen room out to the others. I later found out that the center rooms on both sides were filled with first aid kits and an array of canned and perishable food. For the time being, Katy and I ignored this. We decided the best thing to do was to play the game.

A group of kids played on the lifeless arcade games, pretending to shatter the high scores without even trying. They were the source for most of the noise. The prayer circle in the center of the room was still hard at work. I could see outside the tinted windows, and two decked-out soldiers were setting up some kind of barricade around the front of the building. The door to the far-left box office opened. Hank strolled out with his black ponytail, dangling red beard, and Megadeth T-shirt. Holes decorated the tail of the shirt, no doubt put there by dropped joints, which I know may be unfair to assume, but who am I kidding?

"That our guy?" Katy almost held back her laughter. "Doesn't seem like much of a camper, does he?"

I agreed. "Well, his baggy jeans are pretty dirty. That's probably come from sleeping on the ground, right?"

I got his attention.

"New guys?" he said, not really caring. His accent was thick.

"Peter, and this is Mary."

"Hi," Katy said to him. "Peggy told us to see you about a bag."

"Right, follow me." Hank led us to a closet next to the box of-fice from where he had just come. Inside, the walls were lined with sleeping bags stacked nearly to the ceiling on what used to be shelves for candy. There were countless pillows, and duct tape and the wall facing the door held up a dry-erase board with *Adults* scrawled across the top and *Kids* across the bottom. A thin blue line bisected the sur-face. Each side held a list of names—about sixty on top and less than half as many on the bottom. I later wondered how many of those names were also fake.

"Hey, Hank," a voice said from the walkie clipped to Hank's belt.

"Yeah, Boss," Hank said into the plastic square. In his southern drawl, the word came out more like *bawss*.

"I'm bringing in Mendez. He cut his hand on a window. He fainted when he saw the blood. It's pretty gruesome."

"Right. OK, Boss." He clipped the walkie back onto his belt.

"Everything OK?" I asked.

"Yeah, we're good. One of the hunters just got hurt," he said, wav-ing off the whole thing. "We have blue, orange, red, purple, and green."

"Blue," Katy said, grabbing two plain white pillows from the self. She handed one to me.

"Red," I said.

"Right," he said again. He tossed us our sleeping bags. Then he tossed me a roll of duct tape. "Theater six is the newest cleared-out one. What you do is duct-tape a space on the ground for your area, and use one of the Sharpies hanging on the door behind you to write your name on the tape. How big a square and many times you double tape is up to you. As you can tell, we aren't running out. I'd just make it visible in the lantern light so no one mistakes it. You can double up the tape so you have more room to write if you like."

"So we just tape a box around the space where we want to stay?" I asked.

"Right." He wrote Katy's fake name and mine on the top part of the board.

"Then we double up, make it really thick, and write our name on the tape?" Katy asked.

"Right." He dropped the marker into his back pocket and picked up a bottle of peroxide. He took the lid off the bottle and smelled its contents. For some reason I thought he was going to drink out of it.

"So we just make ourselves at home?" My turn.

"Right."

"Right," Katy said.

"Right, so we'll get on that, and see you around the building, Hank."

"OK." He led us out to the lobby and pointed to the corridor closest to us. "Theater six is just down the hallway there. There will be someone to help you guys in each room if you need anything at all."

The walkie clicked again. "The boss is bringin' in Mendez."

Immediately the door opened and slowly the boss hobbled in with a nearly unconscious Mendez. Mendez was maybe a year older than Danny, if that much, and he was clutching a red-stained rag around his hand. The boss laid him down on the lobby floor. There were groans from the prayer group. The kids playing in the arcade were the only noises in that moment. The boss took off his straw cowboy hat and sunglasses.

"It's fine, folks," the boss told the crowd. "Just a little nick. We'll get him sewn up and back out in no time."

The crowd went back to their activities.

"Hey, Boss," Hank said. "These are some new folks. Came in just a few minutes ago."

The boss dropped the hat and shades on a nearby table. He was wearing camouflage from head to toe, but none of it matched. His boots were dark green, his pants were a desert color, and his shirt was the pattern of fall leaves. He was sunburned around his face, which was only made worse by his bleach-blond hair—even his facial hair was dyed. He had a moustache with gaps and hurtles from start to finish. It made me think of a *Super Mario* level. He was so dirty that I wouldn't have even doubted a few killer mushrooms were starting to sprout on him. His suntan had faded the way a naturally dark person's skin looks after winter months when everything is covered up in the cold weather.

"Hank, could you go to my office and get one of the bottles of medicine out of the top left-hand drawer for me real quick." He handed Hank a cluster of keys.

Hank hustled off to the boss's office. The boss held out his mud-covered hand, and Katy shook it first.

"Mary," she said.

"Adam," he said. Then he shifted to me and held out his hand. "Adam."

I looked at it. I slowly raised mine to me his. "Peter."

It was a lie. I knew he knew it was a lie. He didn't show it, though. His light-brown eyes stayed cheerful and welcoming. His smile didn't waver, and he never called me out on it. I wonder if he saw the same in me—if I was as calm and collected as he was. I know I didn't feel it. Remembering how I actually felt isn't easy, but I know I kept cool enough for anyone looking at us to think everything was normal. As I stood there in the lobby of the theater looking into the boss's eyes, I was overcome with rage. It was an unsettling amount of anger that I had never felt before. My father always told me a handshake can make or break a relationship before it even starts. *Not too firm, not to limp now, Derrick.* I had to keep my father's voice in mind as I shook the hand of the man who had killed him.

Chapter 24

"What do you mean?" Katy asked as she taped the ground in the bottom corner of room six.

"I mean that's Lee." I almost snapped. The anger kept me on edge.

"How do you know?"

"I was at his trial. I saw him in the paper. His face was on the Internet, everywhere."

"Are you sure? Why wouldn't he be in jail?"

"He was declared insane. He didn't even go to jail. Just a padded room."

"That guy wasn't insane."

"Yeah, I don't know what he's doing here. He wasn't blond before, and the red face wasn't his usual color, but I swear that's him."

"He said his name was Adam."

"We said ours were Mary and Peter," I reminded her.

"First of all, come down," she said in a quiet voice. "What I'm saying is maybe he snapped all the way. Maybe he really thinks he is Adam."

I finished cleaning off a path on the ground for the tape and moved the pile of dust, screws, and popcorn to the outside of the square. There was only one other family in this room so far, a Spanish-speaking man and his daughter. "Do you mind if I borrow that?" I asked them.

The man just stared blankly at me. The little girl, who was a toddler, whispered to him in Spanish. I gestured toward the broom and dustpan, and the man handed it to me. I swept the pile into the pan, considering what Katy said. I didn't know the probability of it being true, but I could feel that rage loosen its grip and begin to slide away.

"Do you think that's what happened? Lee just snapped, and now he believes he *is* a whole other person?"

"Could be," she said.

"Has that ever happened to you?"

"I had a grandmother who was teetering with a number of problems when she was admitted. When she was given visiting hours not a week later, she introduced herself as Eleanor Rigby. I thought she was joking because she seemed more normal than she had ever been. Maybe that's what Lee is going through."

I took a breath. "I'm sorry. I lost it a little bit there."

"Little bit," she agreed.

She was finishing the second row of tape, and I started behind her, writing "Mary and Peter" on the silver tape.

"I feel like we have the upper hand here, honestly." She sat with her back against the wall. "I'm going to bet he doesn't want that information getting out. He's probably going to let us do what we want as long as we don't bring it up. And that's assuming he recognized you. If he went off the deep end, that might not even be the case."

"What if he tries something? Like a preemptive strike?"

"We'll always be in each other's line of vision. You take the wall, so even if he does feel like mixing things up, he'll have to get over the idea of waking me up, too."

"We'll just continue what we came here to do until tonight then regroup at Ted's."

"Until then, just don't be alone with him. We won't even have to worry about sleeping."

"Right."

"Right, *Bawss*," she said.

"Right." I laughed.

I walked the broom and dustpan to the Hispanic man and gave him my best *gracias*. I got a cheerful *de nada* in return. "Peter." I pointed to myself then to Katy. "Mary."

"Miguel," the man said. He nudged his little girl. She was playing bashful in the curtain dangling between her and the concrete wall.

"My name is Gabriela," she said, enunciating each word.

"It's nice to meet you two," I said.

Gabriela whispered to Miguel again. Miguel smiled and raised his hand in a wave.

"That's the spirit," Katy said. She stood up from her spot against the wall. "Let's go meet the rest of the townsfolk of the Jackson Theater."

Chapter 25

The townsfolk of the Jackson Theater kept to themselves. Everyone was still in shock from the events of the past two nights and days. It was like entering a wild animal's habitat. I learned quickly that walking up to someone like I would have any other day wouldn't work. The locals were wildly skittish and mistrusting of people they didn't know before coming to the theater. I sat by an older man and what I assumed was his granddaughter. The two immediately stood up and walked out of the lobby, probably to their taped-off square of a viewing room. I tried sitting next to a woman who was by herself on a bench next to a lifeless photo booth—the kind of photo booth that could print fake drawings of pictures as well as the four-picture strip for just a dollar more. Her purse was safely in her arms across her chest, and before I even said a word, it was clear I would have to work to gain her trust.

"I'm Peter," I said as nicely as I could without sounding like a cartoon character.

She only looked at me with wide, sad eyes. She tightened the grip on her purse. Her fingers turned white with the pressure.

"I'm not going to hurt you."

She didn't move. Her mouth opened to say something and then closed again. She looked down at the floor and then back up at me.

"OK, I'm going to leave. Good talk."

A kid sat on a stool by what used to be a butter-dispenser station. I moved toward him, thinking that I should start somewhere, and a naïve kid would probably be easier to befriend than a timid adult. He was using the counter to play solitaire. He had blond hair, blue eyes, and rosy cheeks, and his clothes were very plain—Hitler's wet dream, Sarah would have joked. I figured he was five or six. He played by drawing three cards at a time instead of just one. That only made me think he was better at the game than I'd ever be. No one was around him, and no one passing by made any effort to speak to him. The other kids were in the arcade playing dinosaurs, and the adults spent the majority of their efforts ignoring me or gathering around in a circle for conversation. For some reason I assumed they were talking about me. There were no sideways looks or points, so I shook it off, chalking the thought up to stress-induced paranoia. Although I couldn't imagine them exchanging chicken enchilada recipes, given the current state of things. Regardless, I moved toward the kid at the table.

"You must be good." I leaned against the counter. "I *still* don't play the three-card way. Not even on my computer."

"I'm pretty good." He said it the way a champion solitaire player would say it. Just a phrase he tossed over the shoulder. I instantly got the feeling that this kid was incredibly smart, or at least knew something I didn't.

"My name's Peter."

"I'm James."

"Nice to meet you, James."

"Want to play a card trick?" he asked.

"Oh, it's on, buddy."

Without shuffling, he turned all the cards facedown and stacked them like a Vegas dealer. He laid out three rows of cards on the counter with nine cards stacked in each row quicker than anyone I'd ever seen do it. The cards lay faceup so I could see every diamond, club, spade, and heart. He asked me to pick a card—not to pick it up or tell him, just pick it—and I did, the four of spades. Then he asked which row my card was in, and I pointed to the row to my left. That was when I noticed Katy talking to Lee.

James took a deep breath and picked up the rows. He didn't shuffle them—just stacked the three rows of cards on top of each other. Then he re-created the three rows. This time, instead of making the rows all the way down one at a time, he added a card across each row. When the rows were complete, my card had made its way to the right side. He asked where it was, and I pointed. He repeated this one more time. The card was still on the right. I pointed to the right pile, and he stacked the deck again. Instead of making a fourth set of rows, he made three flower shapes with facedown cards fanned out in a circle. Each flower, like the rows, was made of nine cards each.

"Pick two," he said.

I picked the two outside flowers.

He pulled the middle one out and made a stack with it. "Pick one," he said.

"You're not going to take it away, are you?" I joked.

"I might have to." He smiled at me the way my dad would when I was a kid and he knew the answer to a question or joke I didn't quite understand yet.

I picked the one on the right, and he took the other one away. Then he laid the cards in three blocks of three. I picked two, and he took them away. Then he lined the remaining three between us. I chose two, and he took away the one I didn't pick. James put his finger on one of the cards. For one almost terrifying moment, he looked into my eyes.

Then he smiled a crooked little grin. "Now you can pick either of these cards. I know which one is yours."

"Do you?" I grinned right back. I pointed to the one under his finger.

He turned over the other card. It was the ten of diamonds.

"You have impeccable showmanship, I'll give you that. Let me guess—that's my card?"

Then he turned over the last card. Four of spades.

"That is incredible," I said.

"I'm good at cards."

"Where are your parents, James?"

"They died," he said as nonchalantly as if I asked what happened to the Mesopotamians.

"Oh," I said. "Did they turn into screamers?" His head snapped toward me. I jumped a little. "I—I didn't mean to—"

"They died last year. It was Halloween because pumpkin faces were in the yard."

"Jack-o'-lanterns?"

"Yes," he said as he somberly put away his cards. "They were in the yard when I got home from school and waited for my aunt Donna. She's one of them, now, though."

I felt rotten for making the little kid sad about his parents. Katy glanced at me from around the corner of the hallway across the lobby. Lee came with her. I didn't like that at all. "Hey, do you think you could show that trick to my wife?"

"Sure," he said.

"OK, great. Wait right there."

"Hey, honey." I speed walked to where Katy was talking to Lee. I wanted Katy away from him. I felt sticky from sweat even though I wasn't sweating. The walk across the lobby took an eternity. My mind was on fire. I somehow managed to not trip. "Hey, honey." I didn't know what to do to look normal, so I awkwardly put my arm around her. "I'm sorry, I didn't mean to interrupt."

"It's OK, sweetheart." Katy wrapped her small hand around mine. "Adam was just telling me about their hunting groups. You know how we were talking about that same thing? Getting a bunch of people together to clear out the city. I mean, what better place to restart civilization than right here at home."

"Yes," I said. "Why would you live anywhere else? We were just saying that."

"Yes," Lee said. "You should come. From what your wife tells me, she is a very decorated soldier. We'll be honored to have her on our crew."

"Of course she is," I nearly shouted. My heartbeat was almost a steady hum. That rage was back. Looking at Lee's sunburned face again sent a rush of anger through me. If my arm hadn't been around Katy, the overwhelming urge to strangle him—or at least try—would've been too much to stifle. With Katy there, I had something else to focus my thoughts toward.

"They've invited us to go with them tonight," Katy said, feigning eagerness. "I know you said that since I'm technically a civilian now, I'm not allowed to have a gun, but I think the circumstances have changed quite a bit."

"Why don't we talk about it," I said.

Adam waved us away. He was very neutral on the matter, as if it didn't matter to him whether we helped or not.

"Well, just listen, honey," Katy said as we walked away. "It's all very calculated. It's very similar to what I did in—" She reached into the front waistband of her shorts. She brought the phone out and pressed stop. The phone died almost immediately after that. "Shit," she whispered.

We made it back to the counter where James sat. "Watch this, honey," I said. Then I whispered, "We'll talk as soon as this is over."

"Hi," James said.

"Hey, little guy. I'm Mary. What's your name?"

"I'm James." He was already half finished setting the rows back up.

"I understand you have something to show me."

"Sure," he said with excitement. "Pick a card. Don't tell me. You can tell him if you want. I—" A strange look came across his face. "I have to go to the bathroom."

"That's OK," Katy said. "You go ahead, and we're going to pick a card."

James hopped down from the stool and hurried down the hallway.

"All right," Katy said when he and everyone else were out of earshot.

"Right," I said. She laughed a little and pressed on.

"I recorded our conversation on my phone, but it died. I gotta be honest—he doesn't seem to know who you are. I told him I was a software designer for the army and I served in Pakistan. He thinks I can shoot a gun, but I've never shot more than a Super Soaker."

"Did you have to be in the army?"

"I don't have a problem lying to these people for some reason. I figured it would help get me in on the hunting group. I don't know what kind of weird machismo has started here. They honestly seem like good ole boys. I managed to get on, though. We both are. We'll charge my phone at Ted's tonight when we go out."

I heard a flush then from down the hall. "Does the water work?"

"Apparently, yeah," Katy said.

"I guess if they have manual toilets, you don't need electricity to flush. Just water. I wonder if they realize it will eventually run out."

"Maybe they don't believe it'll take very long to get back to normal."

James came back around the corner.

"I'm telling you, honey"—I made sure he could hear me—"the kid knows how to do a card trick."

"Did you pick a card?"

"I did," Katy said.

"OK, memorize it, and don't tell me. Duh. Which row is it in?"

"This one." She pointed to the row in the middle.

James repeated all the same meticulous actions as before. Stacking the rows and dealing them back out across the counter. Katy's eyes watched the little boy suspiciously. I could tell she was being careful not to be caught looking at her card while the cards were faceup. Then James made the flowers and asked her to pick two. This time he took away the two flowers she picked. He broke the flower of nine into three groups of three. She picked two, and he took them away. She picked two cards from the remaining three, and he took away the other one. He did the same finger-on-the-card show and told her he knew what card was hers.

"Oh, do you?" Katy teased. She looked at James sideways. She flipped over the other card. It was the four of hearts. "OK. So far, so good."

She peeked at the corner of the card still under his finger. He grinned a huge Cheshire cat smile.

"Wow, that is pretty amazing." She was genuinely surprised. It was a moment of real excitement, and in that moment we weren't playing the secret spy game anymore. We were Derrick and Katy, not Peter and Mary, and she was blown away by this little kid and his magic card trick. She tousled his hair and walked in the direction of room six. James was suddenly the poster child for smug amateur magicians everywhere.

The two cards sat on the table. The red four faced the ceiling. The other card lay facedown like a drowned sailor treading water in the ocean. Knowing what I'd see, I flipped it over. The ten of hearts glared up at me. I didn't notice it the first time. Maybe it was the color or insignia on both the cards, but when I saw the four and the ten side by side with all those hearts, realization exploded in my head. My mind was racing with thoughts of the television screen and the person hiding in the shadow of the hotel room.

"You're a lot like me," James said. I was still staring at the cards. "I had to lie about who I was, too. Everyone wants to stay here. They think they'll make it here. I keep seeing things about this theater. What I see tells me they won't. You'll get to where you're going, though. It was nice to meet you, Peter."

I finally looked up. "Do you know my real name?"

"I think."

"You can call me by my real name if you don't tell anyone."

"OK. Derrick. Something bad is going to happen here. I don't know when, but I hope you and Katy aren't here when it happens."

"We won't be. We'll take you with us. We're leaving very soon. You don't seem to want to be here any more than we do."

"I can't stay at the police station either. There are bad people there, too. I think I was supposed to tell you that. And now I have."

I didn't know what to say to that.

Katy called back to me from the corridor. "Are we going to adopt the little guy?"

"Your wife is waiting."

James picked up the cards and slid them back into the cardboard box from where they had come. Then he left. He walked toward the office where Peggy had taken down our fake information. I didn't see him again in Jackson. I walked toward Katy, wondering which of my wives he meant.

"Come on, honey," Katy called loud enough for people to hear her. "We have to get ready for tonight."

Chapter 26

There were two different groups that went out to hunt. Twelve people made up one group, and including Katy and me, the second had thirteen. There were six men and three women who were either police officers or served in some branch of the military. One of the women taught self-defense classes at Jackson State University. She was bigger than I was. The rest were between fifteen and twenty-five. Most were high school students a few days before.

Ted was correct. Their strategy was simple. Flash the light until one of them screamed. Then covertly surround and take down what they called "the enemy" as quickly as possible. The group of twelve consisted of the more experienced members—cops and town locals, if that qualifies a person as more experienced. One group would take night, and the other would take the afternoon.

"And apparently they don't get in trouble very easily," Katy said. "That's why we were greeted by Bo and Luke Duke last night. Apparently, Khakis, whose real name is Bradley Davis, got an 'itchy finger' and someone 'stuck their head up at the wrong time.' Mark should be happy to hear that he has a name. All they did was make them come to the edge of town and take anyone they saw here so the theater would have more people. They *killed* someone—someone normal—and all they had to do is sit in the corner for a couple hours."

We were changing into camouflage clothes in a closet similar to Hank's Sleeping Bag Emporium. Small battery-powered lights hung from the corners and gave the closet a weak-orange look. It was the only room not illuminated by gas lanterns. Lee had "scored some time with our best marksman," and we were getting ready to become flashlight people.

"Did you see either of them?" I said.

"No." She was looking through the shoe containers.

"Are they looking for us?"

"You mean did Khakis and Blue Jeans tattle on us? Yes, but Ted was right. They're looking for two guys and a girl."

"Should we be worried?"

"Well, I should say, they're looking for 'two faggots and some bitch,'" she corrected in a thick southern accent. "But I don't think so. I feel like Lee would have a pretty good description of us. Plus they said we passed straight through town." She was still searching for something on the shelves of shoes.

"Don't you already have boots on?" I asked.

"Yes. But if there are all these shoes, there's got to be..."

"Gotta be what?"

"I'm looking for—Ah! Found it." She pointed the can of shoe polish toward me.

"I don't think they care about that, honestly."

"No, no. Watch," she said unwrapping the can. She put her finger in and quickly applied a coat of the stuff to her face and neck. "Now if we do see him, he won't recognize us."

"That's perfect." I reached into the can. I pulled out a blob big enough to cover my whole body and went to work.

"Not so thick," Katy said. She smoothed out what I had applied on my neck. "You don't want it to look obvious that you don't know what you're doing. This way, we're credible as hunters, and Khakis and Blue Jeans won't easily recognize us." She groaned at the word *hunters*.

"How do you know what you're doing?"

"My real dad was a hunter. Not whatever hunters these people are. All hunting really is, basically, is the ability to fool something into thinking you're not there. It's just as easy to fool people as it is to fool animals. If they see Mary and Peter instead of the two people they saw last night, I think we're in the clear."

"OK, what time are we leaving?"

"We're going around to the back where the Dumpsters are at five when the first group gets back, and the other group leaves as soon as it's dark. So we don't have much time between now and then."

"It's five now," I said. "Am I recognizable?"

"You're good. Me?"

"You look like a genuine aborigine."

She laughed. "OK, we are supposed to wait in the lobby for the others to come back."

I opened the closet door and banged into another kid in uniform. He fell onto his back and almost kept going over to his stomach. His pistol fell out of its holster and slid across the ground. He was the first person we had come across at the theater whose camouflage was the same consistent dark green from top to bottom. A lump of tobacco caused one side of his lip to swell up like a bee sting.

"Whoa, I'm sorry, man." I bent to help the teenager up.

He slapped my hands away. "Watch it, asshole."

"Hey." I tried my best to soothe the anger. "It's OK. Just an accident."

"It's fine," Katy said. "No harm, no foul, right?"

"Whatever. Just watch out. What were you doing in there?"

"We were told to change," Katy explained. "Richie is supposed to teach us the ropes."

"Y'all're the new guys?" he said skeptically. "You're old."

"Experienced," Katy argued. She closed in on him. "I was in the army. We were trained to kill people, and not our own, I should add. We could of course. I mean, we were trained to kill people in their sleep. You could be three hours into your forty winks, and I could get you one time in the neck. There are things we used—I could make a hole wide enough for you to bleed out but thin enough for you to not even wake up. You wouldn't feel a thing. But why would I want that?"

The kid dusted off his clothes with a look on his face like he was looking at his grandparents having sex. "What?"

"Go get Richie is what," she said. "He's late. Stop wasting our time."

"Jesus," I said once the high-schooler was good and gone. "Is any of that true?"

"I have no idea."

"Again, I have to ask, who are you?"

"If we let them talk to us like that, they'll walk all over us until we leave. That's one of the only things I've really learned as a doctoral student. If they can, they will."

"Noted. Jesus, what *is* grad school?"

"Hey," an angry voice came down the hall. The kid was young and accusing, the way bullies were in high school. Then I realized the kid was Blue Jeans. "You Pete?"

"I'm Peter," I said.

"Come on—you're with me." He walked by Katy and me toward a back exit, not giving any sign of recognition.

"OK," I said, and we followed.

The back door opened. I expected a freight train of brilliant light to come blaring through the door, so I prepared my eyes for the worst. Instead, soft, cloudy light eased through the door and down the hall. I hadn't realized how long setting up a place in the corner of the theater had taken until we were outside with the Dumpsters.

"OK, girls," Blue Jeans said with more than a touch of condescension in his voice. "Take these." He tossed us a handgun each. "Aim at the bottles on the top of the Dumpster."

"Do we shoot?" I asked, pretending to be stupid.

"Of course you shoot," he said. "Do it like you were in the heat of the moment."

"So just shoot now?"

"Yes, I want to see your technique and your accuracy. And don't hit the gate behind the Dumpster. You could fuck the whole place."

Against the back wall was a green Dumpster like those that can be found behind every fast-food chain in the world. A crate filled to capacity with empty beer bottles and cans sat beside the dented container. Just behind the Dumpster stood a chain-link fence. The fence created a square against the theater's back wall. Above it I could see the top of a sign that read "Stand Clear of Door." What looked like the tops of the letters in "Emergency Exit" peeked above the fence. Strips of gray plastic filled the holes between the metal wiring, preventing anyone from seeing what was inside the five-by-five-foot area.

"What's behind it?" Katy asked.

"The generator," Blue Jeans said.

"Does this place use a generator?" I asked.

"We will at night. We spent the day scrounging for gas for it."

"Is that back there, too?" I asked.

"No, that's in the boss's office. We can't have someone just come up and steal our gas."

"What if they take the generator? What will you do with the gas?"

"We can still use it to light fires. Just don't hit the generator. We're not even certain it works."

"Why wouldn't you just move the bottles somewhere else so you're not aiming in the direction of the generator?"

A scream came from the woods behind the theater. It was a horrifying thing. The man who created it had gone hoarse over the past few days. He ran at us. A huge shotgun blast echoed around the back lot, and the screamer dropped to the ground, missing a considerable portion of its cranium.

"Better wise up, rookies," Blue Jeans said, loading a shell into the bottom of his gun. "You're going to get yourself killed. You have to be *both* accurate and aware. Now shoot."

I unloaded a full clip of twelve and hit four beer bottles and six cans. Only one of each lingered on the edge of the Dumpster, mocking me. I dropped the clip and slammed in a new one. I used the first two rounds to destroy the remaining stragglers. I turned back to Katy who had a finger in each ear. "See, honey. I told you I was as good a shot as you." I hoped I was getting her out of the chore of shooting her twelve.

"You're getting better," she said. Blue jeans probably couldn't tell she was nervous, but I could.

"That's not bad," Blue Jeans said. The pissed off in his voice had abated, and he looked like a normal teenager. He walked toward me and clicked the safety button for me. "Better than most of the people you will be going out with. That doesn't mean you don't have to listen, though. You're a good shot, but if you're not paying attention, you'll get killed."

"That's what we hear," I said. I was thinking about Khakis and whoever it was that put his or her head up at the wrong time.

"Yeah." Blue Jeans laughed. "Those things will get you without thinking twice. Now pay attention. You can shoot. We've established that. Now you have to know what to do before you shoot. You'll hear *alpha* more than anything. *Alpha* is basically your move word. When you hear it, run, walk, spread out, whatever the situation calls for. Your team will split up into six or seven. Whatever half has gotten up to. Each side goes its own way in a wide circle. When you hear *alpha* from anyone in the other group, it means you've run into each other, and you start over. We have a flag about two hundred yards out. Your team goes an extra fifty or hundred yards out. It'll take about three or four hours. Even a shot like you will need about six clips."

"Thanks," I said sarcastically.

"When you hear *roo*, you be still. You don't move. *Roo* means someone heard something up ahead, and it's probably one of the crazies. If you move, you may get shot. I cannot stress that enough."

"Got it," Katy said. "*Roo* means stop. Even though *stop* means stop."

"*Mars* means someone is under attack or there are more than one and someone needs help. When you hear *mars*, come running like your hair is on fire. Got it?"

"*Mars* is help," I said. "Got it."

"No," Blue Jeans said, his young face scrunching back into anger. "*Mars* means come running. *Mars* is an emergency."

I wanted to tell him that if a person screamed *help*, that would imply some kind of an emergency. Instead, I just said, "Right."

"Right," Katy agreed.

"So we good?" I asked, more in an effort not to smile than really wanting to know.

"Yeah, the group is probably waiting in the lobby already. Don't get yourselves killed. The door locks back automatically. You probably have to go around to the front. Send someone back here to open the door for me."

"OK," I said.

As we rounded the corner of the building, I swear I heard him talking to someone.

"That was Blue Jeans, right?" I asked.

"It was. It looks like the shoe polish was a good idea."

"That's true. Way to think."

She tipped her imaginary hat.

Chapter 27

We met everyone in our group under the veranda. They were mostly kids. Randy—an actual police officer and the chaperone for this field trip—was the only person I pegged older than me, and he was only about a couple years my elder. His skin was relatively young despite the grays poking out in his hair. When I think of a man, I think of exactly Randy. He was tall and broad. To say he had a jaw like chiseled marble would downplay how unbreakable his jaw actually was. I could imagine him in the woods bent over a fire roasting a boar he had run down in nothing but a dirty, tattered pair of shorts. His graying stubble looked like a full beard. Like everyone else, he looked goofy in his multipatterned camouflage, but with the sun setting it didn't matter.

There were good people and bad people on both sides of the Hatfield-McCoy—style feud in Jackson. I believe that because of Randy. He was one of the good guys. One of the very few good ones. He was passing out pistols and shotguns from a wheelbarrow between the front doors and the barriers set up around the edge of the veranda when Katy and I rounded corner. The two of us hurried to the group. He barked orders and did his best to eliminate the horseplay.

"You two the new guys?" Randy asked. He was in a horrible mood.

"That's us," Katy said.

"I hope you guys don't mind a handheld. We're low on shotguns, but from what the boss tells me, you'll be fine with these."

Randy handed Katy and me a handgun each. I engaged the safety on mine and saw that Katy was awkwardly looking for hers. I reached over and clicked it for her, making sure I saw the orange paint of the safety button.

"Shit," Katy said loud enough for anyone who noticed to hear. "I have to get used to the safety button being on this side."

"Are there any questions?" Randy asked. "You know the calls? Everything?"

"I think we understand it pretty well," Katy said. "Nothing too demanding. Just stop and go, right?" She smiled at him confidently.

"If you need to, you can stay close to me. I don't want you two getting hurt out there."

"Thank you," I said. "We should be fine, though."

"That's good to hear." He patted me on the back. "Just don't get lost."

"We'll do our best," I joked, earning a patronizing laugh.

I noticed a number of flames dancing up behind the tinted windows of the entranceway. They were lighting more lanterns for the people who stayed. Probably more than a hundred little fires spread throughout the building.

"We did a good job last night," Randy said. "No one got killed. The other group has gone out twice and lost as many people. I don't want our number to go up. Understand? Even an injury is too much. No one is to goof around. I want your safeties on, and *only* when you hear the call are you to take them off, and then right back on they go. Are we on the same page? All right, guys, spread out and keep an eye out for your six."

Before we had left the parking lot, the flickering light from the lanterns fell over the sidewalk like a living orange sheet of paint.

"What's our six?" Katy asked me when the group set out for the mission.

"He just meant to watch our backs," I said, ducking through low-hanging branches. "Like if you were a clock and you were looking straight, you'd be looking at your twelve o'clock. Your six would be directly behind you."

"Well, that's easy enough," she said.

It was easy getting away from the group in the middle of the night. We could hear their calls for a few dozen yards away and abided by them. Once, a cry of *mars* rang out, and it immediately was followed by *just kidding* and scattered laughter. Randy screamed for a solid minute about the kid's "fuckery," and at one point I was even ashamed for the kid.

Katy and I made it far enough away from the group that they couldn't hear our feet crunching leaves, and we picked up the pace. Getting to the house took at least an extra hour going back. Our limited vision and lack of familiarity with the area slowed us dramatically. Multiple times I reached for my phone to call Mark, and then realizing it would not work, coupled with the fact that I had no idea what his number was, I gave up the search through my empty pockets.

"Where'd you learn to shoot like that?" she asked.

"I was a train robber in a past life." I grinned at her. She tapped me on the arm. "It actually came from a paralyzing fear of snakes."

"Seriously?" She laughed.

"Yeah, growing up on the farm, I saw them daily."

My skin burned with the scratches and pricks from the thicket and thorns when we noticed the gas lantern hanging from the balcony of the huge white house. We passed the house, and it was only when Katy cried out from a thorn in her eyebrow that I saw Ted's place. I hurried over to her and helped pull the two culprits out. Tears welled in her eyes. I wouldn't have noticed the tears if not for the lantern reflecting in them, and I wouldn't have seen the lantern if not for the tears. Funny how that worked out, I think.

"I'm so tired, Derrick." I could feel her slipping back into that panicked state I had met her in. I didn't want that.

"Come on," I said quietly. "We're here."

I put my arm around her shoulders and walked with her around the iron fence to the front yard. Ted smoked a rolled cigarette there as Mark talked about football. It was a one-way conversation. I could hear a slapping noise that came in three bursts, over and over. *Slap slap slap…slap slap slap.* Mark and Ted were playing rock, paper, scissors.

Mark's voice was loud. "I'm saying, Brady's probably one of those things, knowing his luck. That dickhead, I swear to God. As much as I'd hate to, I'd put money on him being one of the ones pulling people apart instead of one getting pulled apart—I have a savings account I'd empty on it. If I win, I get money. If I lose, Brady's in multiple pieces in multiple ditches. Your classic win-win situation, Ted. I'd pay two grand to know he's no longer intact."

"Hey," I said after the short rant.

"Jesus Christ, man." Mark bounced into the garage door. "I just lost weight and inner matter. Come on inside and tell us what happened while I change my jeans."

"How'd it go?" Ted asked.

"I don't think anyone wants to leave," Katy said. "But I do think we got a lot to work with. Do you have an outlet that works? Or a generator?"

"There're plenty at the station."

"Anything good you want to tell us now?" Mark asked. "It's a small world. See anyone you know? Or maybe find out where a certain khaki-wearing fucker sleeps at night?"

"Seriously," Ted interrupted. "This guy has been at full throttle since you guys left. We have got to get him something else to focus on."

"Ted and I are best friends now." Mark put his arm around Ted.

"If we can charge my phone," Katy said, "I have a recording of my conversation with their leader. I don't have my charger, though."

"We'll have something at the station," Ted said. "Let's go."

Chapter 28

"OK." Katy's voice came from the small speakers of her phone. All other outside sound was barricaded out of the station's conference room with one heavy door, making the speakers sound louder than they probably were. There was the windy sound of Katy sliding the phone into the waistband of her shorts. "I'm waiting outside Lee's office. I saw him walk in a minute or two ago. The door is a couple feet down from where we were interviewed by Peggy. There are flecks of bright-green paint on the door." More shuffling. A door opened and closed and locked. "Hey, Adam!" I could hear the extra accent she added to her voice.

"Hey, Mary, right?"

"Yep, that's me," Katy said a little too enthusiastically.

"You need help getting settled in?"

"No, no. I think we have it under control. I did want to ask you about the hunting situation. How can we get on board with that?"

"Why are you talking like that?" Mark asked.

Jackie shushed him.

"Well, now. Isn't that something? The new folks want to help restart civilization," Adam's recorded voice said.

"That's us." Katy sounded a little nervous. "So what do we have to do?"

"Are you sure you want to be involved in something like that?" Lee said. "It's very stressful. A delicate flower like yourself could get injured. Or worse…"

Even after the thirty-minute propaganda, call-to-arms speech from Admiral Mark Phillips upon finding out the man who murdered my parents was in charge of the theater, that anger I felt when I shook Lee's hand and looked into his eyes never came creeping back. But at the sound of those two little words, *or worse*, I could feel the hot sting of hate warming me from the inside out. The best way I can describe it is like a set of teeth clamping down on my nerves and gnawing as if I were its chew toy.

"People have died out there," Lee said.

"From the…" I could feel her trying not to say screamers.

"Those crazies?" Lee added. "Yes, but it's not just them. Accidents happen out there. Last night we had to discipline two of them."

"What do you mean?"

"We had an incident with the day crew. We had one cornered, and one person put his head up at the wrong time, and the other had an itchy finger. We had to send them out to the edge of town. A lot can go wrong."

"Why did you send them to the edge of town?"

"We need ensure that our numbers grow." A rattle interrupted the sentence—like a pill bottle. "Both for the safety of anyone else out there and"—a pause and the sound of a water fountain—"and so that our numbers here grow."

"Do you know if there is anyone else in town?"

"Nope," Lee said matter-of-factly. "Everyone is right here in the theater."

"They didn't see anyone last night?"

"You know what, I'm sorry. They did see a couple of homosexuals and their female friend. They refused help and said they wanted to make it on their own. I have a team of two searching the town now. I never let anyone go out alone, you see. I should actually check on that and make sure nothing has come up." There was a click and a half second of static. "'Ey, Bradley. You find them boys you saw last night yet?"

A pause. Then the static opened up again.

"You mean those faggots and that bitch they were with?"

"Now, Mr. Davis, that's not how I want you to phrase that."

"I'm sorry, Boss. Naw, I ha'n't seen 'em. Should I call it off? Get back with the group."

"Give it an hour." I could hear the forced concern in his voice even through the speakers of the little phone. "After that, we've done all we can do. Next time just make sure they come here first so we can make sure they have everything they might need. Over and out." Then to Katy he said, "We are just trying to help everyone."

I knew he gave her some smug shit-eating grin, and the teeth sank deeper into my nerves at the idea.

"So what do we need to do to help with that?"

"Do you have any experience in combat of any sort?"

"I was a software engineer in Pakistan."

"Military?"

"Army."

"You see any action?"

"Enough to know my way around a rifle."

"Interesting. A looker, and a sharp shot. I'm only kidding of course. Let's see how you make it tonight. You know if this works out, we might even invite you into the Smoking Room. We could even move you and your husband to one of the hunters' lounges next to the office. We have sofas for the people risking their necks."

"What's the Smoking Room?"

"It's just a place to relax that we're building out back. Using a couple things from hardware and outdoor stores in the area. Just a room for cigars and maybe a little entertainment."

"Where is that? I didn't see anything going up on the way in."

"It's going up behind the building. We found a clearing in the woods. Instead of having a place for the crazies to congregate and build numbers, we're going to use it for a getaway spot. A quiet spot, you see."

"Sounds...nice," Katy said. "I guess we'll have to see what happens tonight. Do we need to help with the construction of that instead? The hunting seems to be pretty well covered. I haven't seen a scr—a crazy in the area at all."

"Why don't we see how you do hunting first? I don't mean to pick nits or anything, but you guys are outsiders."

"Clinton is seen as outside?"

"We just want to make sure we're all in this together. You're looking good, though. Don't you worry."

"We'll see, then. Keep our seat warm."

"And your husband? Peter," Lee asked. His voice was deeper. Not Barry White or Lou Rawls deeper, but I know I heard it. It was an accusatory voice if I've ever heard one.

"What about him?"

"What kind of shot is he?"

"To be honest, I'm not one hundred percent on that. I'm sure he'll be able to hold his own, though."

"Here's what I'll do. I'm going to put in a call for our best guy. Richie. He's out right now with the first group. He'll get you set up and give you a crash course in outside behavior. I'll have him meet you and your husband, if he wants to go also, in the lobby in twenty minutes. You can use the camo room to find something discreet to wear."

"I think I'll have to talk it over with my husband first."

"Hey, honey." My own voice came out of the phone speakers.

A moment later Katy pressed stop on the screen, and the room went quiet.

"OK," Jackie said from the center chair at the opposite end of the conference table.

The rest of us had huddled around the phone on both sides of the long table to hear the recording. A white cord that was clipped into the phone disappeared into a hole in the table's surface.

"What are we thinking?" Jackie said. "We can wait a day, make sure people who want to leave are given the chance, or we can pack up tomorrow morning and get the hell out of here."

"Derrick and I have unfinished work," Mark explained. "We don't have to go back to the theater, but we aren't leaving town until what needs to be done gets done."

"We have a day and a half to get it done," Jackie said. "Anything later than sundown the day after tomorrow will be in the dark, and that risks the chance of retaliation, and that's not something we can afford to deal with. And that's only if we kill the power during daylight hours. I think we can manage that with it being so cool outside."

"The inside of the building is pretty simple," I explained. "The lobby is sort of a rec room where most of the civilians, or whatever you want to call the people without the guns, spend most of the day praying and avoiding out-of-towners. Most of them already know each other, and they're all very nervous around new people. I only got a chance to actually talk to about half of them today. Maybe I can tug at some sympathy strings and get some more people to come my way once we get back."

"We know the front of the building is going to be guarded around the clock," Katy said. "Those weird pillars out front have people with guns in them, so if they recognize anyone from the station, they'll probably just shoot you before you get there. The people with guns are teenagers, and they're riled up on a power trip, so they don't have a problem demonstrating their ability to squeeze a trigger. The back entrance may be the best way to get into the building. I don't know how long the hunters will be out or if they know we're gone."

"You said you left at around five thirty," Jackie said. "I think, regardless, we have to come up with a way to separate you two and make it believable enough for it to be the reason you were late getting back. I think the best thing is for Derrick to go back alone. I'd feel more comfortable with that than sending Katy back in alone. You're probably less likely to be raped. I can tell Katy is getting a lot of attention, and the added fact that her husband is missing is just going to make those little peckers that much harder."

No one said anything to that. Mark just looked at Katy and me with his eyebrows up.

"Derrick, you need to sell it, though. Katy got lost or killed or anything."

For a moment I felt bad for Randy's spotless track record, so I said, "We'll say she got lost. They'll probably send a search out for her, right?"

"That's good," Jackie agreed. "The fewer people around, the better. We've passed the point of being civil. I know it's not a very protect-and-serve way to think about this, but I want that fucker in the khakis to get what's his. Seems like you got some demons of your own to deal with, too, Derrick."

"So I'll just walk out like normal," I said. "Maybe even a little in a panic. Then try my best to create a diversion, and once everyone is gone, I'll let you guys in the back. Do we have any other agenda?"

"You're certain no one wants to leave with us?" Jackie asked.

"I don't think so," Katy said.

"I don't either," I said.

"Then I say we go in," Mark began, "exact our revenge, drop the mic, walk out with the bloodstains on our shoes, and get the hell out of Dodge."

"Here, take this." Jackie hobbled to a podium at one end of the long table, using the table to steady her shaky legs. The pain-killers seemed to be working enough for her to be somewhat mobile. She went behind the podium and came back with a small walkie-talkie. It was about the size of a cell phone. "Just keep this on you. We don't want to rush in there too soon. They'll gun us down like terrorists. So when you know they have sent people out, you give a call on the walkie, and we'll head that way. Just keep it on you, and we will let you know when we're at the back door."

"Where will you be?" I asked.

"Officer Carter and I are going to drive you to the theater. Up to the point where we can no longer hide from the towers. That should be a little farther than in the daylight because of buildings' shadows around the place. We're going to come from a different angle, though. Instead of the way you came in the first time, we'll take a car to the other side of town and come from the hotel. Then you sell it. Sell it like your kids need braces. What I'd like to do is check out whatever it is that they're building in the woods. We'll do that while you round the troops into a search frenzy."

"Hang on, now," Mark chimed in. "Officer *Carter* and I? You're saying it wrong. My name's not Carter. You should know that. We came out of the same nut sack."

"No," Jackie said, impatient. "I meant him."

"Fuck *him*," Mark said. "No offense, Theo."

"OK," Ted said.

"I don't want you in there yet, Mark," Jackie started to explain.

"Yet?" Mark said, still calm. "What does it matter when I go?"

"Because, Mark, we have to be very precise with this operation. We have to make absolutely sure no one wants to leave. We can't allow a personal vendetta to stand between those people and a life they prefer to the one they're living now. Besides, they know you. You stand out for so many reasons. Your mouth, your height, your walk...I could go on, but everyone in this room knows—"

"*I have revenge to exact!*" Mark screamed, shattering the calm mood of the room. "I know it sounds petty and childish and doesn't necessarily adhere to the social norms and niceties of a week ago, but that shit went out the window the moment those godless assholes nearly toppled us over the edge of the interstate to our death. I know it's the good-Christian-boy thing to do nothing and allow his soul to atone for his mortal sins, but you can bend that entire way of thinking over and fuck it. We are not in the real world anymore. We have shifted to a real-life dog-eat-dog existence where there is no system for the correction of wrongdoing anymore. It's all up to the wronged to ensure that people don't continue to make this world miserable. When someone runs you over and leaves you for dead in the middle of the road, it's up to you to make it right. Come on, Jack." Mark looked over the table at Jackie. His eyes were red from anger, and they were wet. He slapped the heavy table and stood up. "Come the fuck on. Where does it stop? They've shot you now. Is pulling someone apart like the screamers do too far? Or no?"

I heard every heartbeat in that nauseatingly pure silence.

"Is everything OK in here?" The doctor from the day before had eased into the room without making a sound. His face held an expression of genuine concern when no one answered. To my knowledge no one other than me even looked his way.

"God-fucking-dammit!" The words stabbed the air as Mark stomped to the door.

The doctor quickly evacuated the room.

"I'm pissed off!" Mark slammed the heavy door, and it rattled in the frame. A single wet drop sat on the table in front of the chair where he'd sat.

"That's a tantrum," Jackie said as though Mark's fit came a minute behind schedule. "Is there anything else we need to go over?"

"Should we get him?" Katy asked.

"Nah," Jackie said. "He'll work it out himself. One way or the other."

"Are you sure?" I asked.

"Sure enough to take care of what we have to do." Jackie ran her hand over the gunshot wound. "Where's the gun they gave you?"

I took the pistol Randy gave me from my back pocket and handed it to her. A few clicks later, a spring shot out, and she handed it back to me.

"Here," Jackie said. "If they ask why you didn't shoot. Tell them they gave you a broken gun. Don't say anything else about it. Just that it didn't work. Maybe it'll create some extra obligation to find her. Now we have to move. The longer you stay out here, the harder it's going to be to believe that you two just got lost. Sooner or later they're going to start asking questions and figure out something is fishy."

Jackie, Ted, Katy, and I hurried back to the garage behind the station. The four of us piled back into the Jeep and made in the direction of the theater—only this time it took about twenty minutes longer, ducking through back roads and neighborhoods to get across town and end up on the other side. The scenes outside the windows displayed a terrifying look into the chaotic postnormal age we had been thrust into. The sidewalk-lined streets were littered with bodies and pieces of bodies. Packs of screamers prowled the streets looking for something to wreck. A cat tiptoed out into the road as we strategically maneuvered from street to avenue and back. Two of the once-people stumbled over an iron gate to get at the stray. In their rush to make quick work of the cat, one of the two got stuck on a post and hung there by his jeans, thrashing for freedom, while the other stumbled over the gate headfirst, startling the cat into a full-on sprint. The body didn't move after that. We passed the scene in darkness, not stopping to offer help.

At one point a pileup of people forced Ted to employ the Jeep's off-road features. "We're getting close," he said. "This is where the theater people pile 'em up in this part of town." He pulled off to the shoulder of the less-suburban part of town to avoid the mound. A miasma of nauseous air filled the SUV. I noticed a house with a huge metal windmill. I thought it was a strange thing to keep in a gated yard. The decoration, because that's all the windmill really was, took up a large portion of the small yard. On top of it, where I expected there to be a rooster for some reason, there was a Heisman statue. Not the trophy exactly but a pretty close copy.

"Could do without that smell. That's for sure," Katy said, covering part of her face with Ted's wife's shirt.

"We'll be at the drop-off point in a few hundred yards. How you feeling, Pete?" Jackie turned to the backseat.

I didn't answer at first.

"You there?"

"Oh, geez," I said. "Yeah, sorry."

"We're going to leave you a couple hundred yards away. We'll cover you until we can't see you anymore. Just get on the radio when we're clear to move in."

"Be careful." Katy's voice was quiet. She squeezed my arm when she said it. I couldn't tell if she was looking at me, though.

"Hit the ground running," Ted said as the car decelerated.

I took this to mean hurry, so before the car came to a complete stop, I was on the move. I was completely turned around. I didn't see anything recognizable, but when the Jeep finally stopped, the driver's window rolled down, and Ted pointed.

"Just down the street," he said. "The trees are blocking it right now, but you'll see it."

I blindly proceeded after his finger's trajectory. I couldn't help but wonder what I would've done, where I would've ended up if Mark had not shown up in my barn. I wondered whether or not I would've even made it out of the barn. I could see the tops of the towers shining in the moonlight through the trees. The theater was so far away. I started yelling for help. I remembered to tell myself to enunciate, but I knew that when they heard the screaming, they would come locked and loaded. I certainly didn't want to be the cause for anyone to have to go on border patrol.

I stopped briefly when I reached the edge of the hotel across the parking lot from the theater. I stopped because I was out of breath. I'd never jogged and screamed at the same time, and I didn't plan to get any better at it. I was nearly hoarse. I used the side of the building to prop myself up. There was a very weak thump on the wall. Nothing significant. Nothing that led me to believe I was in any kind of danger, but I could feel them in there. I couldn't hear the screams if they were screaming, but I somehow knew that if I were to peek into a window or around a corner, there would be wall-to-wall screamers. And once

I knew they were in there, I couldn't not know it. I imagine it was like a pregnant belly when the child starts kicking. It was like a faint motion just beyond the surface of the bricks. I heard the thump better than felt it. I couldn't actually feel anything, but I knew there were hundreds, or even thousands, of them in that hotel. I took my hand away from the building, but that overwhelming feeling stayed with me. I looked around the hotel for an easily accessible entrance or a window I could see through. I didn't find anything. Everything on the first two floors was boarded up. I found a drainpipe creeping up the side of the building. It ran right up to a third-floor window and jerked to the side to miss it then continued upward. I started climbing. I was up to the first metal strap bolted to the side of the building before it gave way and threatened to fall over on me. I jumped back down, and decided the best thing to do would be to leave the hotel alone for now. I surveyed my surroundings and continued to the theater.

"Help! Please, my wife! Please help!" I was getting hoarse, but I was also being very careful to speak clearly again. I didn't want to be another guy who raised his head up at the wrong time. I waved my hands in wide arches. I wasn't even acknowledged until I took the first step up onto the sidewalk leading to the box offices. It was Randy who met me at the door.

"Geez, son, where have you been?" He was annoyed but more than willing to help me inside the building.

"We got separated. Me and Mary, we were chased by one of them, and we got separated." I tried to be hysterical, but knowing Katy was fine wouldn't allow me to sell it. I would be terrible actor.

"Hey, hey." He grabbed my shoulders. It seemed as though my attempt at looking frantic was on the mark. "Calm down. We're going to find her."

"Please, help her," I nearly screamed.

"Come back in here, and tell us what happened."

Chapter 29

"It was like a nightmare, Randy," I said.

He sat me down on the same bench I had used earlier that day. The crowd now gathered around me coupled with the lanterns hung all around the lobby had a strong "Kumbaya" feel.

"We were trying to spread out, you know? Make a radius or whatever it's called."

"You mean a perimeter?" he asked.

There was a group of people behind him. One in particular stood out to me: Khakis. He either didn't recognize me or didn't act like he did, but he looked directly in my eyes. I was confident that our shoe-polish disguises had served their purpose.

"I do. Thanks."

Randy handed me a bottle of water. I chugged it, and because I wasn't thirsty, it took much longer than I expected. Everyone looked at me as I drank.

"We were setting a wide perimeter. It was my fault. She told me not to go too far. I didn't listen. I should have *listened!*" At this I threw the half-empty bottle of water across the lobby, thankful for a reason not to have to keep drinking it. "We got too far to hear the calls, and by then we couldn't get back. We were walking in circles for probably an hour. I got stuck in a bunch of mud. The thing came out of nowhere. I distracted it and told her to find a place to hide. It chased me away from her. I didn't even see where she was going. God, I'm so *stupid!*"

"You're not stupid, Pete. You didn't know this was going to happen. Don't worry. It's fine," Randy soothed. "Where were you when it showed up?"

"We made it to a neighborhood. We were so turned around. I couldn't really even tell you where it was. It was back that way, though." I pointed in the opposite direction the group had gone in earlier that night.

Randy got on his walkie. "We got one of them back. Pete's here. He says they were separated in a nearby neighborhood."

"Just make sure he's OK," the boss said. "No sign of Mary?"

"Not yet. We're trying to figure out their path."

"Do your best to get an exact location." The walkie clicked and was silent.

"We've already got a team ready to go," Randy said. There were a few quiet cheers or encouragements from behind him. "We're waiting on the trucks to arrive, and we'll send them out. Everyone give the guy some space. Why don't you take a bathroom to yourself, Pete? Wash your face off and collect yourself. Maybe even try to sleep. We'll make sure she turns up by sunup. And alive. I promise you that."

Khakis said, "Don't you worry. I ha'nt kilt nothin' all day. I'm itchin' to get after something."

"All right, Bradley," Randy said. "Shut up."

Another tiny wave of encouragement from the army of minors spread throughout the lobby. I saw a glimpse of Lee through the forest of torsos and legs in front of me. He was talking to Peggy, the woman who had ushered Katy and me through the theater when we first arrived. He held something. Another glimpse showed me that it was a manila folder. I later realized it was not only Peter Grabowski's folder but Mary Grabowski's as well.

"Hey, Randy," Lee called. The entire crowd around me turned in the direction of the voice. "Before you send another troop out, come see me."

"You got it, Boss."

"Bring Pete with you, please."

Chapter 30

"What do you mean you don't want to look for her until morning?" I was furious, so mad I forgot about the fact that Katy being out among the screamers was a lie. Those teeth bit down on my nerves again. I forgot my fake name and my real one. I wanted to choke him. I wanted to grab him by his overgrown Adam's apple and pull until something came loose. The thought that he would leave an innocent person—let alone my wife and let alone Katy—out there overnight fueled a rage in me I hadn't known.

"I just mean, I think if she isn't dead already, she is probably held up somewhere." He put his hands up in a surrendering gesture. "I don't mean to be blunt or insensitive, but you said it yourself. She is a very resourceful young woman. Ex-military. Obviously in much better physical condition than most of the people we have standing guard. And word around the campfire is that if she taught you to shoot, she'll probably have no problems clearing out the rest of the city for us. I don't want to send out a team in the middle of the night when everyone has already been out there. The troops are tired, and I can't risk it when you and I both know it won't change a thing waiting a few hours until everyone has a little time to rest. Then we'll send everyone out to find her, wherever she has chosen to hide."

I could tell he was trying to reassure me that she was OK, and it might have worked had the situation been legitimate. Given my knowledge of reality, I just wanted to leave the conversation. I glimpsed down and saw my fake name on the tab of the manila file folder.

"Why don't you just take the night to yourself? Get some rest," Randy said. "Maybe if you sleep on it, you'll be able to remember your route a little better in the morning."

"How am I supposed to sleep with her out there?"

"She's OK." Lee's mouth turned up at the corners. His eyes were uncaring and dared me to say otherwise. They were the same dead eyes from the mug shot plastered over the top-right corner of page 2-A of the newspaper.

"Come on, brother," Randy said. His arm fell around me like an army blanket. "Let's get you cleaned up and in a sleeping bag."

Randy walked me to the bathroom. When his hand slid off me, it brushed the tip of the walkie-talkie's antenna. Nervous that he would wonder what it was, I turned to him. I handed him the gun. I'm sorry to say that a little of my anger toward Lee had spilled over into what I said to Randy next. "Oh, yeah. This didn't work. I don't know what happened, but when I tried shooting the thing chasing her, it didn't do anything." It was a lie, and I thought he could tell. I didn't know any other way to explain what would've been wrong with the gun, so I just said what Jackie told me to say.

A look of total self-disgust wore on him and made his face sag. The wrinkles seemed to deepen. The gray seemed to whiten. "I'm so sorry, Peter. Nothing's gonna stop me from finding your wife. Alive."

"Yeah," I said. I was genuinely upset at the sight of his now fifty- or sixty-year-old face. I walked into the dimly lit bathroom and let the door close itself.

I checked the stalls for feet. Under the first one, I saw a pair.

"Don't worry. I'll be out in a second."

"No rush," I said. "Just thought it'd be better to be alone while I'm in here."

"I appreciate the warning." The door opened, and an older man walked out of the stall with a friendly smile on his face. "I thought everyone got uppity when you dress in blackface."

"Oh, no. My wife and I thought it would help when we went out with the group to clear out the area."

"Your wife?"

"Yeah, Mary."

"Oh," he said, his voice tinged with suspicion. His smile fell. He kept his eyes on me as he crossed the bathroom to the sinks. "You Pete?"

"I'm Peter. That's me."

"I see you made it back. Where's your wife now?"

"We actually got separated."

The man stopped washing his hands. He looked at me in the mirror. "Is that right? You need to watch out, Peter. There are things out there that will get you."

He left the room with wet hands.

I powered on the walkie-talkie.

Chapter 31

"You guys there?" I whispered into the walkie in the echoing bathroom.

"Hey, Derrick. I'm here. Are you OK?" It was Katy. The volume was a little too loud for my liking, even though it was probably inaudible five feet from where I was standing. I nudged the volume down a half millimeter and tiptoed to the end of the stalls.

"I'm fine. Where are you?" I asked for no other reason than that being what I usually asked next over the phone.

"We're back at the station looking for Mark," Katy said. The walkie clicked off then back on.

Jackie had it then. "Do we have a time frame yet?"

"They want to wait until morning."

"Morning? Why?"

"Lee thinks that because she's a military vet, she would be fine for one night in the neighborhood. Plus all his teenage minions need a night to sleep before going back out to wreck the town."

"I guess we can wait until then."

"Unfortunately," I said, "I think we have to."

"Did they believe you?"

"They did…Something tells me he didn't, though. He had my and Katy's files in his hand when I got back."

"What do you mean, your file?"

"They have sort of an inventory of everyone here." I reached for Peggy's name. "They interview everyone when they show up and keep track of whatever they have. Like the sleeping-bag board we were telling you about. The person who conducts the interviews is a woman named Peggy."

"Any idea why they're keeping those records? I can't imagine keeping tabs on people means that much nowadays."

"Lee seems pretty set on keeping everyone under control," I said. "It's like he wants to not only have all his ducks in a row, but everyone else's, too."

"If he is who you think he is, I can't blame him."

"No sign of Mark yet?"

"No, but he'll turn up."

"That's odd. Are you sure he's still at the station?"

"He wouldn't go out there. Not for something as silly as a middle-school playground fight. His leg would slow him down."

"They shot you, though."

"I'm not dead."

I didn't know what to say to that.

"Is there anything new to report?" she asked.

"Nothing yet."

"While you have some downtime, ask around. See if we have anyone else who wants to leave. It's past midnight, so you may have to wait until tomorrow. Just keep it in mind. The less we have to do tomorrow, the better. We don't want to be here much longer." Then she paused. "We can't afford to be here much longer."

"I'll get on it." I thought of Lee holding the folders with my and Katy's pseudonyms, and pseudolives inside, and that stupid dead-eyed grin on his face. "I may be under the microscope, but I'm on it."

"All right, round 'em up. We'll be there bright and early. Don't forget."

"You got it," I said.

"Over and out."

I ran some water. Luckily, they still had the manual faucets. I made a bowl with my hands. The water tasted like metal.

"Derrick?"

I almost didn't hear it. The walkie was so quiet that putting it in my pocket was almost as good as muting it.

"You OK, Katy?" I asked.

"I am. I just feel left out. Everyone talks like a cartoon character. Crap like 'Copy that' and 'What's your twenty?' I feel like I'm in a scene from a Hallmark remake of *Lethal Weapon*. It's like everyone is speaking Spanish. I think I'm going to start talking slowly and loudly when I want to communicate."

"Still no sign of Mark?"

"No." She waited with the line open. "I'm worried he left."

"I don't think he's that crazy. I better go. They're going to think something is up if I don't leave the bathroom."

"You can't say you're making a movement?"

"That's the real reason I have to go."

She laughed. "Do me a favor. Be careful. Watch your six, or whatever it is."

"I will. Get some sleep. We're coming to find you in the morning."

"Save me, Superman. Save me," she said like a damsel in distress.

"Be careful tomorrow. I know something crazy is going to happen."

I washed my hands and did what I could to get the shoe polish off my face.

When I left, Randy escorted me directly to my taped-off square with the blue and red sleeping bags.

"We'll get her," Randy assured me again. "And she'll be fine."

"I know," I said. "I'm just scared for her. I won't be able to sleep."

That wasn't a lie. I was worried about my wife. Her name wasn't Mary or Katy, though. I was suddenly overcome with anxiety for Sarah. What was she doing? Where was she? Who was in the dark corner of her hotel room? What did 410 mean? Part of me felt guilty, like I was using Katy as a stand-in for Sarah. I felt like I was cheating on my wife with the first random person who showed face.

"If you need anything at all, you just call me. I'll be in room three with the rest of the group. If not, in room two with the other group. Even if I'm asleep."

"I probably won't need that," I said. I made a mental note of where Mark would be able to find Khakis when he made his way to the theater with flames of revenge burning in his eyes like an angry cartoon character. The thought was enough to make me laugh.

"I'm sorry about the gun, Peter. I really am." He had the sad eyes of a whipped pup.

I bade Randy a good night and retired to my square.

Before I went to sleep, I traded my camo for the clothes I took from Ted's house. I didn't feel right wearing their clothes. The floor was uncomfortable, so I doubled up the sleeping bags. It didn't help much, but I didn't like the rolled-up sushi-style body bag sitting beside me. I fell asleep with Sarah on my mind. Part of me wished we had never stopped in Jackson. I talked myself in and out of agreement with the decision another four or five times before I fell asleep. I didn't feel at ease again until Katy, Jackie, Mark, and I were pulling away from the chaos spilling out of the theater hardly more than a day later. I slept hard. But not for long.

PART 3
THE YELLOW MAN

Steeeroke! Steeeroke!

Chapter 32

"**D**o you know who I am?"

I was still mostly asleep when my head hit something hard. He had me pinned against the wall. A thin black drapery hung along the sides of the room—I assumed for decoration, because it did nothing in the way of protection. The fabric was the only thing between my head and the cinder-block wall.

"Who the fuck are you?" Lee growled at me. His breath was hot in my face and smelled like chewing tobacco. His hair pointed in all directions. The hands holding me against the wall shook wildly. "Don't lie to me either, boy."

Lee's eyes glimmered in the lantern he'd brought into the room. The white dominated the iris. Tears spilled onto his bony cheeks. The collar of his shirt was stretched wide enough to slide a beach ball through. His throat bobbed up and down as he swallowed a crying fit. He bit at his upper lip. The smell of cigarettes on his clothes all but overpowered the stink of his breath.

"Answer me," he snapped in a hushed tone.

"What did you say?"

"I said who are you, goddamn it? Who the fuck are you?"

"I'm Peter Gra—"

He slapped me hard. The sweat from his palm coated my cheek.

"What the hell?" I pushed him away.

Lee rebounded back as if on an elastic cable, and he unsheathed the knife he had stowed somewhere behind him. I had never seen anyone move that quickly and precisely. The knife was a seven- or eight-inch Bowie. The blade reflected enough light to find a person's contact lens in the blacked-out theater room. I didn't say anything after that.

"Now, I want to know who you are, right now."

"I—"

"And don't give me any of that Peter Grabowski shit."

He pressed the edge of the blade against my throat. It was cold, but when it began to dig into my neck, I felt a hot burn surge from beneath my skin. I stared at him, not wanting to be diced. His eyes twitched.

"Answer me, goddamn it. Or maybe I'll shave that pretty face." The knife went from my neck to my cheek. It dug into my skin. "We want you to look good when Mrs. Grabowski returns. Now, I'll ask you again. Who are you? Are you George?"

At the sound of my father's name, I immediately brimmed with tears, and my throat closed. For what felt like forever, I couldn't breathe. I could feel the saliva from teeth as they bit down on my nerves.

"Or Jamie? Or are you Carol? Why aren't you saying anything? Say something, you little shit," he said through his clenched mouth. He threw me into the wall again. My head bounced off the concrete, and my vision wavered.

"Who," I started, "is George?"

"You know what I'm talking about. You're a little shit. George was a little shit. You're just like George. George and Carol and Jamie. You're all a bunch of shit. Who are you? Jamie? Carol? Or George?" His eyes grew even wider then. "You know about the police station, don't you? You do. You do." Tears dropped off his chin as he moved closer. A drop landed on my hand.

I screamed for help, but it was cut off from his grip on my throat. "Adam," I managed to get out. "Please. Stop."

"What the fuck are you saying, boy? Who is Adam? I'm not Adam. Adam is dead just like *you*, George Jamie Carol. And he ain't coming back no more."

"Please." I kneed him hard. I hoped for the crotch, but contact was made in the gut. The pressure released from around my neck.

Lee fell to the floor into the fetal position. The little Spanish-speaking girl stirred. I didn't move. I still don't know why I was suddenly overcome with the fear that if she woke up, she would blow my cover, screaming at the top of her lungs that the stranger was beating up the boss—so throw him out and let the crazies pull him apart. She only turned her face over to the other side of her pillow. Lee stumbled to his feet and charged me again. I jumped to one side. He hit the wall behind me and recoiled like a drunk. The knife hit the ground, and I kicked it into the corner of the room. It bumped against one of the red curtains framing the screen. Gabriela adjusted the top layer of her sleeping bag.

The smack against the wall must have realigned his circuits because he wiped his face and said, "Aw, shit."

"What?" I snapped. Luckily, it was a whisper, so the majority of the anger and threat was taken from it. I picked up the bottom of the curtain and dropped it over the knife.

Lee flinched. "Geez, man. You scared me. I didn't wake you up, did I?"

"What?"

"I'm so sorry, Peter." His voice was no longer angry and accusative. Rather it adopted a slightly higher tone, and he sounded nearly cheerful, the way a neighbor might after receiving a compliment on the house's new coat of paint. "I've been sleepwalking since this whole thing happened. I think it's stress, you know. A lot's been going on the past few days. How are you doing? I imagine you're having sleeping problems, too, with Mary still out there. Don't worry. We're going to find her in the morning."

He smiled. The grin was Adam's, whoever Adam was, but the eyes still belonged to Lee. Now both of them knew that I knew that something was off about whichever one was at the controls.

Lee reached into his pocket and pulled out a pill bottle. He shook it, making the rattle sound, and dumped a few pills in his hand and chewed them. "This should help me through the night. I'm sorry again about waking you."

I don't think I was wrong to force myself into Hank's Sleeping Bag Emporium, which had been left open for the night. To be honest, I'm shocked I was able to still my heart long enough to fall asleep. I feel the same could be said of any night since that one as well. I checked my watch. It was a little after five in the morning. I had only been asleep an hour. Not much longer and the sun would start showing.

On my way across the building, a couple of older women were sitting on a bench in the lobby. I didn't interrupt their conversation as I dragged my and Katy's sleeping bags into the closet, but the two of them offered a timid raise of a hand. Or maybe they were pointing. I nodded my head. The door closed automatically once I nudged the doorstop from under it with my toe. I tumbled to the ground and slid beneath the lowest shelf on the wall. There were boxes of plastic cups nearby. I moved one between my head and the door, whether to block the light that would inevitably come creeping through the cracks or hide me from Hank or anyone else who might come in, I'm still not sure. I pulled the walkie-talkie from my pocket.

"Anyone there?"

No. They were not.

The hole in my leg throbbed. Heat swelled from the wound. I felt very lonely that night. I imagined that's what a refugee felt like, hiding in a dark closet in search of a few hours of rest before fleeing the next day. I wanted to see anyone I knew. Katy, Mark—hell,

Tony would've been a friendly face. More than anything, I wanted Sarah. I missed her most of all. I thought I would have trouble easing back to unconsciousness, but the more I thought about, the less lucid I became. I stopped controlling what happened in my mind, and, eventually, the exhaustion of the day caught up with me. Before complete control was given over to my dreams, I saw Sarah again.

Chapter 33

I was so happy to see a friendly face in the fleeting moments of my consciousness. Sarah sat on the bed of her hotel room. I stared at her face-to-face, or at least what could be considered face-to-face when this happens. She wore thigh-high stockings and a black-and-light-green teddy I had only seen her in once before. For years it hung on a cushioned, velvet hanger. I almost didn't recognize the thing. She definitely didn't look like a nurse in it. Besides the stockings and translucent teddy, she wore nothing but creamy white with two small interruptions of pink.

Behind my view of her, the television shone bright blue. And as if to finally once and for all prove I wasn't actually there, the blue fell over her face like a veil, uninterrupted by a shadow my physical presence would have no doubt created.

She looked straight ahead with an expression on her face of total curiosity. She grinned the way she used to when we first started dating. The room around her dimmed slightly. She hummed a single sweet laugh. Sarah's eyes followed something from directly ahead of her down to the floor. I wanted to look down with her. I wanted to see what was coming, but I could feel the sensation of movement in my eyes and the bending of my head to face downward, but the angle never changed.

Then she glitched. She went back to facing straight ahead with the curious look on her face. She hummed the same exact laugh. Her eyes followed something down. She glitched again. Eyes forward again, she hummed and followed whatever it was down below her. I waited for the jerky twitch, but instead her head snapped back, her mouth open in a scream of pain, but only the sound of a deep gasp of air came out. Her mouth slowly transformed from a howl to a wide jack-o'-lantern smile. Her head eased back down and faced forward. The face became the grinning look of curiosity.

Chapter 34

When I woke, I thought my eyes were still closed. Boxes blocked my view of the crack below the door. Black covered every part of the room I could see. I tried to read my watch, but the luminescence had worn off by that time. I clicked on the walkie.

"Hey, you guys there?"

After a few seconds, Katy was on the line. "Yes—geez, I was starting to worry."

"What time is it?"

"One thirty."

"Shit," I said, scrambling to my feet. My head hit the iron shelves above me. The shock of the impact coupled with its pain startled me so violently that my stomach retched. I'm sure if there had been food in it, I would've had a mess to deal with on top of the injury.

"Is there any news?"

I swore quietly to myself and then answered her. "No, I just woke up. I haven't even been out of the closet."

"And here I am thinking you were straight."

"Very funny."

"Why are you in a closet?" she asked.

"I'll tell you when you get here," I assured her. By this point I had wrestled myself to an erect position. "Something crazy happened with Lee."

"Do we need to come now?"

"Stand by for now. Let me see what's happening."

I clicked the walkie off and hid it in my front pocket. The light spilling through the glass doors into the lobby was brilliant by comparison. I squinted my eyes as they adjusted. When I could painlessly open them again, they opened to the image of Hank, of Hank's Sleeping Bag Emporium, staring me in the face.

"What were you doing in there?" He sounded worried, not angry.

"Sleeping."

"Right," he said, confused. "You may want to go see a nurse or Dr. Ronson if he's not with someone."

"What?" I touched my head where I banged it on the shelf. A small sensation of warmth and a tinge of pain shot through my forehead. A good bit of blood wet my fingertips.

"We've been looking for you," Hank said. "Go see Randy. They need to know where your wife and you got separated."

"Where is Randy?"

"He's in theater two, walking everyone through rescue."

"Rescue? As opposed to what?"

"Clean up and clear out."

That was a strange thought. The troops were changing their plans from clearing the area of people to going to rescue a person. I wondered why that mentality hadn't been employed yet. "Right over there?" I pointed to the place I assumed theater two was.

"Right. Over there."

As I made my way across the lobby, covering the cut with my hand, I noticed a number of people staring at me as if I had fallen asleep at a frat party and had a bunch of dicks drawn on my face. I had a mean crop of stubble growing by then, so I didn't think that was the case. They watched me walk across the lobby until I rounded the corner and they couldn't see me anymore. In the hallway a young woman emerged from a dark theater room and jumped at the sight of me. I credited it to simple jumpiness instead of anything so grandiose as phallic-shaped ink marks—even though it took her longer than usual to continue with her day.

I pulled the door to room two. Inside, both teams of the hunters gathered around Randy and two other real police officers. The female officer was going over safety precautions when inside a closed-in area. Her voice was as stern and commanding as her posture. She wasn't quite broad enough for androgyny, but if she kept lifting in the days after everything changed, she would soon become indistinguishable from her male colleagues from behind. She was dressed in a complete police uniform down to the shoes and hat.

"Once the door is open," she said, "I want two people at a time always aiming in different directions until the room is clear."

As she continued, Randy noticed me walk in and met me at the door. "Come outside real quick," he whispered.

"Sure." I backed out of the room.

His face was grave, almost pissed off. "Where did you go this morning?"

"What do you mean? I was here."

"No," he nearly snapped. "You weren't in your area in the room."

"Whoa, whoa," I said, trying to calm him. "I went to sleep in the room with the pillows and bags. It was too noisy in six. I didn't get in until late, and as soon as I nodded off, Adam came in the room." I didn't know what I could say without causing a stir here. "He woke me up, and after that I just kept hearing every little thing that was going on."

He watched me, looking for telltale signs. "OK, I believe you."

"It's very quiet in the emporium. And dark. Very easy to sleep in there."

"Emporium?"

"That's what Mary and I call the room with all the sleeping bags and pillows."

He smiled and traded it for a very grave look. "Look, we have guys going out there today to help find your wife. I don't want you to think I'm implying anything, but I just need to hear you say that it's not for nothing."

"What are you asking?" I was thinking that somehow he found out Katy and I were not who we claimed to be—that somehow Lee had made him believe it.

"I'm asking if the possibility for us to find her *alive* is real."

"Of course." I was eager to know where this was going.

"You mean that?"

"Yes."

"There's just a lot of talk going around."

"What kind of talk?"

"Just talk," he said. Then he cleared his throat. "Did you know James?"

"Not off the top of my head, no. Who's that?"

"He's a little kid," Randy explained. "The last time he was seen was with you and your wife. They say you were in the lobby with him yesterday after you settled in."

"Are you sure? I don't know any little kids here." Then it hit me. The little kid with the magic trick.

Randy's eyebrows went up as though he saw recognition on my face.

"Actually, you know what, I did meet him. He's the one with the magic trick. But I assure you, Randy, I didn't have anything to do with him coming up missing. I didn't even know who he was. He just did his trick for us and then ran away."

"Yeah. Do you have any idea what happened to him?"

"I have no idea. To be honest, my wife and I have been pretty nonstop the entire time we've been here. Other than my sleep and our little expedition last night, I haven't been out of the public eye."

"Yeah, I know," Randy said. "The only problem is that those have been the only two occasions where someone has come up missing.

Again, I'm not accusing you. I'm on your side. You're one of the most mature people here. We can't get rid of someone just because we're suspicious. We may as well be out there on our own if that's the case. I just wanted to ask and make sure you are aware that it's being linked with you around the place. But don't worry. These people"—he pointed to room two—"they've been in training lectures all morning, so they don't have a clue."

"Well, that's good to know. I would like my wife found."

"I know. I know. Just be careful what you say to everyone else. Tensions are high, as you can imagine. If you need anything, just let me know."

"I will," I assured him. "Do you ever think about leaving here? Maybe going to one of the bigger cities? Mary and I heard on the radio before the power went out that there were groups headed to New York, Chicago, and Saint Louis—places like that—to try and start everything over. Or at least come together to help with the crazy problem."

"Yeah, I heard that." He suddenly seemed a little standoffish. "I don't see why Jackson can't be one of those places, too. You thinking of leaving?"

"It may become the best option if this whole 'killing my wife and some random kid I don't know' situation doesn't work itself out."

"When we find your wife and the little kid, everyone else will just have to find something else to be angry at together. Because we will find them." He held the door to room two open for me. Then he whispered, "Don't say nothing, and it won't be a problem. I believe you."

"Thanks, Randy."

Chapter 35

The people in the group in charge of finding Mary Grabowski were devastatingly young. I wouldn't have trusted them in the time before with the appropriate professional training, and I definitely didn't trust them in that moment of surveying them in the low light of that viewing room. They were too young, and eager for destruction. They looked ornery. Patchy beards and tiny moustaches surrounded me. The room smelled of wintergreen chewing tobacco. I listened to the female officer power through her training lecture from the wall next to the door. They watched her intently, which I took as a good sign.

"And I know this has been said before, but I do not want you running through the neighborhood with your fingers on the triggers. Do *not*—do you understand?" The group droned in agreement. "I'm not so much talking to the late group as I am the first. This is a major point of emphasis because what if Mrs. Grabowski isn't the only person out there? We need to come back with anyone we find who is still a functioning member of society. This is a rescue mission. Murder of an innocent civilian is a felonious act, and you will be charged with such."

Randy whispered in the officer's ear. He made a circling wrap-it-up gesture with his hand even though she could not see it.

"Now, are there any questions whatsoever?"

The group droned again.

"If there is anything I need you to remember from this morning, it's just one thing. No fingers on triggers. Does everyone understand what I'm saying?" The drones droned. "OK, I know it's annoying, but I'm going to need you all to say it with me. One. Two. Three. No fingers on triggers." Surprisingly, through all the condescending, she somehow managed to get the troops to laugh about that, and their laughter brought her laughter. "Mr. Grabowski is here and ready to explain where his wife was last seen. I'm going to turn it over to him now...Shit. You are bleeding."

"Yeah, I hit my face on a shelf."

"When you're finished here, you need to see a nurse." The troops laughed at that. She handed over a handkerchief, and I used it on the wound.

"I probably will." I laughed.

She just put on an obviously fake smile and walked past me. Her face was pretty. I could see her red lipstick and smell her perfume as she passed me. I can imagine the hundreds, and probably closer to thousands, of incidences she was forced to put up with over the years at a checkpoint or on the side of the road. I could tell she was hardened, and I knew she had plenty of reasons to be.

I scanned the group. The kid I hit with the door of the supply closet kneeled at the very end. He looked significantly less annoyed than the first time I had met him. His chest puffed out, and he had a crooked grin on his face as if to say, "Yeah, guys, that's the one I was telling you about." Then a bunch of kids and one adult filled the semicircle around me, sitting, standing, or kneeling behind each other. Right in the center of the group, Khakis stared up at me, still having no idea who I was. Blue Jeans kneeled beside him. Blue Jeans whispered something in Khakis's ear, and I wanted to know what it was immediately. I liked Blue Jeans so much better when he didn't talk. I started talking before I was ready, just to put an end to whatever conversation was beginning between the two of them.

"All right, uh," I stammered. "Um, thank you, Officer. Hey, guys. I'm Peter. My wife is Mary. Um, I don't know if any of you met us before last night, but we showed up a little late in the game yesterday afternoon. We only wanted to help out. Do our part, you know. When we went out with the night group, we kind of got separated. It was my fault for making her go too far. I would hear something and drag her farther from the group. We found a"—I was careful not to say screamer—"crazy in the woods. We tried to fire at it and bring it down, but the pistols didn't work. They just made a clicking noise and that's it. So it chased us through the woods. We, not knowing this part of town very well, became lost pretty quick. We eventually came out onto a road and that led to a neighborhood about a mile or a mile and a half from here. I know that sounds far, but it doesn't take that long to get there when you're being chased by a lunatic. Or when you're being chased back."

A hand in the back went up. It was the clumsy kid from the tower. "Why don't you tell everyone what she looks like? I greeted y'all when you got here yesterday, but I probably can't do as good as you."

"OK, sure. She has thick red hair down to here. Kind of pale skin. She was wearing the camouflage from the closet. She has green eyes. There's a tattoo on her shoulder of a palm tree and a moon. I don't know if you will be able to see that, though."

Another hand went up. "Do you know what road you were on?"

"I don't," I said. "There was no light, and I couldn't read any signs."

Another hand went up. "If you two were together after the crazy chased you through the woods, why did you split up after you made it to the neighborhood?"

"I'm getting there." I became annoyed that they seemed to be looking for holes in my story. So I beefed up the lie. "There wasn't just one of them. Jackson's a fairly large city. Pretty heavily populated. When we got to the neighborhood, they were all over the place. We tried to hide from them, but one saw us. And when one sees you, it runs, and then the others see the runner. They came after us. Eventually, we just got separated."

"What did the neighborhood look like?" This one was Khakis.

"The houses were white so far as I could tell."

"A little crappy and run down?" the clumsy kid asked. His face seemed to say that his brain had started connecting a few dots.

"I honestly couldn't tell in the dark."

"Was there a house with a big windmill?" he followed.

"With a Heisman on top? Yeah."

"Gerald," Randy said from behind me, "that's your neighborhood."

"Aw, right," a voice said.

"Where you at?" Randy called.

"Smile, Gerald, we cain't see you," Khakis said.

Everyone started laughing.

"That's cold, man," Gerald said.

The female officer shined a flashlight in his direction. A black kid with a haircut I know of as a Boosie fade appeared in the beam.

"Y'all need to keep y'all mouth shut about that racist shit." Gerald laughed.

"OK," Randy said. His angry voice silenced the room. "For that comment, Gerald, you can call Bradley a cracker. Just once." The room roared in laughter. Suddenly, I liked Randy so much better than I already did. "Pete, why don't you come with me to a nurse in one of the other rooms? I think they got all the information they need." He led me out of the room, but not before I caught a glance at Blue Jeans leaning over to whisper into Khakis's ear again.

Chapter 36

To say the nurse kept an eye on me as she walked back and forth from the couch where I lay to the table with her nursing paraphernalia is a bit of an understatement. She eagle eyed me with the veracity of a seasoned military sniper while she sutured the small hole in my forehead. Her movements were jerky on purpose. Her indelicate bedside manner led me to believe I probably would've been just as well off doing the repair myself with an instruction manual and a few pieces of a broken mirror.

"Three stitches, huh?" Randy laughed. "Must have been real bad."

"It's a real bad boo-boo," I agreed. Wanting to put an end to the nurse's cross looks, I said, "Do you think we'll be able to find her?"

"I think if you give us an hour, maybe as little as thirty minutes, we'll have you two spooning in your square by sundown." He turned to the nurse, grinning. "Wouldn't you agree?"

"I really hope so," the nurse said in a tone similar to someone who already knew the negative outcome of the planned excursion. "I just don't want people to waste any time and risk their lives for nothing."

"Well, it cain't be for nothing when a man's wife is at stake," Randy assured her. The cop in his voice was sneaking back in. He was helping me keep my name clean.

"Keep those clean for a few days, and we'll take them out when you're better," she said. Before I could respond, her gloves were in the trash, and the door eased shut behind her.

"You handled that well. Neither of us are too stupid to see that she was being an unprofessional twat."

"Why do they think I killed her, Randy?"

"I don't know," he said. I started to feel bad that he was clearly as mad as I pretended to be. "You know how these things start. One person says one thing to someone else, and before you know it, everyone is running out to the shed to grab a pitchfork."

"But who was that person?"

"Doesn't matter, because when she turns up, everyone will change their tune. Hopefully, to some rock 'n' roll. This praying bullshit is starting to give me the creeps. Feels a little cult-y if you want my opinion. As far as you're concerned, I think given the circumstances, they are just eager to have someone to blame everything on. Since there's no customer-care number to call and representative to yell at, they'll take the first person they can to make a scapegoat. That's how it has to be until someone figures out what happened and who did it. Helps people get through the shitty parts. It had to be someone. It does suck that it had to be you. It won't be long, though."

"You don't think they'll rise as one and slay the nonbeliever, do you?"

"What?" he said, nearly hysterical with laughter. "These old biddies couldn't knock a fly off course if they pooled all their strength into one fart. Anyone who could do any harm has been in that room all day and won't talk to the rest of the people until they find her. I've made sure of that. Me and Regina—excuse me...Officer Tamlin—have been through a riot or two before. She hears every single thing, too, so don't call her Regina. But don't worry. She and I know what the angry mob wants. They won't do nothin' unless we give them a reason. All bark. No bite."

"Yeah. I hope you're right." I paused. "Was it me, or did *spooning in your square* sound dirtier than it actually was?"

We laughed together at that.

"Where are you from, Randy? If you don't mind me asking."

"Nah, I don't mind," he said. "I'm originally from Laurel, almost Alabama basically. I went to school in Hattiesburg. Got my first job in Jackson, and been here twenty years in June. Five months to go, and this shit happens."

"And you never think of leaving?"

"Nah, I grew up in this state. I would say my family's here, but who knows. I just like it here. It's familiar, you know?"

"I guess living all over the place makes living in one area all your life seem a bit boring to me. No offense or anything."

"Nah. It's more of a point of pride, honestly. Good ole boy, born and bred." Randy slapped his chiseled stomach. "Oh, boy, here she comes."

Officer Tamlin came into the room. "We're ready. You take Alpha. I'll take Bravo. Officer Williams has Charlie."

Randy paid Tamlin an over-the-top vaudeville-style gasp. Tamlin stopped in her place, concern painted across her face.

"I get Alpha team?" he said with a touch of aggression. "It's almost like I haven't gotten anyone killed, and I'm being rewarded with the better team. Is this heaven or Almost Heaven, West Virginia?"

"Cut the shit, Officer Childs," Tamlin said. She finally sounded like a person instead of a movie script.

"Sure thing, sir." Randy saluted.

I stood up. Not in any attempt to join the group, but I wanted to get to the bathroom and get on the walkie-talkie. I was stopped before I could explain.

"Not you, Shakespeare. I need you to stay here." I could tell what Officer Tamlin thought of me. "Just in case."

"In case what?" Randy asked.

"In case…In case we need to regroup. I don't want him to get lost again if we have to go back out tomorrow. Adam's rules."

With that she slammed the stamp of finality on the discussion. No, because Adam said so. That would become the mantra of the day. Having said her piece, she marched out of the room.

"So I guess I know how she feels about me."

"Nah," Randy said. "She's just...what's the word? Severe. She had the idea to not allow the troops to mingle with the civilians until we found your wife. Adam is just in her ass more than the rest of us. I can't tell if there's a romance brewing there or not. In any case, she was in charge of the Alpha team until this morning. I think the change hurt her feelings. Very competitive, that one. Maybe it's daddy issues. I don't know. That seems to be the problem for a lot of people these days."

"So there are three groups now?"

"We had three to begin with. There were two hunting squads and a lookout. You no doubt ran into them on your way in yesterday. They're the older guys and a few we don't trust in the line of action, if you know what I mean."

Shoes, dummy, I thought, from the day before. "Yeah, sure."

"Just keep your head down. Not much to be worried about but a bunch of old ladies and kids. The kids probably don't know nothing about what's going on, anyway. There are a few bigger guys, but they're all too old to cause a scene."

"I'll remember that."

"Just be careful. We'll get her back in no time. If you got anything else to patch up, just take what you need. We're all in this together."

"Right on. You guys be careful, too."

Before I left the room, I changed the bandage on my leg. The gauze was damp, but not from blood. I took some peroxide from the shelf and poured a little on the wound. It stung at first then eased up. The liquid was painfully cold. I shivered as I replaced the bandage. When I finished, I left for the bathroom.

On my way into the bathroom, someone came out. He ran into my shoulder hard.

"I'm sorry," I tried to tell him.

I only got something muttered under the person's breath in return. Something that sounded a little too similar to *murderer.*

Chapter 37

"Hey, guys," I said, standing in the last stall of the empty bathroom. I waited a beat to see if anyone was on the walkie. There was a click of static. Then nothing, so I moved on. "Everyone is gone. All the people with guns, anyway. They aren't coming back without Mary, so now's your chance to scoot on over here and take care of business."

"Hey, Derrick," Katy said with a hint of distress in her voice.

Jackie was yelling in the background. *That's why I keep it turned all the way down. Lucky me for thinking.*

"What's going on over there?" I said.

Loud swearing briefly came out of the tiny speaker, and then nothing.

Katy said, "Jackie says this fucking thing's battery has gone tits up. I think it's a family vernacular. She says we have to find a way to charge the battery before the car will crank."

"OK, how long will that take?"

A pause on the line.

Katy said, "She wants to know how long it would take to build Rome?"

"What?"

"Hang on. She wants to talk."

"Derrick?" Jackie said, out of breath.

"Car trouble?"

"Yeah, these repos are always a piece of shit. All the cars are spread out around the city, so we have to use these. All of our charges are shot to shit. The closest place I know that will have anything we can use to juice them back up is the crime lab."

"How far is that?"

"It's about four blocks. Normally, we're looking at a ten- or fifteen-minute walk with just the normal number of Jackson lunatics running around. With the screamers I don't know how long it will take. I'm pissed off!" The line cut.

That's a tantrum, I thought, and laughed to myself.

"Take all the time you need," I told the open line. "They're not coming back anytime soon. Four blocks—you might just need an hour, you never know. We won't know until we actually get out there and do it. Anyone there?"

"Yeah," Katy said. "I'm here. The police officers left."

"You're not alone now, are you?"

"No, I have my thoughts and a few people. I'm in the room Mark stomped out of. It's super quiet when people aren't screaming, and surprisingly easy to sleep in knowing the lock couldn't even be shot open. They showed me. Whole lot of testosterone pulsing through this place."

"Any news on him? Mark, I mean. He turn up yet?"

"Nah, Jackie says he likes to hide when he gets in a tizzy."

"That's a little worrisome. Is anyone even looking?"

"Not really. Jackie said not to. She knows him better than anyone else here. Hey, are my clothes still there?"

"I'm sure they are."

"Good. This camouflage su-u-ucks. It gives me mom hips."

"I'll make sure you can find them when you get here." I laughed.

"How are you handling it over there? You makin' any friends?"

"They think I killed you."

"What?" She sounded vaguely outraged yet bored. "You couldn't kill me."

"Yep. You and the little kid with the magic trick."

"Who?"

"The kid with the card trick. James."

"Oh, yeah. Someone killed him? Jesus."

"No, he just wasn't found this morning, so everyone automatically thinks he's dead. Randy, the guy in charge of our group last night, seems to think they just need someone to hate in this epic time of crisis."

"They're probably not wrong to think he's dead. I don't know why you'd be the one to kill him. He actually seemed to like you. He didn't even talk to the other kids when I saw him. I'll keep an eye out for him, though. I don't think he would come here."

There was a separation of the line, and then Katy's tone changed. The cheer had been used up. She now sounded defeated. "I just want to leave. I don't like it here. I don't feel normal. People are shooting cops. I'm starting to worry about you. I just want to be somewhere normal. Do something normal, you know. It feels like everything has collapsed, and nothing's like the way it was anymore. I *know* I'm not safe. That makes me want to cry. That's not a healthy way to live. But the thing is, everything looks exactly the same as before, only now it's just…quieter."

"Yeah, I know what you mean. But when we get where we're going, we won't have to worry about leaving anymore. That'll be one less thing to think about. It'll only be a day at most. Then we're hightailing it to a place where the levies keep the water out and the walls keep the screamers out."

I realized that no matter where we ended up, the chance that there would be groups of hunters sent out to kill the screamers would be staggeringly high. As it turns out, the ratio would be two for two. The second city turned out to be much more welcoming and well put together. But I don't mean to get ahead of myself.

"Just keep track of me over here," she said in a slightly happier tone. "I'm bored. The only people here to talk to act like they're in their sixties. If it's not the cops, it's the old folks who were in nearby houses. I just don't care about what life was like before it wasn't all right to smoke pot out in the open, which believe it or not is pretty much all the old people in Jackson want to talk about. I mean, who cares if it makes you dumb? Let those people be dumb."

"Actually, I don't think anyone would fine you for it now anyway."

"Probably not. You better get going. People are going to think you've made a mess on yourself. You need to get back to looking inconspicuous."

"Yeah, I'll keep in touch. Obviously, don't go outside alone. Or at all."

"Geez." She feigned annoyance. "You're not my real dad. I hate your stupid rules."

"I will turn this car around," I said.

"I want to go live with Mom." She cracked up before cutting the line.

The hole in my leg from Tony's tantrum throbbed.

Chapter 38

The Jackson Theater held a freak show that afternoon. There was only one act, only one person in the entire show. I was that person. The frumpy ladies snuck glances at me behind hoot-owl glasses—literally peeked around corners to get a look at the Amazing No One Special. If looks could kill, my skin would be nothing but scars. I do think they'd keep me alive so I'd feel the effects of their death stares.

I wanted to go back to being the person they were afraid to talk to instead of the person they all judged and damned to an eternity of fire and the room by the noisy ice machine. I thought the longer I stayed, the more hate they would be allowed to generate. I decided to stay hidden. I wanted to go back to my square, but if the Hispanic girl had told her daddy what the bad man across the room probably did to his wife and the kid with the cards, I didn't want to play a game of charades trying to explain my innocence. I didn't feel right knowing that what I was arguing against was just as untrue as what I was trying to make them believe.

I went to the supply closet with the boots and array of mismatched camouflage clothing. I wanted to make sure I recovered Katy's clothes while doing so was on my mind. I opened the door to find a teenage boy with his pants down to his thighs. His body twitched. I quickly shut the door before he had a chance to turn around, let alone explain himself. Even though I guess I understood. When the urge strikes, sometimes you just have to ditch the group and masturbate in a supply closet. I made a mental note to not wear anything out of that room and turned toward the exit.

There were no noises in the empty corridor leading to the exit. The viewing rooms were emptied except for the very last one, which was piled to the brim with the chairs from the other rooms. The bathrooms stood docile. No one randomly snuck out of a theater room to visit the concession stand. There was an overwhelming feeling that something drastically different had taken over, some totally altered societal foundation. And even though that was exactly what had become a reality, I couldn't shake the unease that suddenly lay over me like a blanket. The feeling brought on by the switch of attitude from terrified to judgmental weighed a ton. I wanted to drop it. For some reason I couldn't let go of it. I reached for the handlebar to the exit.

The kid had wiped off and zipped up by that point and burst out of the supply closet swearing about his lateness. I didn't expect to ever see him again after going out into the city alone, even if he left to catch up to the rest of the group. *Something will get ahold of him*, I thought as I pressed the handlebar and walked outside. My eyes weren't used to the light, so they needed a moment to settle. When they did, I saw someone sitting on the ground next to the door.

"What are you doing here?" I asked Mark.

He sat in the corner made by the theater's rear wall and the fence keeping the generator from running free. He flung what I could tell by the small pile beside him was not the first rock. He stood up and dusted off his jeans and shirt. There was another moment where our eyes met, and I could've sworn I saw that light shade of green in them. My eyes were still adjusting, but I knew it was there.

"Just whackin' my pud," Mark said. I couldn't tell how long he had been there, but his voice said that it was long enough to have grown bored waiting. "Waiting for someone to come outside so I could come inside. Incognito and such."

"You know they're looking for you at the station, right?"

"No, they're not," he said as if catching me in a lie, which was what he was doing. "Jackie wouldn't do that. She'd just tell everyone, 'Oh, that's just him. He always does that,' and then when she finds me, she'll act like she's been looking for me the whole time, but I know she isn't."

"Good point."

"What happened to your forehead?"

"Oh," I said. "I slept under a shelf. I hit my head on it when I realized how late I had slept in."

"Don't do that, then."

"Noted," I said. "Did you just walk all the way here?"

"Yeah," Mark said. "Surprisingly little things to worry about in this part of town. It's infested as close as Ted's place, but for some reason they're not coming here. Or they're not staying very long, at least."

"The teenagers around here are killing them."

"I guess that makes sense. I had no problems sneaking my way here. Took a while, though. This place is not close to the police station."

"You're not being very stealthy now."

"Well, it's been about an hour." He put on that face people have when they are waiting for something obvious to be said. Eyebrows raised, eyes wide, corners of the mouth back. "Aren't you going to invite me in?"

"I guess." I laughed. "But look, people here are really weird about me, so I suggest you go around front and come in. Khakis isn't here, so no one will recognize you."

"The fuck—really?" he said. "The only reason I came was to stomp ass and head out. Do you at least know where to find him? Where he sleeps?"

"Yeah," I said. "In the middle of a big pile of other people who are too young to be carrying guns. You're going to have to come up with a strategy of some kind. Even if it is thrown together. You know, something to work with. You can't just raw dog something like this. I'm being serious. Go around front and act like you came from somewhere nearby. You'll have to jump through all the same hoops we did, but at least you won't have to sneak around. Everyone with a gun is gone, so no one is going to tattle on you. No one is going to shoot you while they're gone either, so you don't have to worry about that."

"That seems dumb."

"What does?"

"Why wouldn't they leave a couple behind just in case?"

I thought of the kid in the closet.

"I don't know," I said. "Maybe they gave some of the old ladies a gun."

"You didn't say there were old ladies here." He licked his fingers and straightened his eyebrows.

"Gross. And kids. Seriously, they're not OK with out-of-towners."

"Oh, kids? Then it's game over. Mark is here." He breathed into his cupped hands and sniffed. "I'm good. It's so on, Derrick."

"OK, I'm shutting the door. Go around front while working that out of your system—don't be too crazy. Peggy is going to take you to an office and sit you down for a get-to-know-you kind of thing. She's the short, fattish one with a bob haircut. I'd use a fake name if I were you. Especially since I'm pretty sure Khakis knows your name."

"Peggy?" he asked.

"Yes, but obviously you don't know her name yet."

"What color is her hair?"

"Reddish brown, I think."

"Do the drapes match the carpet?"

"Oh my God." I shut the door and trusted him to handle the rest on his own.

I walked back to the camo room. I found Katy's clothing, dry and free of stains, on a shelf next to the door. I understood why the kid was overcome with the urge to self-complete. Her smell had filled the closet. The smell of sweet perfume and shampoo taunted my senses. After leaving the closet, I dropped the clothes off in room six. I hid them in her sleeping bag.

I slowly made my way back to the center of the building. The freak show continued in the lobby. At first I thought time had slowed to a halt as they glared at me. Mark took his time getting to the front of the building. I had time to take a seat on an empty bench and scan the room two or three times, watching glances suddenly shift to anything other than me. The tension built inside me. Minutes piled on top of each other. The kids and their perpetual vigor carried the energy of the room now. The adults had settled into the routine of their new lives. I came up with the idea of putting the kids on gigantic hamster wheels and connecting them through the magic of mechanical engineering to the building's fuse box. I wondered if there was anyone I could bring the idea to in order to get production in motion. Technology does not manifest itself, after all. I took a look around the room. Stares darted away as I scanned the room, and I thought, *No, there isn't anyone who would be interested in my idea. What a shame.*

Eventually, my mind wandered even farther. I considered how unjust my situation in the theater was—that because I was new in town, I had to deal with the stigma of automatic murderer. How fair was it that this bunch of gossips, who knew nothing about Katy or me, got to pass judgment with no information whatsoever? I wondered how people ever got away with murder. I started feeling those teeth gnaw at me, taking me from irritated to mad and then furious. Then I became aware that I was getting mad, and how silly of a reason to be mad it was. I stared at my feet and thought of ice water to help cool me down. Believe it or not, that works nine times of ten. I was slowly draining my anger until there was a metallic tap on the double glass doors between the box offices. That heat was gone in a flash. The crowd of people turned toward the door. Mark stood there with a rock in his hand, tapping on the window. I wondered if they had done that for Katy and me. I didn't think so.

Mark sold pity like his family depended on it. Peggy crossed the lobby on her squat legs with enthusiasm, oozing her southern charm. Her cheerful accent filled the lobby. She asked if Mark was OK. It was all a show. My mom would have said that she was an old soul trying to get into heaven, and if I saw fat little Peggy sitting in the prayer circle even once, I would have agreed with my mother.

I couldn't hear what Mark said to Peggy after she greeted him. I saw him though, and his body language definitely warranted the question. He had rolled in the dirt and tore a sleeve of his shirt before making his way around the building. He hunched over and carried the black Dolphins cap in both of his shivering hands. It was the only thing he had that hadn't gotten dirtier or damaged. Peggy hustled him to a concessions counter where she handed him a room-temperature bottle of water. He thanked her kindly. She escorted him down the hallway toward the office. He looked like a giant standing behind her. Mark and I made eye contact as they turned away from me. I swear I saw crocodile tears dripping down his cheeks, but behind them was a tiny grin.

Chapter 39

"New here?" I asked. I lifted my hand to shake with Mark. He was carrying a sleeping bag, a marker, and a roll of duct tape. "I'm Peter."

"Thaddeus Clementeal."

"Jesus," I said under my breath, but I think Gabriela heard me anyway. I gestured toward Miguel and his daughter. "Well, that's Miguel and Gabriela. We'll be your new roommates."

Gabriela whispered to Miguel. He nodded, and she bounced out of the room.

"Thaddeus Clementeal?"

"Aren't you supposed to not know me?"

"He doesn't speak English."

"Did you actually ask him, or are you being racist?"

"Yes, I did," I said. "I have tried to talk to him. The little girl translates for him."

"OK," Mark said, satisfied. "And, yes, Thaddeus Clementeal. It's an homage to my mother's grandfather or something."

"Do you go by Thad, or do I have to say the whole thing?"

"He actually went by Rudolf. Rudy."

"Why?"

"I don't know," he said. "The more I think about it, I think I'm mixing up two different people."

"What's the plan?"

"Actually, I had one going wherein I would blackface my way into the hunting club like a marauder in the night, but then I noticed something far off in the woods behind this place."

"What do you mean?"

"I saw something moving," he said. "Two guys carrying a long piece of metal from the back of a truck is what it was. I shit you not, Derrick, it had a dangling nut sack on the back of it. Big white thing—that's how I knew where to go. I saw the white. The reflection of the sun on the metal got my attention, but I followed the white truck."

"What'd you see?"

"There's a building back there. I mean, a shitty one. I wouldn't live there. But something is going up there. It's pretty big, too. Little smaller than the place I found you. When they left, I snuck around to see. Big, open, just not nearly as tall. Real shoddy. It doesn't have a foundation—basically, just a wooden frame with a load of tin-roof material fashioned to the outside of it. It could go over in a big enough gust of wind. The weird thing though is the cages they have in there."

"Cages?" I asked.

"Yeah," he said, laying down the tape for his own square on the floor. "And they've got crazy-thick bars. Not like some wimpy kennel you put your dog in when you leave for work. These things are basically portable prison cells. Way better quality than the crap shack they put them in, for sure. They're not rooted to the ground, but I tried to shake one. They don't move. It must have been two hundred pounds at least. There are three of them against one wall. Even creepier than the cages, right in the middle of the place is a sharpened log. I don't know what it's for. It looks like someone took a huge pencil and jammed the eraser end into the ground and left the rest sticking up. Something fucked up is going to happen. I feel it in my bones."

"Hang on. Your square can't be bigger than ours."

"I'm bigger than both of you."

"Not combined."

"Are you listening? We have got to check that thing out."

"What are we going to do about it?" I asked.

"I don't know," he said passively. "I figure if they're going to start locking people in cages, maybe we should take a peek before we leave. See if it's something we could dismantle for these welcoming folks. We don't even know what it is. Although it does sound like a sexy seventies strip club."

"Could be the smoking room Lee was talking about. I don't know why they would need cages for a smoking room."

"I don't either." After a moment Mark said, "Did you ever find someone who wants to leave?"

"No. I haven't been able to talk to anyone."

"What do you mean? Just talk to them. They're all out there."

"They think I killed Katy, and a kid who is missing."

"What kid?"

"He's a little boy who showed Katy and me a card trick yesterday. That's really all I know about him. I didn't even see him with anyone else. No one did after Katy and I saw him. That's why I'm the automatic culprit."

"What about these guys?" Mark gestured toward Miguel who lay on his sleeping bag.

"I don't know. I haven't asked them."

"That's rude. Were you just going to leave them here?"

"I don't speak Spanish. I just haven't asked them."

"*Hola*," Mark said to Miguel. "*De dónde es usted?*"

His Spanish accent caused a burst of laughter to shoot out of me that I couldn't stop.

"That's enough," he said to me over his shoulder.

"*Zihuatanejo.*" Miguel stood from his sleeping bag.

"No shit? That place is real?" Mark said.

"What'd he say?" I asked.

"He's a Mexican."

"I don't like how you said that," I said.

"I said it normally."

"Yeah, but it had some stank on it."

To Miguel, Mark said, "*Quieres un gatito?*"

Miguel's face collapsed in confusion. "*Qué? Lo gatito?*"

"I don't think you did it right," I said.

"Shit," Mark said. "I thought I was better at Spanish. Um, *Dónde está tu hija?*"

"*El baño.*"

"The little girl is in the bathroom," Mark told me.

"I got that much," I said.

"We'll get her to translate."

"Good call."

I turned to sit down back in our square on the opposite side of the room, but Mark didn't follow me, so I stayed where I was. After a second I nodded to Miguel as a way of being polite in the uncomfortable silence as we did our best to look anywhere but at each other. Miguel shifted his line of sight from Mark to me and back with a toothy smile on his face.

"I get why you can't talk to these people now," Mark said.

"I feel like you kind of brought this on by yourself."

The man gave us an expression as if to say, *Qué?* and Mark waved him off.

"Not you," Mark said and shook his head.

Miguel made a circle with his thumb and forefinger. It stood out to me because it was the same way I used to motion OK with my hand when I was growing up. I don't know why it looked the way it did coming from someone who didn't speak the same language as me. Some things are just universal. A flushing sound seeped through the walls. Shortly after, little Gabriela walked back into the room.

"There she is," I said.

Miguel said, *"Te lavaste las manos?"*

"Sí, papá," Gabriela said, hiding something behind her.

"Lavarse las manos," Miguel said, pointing to the door.

Gabriela stomped once and went to leave the room.

"Oh, no, no, no," Mark said loud enough to make Gabriela jump. "Jesus Christ, no. *Un minuto. Un.*" He held up a finger to Miguel. Then he kneeled down to Gabriela. "Hey, sweetheart. No, no, I'm not going to hurt you. I'm a good guy, see." He pointed to his smile and circled it with his finger. "My name is Thaddeus. I just need to ask your daddy some questions. The only problem is, I don't know how to speak Spanish. But my new friend, um…" He snapped his fingers, trying to think of my fake name.

"Peter," I said.

"Peter! My new friend Pete tells me that you do speak Spanish, *and* English. Is that right?"

Gabriela didn't move. She just looked suspiciously up at Mark.

"You do understand me, yes?"

She said nothing.

Mark repositioned himself from his bad knee to his good knee. He rolled on an ankle and slipped backward. The sloping floor caused him to land awkwardly so he couldn't easily get back to his feet. He struggled for a second and gave up. He flopped over from butt to back. This made Gabriela giggle. She had a couple gaps in her smile from missing baby teeth.

Mark laughed as he got back to his knees. "See, honey. I'm just a silly clown, but without all the creepy makeup. I really need your help. You're super important to this situation, you know? You're like Wonder Woman right now. It's your time to shine. Whaddya say?" Mark made a goofy face. Gabriela laughed.

"OK." She walked around him to hide behind her daddy's pant leg.

"Great!" He spoke like the host of an early-morning kids' show. "Thank you so much. Can you ask your daddy if he knows of anyone still out there?"

"My *abuela*. She is in church. Back home."

"Do you know what you guys plan to do about her?"

"I don't know." She buried her face in her daddy's pants leg.

Mark stared at her waiting for her to translate.

She looked sad. Miguel had a concerned look on his face. They spoke Spanish to one another for a minute or two.

"I think you may have found someone," I told Mark.

"First try, too," he said. "How does that make you feel?"

"I could take it or leave it," I said.

"Oh, he's in denial." He was looking at me but talking to himself. "So cute."

"Um," Gabriela said. "*Papá* says he wants to go back, but we can't."

"What if we had a way to get you back?" I asked.

Gabriela said something to Miguel. Tears welled in his eyes.

"*Sí, sí,*" he said. He wiped his eyes with trembling hands. "*Sí.*"

"Tell him we're going to get you guys back home," Mark said.

I guess there was something universal in Mark's tone that Miguel read because Gabriela didn't have to translate that. Miguel rushed over and embraced Mark.

"*Gracias, Thaddeus.*" Miguel's tears dropped onto Mark's shirt. "*Muchas, muchas.*"

"Hey, we're friends." Mark pulled Miguel back. Mark put his hand on his chest. "*Me llamo Mark. No Thaddeus. Él es Derrick. No Peter.*" He pointed to me.

Miguel kissed Mark on both cheeks saying, "Marcos, Marcos."

"N—no," Mark started. "OK, Marcos is fine."

"Well, it looks like we got two people coming with us." I couldn't help but smile.

Miguel's elation made it all worth it. The throbbing pain in my leg from Tony's rampage had momentarily subsided. The intensity of my longing for Sarah was cut in half, and I didn't care at all about Lee or what the people in the theater thought I did to Katy or that little kid. Miguel picked up his little girl and rested her on his forearm. He spoke to her in Spanish, and like a parrot on his shoulder, Gabriela translated what he told her.

"*Papá* says thank you. And..." She looked at her father. They whispered to one another, and then she said, "And just say we can leave."

"What do you mean?" I asked. "We're just going to leave."

"The yellow man won't let us leave." Gabriela wrapped her arms around her daddy's neck. I knew already whom she meant, with his bleach-blond hair, jagged moustache, and his yellowing skin.

"Who's the yellow man?" Mark asked.

"She's talking about Lee," I said.

"Lee is the yellow man?"

"He's the boss," Gabriela said from her perch in Miguel's arms. "He won't let us leave. *Papá* says it's because he wants to be like a king. *Papá* says he was in jail not because he was bad but because he was sick."

"What do you mean?" I asked.

Gabriela spoke to her father, and for the first time, the happy smile fell. Miguel said no a few times. Mark said something to him in Spanish. Miguel put Gabriela down. He said something that sounded like it might mean jaguar, and Gabriela went to their square on the floor. She played with a naked doll.

Miguel spoke slowly and tried to use as many English phrases as he could. He used his hand when he talked and mimed a number of things. I only caught three Spanish words. *Raparador, el hospital,* and *manicomio*. I knew what two of them were. *Raparador* means repairman. I knew that one from my life on the farm, and I knew the other because it was just like the English version of the word, but with *manicomio* I was clueless. The word only stuck out to me because Miguel said it over and over. Finally Miguel ran out of words.

"You getting any of that?" I asked.

"Yeah," Mark said, but he didn't sound very confident. "He was a maintenance man somewhere, a place that *el hombre amarillo* either lived or worked. He says he's seen him there a number of times, but I don't know what one thing he keeps saying means, though. I can't quite guess what it is."

"*Manicomio?*" I asked.

"I never heard that word in class," he admitted.

"Is it a bad word?" I asked.

"I don't think so. Those were the first ones I learned. It's something like a hospital. He keeps said them interchangeably. *Que es un manicomio?*"

"*Es un asilo.*"

I looked to Mark for clarification. He had none. His face turned up as if straining to understand.

"*Whitfield,*" Miguel tried.

"That's English, right?" I asked.

"I think so. I don't know what it means, though." Then to Miguel, "*No entiendo.* That's not my field, bro."

Miguel had a reluctant look on his face as if he was embarrassed. Really he was trying not to seem insensitive. He crossed his eyes, stuck out his tongue, and circled both ears with his pointer fingers. "*La casa de locos.*"

Realization dawned on Mark and me at the same time.

"Understood that," Mark said.

"So he was in an asylum?"

"I guess so," Mark said. "He says Lee doesn't look the same, but he knows it's him. Lee used to have black hair and sideburns. Miguel says his name isn't Adam, but we knew that. At least that's what I understood of what he said."

"*No Adam,*" Miguel said. "*Jamie.*"

"Clearly Lee has some kind of identity crisis he's working through," Mark said.

"Can you ask if he has ever seen Lee sleepwalking?"

"Yeah, it's just el sleepo walko." Mark laughed to himself and spoke his broken Spanish while miming walking in his sleep.

Miguel looked a little confused but was able to decipher the information. He spoke back.

"No," Mark said. "But he's always taking pills. Probably for that. I'm paraphrasing of course. Why, did you see him?"

"Yeah. He came in here last night. He tried to kill me. He ran into the wall, and I guess that woke him up." I walked over to the curtain in the corner of the room. When I raised it off the ground, the knife glimmered in the lantern light.

"Jesus Man, Woman, and Child," Mark said. "That'd-a killed the shit out of you."

"He kept asking who I was," I said. "He must be totally gone, but the part of him that's homicidal keeps poking its head out. Those pills probably keep him at least sort of stable." I dropped the curtain back over the knife.

"We have to get the hell out of here," Mark said. It was all one word again. "We can't literally sleep with our eyes open."

"We're waiting on your sister to fix the car."

"What's wrong with the car?" Mark asked.

"Something about the battery's tits."

"They've gone up!" Mark exclaimed as if it was the worst news he could imagine.

"It's going to be all right," I said.

"I don't want to be stuck here with all those tightwads," he said. "You know how difficult it is to cross town in these conditions? God, I miss Ted."

"Would Ted know what to do?"

"I don't know," Mark said. "I could tell I was getting on his nerves, and that would give me something a little more fun to do. I get stressed when there's a chink in the plan. And that's not a racist thing. I just wanted to come in, do what I gotta do, and then head out." Mark stopped and posed like Superman, chest out and fists on his hips.

"What are you doing?" I could hardly keep from laughing.

"Standing like this helps configure your brain to deal with stress better."

"That works?"

"It's scientifically proven. I have a book. I guess I left that at my place, too." After a few seconds, his shoulders fell, and he shook his arms. "Let's get the little girl to help us work out a plan with Miguel." Mark called Gabriela back over to the triangle.

It took a while, but we made a plan. Miguel didn't trust Lee, so he stayed in room six nearly all of his time at the theater. Because of that and the level of disconnect brought on by the language barrier, Miguel hadn't heard any of the rumors that I killed the kid or my wife. More importantly, neither had Gabriela. Convincing him to put a little trust in me was easier than it would've been with anyone else in Jackson. Thankfully, I didn't have to tell him how I knew Lee.

The plan was easy, like most. All Miguel and his daughter had to do was not change a thing. In his part of the room, there were books he used to teach him how to speak English. He had swiped them from a bookstore not too far from the theater. I complimented his resourcefulness and suggested that he start working on them, if for no other reason than to pass the time. Since theater room six exited toward the front of the building, when Jackie finally showed up with the Jeep, we would simply pass through and get Miguel and his daughter. I asked if he knew where his truck was. He didn't. His daughter only said that once they were here, members of the hunting groups took the truck and moved it away from the theater under the guise of a safety precaution, so nothing would be blocking the line of sight in case a bunch of screamers decided to charge the building. What I believe now is that Lee didn't want anyone leaving.

Chapter 40

The freak show continued after the four of us hammered out a rough outline of a strategy. I left the room a few minutes before Mark so no one would get the wrong idea and lump the two of us together. Before I left, Mark said it would be a good idea to make a signal to meet back at our room. If I wanted to give Mark the signal, I had to make eye contact and put my hand over my mouth and tap my lips twice.

I could feel the blazing heat vision and hear the disapproving scoffs and eye rolls over my still being alive. One thing I did notice was that about half the people from the earlier show were gone. There were a few women who stayed behind, and all the kids were accounted for and present except for James. A man headed up the prayer circle. The lobby stood nearly quiet. The prayer circle had shrunk to a meager five members. The emptiness of the lobby was intensified by the empty chairs around the small group sitting in a circle on the floor. The sight made me think of an eyeball, which was also glaring at me. I decided I would try to make nice.

"Where is everyone?"

No one said anything. They stared at me for a moment longer and continued with what they were doing.

"Surely, everyone didn't leave," I said louder than I normally would have. For some reason I wanted the remaining members of the prayer group, who were doing a fine job judging me, to hear it.

I knew the adults had made up their minds about me, so I thought I would employ the same strategy as the day before and try talking to a kid, even though that was part of the reason I was in the theater people's bad graces. I strolled over to the arcade where most of them were playing. I took my time so I didn't seem as eager. I glanced around the arcade. Kids ran from one end of the room to the other in what looked like sugar-induced mayhem. When I turned around, the members of the prayer group had perked up in their seats.

Two kids sat coloring on a small table that looked straight out of a McDonald's playhouse. The plastic table was yellow and red, and its edges curved greatly to prevent corners where a kid could bang his or her head. The boy and girl looked like twins, and if they weren't, they were at least related. They were both small and brunette. They both had chubby toddler faces and gaps in their smiles. I kneeled by them. The boy colored, and the girl sat beside him looking over his shoulder. "Hey, guys. What are you coloring?"

"Dinosaurs," the boy said. He stuck out his tongue. I guess it helped to really hone his craft.

"I'm watching," the girl added.

"Wow, that's great." I added a good deal of fake excitement and patronage to my voice, but the drawing actually wasn't bad. I'd put it on my fridge. He could've been a real artist in the old world where he could actively nurture his gift. "Say, do you guys know where everyone went? The lobby is pretty much empty, and I have to tell them something."

"They went outside to look for a lady," the little boy said.

"She's like Red Riding Hood," the girl added. "Because her hair."

"That was earlier today," I said. I wondered briefly if Little Red Riding Hood had red hair as well as a red hood. I picked up a crayon and scribbled on a separate piece of paper. "Do you guys know what happened to the people who didn't go looking for her?"

"They throwed up," the boy said.

"Nuh-uh, they went number two," the girl argued.

"Nuh-*uh*," the boy said, stabbing the crayon into the heart of his drawing. "Mom said they were sick."

"No." The girl affected a tone she could've only gotten from her mother scolding her. "They went number two, *Tristin*. I went in the bathroom. It smelled like *poop*."

The other kids running around in the arcade laughed and started chanting *poop, poop*.

"It's OK, guys," I said, trying not to laugh. "I can just wait for them to feel better."

"Tristin! Avry!" I heard from a shrill voice emanating from behind me. "Get over here right this second."

"Mom," they groaned simultaneously. They made cases for their innocence in their own ways. Their mother was pale and had bluish rings around her eyes, like thinly applied makeup. She was sweaty, and sprigs of black stringy hair poked out from her short, tightly made ponytail.

"It's OK, Mom," I said. "They weren't bothering anyone. I just asked them a question."

"My children are not who I'm concerned about," she snapped.

"Whoa, I'm sorry. All I wanted to know is where everyone went."

"Everyone's sick."

"What from?" I was getting annoyed because I knew I was the cause of whatever the new bug going around happened to be, whether I was aware of it or not.

"Oh, you don't know?" she snapped.

"I don't."

"Well, why don't you try the coffee you made for everyone? See what a good job you did there."

"I didn't make the coffee." I had to make a point to stay calm, which took a great deal of effort. I could tell she wanted to get a rise out of me. "I slept until one and was with the hunting groups the rest of the day."

"I'm sure that's what you'll have everyone believe."

"What's wrong with the coffee?"

"You tell me."

"OK, I don't know what you're talking about. So let's assume I'm someone else. What would you tell them is wrong with the coffee?"

"I don't know what you put in it, but everyone is vomiting"—she lowered her voice—"and shitting all over themselves."

"And what makes you think it's the coffee?" I asked, making an even more calculated effort not to laugh.

"Because it's only the people who drank the coffee who are sick. I haven't seen *you* near the coffeepot today."

"Have you seen me anywhere today?"

"It burns when it comes out, you know. I don't know how you got it to do *that*, but congratulations. Everyone's sick. I hope you're happy. Amateur little prank you pulled. You'd think we were in junior high with that sort of nonsense. Some people never grow up, I suppose."

"Look..." I said quietly.

The other people were watching the freak show again. They seemed amused with the new addition.

"I didn't do this. I don't know who did, but I've been with people all day since I got up. Someone can vouch for everything I've done today. How did you even get coffee with no power anyway?"

"We turned on the generator," Lee said as he emerged from the hallway leading to his office. His voice was soothing already as he made his way to the woman's side. He wrapped an arm around her. "Now, Mrs. Gillespie, don't you think that's enough?"

"He poisoned the coffee. He's trying to kill us."

"I will deal with this, Mrs. Gillespie." I noticed he didn't defend me, only assured the borderline-hysterical woman that I would be dealt with.

"He's trying to—"

"I will deal with this." Lee's voice became significantly more threatening.

Mrs. Gillespie gathered her kids and marched them to their own taped-off square of the theater.

Lee turned to me. "I see you've discovered the problem we're facing."

"Yeah, I don't even know what she's talking about. I didn't know we got the power going this morning."

"We did," Lee said. His face and gestures were angrier than his voice.

I think he was actually making an effort to help me. I'm certain that looking at the scene from an outside point of view, the conversation looked more like he was chewing my ass. Just to keep up appearances, I shrank a little. Just enough for the onlookers to notice.

"The only problem is, the generator crapped out, and we have to find another one. No one here is a mechanic, so we won't be lucky enough to fix it and let that be that. We already threw it out."

I was certain that I could fix it, and under normal circumstances I would've. But under normal circumstances my name was Derrick, not Peter. So instead I just said, "That's a shame. What are we going to do about that?"

"I've sent a few of the less-important troops to a hardware store to pick one up, along with some material to make barriers out of. I doubt those windows will hold up forever."

That less-important-troops comment stuck with me.

His face was very serious. He gripped my shoulder. "Don't let these people get to you. We'll have your name clear in no time."

"I appreciate that." There was no feeling to what I said, only the act of going through the right motions and jumping through the right hoops. "At least Randy's on my side. He seems pretty confident in finding her."

"Randy you said?"

"Yeah, the cop. He's doing a good job keeping everything hush-hush."

"Yes," Lee said. "Watch out for yourself."

Lee disappeared down the hall. At the same time, Mark materialized out of the darkness in the opposite hallway. His face asked the question all by itself: *Was that him?* I nodded. He nodded back and continued to the prayer circle.

"Hey, everybody. I'm Thaddeus."

They looked up and cautiously greeted him.

"That's the way you do it," he would later tell me. "Just shove yourself in and don't give them the opportunity to tell you no."

I always wondered what else he knew but didn't say.

Chapter 41

I made the executive decision to put a temporary suspension on the freak show for the afternoon. I retired to a bathroom and clicked on the walkie.

"Anyone there."

No. I left the walkie on the sink, which was just as wet as the sinks in a theater always are. I did what I actually came into the bathroom to do, and then I washed my hands and gave the walkie one more try. I repeated the call, waited a second, and just as I was going to give up for the time being, Katy came on the line.

"Derrick?"

"I'm here. What's the matter?"

"They just got back with the battery."

"That's great news." I could tell I was being a little too cheerful. I guess I was refusing to believe that her mood wasn't the result of something terrible.

"Something bad happened. We'll be on our way soon." She sounded like someone had hit her puppy in the street.

"What happened?"

"Hang on. Let me get Jackie."

I waited for Jackie to come on the line. She was apparently no-where near Katy because getting her took a while. "You there?" I asked just to make sure the walkie still had power.

"Here she is."

"That you, Derrick?" Jackie was only kind of gloomier than her normal self.

"I'm here. What's wrong with Katy?"

"The mission to bring back the equipment for the car was slight-ly botched."

"What do you mean botched?"

"We arrived at the lab without a problem."

I wanted to tell her I wasn't her superior and that she could talk to me normally, but I didn't.

"We didn't even see anything but what the screamers left behind. There were parts along the sidewalks. There were five of us: Ted and Officers Bryant, Cooper, and Jacobson, and myself. We would've only needed one person to carry the charger and someone to carry all its cables in the pack. I could wear the pack and make a one-man job out of it. I had four extra people there just for safety's sake.

"We made our way through the building, following the flashlight beams with guns at the ready. Nothing to see. Just dust. The locker room we were aiming for couldn't have been farther from the en-trance we employed. We made it all the way across the building with-out a single shot fired. No problem. We got the charger and the pack. No problem. We crossed the building in the dark again. No problem.

"The lobby of the building had glass doors. We saw them com-ing. There were at least ten of them. It was like they trapped us in the building. They were coming to the glass door at the front of the building. We thought we could just backtrack and go around. We'd avoid them entirely. No. They came in through the stairway. Once one saw us, the rest followed. We couldn't go back, and we couldn't go forward without blood getting spilled. So we opened fire. We had to pick them off through the door. We lost Cooper to the ones coming from behind. We lost Ted to the ones in the front. They were relentless."

She sniffed. "I hadn't seen them do it yet. It's a lot. They just rip and pull whatever they can get at. An arm. A jaw. It's like the only life in them is rage."

"Look," I said. "Just take your time. We're not in a hurry to get back. Mark is making his way through the people, and I'm doing my best to lay low."

"Yes, we are in a hurry. We're not wasting any more time or people. I don't want anyone else to go down for nothing. No more wasting. Not another officer. Not a civilian. Thank God Jacobson was there."

"He the one that got you guys out of there?"

"He was just ready." She was more colloquial now. We were just having a normal conversation. "Like he was eager to do it. It was like he was happy to be in action again."

"I do have good news." I didn't have to make an effort to keep my excitement down this time. "We found some people who want to leave. Two. They don't speak English, though. Well, the little girl does, but I don't think she knows the swear words yet."

She clicked her walkie on at the end of a sad laugh. "That's very helpful. Thank you for doing what you're doing. That is incredibly brave for someone who has no reason to care about those people and already knows what's out there. I'm really sorry this is taking so long. And I'm sorry for what you're going through over there."

"So I take it you heard they think I killed Katy."

"I heard," she said. Her mood changed drastically. "We're on our way. The chargers are hooked up, and we'll be there in less than half an hour. Did you see which direction the group left in?"

"Yeah," I said. "I have no idea as far as north, south, east, or west. But if you're facing the parking lot from inside the building, they went left toward the spot where you guys dropped me off last night. They went in the direction of a neighborhood that way."

"OK, we'll plan accordingly."

"Come to the back of the building. No one seems to notice when people go back there."

"How do you know that?" she asked.

"That's where I found Mark," I said. "No one even saw him. He's actually the one who found out the Mexican father-daughter team wants to leave."

"Oh, good. So we can stop looking for him." I didn't press the button to let her hear me laugh. "So get him and meet us at the back of the building in half an hour. I'll have the radio on if you need us. I'm bringing Katy, too, for no other reason than to stop the mob from lynching you. We'll have to adjust our plan, but only a little."

"That's appreciated," I said around the stifled laugh. "I'll get Mark, and we'll see you guys in half an hour."

"Over and out."

I expected Katy to come back on the line. I waited a few moments, and when she didn't come back, I turned off the walkie and slid it back into my pocket.

I swiped at the water on the sink. It didn't help much, but the puddles turned into streaks, and I felt somewhat like I had done a good job. I ran the water to wash my hands. The faucet hiccupped and hissed before spurting out a reddish muck that looked black in the dark bathroom. I jerked my hands away and refocused my eyes. For a moment I thought I was hallucinating, but the water faded to orange to yellow and clear again. *The water is about to stop*, I thought. *And that'll be it.* The paper towels were empty, so I shook my hands dry and wiped them on my pants.

When I left the bathroom, I knew the freak show was about to start again, but a confidence filled me that it was the last time I would be going onstage. Before I made my way to the lobby, I took a brief detour into room six to ensure that Miguel and Gabriela would be at the ready in case we had to make a quick getaway. Then I stepped into the spotlight once again.

The show must go on.

Chapter 42

I took a cursory lap around the lobby just to appear normal. Mark was waist deep into a spirited conversation with the remainder of the prayers in the circle of chairs. He was making jokes and sympathizing with their worries, all the while making direct surreptitious eye contact with me, never for more than a second. He faced me so the people he talked to had their backs toward me. Eventually, I got tired of waiting for enough of his attention to tap my lips twice, so I just constantly tapped them until it earned me a nearly unnoticeable quick look of total bewilderment. I gave up and just waved him over. He made a face of irritation. While I ducked back down the hallway, I heard him breaking up the conversation. There was a moment of protest, which he put an end to with a declaration of a full bladder.

"The hell was that?" he asked, confused. "I thought we were being discreet."

"I tried giving you the signal."

"No, you didn't."

"That's not true."

"What was the signal?"

"Tapping my mouth." I showed him.

"Oh, yeah." He laughed. "That's why you were doing that? You looked so goofy. I was like, *God, he's being so weird right now.*"

"Oh my God." I opened the back door to the theater. Much like before, the light was a little harsh, and my eyes needed a moment to settle. "It was your idea."

"No." He laughed. "My idea was cool. Like James Bond. The execution was just silly. If they see that, they'll think you've lost it. So these guys are really uptight here, and, Jesus, they do not like you."

"I'm aware. That's why I can't talk to any of them to see if any want to leave. They're already skittish, and on top of that, they don't trust me."

"What did you do?" he asked. "I mean, other than poison the coffee of course."

"I told you. They think I killed Katy and the little kid."

"OK, wait. So you're telling me they're sending a group of guys out into the wild looking for someone they think is dead?"

"Well, the people out there haven't been exposed to that information campaign yet. They were in meetings all morning. I'm pretty sure they just want something to shoot, so it's good news for my sake that they're out there."

"And now you're in lockdown because some latchkey kid goes AWOL?"

"That's the gist of it," I said. "But I don't think it's the people. That doesn't seem like something those people would have come up with by themselves."

"What do you mean 'those people'?"

"I think last night when Lee came into our room, part of him recognized me. He mentioned my parents and the guy he killed and swapped lives with by name. I think part of him knows that I know who he really is, and he spread that information to turn everyone on me. If he didn't, I certainly don't think he did anything to stop it from spreading. I wouldn't be shocked if he wanted me out of here. The coffee thing was probably the happiest coincidence he's ever run into."

"That's bullshit," Mark said. He reminded me of a teenager who was reprimanded for riding a skateboard where signs prohibited it. Then, as if instantly growing into a strong, confident adult, he said, "You know, I've been through worse. If we can handle getting here with only a few nicks, then we can get past this. Any ideas on how to fix it yet?"

"That's why we're out here." I leaned against the back wall of the theater, trying to get a view of the cut on the palm of his hand. I didn't see anything. "Your sister is on her way. She told me to meet her back here."

"She bringing Katy?"

"Yeah."

"Good," Mark said. "Hopefully that'll defuse some of the lingering tension."

A scream echoed from within the woods. It was a few hundred feet deep. It was only one, but something told me that wasn't the whole story.

"I just know we're about to go check that out," Mark said unenthusiastically.

"Didn't you say that's where they made that shack?"

"No. I said that was on the other side of town. You are changing my words around."

"How deep into the woods is it?"

Mark deflated. "About a football field."

"If we start now, we'll be back by the time Jackie and Katy get here."

Mark bent over and took three deep breaths. He combined that with a brief Superman pose. "And you're sure you don't want to bring them with us?"

"I think the fewer people running through the woods, the better. You're welcome to stay," I said.

"No. God, no," he said. "You have no idea how boring it is just sitting there. Waiting."

I laughed at him. "We better hurry, then. Just stay quiet."

Chapter 43

A hundred yards at a snail's pace takes quite a while. We moved slowly to avoid too much noise from the fallen leaves. Luckily, most of the trees in the area were pine, so we could walk normally for more than half the way into the woods as long as we avoided the branches and vines hanging over roughly every step of the way. Pine needles were relatively silent, but crunchy leaves were like auditory landmines.

"These fuckin' stickers, man," Mark said. "I'm going to lose my shit if another one hits me in the face."

"Shh, I think I hear someone up ahead."

"Right," he said.

That made me chuckle.

Mark had a confused look on his face.

"Oh, yeah, you weren't there for the 'right' thing."

"OK, weirdo."

Something metal and heavy banged up ahead. Mark and I were silent. A truck's tires spun out on grass, and the woods fell still except for the occasional banging of a jail-cell door against its lock. I heard a muffled cry for what I assumed was help.

"Come on," I said.

Mark and I ran. The building was almost exactly as Mark described it. Whoever had thrown this place together took strips of tin roofing and affixed them to a wooden frame on all sides. Rope and loosely tightened screws were used to adjoin the metal slabs to the frame. Instead of a door, there was just an open space between strips. The only difference between my vision of the place in my head and the reality of it was the size. I thought it would be a small fifteen-by-fifteen box, but no. Mark said it was the size of my barn, but it was easily twice that size. And inside there were cages. It looked as though they had removed three jail cells, dropped them in a line, and built a metal cage around them.

The moment we crossed what could be considered the threshold into the shack, the muffled screams were revealed as muffled shrieks of rage. Screamers had been placed in two of three cages. That was all they were—essentially, huge metal kennels. The only things separating this from an actual jail cell were the locking mechanisms. Where a jail cell would have a key-activated lock, these doors were held on by a thick metal bar, like a bathroom stall or a dog cage. Each bar had a hole on one end where a lock kept the door from being opened.

The screamer on the right was a woman, roughly Katy's size before the switch, and the one in the center cage was a teenage boy. Someone had trapped them, gagged them, and tied them up. They lay on the ground with their hands and feet entwined with thick plastic zip ties. The same was done to their knees and elbows. They squirmed on the ground. In the center of the room—if it could be called a room—the sharpened log stuck out of a bald black spot in the grass where people used to build fires, probably for high school parties rather than camping. A circle had been screwed into the tip of the point. I recognized it as a larger version of what Sarah used to hang plants with on our front porch and patio, only instead of hanging down, this one was pointing upward.

"Jesus Man," Mark said.

Before we could enjoy our stay, tires screeched down the road. We started for the woods, but we would've had to cross the trail leading out of the clearing to the road. Mark grabbed my shirt and pulled me back.

"Nah, bro. They'll see us. Come on."

We hid behind the building. Careful not to be visible between the cracks between the strips of roofing, we lay on the ground. A corner of the room had an open hole a couple inches wide. We used it to peer inside. We heard the sound of tires on a road turn into tires on dirt and then just a motor and branches slapping and scraping the side of a truck. A black Hummer emerged from a narrow trail. The engine died. Three people got out. Two I immediately recognized as our gun-toting friends from the overpass: Blue Jeans and Khakis. From the driver's side, Lee dropped out of the tankish car.

"That's him," Mark whispered.

"Don't you fucking dare. They have guns."

Mark rolled his eyes, but I could tell he wasn't planning to do anything, anyway.

"I have got to see this," Lee said theatrically.

I peeked through a crack. A huge gleeful smile decorated his face. He nearly skipped inside.

"My God. This is perfect. You boys are just—jumpin' Jesus. Consider yourselves pardoned. This and what you did to that police bitch has more than made up for what happened in the woods that first day. How many of you put this together?"

"Us and four others," Blue Jeans said.

"Well, I absolutely love it. Boys, wait in the car. We're going to need a distraction. Take one of the shitty generators and use it to play a movie tonight. The people will love it. Whatever Disney thing you can find. They'll keep clam as long as the children are happy. Start the popcorn machines, too. You still have that iodine on you?"

"I do," Khakis answered.

"Maybe put a little extra butter on the popcorn, if you get my drift. And I don't have to tell you boys to keep it quiet, do I?"

"No, sir," they answered together.

"You boys know why I'm doing this, right?" They were quiet. "I just don't think he is a stable presence. I can't say for sure, but I feel very strongly that he is a bad egg. Once he is gone, we will be able to move forward." A pill bottle rattled. "Call everyone in. If they haven't found her yet, they won't. Just as well. I don't want to risk anyone else. Besides, her not turning up will help us send him on his way. Out of sight, out of mind. Now, you boys keep in mind what I want you to do. I'll see you back here when it's done. Just call 'em back in."

Khakis got on the walkie-talkie before he left the building. He asked for their progress, and by the time the Hummer roared to life, he had told the troops to come on back. A regular Vietnam. As they left, I only had one thing on my mind.

"What is iodine used for?" I asked Mark as we weaved through the trees back toward the theater.

"It's usually used to kill bacteria, fungus, shit like that."

His normal, playful attitude had been taken over by something different. Something angry. Something that made me very uneasy as it took the real Mark away. He walked fast. I had to hustle to keep up.

"It's used to treat thyroid problems, skin disease, diabetes, cancer, radiation, stroke, you name it. You can find it in pretty much any hospital. *Any* hospital. Even *la casa de loco*. Get too much of it, and you'll spend the day vomiting and shitting yourself. So what I think they're using it for is making coffee." He stopped and turned to me. "I don't like this. Those fuckers are poisoning these people. We need to stop whatever it is they're planning to do and get the hell out of here."

Chapter 44

Getting back to the theater proved much easier than getting to the shack. Mark was silent. Part of me was glad that he affected a new, serious attitude. Not worried about making a lot of noise, we could walk as fast as we wanted. That was for the best because there was nothing I could do to slow Mark down.

Jackie and Katy waited for us behind the theater. Jackie spoke into her walkie as we appeared from the edge of the woods. Mark didn't stop. As soon as she saw us, Jackie hounded us with questions of where we were, how we were going to get in if the door was locked, why Mark looked so pissed, and a number of others. I noticed that for the first time, she wasn't wearing any part of her uniform. Just jeans and a black T-shirt, the same thing Mark wore when he picked me off the floor of the barn back when this started. I half expected her to bring a dirty cap of her own, poking out of the back waistband of her jeans. Mark hugged her so hard her voice rose in pitch. She stopped talking. I could tell this wasn't the first time this method was used.

"You have to shut up now, OK?" he said before letting her go.

She closed her mouth and nodded against his shoulder.

"Something shitty is about to happen. We have to stop it. This isn't just about revenge anymore. It's about making sure bad people don't win."

"What happened?" Jackie asked.

Mark finally let her go.

"Katy, why don't you and I go around?" I said. "Let's give these guys a minute. I'll tell you what we just saw."

PART 4
THE WORST THING THAT EVER HAPPENED

Someone's rocking the boat to the beat of our favorite song about murder.

Chapter 45

The worst thing that ever happened was actually two separate things. I don't know which was worse, but I watched both of them unfold right in front of me, and I had to turn away by the end of both of them. If it wasn't for me, I doubt either of them would have happened in the first place. Like I said, I don't know which is worse, but I know which one keeps me up—and wakes me up—as I work my way through these pages.

I walked Katy around the building to the veranda. I helped her over the barricade that was set out for the screamers, but it did literally nothing as far as we could tell in the way of protection. It only came up to my waist, and there was nothing sharp on which someone's clothes or body could be snagged. A screamer would only have to put minimal effort into jumping over the sand-filled wooden box. It would only have to raise its legs a little higher than a normal running stride. The theater people were a very slapdash organization. That actually may be exaggerating how well things were run.

Katy put her arm around my neck and allowed her legs to give way. We almost fell over because of the sudden balance shift. The doors were locked, so we waited for someone to come to the door. Peggy was that someone. Angry glares on the other side of the window waited for us. The spiteful disbelief painted across Peggy's face made her look like a caricature of herself. She opened the door and stood so I couldn't get past her.

"What did he do to you, sweetie?"

"I found her," I said, trying not to let myself get angry. "What do you mean?"

"*You* found her? That's convenient."

"Yes. It really is."

Katy groaned. Standing on the sidewalk, she worked Peggy over harder than Thaddeus Clementeal ever could.

"She looks beaten," Peggy added. "And starved to death."

"I'm hungry," Katy said. It was hardly even a whisper.

"What'd you say, sweetie? Did he hurt you?"

"Are you kidding me? She said she's hungry."

"I'm hungry," Katy said louder. "And tired. They chased me. My husband found me."

Peggy glared at me. "Do you want my help, dear?" she asked Katy.

"I want my husband," Katy said.

She made her voice weaker the more the conversation wore on. She still had the wherewithal to affect her overly southern accent, which impressed me. I still had to concentrate to tell people my name was Peter.

"Can I please have some food?"

"Of course, dear." Peggy tried to take Katy from me. I had a strong feeling that if she did, I would be locked out in the cold. She slid under Katy's arm, which only made Katy pull me tighter.

"Peter, can you take me to lie down?" Katy laced her fingers around my neck.

Instinctively, I picked her up the way a husband does his bride. Peggy had moved away from the door enough for me to squeeze by her. I can't say for sure, but I think I felt Peggy make a move to get in front of me again before I walked inside. Regardless, she wasn't quick enough to stop me, and I carried Katy inside. The prayer circle turned, and silence froze the air. A number of the pale, sickly faces had returned from their bathroom vomit party, ready to judge me. I don't know what they made of Katy's presence, but they weren't giving her a standing ovation. Not even an attempt at a slow clap. No one moved at all. Not to help or hold open a door or clear a path. Nothing.

"Is there anything I can get her to eat?" I wanted to keep the story going and feed Katy, but the truth was, I hadn't eaten anything since the feast of chips at Ted's. I was hungry. "My wife is hungry."

"There is some candy," Peggy said.

"That's fine. Her blood sugar is low, anyway." I didn't know if that was actually how it worked, but I made my way to the concession stand. I heard Katy quietly laugh against my chest, which almost sent me into a laughing spell. I had to struggle to force the corners of my mouth down. "It's OK, honey. Don't try to talk. Just rest."

"We're trying to ration everything so it lasts longer," Peggy argued. She followed behind me like a barking Chihuahua nipping at my heels.

"That's fine. We haven't eaten since we've been here. And she can have my share if there isn't much to a ration."

Peggy opened her mouth to protest.

I interrupted her loud enough for everyone in the lobby to hear me. "Is there a problem? Do you think there is something better than keeping my wife alive right now, *Peggy*? Look, I know what you people think I did, but you're wrong. The proof is right here in my arms. My wife has spent more than her share of time out there trying to help you people, which I think is deserving of a little something to eat. I'm going to get her some food. Thanks for your gracious help."

I know technically it was a lie just like pretty much everything else I said to the theater people, but in that moment I needed those people to stop hating me or at least see that the rumors were wrong about me. I worried that if whatever Lee planned on doing required a lynch mob, it wouldn't be too difficult to scrounge one together. The sooner I got them on my side, the quicker I could stop looking over my shoulder. None of them had shown me they would do anything if it came down to it—just a lot of nasty looks—but the way they reacted to Mark's arrival, coupled with their complete submission to Lee compared to the way they reacted to me when Katy was missing, kept my comfort level lower than I had ever noticed it.

I walked behind the counter, throwing the hinged partition counter top open with Katy still in my arms. A drawer, which had been neither labeled nor colored in a way that would make me think candy hid inside, was cracked enough for me to see a brightly printed wrapper in the fleeting light. I grabbed a handful of anything I could pick up and stomped back to room six. As I reached the door, Mrs. Gillespie entered the hallway from a bathroom. The blue around her eyes had faded a little. She seemed to be feeling a lot better. We made eye contact for a moment, long enough for me to catch the expression of realization on her face, and I continued into the room.

I pushed the door to room six with my back but bounced off it. The door opened outward, and that was confusing to me. I understood that not everyone entering the theater was carrying a full-grown woman, but it could probably be conceived that a few people a day entered the theater with armfuls of snacks and drinks, so why didn't the doors open inward so people could just back into the room without spilling anything? Maybe they could just build them to swing inward and outward. It may have been too late to ask, honestly.

Regardless, I laid Katy and the candy on the ground.

"Is she sick?" Gabriela kneeled on the side opposite of Katy from me.

"Oh, I'm fine, sweetheart. Just tricked this big, strong man into carrying me around." Katy patted my arms. "Just look at those muscles. I'm gonna teach you how to get a big, strong man. Oo, let me get them Sno-Caps!" She said it like the hype man for a hip-hop artist.

I turned to the door again and saw a head peeking through the window.

"I'll be right back," I told Katy. I got up and walked to the door.

"Yes, Mrs. Gillespie?"

"They found her?"

"No, I found her."

"Well," she said. I could tell she was choking on the metaphorical crow. "I owe you an apology."

"Not necessary." I tried to wave her away.

"No. There were rumors going around that you had killed your wife and the little boy you came with. Now, I didn't make up the rumors, but I also didn't do anything to stop them."

"We didn't come here with a boy. He was here already."

"He showed up when you did."

"Just the same, he isn't ours."

"I just assumed he was."

"Well," I said. "You see where that gets people."

"If I can do anything," she began.

"Thank you, Mrs. Gillespie." I pulled the door closed. It would have taken no effort for her to open the door because there was no lock. Instead of forcing her way back into the room, Mrs. Gillespie walked away.

I turned back to Katy, who was already making friends with Miguel and Gabriela. "You play nice now," I told her. "I'm going to let Mark back inside."

"Are these the guys coming with us?"

"Those are the ones."

"Aw, yay!" Katy said with wide eyes. She spoke to Gabriela the way all adults say things to toddlers: "'Cause you are cute as a button." Katy tickled Gabriela, completely ignoring the tears of laughter already rolling down her chubby cheeks.

I opened a box of candy while heading back to the exit. Light in the theater almost didn't exist by then, but I noticed on the opposite end of the building two people lighting gas lamps lining both sides of the side corridor. A faint orange glow flickered and grew down the ominously dark corridor as the two silhouettes made their way toward room six. I popped a couple pieces of chocolate in my mouth and continued to the back exit. That was the first time I smelled gasoline in one of the rooms. The smell wasn't overwhelming, but there were definitely a lot of full cans somewhere on this side of the building.

I opened the rear door to a cacophony of roaring truck engines and rebel yells. Sporadic pistol fire and diesel-fueled engine clatter bombarded my eardrums. I suddenly wondered if I had opened a wormhole to Talladega.

"They're back," Mark said. "Khakis and Blue Jeans have a pile of generators and gas cans stacked up in one of the trucks. Two more are full of idiot kids. Those are the ones spinning wheels and shooting pistols. I guess they found something to kill, and the testosterone hasn't worn off yet. *El hombre amarillo* is walking inside."

"You need to move." Jackie slid past me.

"I do?"

"It's number six, Jack," Mark called up to her. His new attitude unnerved me.

"No, Mark." Jackie marched down the dark hallway to room six. "I can't be out. It risks my cover. People are here who I've either worked with or arrested, and someone could recognize me. After the police station split, most people aren't happy with anyone who stayed. I'll get Katy on duty, too. You need to stay close to me. With Lee obviously planning something for you, I don't want you alone or surrounded by a group of people who think you just killed a child and your wife."

"I made a pretty big ordeal of making sure they saw that Katy wasn't dead," I told her, trying to keep up with her pace.

"I don't have time to decide if that was the best thing to have happened, but maybe that will help. It's not going to be an immediate switch in attitude regardless. You're still the out-of-towner that no one trusts. They're going to have their eyes on you."

We reached room six without anyone noticing the extra member of our party. Jackie pulled the door open, and before I realized she wasn't speaking English, she and Miguel were in a full-on conversation.

"She seems a little better at that than you," I teased Mark.

"She was paid to learn it." Mark's voice was all business. "I did it for fun."

"OK," I said. "We still have to fill Katy in on everything."

"Yes, you do." Katy stood up. Her body language said that she was nervous.

"Basically, Lee is planning something fucked up," Mark explained. "We were in the woods because we heard some people way back behind the theater. They've built some psychotic shed back there, and they're keeping screamers tied up in cages."

"Jesus," Katy said. "Can they do that?"

"I'm not sure there is anyone to stop them," I said.

"What are they planning to do?" Katy asked.

"We don't know yet," I said.

Mark said, "What we are going to do is have you and I go out and see if anyone else wants to leave."

"We're going to give it another hour, and we're going to go together. Jackie doesn't want you straying too far from me just in case someone comes at you. We're going to stay close to the room in case we need to bolt. There are a couple kids who may even be orphaned that we need to talk to. We just have to be quick."

"All right, let's go," Katy said.

"I'm going to go out first," Mark said. "Give me a couple minutes, then you come out. Jackie said if anyone was watching us, it would look less conspicuous than if we came out together, even if we're close to one another."

"Right," Katy said, and glanced at me with a nearly unnoticeable sideways grin.

Mark left the room. As he did, he bumped into one of the silhouettes. He told her he was sorry and even held the door for her as he left.

She caught the door before it closed and turned her attention to the inside of the room. "Here's some extra kerosene for your lanterns," the bitter old woman said. She tossed the tin cans into the room. They clunked onto the floor and slid, leaving a wet trail behind them.

"Ain't she sweet." Katy picked the cans off the floor and laid them on the opposite side of the door.

By then, Jackie had reached the end of her conversation with Miguel. We could tell by the cadence in her speech that she was about to switch back to English. She reached for her waistband where there was a line of three guns, not just one like the movies. She handed Miguel one and said something else in Spanish. Miguel carried his daughter out the exit next to the screen. I never saw him after that.

"OK," Jackie said once the world was shut out again. "Here's what's going to happen. We're going to try to move in an hour. Shouldn't be too hard unless something unforeseen happens. Katy, just give Mark a few minutes, as I'm sure he said. Then you go out after him. I have Miguel and his daughter taking our car to the police station. They're going to send the word to prepare the buses for an early-morning departure. We're going to leave here, get a full night of sleep, and head out to New Orleans in the morning. Hopefully, we can do it completely unscathed."

"What do you and I do until then?" I asked Jackie.

"Katy and Mark are going to send the people they find to me, and I'm going to get them ready to go. What you are going to do is find where they put the keys to the cars and trucks that they moved when people started showing up. We saw a group of cars that was too organized to be there when everything happened. If he's trying to be totally in control of everyone here, he'll have all the cars in one place. Katy, you remember where we saw them, right? The Wendy's across the street at the end of the road."

"Yeah. Did you"—Katy grasped for words—"confirm that's where they are?"

"The bluish-green one with the overhead lights and bullet-hole stickers is the one outside doing doughnuts in the parking lot. So we know they used the cars from that lot."

"Sounds about right," Katy said with a dry tone.

"Miguel has a silver Nissan Frontier in that lot." Jackie turned to me. "Derrick, all you have to do is find where they keep the keys. His set has a cartoon-turtle key chain and a blue dinged-up carabiner."

"What's a carabiner?" I asked.

"It's a hook you use when you go mountain climbing."

"Oh," I said. "I didn't realize those had a name."

"Me either," Katy said. "I always called them hooks."

"We'll leave as soon as we get the keys," Jackie said.

"I understand," I said.

"If there are no other questions, we're all set," Jackie said. "I think you're fine to go out there now, Katy. It's been a couple minutes."

"Just find out if they want to go, and then send them in here?"

"That's all you have to do," Jackie said.

"We'll keep an eye out for you," I assured her.

Chapter 46

After a few minutes, I also left room six. I guessed there were probably four places the collection of car keys would be. I excluded the sleeping-bag emporium because when fumbling my way around the room in the perfect dark, I would have probably noticed a pile of about forty sets of keys. My first official stop would have been any of the three box offices, but knowing Lee's teenage army was headed back to the building, I decided to make that a do-or-die decision. I tried to remember if Peggy used a key to unlock the door to the welcome room marked Office. I didn't think so. I snuck across the building to that room.

I jiggled the handle to the office door. It was unlocked, so I pushed the door. It thumped loudly in its frame. The loud noise caused me to flinch. I jerked the handle down farther after a surreptitious glance around to see if anyone had noticed the man in the poorly lit hallway sneaking into the darker room. The door opened without a sound, and I closed it behind me. The room temperature jumped at least ten degrees from the hallway. The lanterns had burned out, and there were no windows or emergency exits or even an air-conditioning vent in this room, so I guessed the temperature was to be expected.

Only one lantern in the office kept a flame. It flickered weakly from the short wick inside. I wondered, and not for the first time, why the electric lanterns weren't put to more use. It had crossed my mind multiple times so far that I hadn't seen any. I banged my knee on a stool. In the orange light, I was able to see where the desk was, but I couldn't make out anything written or printed on the pages lying on it. I rifled through the drawers, most of which only held a couple pieces of paper or a wadded bag of chips. The contents of the bottom right-hand drawer made a plastic rattling sound when I opened it, like an empty bottle, which turned out to be of the orange pharmaceutical variety. I grabbed it and continued through the desk, finding nothing but a desk plate. I traced the letters with my finger. One by one the letters spelled out Adam Barthidge, and below the name, in smaller letters, read Manager. I dropped the nameplate back into the top drawer and left the room, confident that what I was looking for wasn't there.

As the lobby grew closer—I didn't walk, my feet carried me without my being involved at all—I realized that checking the welcome room, the emporium, or either of the three box-office rooms would be a facile waste of time. I had learned only one thing about Lee in my time at the theater. He wasn't going to allow anyone to leave. I knew where the keys were. In the light of the hallway, I read the bottle. The prescription on the label was made for thirty twenty-five-milligram pills of clozapine, which was the first time I had ever seen the word. Under the prescription information, the bottle read, "Use as directed. Do not overuse." I meant to take the bottle back to room six. On my way I bumped into Randy.

"Hey, it's Peter!" Randy's excitement was very apparent. He wrapped his arms around me and bear hugged me. I dropped the pill bottle into my pocket before reciprocating.

"It's also Randy!" I returned the enthusiasm.

"I hear Mary came back home. Great timing, too. The boss just called us all in."

"Yeah, I found her when I went outside to get away from the hate," I explained. "It's got me thinking, though. What if there are other people trapped in those houses? Or any other place around here. Shouldn't we be heading up teams in big trucks, going around town?"

"That's actually a great idea, buddy," Randy said. His excitement finally outweighed his normal angry demeanor. "I'm going to run that by the boss, and we'll put you in charge if you're up for it."

"Right on. Do we have any cars available? I can start tonight."

"All the keys are in the boss's office," he said, rubbing the stubble on his face. "I have to get the key. He shouldn't have a problem with it. He wants to find as many people who aren't crazy as he can. The more people we have here, the easier it will be to get back to normal. We'll get the key from him, and you can start immediately. Cool?"

"Right on," I said. I hoped I didn't come off as annoyed as I really was. Of course getting the keys couldn't have been easy. No, sir. Not with all these hoops to jump through. "How did he get to be the boss, by the way? Adam, I mean."

"Oh, man," Randy began. "You should've seen him. When this whole thing went down a few nights ago, he was just on, ya know? We had already thought it was a great place for everyone to stay until we figured out what to do. It was Monday night, and we figured everyone would be at home watching the game instead of paying twenty bucks to see a movie. Adam was so welcoming and giving to the people here. He's only been the manager for a week or two. Just transferred from Minnesota or Wisconsin. I forget which. He didn't know anybody, but he put everything into motion. It was his idea to make notes of everyone here, his idea to clear the area and start over. When the police came here with civilians for shelter, he only asked to make the rules. We let him, and he hasn't let us down. He's keeping this thing from falling apart. Adam's a great person."

"That's great, man."

"You going to be around?"

"I have an appointment in town, but I can move it to tomorrow."

Randy laughed. "I'm about to make an announcement that we're playing a movie and turning the power back on. At least for the night. We just wanted to make sure we have enough gas before we tell everyone. No point getting everyone's hopes up before we know what we're capable of, know what I mean? Maybe you and the missus can find an empty room when everyone else is watching whatever Disney crap they have here." He nudged me with his elbow.

"I heard that. Spoon her in my square."

"Keep an eye on her this time." He clapped me on the back and headed off in the direction of a group of camouflaged teens.

I caught Katy's attention and motioned for her to follow me. She hurried beside me and wrapped an arm around my waist. I noticed Mark having fun with a group of kids despite his recently adjusted attitude.

"What's that?" she asked.

"It's a pill bottle. The name is scratched off, but I have an idea whose it is."

"It doesn't say Adam on it?" she joked. "Any idea what it is?"

"It's called clozapine. Any clue?"

"That actually sounds familiar," Katy said. She pushed open the door to room six. "Hey, Jackie, have you ever heard of clozapine?"

Jackie's eyebrows rose as if she'd been caught doing something she knew was wrong. "I've heard of it. Yeah. Why?"

"Derrick found this bottle." Katy handed the bottle to Jackie. "The prescription is for clozapine. It sounds familiar. I think my grandmother was on it."

"What was wrong with your grandmother?" Jackie studied the label.

"Everything. Dementia. Anorexia. Schizophrenia. Diabetes. I think she had a tumor."

"This could have been one of the things she took. The name is scratched off of this one." Jackie tossed the bottle onto a sleeping bag in the corner of the room. "Whose is it?"

"It was in an office. I don't want to accuse anyone, but there's only one person regularly taking pills out of one of these bottles."

"I think we need to get Mark back in here," Jackie said.

I moved to the room's entrance. When I opened the door, there was a loud noise like someone dropping a heavy piece of mechanical equipment. Everyone was quiet, and then someone gave the generic "I'm OK," and everyone went back to what they were doing. What happened next sent everything into motion.

Chapter 47

A low rumble of conversation hovered like a strange smell in the lobby as a single voice rose to bring the noise down. The teenage troops continued to move equipment. Eventually, the rumble became a purr and then nothing but the single voice.

"Now that I have your attention…" It was Randy. His tone was as playful as ever. "Look, folks, we know this is a difficult situation. I know people have been sick and tempers are high. However, there's some good news. I'm being told that Mrs. Grabowski has been found, so there is one silver lining behind this horrible event. No one was injured while trying to find her, so there is a lot to be thankful for tonight."

Someone in the crowd asked where the boy was.

"Now, as a special treat to everyone, just to lighten the mood, we are going to fire up the generators, cook some popcorn and snacks, and play a movie for everyone. We're even going to get the heat going in this place so we're not all shivering. How does that sound folks?"

A cheer went up.

"Who's ready for a movie?" Randy shouted.

Applause and laughter carried through the building. As well it should. A family reunited. The troops came home. On top of it all, we were getting the power back, even if it was a temporary return. The feeling of a reemergence of normalcy even tricked me into believing things were going to start moving upward from there. Luckily, I was able to come back before it sucked me in entirely.

"We're just going to ask everyone to find a friend—or stranger if there are any left—and mosey on over to theater ten while we get everything set up. Tonight we're going to have *power*!" Another cheer went up as the herd of people slowly made its way to room ten. The energy in the building began to pick up.

"Well, shit," Mark said when he emerged from the crowd of passersby and into the room. "That's going to throw a wrench in the gears."

"We're going to be fine," Jackie said. "The plan is going to continue as we laid it out. In fact this will probably make it easier to talk to everyone if they are all in the same place and not talking to each other."

"No, did you see that?" Mark asked.

"See what?" Katy asked.

"Derrick's cop friend." Mark pointed to the hallway as if he were just beyond the door. "Khakis and Blue Jeans. They just walked him outside. Not really forced him, but it didn't look like the guy had much of a choice."

I ran. I pushed through the crowd and frantically scanned the lobby for Blue Jeans, Khakis, or Randy. I saw nothing but the tail end of the herd and a bunch of teenagers hauling plastic red-and-yellow gasoline cans by the twos and a few extra generators into the lobby. No one looked up. There was no sign that Randy had been there at all. One of the double doors opened again, and the shrill of a screeching tire ripped through the building. No one else noticed the banshee shriek from the parking lot.

Chapter 48

"What do you think they're doing?" Mark asked.

"They're trying to get to him, right?" I said. "I mean, they know he's sort of on my side with this whole thing."

"They took him out of the building, though." That shade of green I had noticed before reappeared in Mark's eyes. Mark straightened up. "You don't think they're taking him to the shed, do you?"

I didn't answer. I just charged forward in a blind panic. All I knew was that I was going in the opposite direction of room ten. "Get a gun from Jackie." I felt like the hinges were going to burst off the frame when I slammed through the door. The door recoiled off the wall and slammed behind me. I made my way into the woods a couple feet, at a pretty high speed, before a vine of thorns caught me above my left eye. I cried out. The back exit opened again. Water in my eyes blurred my vision, but I could hear Jackie's voice.

"Where'd you go, Derrick?"

"I'm right here." I pulled the thorns from my skin and wiped the driblets of blood from above my eye. "I'm in the woods."

"Is someone attacking you?"

"No," I said. "I got caught in a briar patch. I really hope that's not how you would react if someone was attacking me."

"I was actually trying to find you easier without telling you to keep talking. It's less awkward that way." Jackie emerged into the woods. "Mark told me to bring a gun. Are you going to be able to find the place in the dark?"

A tire squealed again. It was off in the distance but unmistakable just the same. This time the brakes, instead of acceleration, caused the noise.

"Shouldn't be too hard." I continued through the thick brush with my hands in front of me to block oncoming bogeys.

"What's the plan here?" Jackie asked from behind me.

"I don't know."

"You can't run in there with your ass out. They've got guns. We have *a* gun. And there are screamers back there. What if they let them loose?"

"I haven't thought about it. But how am I going to know how to help unless I can see the situation play out? I may not be able to do anything at all."

"Then why are you going?"

"Because what if I *can* help? You knew Randy, right?" I asked her.

"I did. Yes."

"Don't you want to help him if you can?"

The woods were silent then. Not even the crickets had anything to chirp about. I immediately attributed that to the time of year and forgot about it. My eyes continuously fixed on trees farther and farther ahead to avoid walking in circles. After a minute or two, something visual clicked. A sudden brightness up ahead peeked through the woods. A brilliant white glow reached between trees and guided me in the direction of the shed.

"I think we found the place," Jackie said. "Better be like church mice from here on out."

The light grew more and more intense as we made our way through the woods. Eventually, the brightness reached a peak. Voices came from the direction of the light. We slowed our pace even further until we were able to understand what the two voices were saying. They came from two younger kids, of course.

"What does he want to do with this extra one?" the younger of the two said.

"I don't give a fuck," the other said. He sounded like a teenager who just learned how to swear.

"Well, we can't just leave it out of a cage."

A gunshot rang through the air. "There. Now, just clean the fucking thing up, and get it the fuck out of here."

The shed came into view through the trees, and the inside was lit up like my garage back in California when I worked late nights, and I realized then where the LED lanterns had been taken. We inched to the edge of the woods where the shed stood in plain sight. Jackie yanked me back.

"Do not step on that." She pointed to a deer trap covered in pine needles. She pointed to about six other ones to keep an eye out for. "Probably wouldn't hurt too much for too long, but we don't want you to yell."

"Right."

A truck engine revved from the trail on the opposite side of the clearing. The sounds seemed to come at us like a monster from the ominous dark on the other side of the building. I pulled Jackie with me, and we hurried to the corner with the crack to look through and lay on the ground just as Mark and I did before. We waited. Amazingly, when the younger kid managed to drag the surplus screamer's body to the edge of the building and toss it aside like a sack of garbage, he didn't see us. I guess his eyes hadn't adjusted to the darkness outside the shed. The sound of the engine drowned out the sound of the tires going from road to grass. The headlights ruined any chance of surprise.

"Go get me three more," Yellow Man called down to the two younger troops from the driver's window of the jacked-up truck. The two piled into the smaller of the two vehicles and sped off into the black night. Lee rolled up the window, blocking the light out with a tint so dark even the mass of fifteen LED lanterns couldn't penetrate the glass.

Four people got out of the truck: Khakis, Blue Jeans, Lee, and Randy. Lee marched to the thick post in the center of the room. At the sight of him, the screamers in their cages started to stir. Lee held a hammer and handcuffs in his hand. He ran the chain of the hand-cuffs through the hook screwed into the point of the sharpened log. He then used the hammer to beat the hook down into the log so the handcuffs couldn't move.

Behind him two people, hardly more than teenagers, kicked a gagged and blindfolded law enforcer to a point of near unconscious-ness. He groaned around the gag loud enough to be heard on the opposite side of the shed. When he stopped moving, they both got another two hits in. They dragged him by his elbows to Lee. Randy's wrists were slammed into the metal rings. Blue Jeans cut off the zip tie his wrists were in and slugged him one more time. He fell over and hung by his wrists. I couldn't tell if that laid him out, because of the blindfold he still wore. Blue Jeans and Khakis went to the three cages. They reached through the bars and cut the ties on the scream-ers. I really wanted Randy to be out for what was going to happen.

"Listen," Lee began. He had to shout over the commotion of the screamers. Lee bent down and ran his fingers through Randy's short hair. "This isn't personal. I can't have you standing in the way of what I'm trying to do. Trying to rebuild. I know and understand that you are not any immediate threat to me, but you're on the side of someone who is. Someone who could ruin *my* kingdom. I see the way you buddied up with him. The way you became friends, and I hate to say it, but that is exactly what brought you to where you are. You two could have been a lot of help to me."

Randy still didn't move. Fortunately, I couldn't move. If I made any sound whatsoever, Jackie and I would be caught and strung up the same way. I had to sit and watch as the one person who actually made me feel welcome was beaten and strung up for the wolves. Thankfully, I never saw Randy move either.

"When you're done with that, hit the music," Lee said.

"You got it, Boss." Khakis left Blue Jeans to tie a thin white rope around the cage's locking mechanisms. A few seconds later, a car door opened, and heavy-metal music raked against my eardrums. Lee and Blue Jeans left from view.

The rope connected to the locks on the cages pulled, and two of the doors unlocked, leaving one screamer captive and slamming his body into the cage. The other two, banging on the doors of the right and middle cages, sprinted out of the cages. The once-man picked Randy up by the ankles and yanked. The handcuffs snapped, sending chain links flying in all directions. I closed my eyes after that. Cutting through all the racket, a scream of absolute pain sounded. It was Randy. Unmistakable. I plugged my ears, but even with the music, the screams, and my fingers so deep I could almost touch my brain, I still heard the thumps and breaks that accompany a bare-handed murder. I felt him banging against the wall. Eventually, the sound of homicide stopped, leaving just the music and the almost-appropriate screams. Shotgun blasts interrupted everything.

"Well, this one didn't get any fun." Lee shot the screamer trapped in the cage. At close range the spray of metal from the shotgun eviscerated the thing behind the bars. Lee stepped back into view. He was visibly shaking. He dropped the shotgun onto the grass and reached into his pocket. A toothy grin stretched across his yellow face.

Khaki and Blue Jeans moved to the pieces of Randy.

"No. Leave him there. When we bring the others here, I want them to see that and be afraid." Lee twitched as he fumbled the bottle open. He shook the last of its contents down his scrawny throat and threw the bottle into the corner where Jackie and I stared in horror. "Here's what I want. Richie, I want you to help those other two shits wrestle up some more of these. They'll get themselves killed if you don't help them."

"You got it, Boss," Blue Jeans said.

"Bradley, we're going to find those other two and drop Richie off with his equipment. Then I have to make an appearance among the people. Give a speech—'all that fine work has paid off now we can enjoy some electricity'—and what have you. While I'm doing that, I need you to go into my office. In the top-right drawer, get me one of the bottles. The fifty-milligram bottle. The twenty-fives run out too quick."

"You got it, Boss." Khakis dragged the screamer in the cage onto the sacrificial area and dropped it. The hollow thump it made was disgusting.

"One more thing." Lee scratched at his neck. "They found the wife, you said? Do you recognize her, too?"

"Haven't seen her yet without face paint," Blue Jeans said.

"And I don't suppose you were able to catch a glimpse at the new guy?" Lee asked. "He's a big one. Fits your description of the other one pretty well. He looks like he wouldn't have a rough time humiliating some of our people by jumping them in the dark and holding them at gunpoint. We may need a few people to get *him* here, though."

"I think we laid on enough suspicion to be able to work the people into a frenzy if we need to," Blue Jeans said. I liked him so much better when he said nothing. "We'll do whatever you need. Just say the word, Boss."

Khakis chimed in. "If the other one is in the theater, I want a shot at him myself."

"After we drop him off," Lee began. "I want you to go in and get the bottle for me. Then come back out to the truck so I can get the shakes under control. While I'm addressing the folks, I want you to get her and escort her back to the car. Tie her up and gag her if she won't play nice. She's got military skills, so be careful. We'll find a way to pin her on Pete, and we'll get it right this time. And if you boys come up with anything else, you just say the word. We have to keep our people safe."

The three of them walked back out of view. I heard one of the other two say something that sounded like generator. But they were gone before anything else coherent came through.

"Come on," Jackie whispered. "We have to move."

The truck roared to life, and we made a mad dash through the woods back to the theater.

Chapter 49

We almost missed the theater. The woods were so poorly visible that we broke out of the tree line behind the hotel on the opposite end of the parking lot. I looked through the glass back door, cupping my hands around my eyes. I saw a stack of sofas blocking the door. Beyond that something moved. There wasn't a scream, but I definitely saw something move. The air was empty and still, but that didn't mean Lee and his cronies hadn't driven around to the other side of the theater.

"Come on," Jackie said. "Get away from there."

I ran behind her, but not before feeling the strange sensation of knowing they were in there come over me. As we ran across the parking lot, I heard an unmistakable thump on the second or third floor.

"Get Katy and anyone else they found," I said between breaths. "I'm going straight for Mark. We'll meet you in room six, and we are getting out of here."

"How are you going to get in the office without a key?"

"I don't know yet. We'll kick it down if we have to."

I tripped over the barricade when the two of us reached the veranda. Jackie's training kept her in much better shape than my occasional workout, which consisted mainly of chasing homeless people off the farm. I caught my balance by plowing into the front doors. The guards, who should have been in the *Jetsons* suites, were gathered in the lobby. We banged on the glass until one of them opened the door for us. It's only now that I realize how lucky we were that the other two police officers had just finished giving orders and left the room. The clumsy, nervous kid from the day before pulled a set of keys out of his pocket and let us into the building. We blew by him.

A number of things had changed inside. The most obvious being that the fluorescent light bulbs illuminated the place instead of lanterns. I could almost hear the faint echoes of the weak cheer as light filled the theater again. Behind the counter, two of the troops made laborious work of connecting and properly assembling the already-put-together popcorn machine. I have to give them credit. It is rather difficult work pouring cooking oil, butter, and popcorn kernels into a bowl, flipping a switch, and waiting. I wondered if Khakis had done his work on the process yet. Regardless, I wasn't going to allow anyone I was with to sample the kids' work. Another change was the hum of generators in other rooms. I wondered if they would be able to hear the movie with all that racket.

The most important change in the general atmosphere was the smell. The scent of gasoline lingered like the smell of the ocean in beach towns. A quick glance around showed me dozens of gas cans lining the walls like ants in a line in the corners of a kitchen. One followed another every six or seven feet. I wondered why the lanterns were still lit and hanging if the power was back. When Jackie and I reached room six, I had forgotten all about it.

Chapter 50

"Who's this?" I asked. There was a blue-haired white woman in the room. The lights were dim, but I couldn't help but notice the new addition. She wore a purple dress and red shoes. I thought that was a strange color scheme. But she was at that age where it didn't matter anymore.

"This is Evelyn," Katy said. She wore the clothes she had come to the theater wearing. "She has family in Nebraska. Her son owns a place called the Rusty Nail. Isn't that nice? He says they're held up in a football stadium."

"It's a hole, that bar of his," Evelyn said. "It was when it was his father's, too. I have to go there, though. My Daniel is all I got now. I owe you an apology, Derrick. Just like everyone else, I believed what they said about you—Adam and Bradley and the rest of them."

"It's fine, Ms. Evelyn," I assured her. "No harm, no foul."

"It's the teenagers, you know." She spoke with her hands, waving them around and nearly hitting anyone standing nearby. "I don't mean to sound like your typical old woman, but they don't know what they're doing. You know they murdered a police officer on one of their testosterone-fueled outings? I never thought I'd see the day where we'd start openly hunting people."

"Did they..." Mark made a slicing gesture with his fingers across his throat.

"He's gone," I said.

"How?" Katy asked.

"I don't think that's important," Mark said. And I bet his eyes were green.

"We were out at the shed," Jackie said. "They've got a little group forming. It's not just Khakis and Blue Jeans anymore. There were at least two other ones helping."

"They capture the screamers and lock them in cages, as I'm sure Mark already told you," I continued. "Then they tie you up, leave the room, and come back when the screamers are done with you. Not even cleaning up the mess."

"What's the next step?" Mark asked.

"They're planning to come for Katy."

"What?" she said, panic creeping into her voice.

"Khakis and Blue Jeans have all but let Lee know that we were the ones they ran into on the overpass," I said. "He's still trying to frame me for your murder."

"I'm not dead though," Katy said.

"Not right now, you're not," Jackie said. "They're planning to remedy that, and that's why *you* two have to get into that office. Whatever it takes. And hurry."

All at once the lights in the entire building went out.

Chapter 51

Mark and I followed our memory to the door of room six. The one still-functioning lantern in room six wasn't bright enough to see much as our eyes adjusted to the sudden darkness.

"Be ready to move," he said. "We'll be back in five."

Down the hall a low, angry rumble emanated from room ten. A voice rose among the crowd. The voice sounded like it was coming from the hallway, and it sounded like Lee's. The rumble hushed to a palpable silence.

"It's OK, folks," the voice explained. "Someone probably accidentally cut the power. Incidentally, where is Peter?"

"He is an adamant son of a bitch, isn't he?" Mark asked. "We better hurry."

I followed Mark down the dim corridor toward Lee's office. We passed a suspiciously occupied room two. A group of about eight or nine troops congregated on the other side of the door window in the dark room. We didn't stop to hear what they were huddled together over, but I wondered who the person in the center of the circle was, and what that person was saying.

The room we were after was one door past a women's restroom. We came upon the door just as Khakis emerged from the opposite side of it.

"Oh, hell yes," Mark said under his breath.

In the movies when a character head-butts another character, the motion looks like a face-to-face contact, and there is usually a moment of levity immediately following when the striker makes a silly face in pain and the strikee falls unconscious to the ground. When Mark head-butted Khakis, it was nothing like the movies. Khakis turned around after locking Lee's office, and Mark was already on top of him. Mark grabbed Khakis by the front of his camo shirt and pulled Khakis toward him. He tilted his head forward so that the top of his skull met Khakis right in the center of the face. Blood burst out of Khakis's nose, and his head rebounded back into the door. The keys and an orange bottle of pills fell onto the floor. Mark covered Khakis's mouth and slammed his head back against the heavy office door. Reddish-black liquid ran over Mark's hand. Khakis didn't try to get away. He instead went limp. Mark held Khakis up long enough to take two more swings. When he was ready to let Khakis succumb to gravity, he allowed him to fall to the floor.

Mark put a row of fingers in Khakis's mouth and dragged him by his upper jaw into the women's bathroom next door, knocking him into a gas can on two separate instances. I followed.

"Mark, be calm. You can't kill him. You know that, right?"

Khakis reached for the walkie-talkie clipped to his belt. Mark slapped it across the room.

"The fuck you do," Mark spat at him. "Get out of here."

"Don't kill him." I tried placating his obvious rage.

"Oh my God," Mark snapped. "I'm not going to kill him, OK, Mom? I'm going to hurt him. Get the keys, and get in the office."

Mark straddled Khakis on the floor and whaled on him. I eased back into the hallway, and the door, like a curtain, slowly closed, but not before I saw two more blows connect with the side of Khakis's head.

The keys hadn't moved when I found them with the edge of my shoe. There were only four on the ring, which I considered a blessing. I wasted no time trying them. The third key went into the hole when I heard a weak groan from the bathroom next door. The handle twisted, and the office opened.

Only it wasn't an office. The room was nothing more than a closet. Lanterns hanging at eye level from a pipe running across the ceiling created a yellow glow inside the hovel. There were a couple of gas cans in this room, too, and a pallet made from sleeping bags and sheets, and a black dairy crate with a collection of keys and a pill bottle. There wasn't any room for anything else in the cramped space. I guess living in and out of padded rooms and jail cells gets a person used to a specific type of living.

I dug through the crate looking for a Nissan key. I had forgotten what Jackie told me to find. I found two sets of keys with the logo, and, luckily, at the same time because the first set I saw was obviously not Miguel's. It had two keys on it and twice as many key chains—a *Diary of a Mad Black Woman* lanyard, a grocery-store discount card, a cross made out of yarn and different-color beads, and a pink breast-cancer awareness tag. I would have absentmindedly taken this set without examining it because it had the trusty logo I needed. When I picked it up, a second set lay beneath it. The other was a rusty ring holding about twenty keys, all in different degrees of dirty. On it was a frog key chain attached to a blue carabiner.

I took them both. There would be no way of getting me back to that theater once the four of us—five, counting Evelyn—left. I dug through the crate a little more just to be certain there were no more Nissan emblems hiding at the bottom. When I was satisfied, I still held only two sets of keys. That was going to be it, but as I turned away from the crate, I caught a glimpse of the corner of a picture frame peeking out from underneath the pallet of sleeping bags. I took it out. The picture behind the glass was of a big man with a round face, gelled hair, and a little girl in his arms. I knew immediately that this was the real Adam Barthidge. I wondered if Lee shoved him into a dark corner in the theater he managed before the switch or if Lee had the wherewithal to lock him outside to face the same fate as Randy. My heart went out to him and the girl in his arms.

I put the frame back where I found it. I took one last look into the crate and saw the pill bottle. It was harmless sitting in the crate among a pile of carved metal and plastic, but I knew that pill bottle, and the one on the ground outside the door, were well on the way to creating a small-scale dictatorship. I thought that if I picked them up and tossed them in a sewer drain on the way to the Wendy's down the road, I would single-handedly put an end to Lee's reign. So that's what I did. I plucked the pill bottle out of the crate and went outside to search through the dark to find the other one. When I did, I put them both in the pocket of Ted's baggy work-out pants I was wearing. Shortly after, Mark opened the bathroom door. He was drying his hands on a cluster of paper towels and looked completely normal to the point that I expected to hear the sounds of a toilet on the back end of a flush.

"Water's out." He shook his hands dry. His silly temperament was slowly returning. "Ready?"

"Who's he talking to?" I asked.

"I don't know. No one else was in there."

He opened the door to the bathroom and peeked at the body still on the floor. Khakis spoke feebly. I couldn't see anything but movement in the dark. Then I noticed a small red dot. The walkie-talkie Mark had slapped out of his hand.

"They're down here," Khakis said into it. "By the boss's—"

Mark kicked the walkie out of his hand, and it smashed against the cinder-block wall. Mark swore and dragged me the first few steps down the hallway to the exit. As the door shut behind us, I could hear the footsteps of the small army coming our way.

Outside, Blue Jeans had torn down the fence keeping the generator safe. The orange glow of a gas lantern gave away his position. He banged on something metal with a sledgehammer.

"Hey," Mark screamed. "What's going on? Are you hurting someone?"

Blue Jeans jerked toward him. His eyes widened to golf balls. "I knew it," he said. "You jumped us."

He charged, swinging the hammer, and missed me—just far enough away for me to feel the wind from the swing. Mark and I ran around the corner of the building. Blue Jeans followed.

"It's them," he cried. "Help!"

He was fast. He gained on us quickly, and he was close enough to hit us if he tried. I looked back as Blue Jeans reared the hammer to swing. As he did I halted and punched him in the stomach. He writhed on the ground, gasping for air. He reached for the hammer, but Mark snatched it from his weak grip.

We ran to the front of the building. We ran up to the doors under the veranda, and instead of shaking and waiting for some kid to unlock the door, Mark smashed the door open with the sledge-hammer. The glass shattered into tiny pieces. Pieces hung by the tinted film. He swung one more time to clear a wider entrance and knocked the handrail off the frame. We stepped through unscathed. No one gathered around waiting for us in the lobby. No one waited in the lobby at all. We thought it would be a clean break, but a kid came from one of the hallways and announced our location.

We ran toward room six but were cut off by a second group. They circled us and moved in. Mark took one out by jabbing the handle of the hammer into his stomach. The kid fell to the ground. He gun fell out of his waistband and slid across the floor. The troops rained down on us. I imagined us as a dust cloud of flying limbs like a cartoon. Eventually, Mark dropped the sledgehammer, and we were no longer able to hold our own against twenty kids. Slowly, the troops realized this, and their limbs began flying with confidence. Four of them held us up so the others could take turns running up the score on us. Fists flew. Legs swung. I saw a kid weaving through the crowd, holding a long piece of rope.

Pistol shots rang through the lobby. Everyone stopped. Jackie and Katy stood at the mouth of the hallway, pointing guns into the crowd.

"Let them go," Jackie said.

"Right now," Katy added. She wasn't nervous at all. She shared the look of fury that Jackie wore on her face.

"They can't shoot us all," a voice from behind us said.

Jackie pulled the trigger, and a kid who held the sledgehammer fell to the ground gripping his shoulder and crying.

"Nope," Jackie said. "But we have eighteen more bullets, and we can thin these numbers out. I know where to shoot you so you don't die. Do you really want to be on the ground in the middle of a brawl? Trampled to death holding a bullet wound?"

Coming from the hallway leading to the broom closet and women's bathroom, there was a commotion like someone throwing things in another room. Then the mad shouting of people in pain filled the theater, and the hallway leading to Lee's office erupted into flames.

Chapter 52

I'll be brief. After all, this isn't my story to tell.

A few minutes after Mark and Derrick left room six, Katy told Jackie she had to use the bathroom. Initially, Jackie wouldn't let her go, but when the argument came down to Katy using a corner of the room, Jackie decided to let her go the normal way—only she had to carry a gun and make absolutely sure to disengage the safety. So Katy left, leaving Jackie to anxiously babysit an exuberant and feisty Ms. Evelyn.

At the same time, Lee was speaking in front of the townspeople. Katy heard his exultant voice assuring them that whatever the problem was, he was going to make sure it was fixed and punish anyone responsible. Derrick, essentially. Somewhere in the middle of his speech, a member of the troops tapped him on the shoulder and whispered in his ear. The soldier said that Khakis—or Bradley to that side of the theater—had been jumped in the bathroom. Lee excused himself, asking the people of the theater to please be patient and not leave the theater; it seemed as though the problem had been found. Nobody moved as their fearless leader exited the room.

By the time Blue Jeans chased Mark and Derrick around the building, Lee had made his way through the crowd of teenagers to see the swollen, bleeding face of his right-hand man. He told them to find Thad, Mary, and Pete and bring the three of them to him. The troops broke into two groups and searched up and down the theater hallways. When they got to room six, Katy was in the bathroom, so all they saw were two females sitting in a dark room, and they were looking for neither of them. Lucky for Jackie, the real police officers were making sure the townspeople stayed calm. They moved on to the next room. Because the social norms of the old world clung desperately to the new reality, the troops skipped over the women's restroom across from room six. When the front glass shattered from the sledgehammer, both groups of underage soldiers swarmed to the lobby, leaving Khakis and Lee to the left hallway and Jackie and Katy to the right. In the skirmish a kid-cop lost his gun. Katy nervously picked it up and shot into the ceiling. Her hands trembled. The people in theater ten still waited, even with all the commotion. Most of them silently wanted that murderer Pete to be caught.

When the pistol shots came down the hall, the kids holding Mark and Derrick let go. Then the shouts began. Derrick and Mark ran against the flow of traffic toward Jackie and Katy. Behind them there was a low pop. Derrick turned and watched the fire spread like a wave down the hall. The crowd of teenagers clogged the hallway. Waves of fire swept between their legs. From the other end of the crowd, a projectile gas can flew across the lobby. It was a flaming missile. Gas leaked out of the nozzle, dripping burning liquid along its path toward Mark and Derrick.

"Put 'em out!" one of the older troops ordered.

"Get a hose!" another yelled.

The cans of gasoline were melting and leaking onto the floor, allowing the fire to spread at a vigorous rate. Just as one can's contents were spilled and burning, the heat would melt another can, spilling its insides onto the floor. Eventually, the fire was so hot that the cans would blow up in a *woof* of red, orange, and yellow.

Mark, Jackie, Evelyn, Katy, and Derrick exited out the back of room six. They ran across the parking lot and waited near the hotel.

"Oh my God," Katy said. "What happened?"

None of them could say anything.

When Lee saw what Mark had done to Khakis, the stress of the situation exacerbated whatever caused Lee to sleepwalk, whatever made him need the clozapine, whatever forced him to kill Adam, Jamie, Derrick's parents, and the number of others before and after the change. He went to his closet to find the pills he had been overusing. When he realized they were gone, he snapped completely. Derrick was correct in assuming that those pills were the only things keeping Lee firmly planted at the top. Lee knew it too. And suddenly they were gone. He started banging on the walls. He threw the dairy carton. It bounced around the walls of the closet. Keys flew around the room. He slung the makings of the pallet into the hall and then knocked over a lantern. Then he knocked all of them down. The oil spilled out, and the flicker inside the lanterns came outside. In his hysterical fit, he slung the lanterns out into the hallway. They cracked and leaked down the walls and into the carpet. Instead of helping the troops put out the flames, he knocked over a few gas cans. The rest was just nature.

"Should we save them?" Evelyn asked.

"I don't think we can," Derrick said.

"The water is out," Mark said coldly. "There's nothing we can do."

Heat vapors slowly surrounded the entrance to the theater. The tips of the flames licked the top of the doorframe. Then, with almost no notice, the rest of the glass doors broke open, and a huge mushroom of black smoke and red inferno rose from the doors. Standing a hundred or so feet away, they could feel the flames warm their faces in the chill of the winter night. Three pops sounded from inside the theater. Then nothing. The light spread across the parking lot. Pounding on the walls of the hotel began. The screamers wanted out. Now they had a reason to break their bodies getting through the walls. A window in one of the top floors broke. A few seconds later, a body thumped onto the concrete sidewalk. Furious screams from a few dozen feet up. Shrieks poured out of the room and into the night. Oddly enough, nothing came from the theater. No people. No shouts of pain. No sounds at all but the susurration of a hungry fire. The group in the parking lot would remember that. They would never forget that silence.

"We have to get to the Wendy's," Jackie said.

Derrick turned away from the scene.

The small group of survivors fled the parking lot to the end of the service road where only the street separated the little unit from the Wendy's. Derrick could still hear the banging on the hotel walls. The screamers boarded up inside were pounding their way out. He wondered why only one person left the flames. The kids in the lobby tried to leave, but the pops they heard from their place in the parking lot were the sound of a handgun. When the ones who were burning finally dropped to the ground and expired, the few left made their way to the door. Lee gunned them down. Then he tossed a few more cans of the gasoline down the hallway where his loyal following waited for death. Derrick thought maybe they stayed in the theater because they were afraid of the things that waited out-side the door. Maybe there wasn't any time to leave the room before the flames swallowed them whole. He was wrong. Their reason for not leaving the building was because Lee told them not to. In that crazy time, it was enough for them. Most of them were able to justify their immobility with the idea that God had finally decided to take them after all. And in some overromanticized way, they weren't far off. It wasn't time to take them to heaven, but time for their lives to end. Only one person left the building as the flames conquered the walls of the theater and its inhabitants. Derrick saw no discernible face from that far away. There was no voice to its screams. But he knew who it was. Even consumed in red, blazing fire, the man was yellow. Lee stopped as if looking at them, watching them leave the kingdom he created under the pseudonym of Adam Barthidge. The only reason he left the building was one last effort to bring them back. He needed control. He fell to his knees, and it was over. The doors of the hotel gave way, and the madness inside spilled out into the parking lot. Derrick felt those teeth of rage release. The warm place where they had been clamped cooled in a river of sudden relief.

He ran.

A simple click of the red button marked "!" on the Nissan key gave the group a direct path to the truck. Derrick tried his best to ignore the license plate that read, "H41 0JM." They piled into the cab and left for the police station. No one said anything, not even Evelyn, until the car reached the station.

Chapter 53

If someone had told me that I would be sleeping on a tabletop in the center of the station after what I just went through, I wouldn't have been excited. I would have thought I'd be spending a night of indefatigable rolling around on a card table with my feet and head hanging off opposite sides. I would have been certain that the last known inhabitants of the city would have marched up and down the halls of the police station making every kind of noise imaginable. Luckily I was wrong. In actuality the table was covered in a number of thick blankets, the power was cut within an hour of our arrival, and I was sleeping in the quiet meeting room where we once huddled around Katy's cell phone. The table was large enough for Katy, Mark, Jackie, and me to sleep on comfortably without anyone invading anyone else's space. That's not what happened, though. Katy and I slept on the conference room table while Mark and Jackie slept in the adjoining offices on either side.

"You OK?" Katy asked after the station fell dark and muffled voices around the building were no more. Our heads were on opposite ends of the long table, and when she spoke, her foot nudged mine playfully.

"I was actually almost asleep."

"I can't sleep. I feel like we did something wrong."

"We didn't. We tried to help them."

"It just feels that way. The police officers here went up and down the streets trying to find more people. There are only about twenty leaving on the buses tomorrow. That's including the ones who plan to leave in their own cars. There're not many people here. It makes me feel very alone. I miss my friends."

"The ones from your apartment?"

"No, the ones those people used to be. We had fun. Bowling, drinking, watching overpriced movies at a nonhomicidal theater."

I laughed. "Yeah, eventually things will be normal again."

"How do you know?"

"Well, nothing is ever different for long. Eventually, change becomes a regular part of life. And that becomes normal."

"God, I miss normal."

There was a moment where we didn't say anything.

"Are you guys going to bone?" Mark asked from behind the open office door.

"Well done, buddy," Katy said.

"If you need some rest, we can just shut the door." I got up from the table.

"Don't be that way, guy," he said. "No, it's cool. I can totally let you—"

I closed the door and felt my way to the table. I climbed up and noticed that Katy's feet were no longer where they had been. Instead a pillow rested in the middle of the high-rise bed.

"Please don't kick me," she said from the pillow.

"Did you switch places?"

"Yes. Bring your pillow this way. These shitty things are too thin. We may as well be laying our heads directly on the table. You don't mind sharing, do you?"

"I don't." I moved my pillow to the center and stacked it first over her face. That got a laugh and she adjusted the stack beneath her.

I lay beside her on the pillow, our feet at opposite ends of the table now. We listened to each other breathe in the dark, cold room. I pictured my wife in her hotel room. I wondered again what the significance of 410 was.

"That was the worst thing that ever happened to me," Katy said.

"What was?"

"Everything. From the past couple days."

"I'm sure it was the worst thing to happen to a lot of people."

"I don't mean the change, or whatever happened, or the people losing it. I'm talking about the theater. The people who didn't change. I know for the most part they were out to get us, but a lot of them were innocent. They were just stuck in a bad situation. I talked to them. Some of them were kids. Do you remember the little boy with the cards?"

"Yeah, James."

"They really thought you did something to him." In the glow of the moonlight coming through the window, I could see her breath plume up toward the ceiling. "I know you didn't. So what did happen to him? He had nobody. He was just an orphan."

"I really don't know. He said he was just going to leave. Come to think of it, I'm pretty sure he didn't even say it. He just left."

"What if he's still out there? What if he's in a ditch scared?"

"I don't know," I said. I knew one thing, though. That kid wasn't scared to be out there.

"I don't mean to get heavy or anything. It's just something else to process."

"I get it." I tried to put a hand on her shoulder. In the dark I just found the top of her hair. The consolatory shoulder pat became an upside-down tousle. That made her laugh.

"It's a shame we didn't meet under better circumstances." Katy turned to face me.

"Yeah," I said as I turned my face to her. I couldn't see her very well, but I pictured her upside-down head resting on the pillow. "I don't know how that would have worked, you being from South Carolina and me being from California."

"It's weird how we ended up together, y'all saving my life. I don't know what I would've done if y'all hadn't been there. That's scary to think about."

"But we were there." We were both falling asleep. "And now we're here."

"We made it," she said. She was already dreaming.

"We made it."

Chapter 54

Katy was still asleep when I woke the next morning. The lights were on in the building for the last time. I could smell coffee brewing from somewhere, and that made me unable to close my eyes. I slowly drew the blanket back and eased off the table. I followed my nose to the office where Jackie had slept and shut the door behind me. I was disoriented from the amount of sleep I had gotten. I've never been someone who wakes up past nine in the morning.

"Mind if I get a piece of that?"

"What?" Jackie said defensively from behind the desk.

"The coffee?"

"Oh," she said. She pointed to a collection of plastic cups next to coffee maker. "I thought you were asking for something else."

Most of the cups had already been used.

"What time it is?" I poured some coffee.

"You just drink it black?"

"I like my coffee like I like my woman."

"In a plastic cup?"

"Exactly." We laughed tiredly at the shared reference.

Jackie looked at her watch. "It's nearly noon."

"Seriously?" I asked. "I usually wake up at seven."

"People are wired to a natural sleep cycle that lasts longer than a twenty-four-hour day."

"Is that true?"

"I don't know," she said. "I read an article about it once."

"Never knew that. What time do we set sail?"

"When everyone else wakes up. Hopefully within an hour."

"Did Miguel and his daughter make it here?"

"They already left. They had packed his truck and were headed south before most people were up."

"You think they'll make it?"

"If they get out of Louisiana, they have a pretty good chance. He's got nothing but dirty highways for hundreds of miles to look forward to."

"What if he runs out of gas?"

"We're ahead of schedule, and we shut the power off last night, so we were able to spare enough for an extra tank, maybe a little more. If New Orleans is as far along as we suspect, he may be able to stop for a fill-up."

"Well, all right," I said. "What's our plan then?"

"We're going to finish loading up the buses with as many gas cans and as much food as we have. Then when everyone is up, we'll head out. One bus headed north, the other west."

"What was that face about?" I asked.

"It's just unsettling how ready to be outside Jacobson is," Jackie said. "I'm worried that the only reason he stayed here was to move on to a bigger city with more of them."

"Why did the police split up?"

"I thought it would be best to keep everyone together and move on to a bigger city. Officer Tamlin wanted to stay in Jackson. Normally, the chief of police would have made a comment about our periods syncing up, but he was one of them. We argued and argued for about an hour. The only thing we did agree on was to have everyone who could meet us in the theater. It was empty. There was food and space to lie down. So we put it to a vote. The majority of the police officers voted for leaving. The rest took out their guns and said if we were seen anywhere near the theater, that'd be all they needed. They wanted to stay. Their lives were here, and they refused to leave it behind. We made the case that there was no life here with so few people. No one listened. That's the problem with debating. Without neutral parties with nothing to gain, no one changes their minds. It's just yelling for the sake of yelling. Those people would still be alive."

"No, those people were stubborn. Some change is mandatory. What would they have done with fifty people? Most of them were either too old or too young to be able to really contribute. After the testosterone wore off and it was time to really move on, what could they have done?"

"I guess you're right. They could've had a chance if they'd just listened."

She was right. Debates do nothing in the way of changing a person's mind. I figured the only thing this conversation could do was get worse. After a moment I asked, "So which way are you going? North or west?"

"With you guys. Was that not obvious?"

"I assumed. I just didn't know if you had somewhere else to be."

"Cheers," she said. We raised our plastic cups.

Mark walked into the room with his eyes nearly closed and his hair reaching in all directions but down. He wore only a T-shirt and underwear. He shambled from the door to the coffeepot, poured a cup, and left without saying anything. He held up a peace sign as he pulled the door. It swung shut as slowly as Mark walked. The door caught on the threshold and didn't close.

"If you want, you can come downstairs with me. I'm going to check on the progress of loading the buses. It should be finished by now."

"Sure, let's go." I downed the rest of the coffee. It burned my throat, and my eyes watered.

The corridors of the police station were surprisingly lively considering the lack of noise. Just outside the parking garage, there were two buses pointed in reverse directions, like two men in a duel. Police officers at each locked the back doors and made their way back to the building. Officer Jacobson stood in the road with a shotgun. The red scruff on his face had been shaved since the last time I had seen him. He stood like a gorilla in the street. Jackie was right. He was a little too ready for something to happen. The shotgun he carried looked like a popgun a child would use in the backyard to play army. His hair still looked wet, but it was slicked back instead of reaching like fingers down his forehead.

"Seems a bit ballsy right before we blow town," I told Jackie. "Are we not worried about the screamers anymore?"

"They're all on the other side of town."

"How do you know?"

She pointed to huge black cloud lingering over the approximate area of the theater. "They followed the smoke. I guess they saw movement and went that way."

"So I guess that wasn't a terrible dream." I touched the bandage on my head.

"I don't think it was."

"I can't believe it's still burning."

"No one was there to put it out," Jackie said with a tone of boredom. "It's probably spread to the woods by now. Maybe even farther."

"How far do you think it will go before it stops?"

"I don't know. The good news is, it's not our problem. We're not from here anymore."

Only thirty minutes later, the buses were loaded with people as well as supplies. The buses looked pitiful with only about a dozen people in each one. Jackie told the rest of the police officers that it wouldn't be a bad idea to bring the Jeep with us to New Orleans because there was enough gas in it to make it far beyond that, and it may even come in handy if the bus were to break down. With that the driver of the bus tossed her a walkie-talkie and told her to keep in touch. Mark took the shotgun seat beside her in the Jeep, and Katy and I took the back again. The black smoke cloud filled the city with a sorrowful gray haze. As we left, I surveyed the disarray outside my window. Pieces of people and buildings had been strewn all over the streets. Jackie weaved through pileups and around broken-down cars. The smell of fire stayed with us until we were well out of Jackson.

INTERMISSION

We play games to pass the time.

It wasn't all bad—the time between what happened and now. Once the four of us were together and back on the road to New Orleans, I felt much more at ease. The drive from Jackson was a straight shot down one interstate all the way to the Gulf. After the initial departure from the city, we didn't have to radio to the bus ahead at all. Even if we separated from the big yellow escort, we would've found our way to Louisiana on our own. Just keep true, Cap'n. We'll being hitting land by sundown.

"So what are you good at?" Mark posed to everyone in the car. "Or what were you good at, I guess. Technology pending."

"Farming," I joked.

"No," Mark corrected. "That was your job. I'm talking about a skill or something totally separate from everything else in your life. Something we probably wouldn't guess."

"OK." I thought about it.

"Derrick can shoot a gun," Katy chimed. "Give him three bullets, and he could circumcise you with two. I've basically seen him do it."

"Well, good thing I don't need that service. I can't imagine recoil helping too much with the steady hand. I was thinking more like something we didn't know already about you."

"I can punt a football," I said.

"Wow," Mark said, totally unimpressed.

"I'm talking NFL-quality kicking."

"No, keep going," Jackie said. "You're only getting cooler, Mr. Guy."

"I wish I was Ray Guy."

"And what's your thing?" Katy asked her.

"I can do a backflip on a bicycle." Jackie mimed dropping a microphone. "Off the trunk of a police car."

"You still do that?" Mark said, more bored than amused.

"Of course I still do it. That's how I know I can still do it."

"I'm really good at bowling," Katy said.

"What?" Mark said. "There are no bowling alleys anymore. That was a thing in the nineties."

"I'm serious. I went the night all this happened, actually. Two eighty-nine."

"Little thing like you could not throw a bowling ball, let alone score a two eighty-nine," Jackie declared. "Unless you mean in two games you scored eighty-nine each time?"

"No," Katy's matter-of-fact tone was nonconfrontational. "I've hit a perfect game."

"That's awesome," I said, although I was still on the fence about believing her. "I would love to see that. Especially from you."

"What do you mean especially from me?" she asked.

"You just don't look like a bowler," Jackie said for me.

"What do you think bowlers look like exactly?"

"Lesbians," Mark said.

"Wow," Katy said.

"I'm just saying," Mark began. "The only way to tell the difference between softball players and lady bowlers is whether or not the shirts have numbers on the back." He chuckled. "I feel the women in the car hating me now, so I guess I need to actually say that I'm just kidding on this one."

"Probably a smart move." Jackie punched his arm.

That was pretty much where we left the conversation. Mark claimed that his secret skill was the ability to make any woman fall madly in love with him, and the conversation changed. It wasn't until nearly an hour and a half later that we saw the sign. In huge, glittering, space-age font, a billboard declared with wild fervor: 4TH DIMENSION BOWLING! BEST LANES IN THE STATE NEXT EXIT. Jackie picked up the walkie-talkie.

"Officer Jacobson, this is Officer Phillips. We're experiencing that trouble with the battery again. I'm going to pull over and adjust."

"Do you need us to stop?" Officer Jacobson asked.

"No, I think between the four of us, we'll be back on the road in a matter of minutes. Just continue toward the Easy."

"Roger, Wilco."

"Who's Roger Wilco?" Mark asked.

"He won an Oscar for *Casablanca*," Katy said. I laughed.

"Do you really want to know?" Jackie asked, activating the blinker.

"Sure," I said.

"Roger stands for the letter *R*, which is short for 'received.' And Wilco is a shorter way of saying 'will comply.' The more you know, right?"

"Hmm," I said, having learned something new. "What's wrong with the battery?"

"Nothing," Jackie said. "We're going to have a little fun."

She took the car off the exit and headed in the direction of a building that I thought was the largest one-story building I had ever seen. The sun reflected brightly on the huge glass entrance, which spanned most of the front of the building. Maybe twenty feet of brick stood on both sides of the entrance to keep the glass erect. The roof was more brick, but there was a staggeringly massive sign blocking most of it.

The sign was a black bowling ball wearing a crown tilted jauntily to one side with a red, a green, and a blue gem, each on a spike of its own. The closer we came to the building, the easier it was to see the starlight pattern painted on the ball. Above the crown read, 4TH DIMENSION BOWLING! And of course at the bottom of the ball was BEST LANES IN THE STATE! The font was white with black stars and tilted at an angle so it looked like it was coming right at us.

Jackie parked the car right at front of the building—nearly close enough to check to see if the door was locked without getting out. From where we sat, I could understand why this place would be considered the best lanes in the state. The location was right in the middle of nothing but grass and the occasional tree for miles and miles. There was nothing but the interstate north, south, east, and west. Not even a house off in the distance. There were trees blocking most of the building from the view of the road, so I would've agreed then and there that when any random person stumbled across this place, it had to be the best thing in the state. There were only two cars in the lot, and if *it* happened on a Monday night, I suppose that made sense. I don't assume however many operating bowling alleys there were when it happened had much business when the week started back up.

"What is *boweling*?" Mark asked. "Am I saying that right?"

"What do you say?" Jackie proposed. "Perfect game?"

The three of us looked at Katy. She smiled so wide I could almost see her back teeth. I think I could almost see tears welling up in her eyes. She wanted that moment as bad as I wanted her to have it. This was the normalcy she needed.

Katy said, "It's why we're here, isn't it?"

"That's the spirit," Jackie said. "Mark, go see if the door is locked."

"Uh, yessa, Massa," he said as if he was annoyed but did it with a smile on his face. He got out, and we watched him pull on all four doors. "It's locked," he said, coming back to the car. "Maybe next time."

The moment he was out of the direct path of the Jeep, Jackie floored the accelerator. The big SUV smashed through the glass windows, and before I could process what had happened, we were parked in the lobby of the best bowling alley in the state of Mississippi.

"That's my fault, guys. I thought I was on the brake, not the accelerator."

"Sure thing, Officer," I said.

"At least count to three next time. *Fuck!*" Mark said.

"I'm sorry," Jackie told Katy and me as she unbuckled her seat belt. "What do you say we knock this out? What size shoe do you wear?"

"Uh, seven," Katy said nervously.

"You guys good back there?" Jackie said.

"Yeah," Katy and I said at the same time. My heart was drumming.

"Then let's do it." Jackie left the car.

"You left the lights on," Mark said from behind us. He was right.

I reached forward and shut them off. The lights and the chirping from the car both stopped at the same time. Katy and I both stared forward from the backseat.

"That took me by surprise," I said.

"Yeah."

We slowly got out of the car.

There was hardly a scratch on the car. I don't know why, but that stuck out to me the most. Aside from the chaos created by the Jeep, the alley looked innocuous enough to pass for normal. There were forty lanes sweeping across my vision from far left to far right, and all of them in perfect order. All four hundred pins stood at attention. The floor was a bright-white carpet with bowling-meets-space-travel designs on them. There were pins with flames shooting from the bottom like a rocket. There were bowling balls with meteor divots like the moon. Pins dressed in space suits. Pins riding rockets as if they were bucking broncos. One piece of clip art was even on the posters and curtains. It was the ball with the three-jeweled crown with a rocket pin swooping around it as if in orbit. 4TH DIMENSION was written above it and BOWLING written below, and the font was tilted so that it looked like it was coming right at us.

Two televisions hung above each pair of lanes. I imagined that typically they kept score and played animated graphics when a bowler made a strike or spare or gutter. For us they were solemn and black. Jackie rummaged behind a taller-than-usual counter looking for shoes. There was a lifeless arcade to my left and a pool hall to my right. Both had more things to play on than I ever would have thought necessary. Dividing the lobby area from the bowling area, there were racks of balls three shelves high. Each shelf held six balls, and each lane had its own rack. Glancing across, I noticed that every single ball on a rack was the same color.

"I'm going to make sure no one is here." Mark made his way around the building.

"Want to help me look for a ball?" Katy asked.

"Yeah, let's do it." I followed her to the ball racks.

Going through the racks, I noticed each rack was meticulously organized by size. The top row held the smallest, and the balls were heavier in descending order. I picked up the first ball. It was maybe three or four pounds. The holes were very close together, and the tip of my pinkie stuck in the thumbhole. I picked it up and turned to Katy.

"This one good?" I asked and dangled the ball in front of me.

She laughed. I pulled the ball off me. It made a comical sucking pop. I saw that even the balls had the 4TH DIMENSION BOWLING logo engraved between the three holes. Below the place for the thumb read, "Size 1."

"I think I found one," Katy said from behind. She lifted the ball over her hand with one arm and sang a note like an angelic choir. She walked to lane one and haphazardly rolled the ball down the gutter. "No, I need to come down one." She picked up the ball next in line on the rack and rolled it down the opposite gutter. "Per-r-rfect," she crooned.

I heard the balls clunking together behind the pins.

I was looking at the engraved logo on another ball. It was bright blue. The way the television in my head was. I knew what size she wanted before she said it. I looked from the four in the logo to the "Size 10."

"Why don't we do this," Jackie said, handing Katy a pair of blue-and-red bowling shoes. The white tongue and rubber soles had browned over time. "There are forty lanes. Why don't we put a ball at each lane? No waiting, just chucking. You only need ten, right?"

Forty divided by ten is four—410, I thought.

"Actually, twelve is plenty," Katy corrected. "Two extra to finish out the tenth frame."

"Right."

Katy and I glanced at each other when Jackie said it.

"So you have at least twenty-eight rolls to warm yourself up. You think that's enough?" Jackie said.

"Just the twelve is fine," Katy said again with a cocky grin.

"I think we're clear," Mark said from the pool hall. "What are we doin'?"

"We got your shoes. What size ball do you need?" Jackie asked.

"Eleven," Katy said.

I flushed with relief without realizing I was tense in the first place.

"Take all the elevens from the racks and put them on the weird conveyer belts." Jackie handed Katy the shoes. "One for each lane. We're going for the perfect game. Batting a thousand."

Mark jogged to one rack of balls. "What size?"

"Eleven."

"Seven?"

"Eleven," the three of us corrected.

"Do I have to say that I'm kidding every time? There's no one here. Of course I heard you. Does it matter what color?"

I handed Katy the blue eleven from my rack. She compared the weights and finger holes like an old scale. "Nope, they're all the same."

"What else can we do while we get set up?" Jackie said.

"I feel goofy being the only one dressed up," Katy said. "Do y'all mind if we all wear the shoes?"

Jackie took our shoe sizes and jumped behind the counter again. A few minutes later, all the preparations had been completed. All the demands had been met.

"Batter up," Mark said. He was watching casually, like someone flipping through the channels who had finally found something that wasn't a commercial.

Katy picked up the first ball. It was green. Standing beside the conveyer belt thing—I still don't know what to call it—she raised the ball to eye level. She stepped forward. The normal bowler has more of a straight-arm rear back than a bend, and there is sort of a sliding motion to the roll. Katy's motion was much different. The ball never really fell past her waistline. She bent her elbow first, then her arm came back, and rather than a slide, she pushed the ball forward with a twist of her right hand. The ball hit the edge of the wooden lane, spinning almost completely to the left. It teetered over the edge of the gutter for most of the length of the lane, and then right at the end, the ball snapped across and charged through the pins. It was like watching fireworks. I could see the burning fuse float up into the air and the burst of color. A scatter of white jumbled like flailing fingers in the dark. Then they all lay, a few spinning as if giving a courtesy wipe for the next set of pins to collapse without getting their bottoms dirty. I imagined the paint on the ball melting and the wooden remains sitting in a pool of green.

"Holy shit," Jackie said.

"Yeah, no kidding," I said.

"All right," Katy said, finally turning to us. "I think I'm ready to go."

Mark didn't say anything, but I could tell he was at least a little bit interested in what had happened. Katy continued five more rolls, getting two turkeys in a row. Then fate's dirty hand swooped down and held up one defiant seven pin. The air left the room.

"Dammit," Katy said under her breath.

"Oh, fuck that," Mark said. He ran down the lane, slipping in the grease, and slid into the last remaining pin. He groaned in pain as he landed on the other nine pins, the ball, and whatever machinery lay in the darkness beyond the pins. "I ate it. Oh my God. I ate it so hard. Oh, I hate that I just did that."

He came back out with three pins. His limp reappeared, and he fell once walking back to us in the grease. "Have you guys ever felt one of these things? They weigh like ten pounds."

He tossed one to me and I nearly dropped it. They were heavy. Much heavier than they look bouncing around at the other side of the room.

"Could you imagine juggling these things?" He tossed one up; it flipped multiple times, and he caught it by the small end.

"All right, I just have to start over," Katy said. "No big deal."

"You want to wait a little?" I asked. "Let your arm cool off?"

"I'm warmed up now."

She got all the way to eight in a row. The ninth throw left the five pin and the seven pin.

"Shit!" Mark screamed. "What the hell, man. It was shaking! They have dirt at the bottom. Someone is a cheat."

"You want to go knock them down for her again?" Jackie asked.

"I'd rather not, honestly."

"Damn, I thought that was it," Katy said.

We all thought that was it. "Take a second this time," I advised. "We're in no hurry."

"You're right. I'm starting to feel it. Maybe I should go down a size."

I nervously went to the rack and picked up a size-ten ball. I handed it to Katy. She rocked it back and forth like a normal bowler's motion. With twenty-four frames to go, she started over. The first frame, down. Second, third, no problem. Katy's fourth throw was probably the most fun to watch of the entire day. The yellow ball reflected even the most microscopic amount of light and multiplied it by five. Eight pins went straight up and back. One pin from the right spun like a propeller across the lane and knocked the one remaining pin back toward Katy. It was electric. Five went down without a problem. Six was a black ball, so when the flare of pins went up, it was kind of like a magic trick. Seven dropped like a bag of hammers. Eight went down even harder. It wasn't until the ninth frame that a problem arose. In lane thirty-nine there was a commotion, or more accurately, a fallen body. It thumped hard onto the wooden floor. Pins toppled over into the lane. Mark jumped to his feet.

We turned toward the sound. The screamer flailed and slipped on the grease. Jackie, Katy, and I perked up. We stood very still as it struggled to stand. Mark immediately laughed so hard that his legs gave way, and he fell back into the chair.

"Mark, come on, man," I said.

"Don't worry." He picked up one of the three pins he had been using to practice juggling. He strolled arrogantly toward the slipping and sliding man, probably the owner of the best lanes in the state. He certainly dressed for the part, even down to the red-white-and-blue shoes. Two lanes away Mark pulled back and let the pin fly. It was quick. When the sound of the spinning pin silenced, Mark turned back. The ninth frame ended with a third consecutive turkey.

Tenth frame. The homerun. The breadwinner. Three hundred. First ball, solid as a rock. She was automatic. The blue ball barreled through like a monster. We cheered for Katy. When those ten little white shapes hit the ground, we roared. None of us knew how to encourage bowling, so we could only offer words of encouragement from other sports. Knock it out of the park. Going long. Slam dunk. Whatever came to mind, we threw it out there for her to accept as roses after an encore. And that's where we were. The end of her set. She had nailed the performance, and now she was coming back for two more songs. Her greatest hits. If two rolls of a bowling ball could ever be considered as much, that was the appropriate time for it.

The eleventh roll ended with the boom and shatter we had come to expect after the bang of the ball hitting the floor. Pins rained down on the empty stage at the end of the lane. We cheered again, loud enough for even a screamer to hear. Katy jumped and slapped one of the nonfunctioning televisions hanging overhead. Mark, Jackie, and I cheered and applauded.

"Only one to go," Katy announced as we moved down one more lane.

"Hell, yeah, only one more. You can do it. You've done it more than twenty times already in a matter of minutes. You take this yellow ball, and you shove it up those pins' asses." Mark slapped Katy on her behind and took a seat next to me. "Goddamn it! I can't believe you made me care about this."

Katy stood at the conveyer belt like a statue. She breathed deeply. Her shoulders rose and fell. She took one step, stopped, and readjusted the ball. Jackie punched Mark hard on the back of the arm.

"The fuck?" he screamed.

"I'm sorry! I'm just so excited." Jackie's hands were shaking.

My hands were shaking.

Katy repositioned herself next to the conveyer belt. We were stone. Nobody moved. Nobody breathed. Katy's shoulders rose and fell one last time. She stepped forward; bent her elbow; pulled her arm back; and with the flick of her wrist, the yellow ball flew. It stayed there in midair for a month, maybe twenty. We stood from our chairs. The ball came down. It rode the edge of the lane all the way down. Then just at the last second, it jerked left and hit home. The pins erupted.

We lost control.

We cheered. We yelled. We ran to Katy and hugged her as tightly as we could. Mark, in a fit of excitement, ran to the nearest rack of balls, picked up a size one and overhanded it toward the first full set of pins. It crashed into the barrier between lanes and bounced back. We filled that empty bowling alley with jubilation. I don't think that I'd felt more happy than in that moment. To think I had only known them a matter of days. It was an incredible feeling. It was the exact release we needed. Four people who one week before had never so much as pretended to murder someone in their minds, who had suddenly been forced into a situation in which murder, now necessary for survival, unloaded. We fell to the floor.

Then the screamers stumbled out from behind the pins. There were eight of them when they finally stopped piling out from the darkness. They were screaming louder than we ever were. They slid for a moment in the grease, but when they realized the gutter had good enough traction, they had no problem making their way toward us.

"Run!" Jackie called. She and Katy sprinted to the car.

Mark and I heaved a size one each. Mine caught a leg and sent screamer tumbling into another one. Mark's found a face. Only one screamer found purchase on the carpeted lobby floor, and it bolted after us. It caught Mark by the shirt. It dragged him down and started pounding and ripping at his face. It pulled a chunk out of his beard. I ran back for him. The thing bent over him looked up just as my foot connected. I felt its nose crunch. Mark got to his feet just as the Jeep roared to life and the wheels spun on the carpet. Mark and I dove out of the way. Suddenly, the thing's broken nose was the least of its worries.

"Get up!" Jackie commanded, and we did.

We piled into the passenger side and locked ourselves in the car. The Jeep fishtailed around and plowed through another plate-glass window. The car bounced violently over the threshold. In a matter of seconds, we were back on the interstate.

"That asshole." Mark checked his swelling face in the overhead mirror. "Son of a bitch fucked up my beard. Took a month to get it this thick."

"Everyone all right?" Jackie asked.

"We're good," Katy said.

"I'm fine," I told her.

"Good thing you switched to the ten when you did," Mark said. "I don't think we could have afforded to try it again."

"Yeah," Katy said. "That was really nice, you guys. I'm sorry you got hurt, Mark."

"You should see the other guy."

"It was just nice to have something normal," Katy said. "I don't know if I'll ever be able to do that again."

"If that's the case, you went out in style. You told us you were going to get a three hundred, and then you got a three hundred," Jackie said. "That's like the Babe pointing to the outfield and knocking one out of the park."

I looked down at the bowling shoes we had now stolen from the abandoned alley. That was the moment I realized that the number 410 wasn't foreboding some destructive event to fear. I truly believed that Katy never would have knocked down 120 consecutive pins if she had stayed with the size-eleven balls. That was when I decided the best thing to do would be to steer into the skid. Let the number show me what it wanted. I still didn't understand the validity of forty lanes, though. We didn't need that many. I guess the extra ones were only there to prove that no matter what we're given, too much or not enough, we find a way to make it work. The car eased back onto the interstate going south, and those precious idiosyncrasies of normal human behavior took over again.

PART 5
NEW ORLEANS

Land Ho!

Chapter 55

After the worst thing that ever happened, I didn't think anything would ever be normal again. The Big Easy, as usual, did not disappoint. Between Jackson and the outskirts of New Orleans, there were almost no cars. The visual droning of passing trees put me in some sort of trance. Roving through the spider's web of highway and exit ramps proved to be absolutely boring, to be perfectly honest. After an hour from the middle-of-nowhere bowling alley, the conversation inside the car tapered off. I was lost in thought, looking out the window at the passing trees, when eventually Mark broke the silence.

"You know, you could fog a mirror, but I wouldn't exactly call you alive." He spied on me from the gap between the seat and the door.

"Very funny." I rubbed my eyes in an effort to wake myself back up. "Any idea how far out we are?"

"I'd say less than five minutes if we were following the speed limit," Jackie announced. "I can haul ass with no one in our way. I don't know how wide open we can get in the city. Might as well get it out of my system."

I looked between the front seats at the dashboard to check her speed. The car was pushing one hundred. Maybe it was boredom or maybe it was the comfort of knowing she was a cop, but instead of worrying, I just sat back in the seat and enjoyed the ride. Katy slept next to me. I nudged her arm to wake her. She looked at me sideways, and without lifting her head, she announced that she had to use the bathroom.

"We're almost to a potty, teddy bear," Mark said as though he were talking to a toddler. "We're gonna pull over and let you have a tee-tee. Does that sound good?"

"Ew." Katy groaned.

"You're the one who's gotta do it, man." Mark turned his attention to Jackie. "I know we weren't at the bowling alley very long. You've had it to the floor this entire time. Shouldn't we have run into Jacobson and the bus by now?"

"I would have thought so," Jackie said, narrowly avoiding a screamer running at the car from the trees. "Maybe he was speeding too."

"Would that have been safe in a bus?"

"No," Jackie said. "Come to think of it, school buses have a governor on them that prevents them from going over sixty-five." Jackie picked up the walkie-talkie and clicked twice. "It's probably out of range, but it doesn't hurt to check."

"Do you think something happened?"

"I can't imagine what could have happened," Jackie said. "It's a straight shot. We would've seen the bus if they had to pull over or something. I'll try again in a minute."

"Do you think he would know how to override the governor?" I asked.

"That would put those people in danger," Jackie said. "I just don't think he'd do that."

Jackie eased off the accelerator and narrowly avoided a pack of screamers. I thought about what she said after her team made the jump-starter run. About how Jacobson seemed a little too happy to be in action.

"They're showing up more and more," Mark said. "We must be close."

Up ahead a metal structure displayed a number of green signs directing drivers to different locations in town. Dangling from the fixture was a white tarp that stretched across multiple lanes on both sides of the road. In huge black spray-painted letters the sign read

WELCOME, FOLLOW THE SMOKE

"What smoke?" Katy asked. She and I leaned forward between the front seats.

"Do you not see it?" Mark asked. He was pointing forward to the center of the city.

The skyline of New Orleans isn't the most impressive in the country. It is dwarfed in comparison to cities like New York, Seattle, or Chicago. But when I saw the red smoke billowing up from the roof of a thin, white skyscraper, my jaw dropped. It was like looking at a burning match. I had never seen anything like it. So much went through my mind.

Chapter 56

As we drove deeper into town, the building with the red smoke seemed to never get any closer. Jackie maneuvered the car through roadblocks and pileups through a residential area just outside the city. There were neighborhoods and convenience stores on both sides of the highway. An ominous lifelessness filled the air. There were no people, no screamers, not even a bird flying overhead. That, of course, changed. We mounted the crest of a hill and saw the yellow bus stopped on the line dividing the lanes.

"What are the odds that's a good thing?" Mark asked.

"We don't know if it's the same one," I said.

"Mississippi plate," Katy answered.

Jackie stopped the Jeep alongside the bus. I never noticed how big those things were until then. So long and open. So many opportunities for a homicidal invalid to come shrieking forth, ripping and clawing. I never rode the bus as a kid, nor did bullies ever pick on me. But staring through the side window, knowing that within five minutes I'd be walking on board, I suddenly understood how someone dealing with both might feel.

"Do you see anything?" Katy asked.

"No," Mark said.

I opened the door an inch or so before Katy reached over the seat and jerked it closed again.

"Are you crazy?" she asked.

"I'm just going to get out and look around," I said. "I feel like we need to know."

I opened the door again, and Mark followed. "OK, Robin, let's go."

"Robin?" I asked.

"You're not Batman," he said. "I'm taller."

"I'm not Robin."

"OK," he said. "Li'l Bat. Leave your door open like with the truck. Anything moves, we're taking off."

Jackie eased the Jeep forward so that we were clear of the front of the bus. Mark and I crept along the side, looking for feet on the other side of the undercarriage and the tops of heads over the Jeep and inside the bus's windows. I only saw a lot of fluid on the ground beneath the bus. No one inside the bus. No one anywhere else. We were in the clear. My heart pounded enough to ache as we walked along the side of the bus toward the door. The engine radiated heat. The outside of the vehicle was almost too hot to touch. The accordion door was flat across the opening. I pushed the centerfold, and the door folded inward.

"Hello," I called. My voice shook as though I were freezing.

No one answered.

I put one foot on the bottom step. The hydraulics on the old bus creaked. I looked under the seats. All the way to the back, I saw a box of candy that had fallen out of the seat and lay on its side. About midway back I saw pale, white fingers hanging from one of the seats. I counted seven seats back. I called out again with no answer. I stepped all the way onto the next step and peered around the front seat. I saw no one. All the way to the back in a pile against the back exit sat three cans of gasoline, which now that I became aware of them was all I could smell. I slowly walked toward the back, surveying each seat before moving on to the next. Nothing stood out to me as odd, other than the remarkable emptiness. I reached the sixth pair of seats and stopped. My hands trembled at the thought of what would be there. My heart pounding, I jumped to an attack position in the aisle next to the seat, and everything in me dropped. A rubber glove hung over the edge of the bench. The fingers swung back and forth like a child's legs in the commotion I had caused.

"What do you see, man?" Mark asked from the door.

"Nothing. It's empty."

"The food and gas gone, too?"

"No, it's still here."

A beat and then, "You think you could grab me something?"

I walked to the back and picked up the box of candy. I rose back up, and something dense slapped against the back door of the bus. It hit so hard, the top can of gasoline toppled onto the floor, and liquid poured out. The smell of gasoline permeated the air. Two screamers built like Saints linebackers were pounding on the door. They slapped and punched at the glass. I tripped over the leg of a seat. The candy spilled out of the box. I grabbed a handful and bolted down the aisle to the door.

"*Fucking shit!*" Mark cried.

The back glass gave way. Hands reached through and knocked over the other gas cans. Blood ran down from their elbows to their fingers and dripped onto the floor. The two screamers pulled at the door. I stood at the driver's seat, watching them beat on the back of the bus. The door popped and slammed against the lock.

"Come on!" Mark screamed at me.

"I think they're stuck in the door."

"Good, let's get the fuck out of here."

Just then the metal door bowed outward. I flinched and ran into all the levers and handles at the front of the cabin. I caught my balance on the gearshift. I knocked it out of gear and fell farther toward the ground. The door cracked open. I saw part of a face in the open-ing that belonged to someone who wanted to kill me.

"Holy shit." I jumped out of the bus.

Mark took off as I closed the accordion door from the outside. I heard the door give as I sprinted across the front of the bus. Marked jumped into the shotgun seat of the Jeep, and I went in right behind him.

"Punch it," Mark said to Jackie.

The tires squealed. We raced down the hill.

Katy and I looked out the back window as the bus became small-er and smaller. It rocked back and forth on its shocks.

"Jesus," Katy said. "They're going to tip the damn thing over."

"Everyone OK?" Jackie asked. "Let's get some seatbelts on. I have a feeling this is going to get rough."

At the bottom of the hill, there was a brick building and a yel-low sign in front of it with a black palindrome arrow pointing left and right. Jackie slowed to make the left. Two more screamers ran at the car. Jackie jerked the wheel. The car went into a skid. The screamers hit the grille and stayed there for the rest of the trip. Katy grabbed my hand. The Cherokee slammed into the wall head on, ending the screamers. Everyone jerked forward. I bounced off the back of Mark's seat hard. The front airbags deployed. The wind-shield busted. The doors bent outward.

"Are you *fucking* kidding me?" Jackie slapped at the airbag. Mark unclipped her seatbelt and told her to stop pillow fighting and get out.

"Are you guys OK?" I asked.

Katy had tears in her eyes. "Yes." A red welt had already formed on the side of her face from the back of the driver's seat.

"Are you hurt?"

"No, I'll be all right." She released her grip on my hand. It was so tight that the skin on my hand turned white and rushed back to red.

"Let's make sure you can walk."

Katy, Jackie, and I left the car. Mark's door wouldn't open. I pulled on the handle, and it freed with a good bit of effort.

"The car is on fire," Jackie said. "We better move away from it."

"How is this fucking engine still running?" Mark asked. "You know what I bet it was. Those two cushioned the blow. I tell you one thing. My next car: Jeep. This thing has taken some shit from us today."

"You guys hurt?" I asked over the car.

"Everything looks all right," Jackie reported.

"I guess we just hoof it again," Mark said.

"Move!" Jackie screamed.

"Fuck," Mark said. He yanked me with him away from the police car.

Coming down the hill was the bus. It raced straight ahead for the brick building. Another screamer came out of the alleyway, and the bus took it on the journey to expiration. I could see the two linebackers pounding on the windshield. The bus jerked toward the left. It took out a number of light posts. It slowed a little but didn't stop. The bus crashed into the back of the Jeep, ending three more screamers against the brick building. An explosion ignited the gasoline, and within seconds the two vehicles were consumed in fire. The Jeep's engine finally stopped.

"Bullshit. That didn't happen," Mark said.

"Katy? Jackie?" I tried to fight off the panic. The rage I had felt when I saw Lee was coming back. "What's going on over there?"

"We're alive," Jackie said. "Can you come around?"

The front was an obvious no. Twisted metal threatened to sever an artery no matter which way I tried to climb over. On the ground was a pistol from beneath the seat of the Jeep. It was almost too hot to touch. I ran to the back of the bus. When it crashed into the building, the bus had wedged itself between the drugstore on the corner of the street and the brick building. I moved to see if I could somehow fit between it, but a burst of flame rose out of the dented back door. I tried going under, but the frame was bent, and the bus sagged down and all but touched the ground.

"I can't get to you," I said.

"What?" Katy asked.

"It's OK," I said. "We'll just wait it out and come over when the fire dies down."

Multiple screams echoed through an alley.

"They're coming, Jackie," Mark said.

"No!" Katy screamed. The panic of being separated in a strange city with an unknowable number of screamers brought back her obvious fear. It reminded me of when we first picked her up. I hated the idea of leaving her that way.

"Listen to me," Jackie said to all of us. "That building with the smoke is the Shell Square. It's less than a mile from here. It looks like a white rectangle stacked on top of a white square. Just get there. We'll meet you there."

"Do you both have guns?" I asked.

"I have one," Jackie said.

"Here is an extra one." I tossed the gun over the fire.

"We have to run," Mark said. "Get to the Square. We'll see you there."

"No!" Katy cried. "Please!"

"Run," I told her as Mark and I started to run away from the bus. "You have to get to the building. You have to promise you'll get there."

"Don't go!" She was in tears.

"They're coming," I said. "Get to the building! Run!"

"If you get in trouble," Jackie said, "find a way to get on a roof. We'll see you at the Square."

We ran.

Chapter 57

The majority of the screamers filtering in from the alleys and streets leading to the crash site ran toward the fire. I didn't concern myself with finding out what they planned when they reached the bus because a small group saw Mark and me. We fled the scene, and they came after us. Luckily, we had enough space between us to find a hiding place. My first inclination was to circle around the building to meet up with Jackie and Katy. We tried, but at the second turn down an alley, we encountered a chain-link fence topped with barbed wire.

"We don't have time for that," Mark said, pulling me back down.

Down the next alleyway, a Dumpster stood perpendicular to the next building's wall. Mark opened the lid. Garbage was piled to the top.

"Really?" Mark said. "No fuckin' jobs, America? And no one could take this shit to the dump." He kicked the side of the Dumpster.

I pulled him around to the side away from the road. Not two seconds later, four screamers ran past the opening between the buildings. They found something else to run after. Once we were certain we'd be clear to move, we got up and started walking roughly in the direction I figured Katy and Jackie would be.

Mark called their names. After the echoes subsided, Jackie called back asking for our location. Mark told her we were two blocks down from the wrecked bus. Then he screamed, telling her not to come this way.

I didn't see it at first. I only saw the dirty, hazy afternoon sunlight peeking through buildings. Mark turned back for the road. Then I saw it—a wave of them about a football field away. They were marching down the street as if in an actual army platoon. They didn't see us at first either, but by the time we rounded the corner back into the street, the alley was filled with horrible shrieking.

Mark and I ran, looking for anything to hide us.

"Look," Mark said. He raised a finger long enough to aim it at a maroon building with a black fire escape leading to the roof, and then his arm fell back to a running stride. "Get to those apartments. Do what Jackie said. I need a rest. My leg is killing me."

It was a simple plan, but a car pileup and three more screamers encumbered us on our way to the building. Mark was slowing down. I told him to go straight for the ladder. I waved my hands over my head, hoping to attract more attention both in front of and behind me.

The wave behind us had poured out into the streets, and I heard the stampede gaining ground. Two of the three screamers set their sights on me, still carrying pieces of an animal. The other paid no attention to anything going on as it faced the building with the red smoke. That one ran down the street, chasing I don't know what, leaving Mark and me with the remaining two to avoid. He took the direct path to the escape ladder. He ducked behind the pileup while I went the long way around the cars.

Still waving my hands in the air, I jumped on the hood of a low-rider with a huge protruding bumper. There were enough of them circled around that I could leap from one to another all the way across the street to the building. Mark jumped for the ladder once, twice, and on the third attempt, he grabbed the bottom rung. It fell so fast that Mark wound up on his back momentarily pinned below the lowest rung. He got to his feet swearing. The screamers were almost on me then. The two in front climbed up the car. I kicked one. It fell back onto the street. The other lost balance, and I ran the opposite way along the roofs and hoods of the cars. I stayed a little too long on a police car that had a row of lights. They caught up to me, so I ran around the building, hoping they would follow my direct route and trip over the red and blues. I had no idea if I was lucky.

"Where are you going?" Mark called to me.

"I'll be back."

In the alleyway, there was another escape ladder. I hurdled in midstride but didn't even come close. I continued around the building, knocking anything down that I could: trash cans, a metal shopping cart, even a bookshelf. That one fell slowly, but I heard it crash onto them. They were too close. I rounded the corner at another street. A bus stop waited on the sidewalk. Its walls were glass but with enough posters and graffiti to hide behind. I watched through the grimy glass walls as the screamers came into the street, and almost immediately they stopped. The stampede had tapered off to no more than ten or twelve. A few of them turned around and walked back down the alley as though they had made a wrong turn somewhere. I realized that they no longer possessed much, if any, object permanence. If they didn't see me, they didn't know I was there. When I thought the few remaining in the street were not looking my way, I fled the bus stop for the corner. I heard them scream. I had confidence though that by the time I reached the fire escape, only one or two would still be behind me.

"Fuck, bro," Mark said as I ran toward him on the sidewalk. "When they stopped screaming, I nearly lost my shit."

I ran up the ladder. I was correct to assume there would only be two left chasing me. Mark pulled up the ladder just as one of them grabbed it. Mark held the ladder midway to its full extension. One of the screamers used the other to climb up to us.

"Grab the rock," Mark said.

"What rock?"

"The one in the corner. Grab it." He then let out a high-pitched yelp.

Behind me there was a big concrete chunk by the doorway. There were ashtrays around it, and I assumed people used the rock to keep the door from locking them out as they smoked. I picked up the rock. I raised it over my head, nearly running it into Mark's face. I spiked the stone down the hole around the ladder. The weight Mark held dropped. He yanked the ladder up until it locked in place.

"I just made a discovery," I said between gasps of air.

"Yeah?" He sat on the floor of the landing.

"If they don't see us, they don't know we're here."

"You think if we're perfectly still, they don't see us, too? Like a dinosaur?"

"I have no idea."

"That seems like a bit of a flaw. Literally, all they do is see and kill? Don't even think. They don't even eat. How are they still alive using all that energy?"

The roar from the wave of screams started again. This time they were on the other side of the building. Then the sound of a small engine, which I mistook for a Weed eater, cut through the air from almost directly above us.

"I guess we're going to check that out," Mark said.

Chapter 58

At first I didn't notice the middle-aged man in the white scrubs leaning over the edge of the building. The first thing I saw was the thick rope. The man in the scrubs had tied one end to an air-conditioning unit, and the other end hung over the edge. The rope was pulled tight as if there were something heavy tied to the other end of it. The man climbed onto the ledge. He'd zip-tied the trigger of a chainsaw down so that the chain wouldn't stop spinning. He held the chainsaw out over the street and dropped it. He looked bored. He brushed his silver, shoulder-length hair back over his head. The chainsaw hit something and then hit the ground. The impact was enough to kill the engine. He grabbed a cordless saw.

Mark whispered, "I feel like this is one of those times we should just fuck off."

"He's got a lot of tools over there."

"Yeah, and he doesn't seem to be against using them."

"What if he can help us? He had to get those tools here somehow. What if he knows a better way to get to the building?"

"OK, we're obviously going to do it, so let's just do it." He didn't move. He just looked ahead. Then he turned toward me and said, "I'm not going first."

I stepped from the landing onto the roof. The man in the white scrubs stopped. The full-throttle engine of the saw buzzed loudly. He dropped it. A thump and bang, and the engine died. The man on the ledge adjusted the gardening gloves and pivoted on his heels to face me. Black sunglasses covered his eyes. Blond streaks divided his graying beard.

"Come on out if you want to." His voice was much younger than the rest of him. "I won't hurt you. I'm not here to hurt *you*. Your friend either."

"What are you doing up here?" I asked him.

"The same thing you are. Getting out of the elements." He chuckled.

"I'm—"

"I know who you are. And don't give me any of that Peter shit either." Louder he said, "You, too, Thaddeus." He stepped down from the ledge.

"How do you know that?"

"Ah, I used to know more. Years and years ago, I could tell you exactly how many atoms you were made of. I could tell you when your kids were going to be born before you were. There once was a time when I didn't even have to say a word, and I'd have you jumping off this building. Ain't that right, Green Eyes? We used to all be like that. It's a shame now. It's all gone. You would have been one of us, you know. Those pictures of your wife you see. Not everybody has that. I know you've always wondered. She has them, too. I came here to find the person I shared that connection with."

"What's he talking about?" Mark whispered.

The roped tied to the AC unit jerked and twitched. Something alive dangled over the edge on the building.

"Who are you?" I said.

"I'm no one." The man ran his fingers through his hair again. "Someone the world forgot. I used to be a force. I had the world in the palm of my hand. But I tried too hard to make the world what I wanted it to be—what I thought was best. I made it to the top when I was just a kid. Making it is the easy part. It's maintaining that becomes the problem, and I fell. When you fall, you don't go from the top to right below the top. When you fall, you fall all the way down. I can't even see now. I was locked up and blindfolded for months at a time. I have to feel and hear my way around the world. I was on the *top*."

He stepped back onto the ledge and felt for the next item to drop. His foot bumped against a hedge trimmer.

"How did you get here?" Mark asked.

"I found a way. I appreciate you boys bringing the crowd. That helps me a lot more than you realize." He pulled the cord on the hedge trimmer until the engine swelled to life. He bent down and cut the rope dangling over the edge. The rope snapped and was gone. He dropped the trimmer over the edge. Slowly, as if telling a child, he said, "I am so old." He spread his arms. Screams rose up from the street. He leaned back.

"Whoa!" Mark said, and we ran toward the ledge.

Of course it was way too late. He was gone before we took the first step. There was no thump against the sidewalk below. Only the sound of a pack of animals tearing apart its prey.

When the noise died down, Mark and I still stared at the place the man had stood.

"W—What?" Mark asked.

"I have no clue."

"Hey!" a voice called from a few blocks away. "Y'all are OK."

On the top of a building, Katy and Jackie waved their arms over their heads. We were on a taller building, and the two buildings between them and us had only one floor. The air was cool and clear as the sun began its decline.

"Yes, we are." Mark's booming yell caused me to jump. "We're pretty surrounded over this way. What about you guys?"

"The same," Katy said.

"Well, I guess we're here for a while," I said.

Mark sat on the ground against the ledge. His feet were straight out. His shoulders hunched. I suddenly imagined what he looked like when he was a child, tuckered out after a little league game or a long day at the park.

"How's your leg, Mark?" Jackie called.

"It's super great. I wish we would've done this sooner."

"You're a shit, you know."

"I love you, too."

"We're going to take a rest," I told them. "If you find a clear spot to come here or move forward, take it."

"Already making plans," Jackie said. "You better find a warm place. The sun is going down. It's going to get cold soon."

"We'll be drinking hot chocolate in the Square before you get off that roof," Mark said.

"OK, teddy bear," Katy mocked. "We'll send a helicopter to come back to get you."

"Thank you," I singsonged.

I sat down next to Mark. He massaged the soreness from his legs. After a short while, the crowd below us disbanded, leaving only a few stragglers. I planned our route.

Chapter 59

An hour passed before Mark felt up to walking. Jackie and Katy had an opportunity to move forward toward the Square, so they reluctantly took it. The path to Mark and me was blocked, and there was no telling how long it would be before they got the chance to make a run for it again. So they moved toward the skyscraper.

"I'm sorry about this." Mark got to his feet.

"It's not a problem. I could use a moment, too." A deep throb started in the area of my leg where Tony got me with the pickax. I knew that couldn't be great news.

"I think I'm ready."

"Well, we don't have a clearing yet, so just stay down."

"Done," he said. "What was that guy talking about?"

"I have no idea. It was all gibberish to me."

"What did he mean by the pictures that Sarah has? Are they dirty pictures?"

"I don't know." I could tell he knew I was lying. He didn't press the subject, though.

"That green-eyes stuff was cute. I'd say your eyes are closer to blue, though."

"You think he was hitting on me?" I humored.

"You could've hit that. Should've got his number."

"We'll hit up missed connections on Craigslist when we get there."

"He'll turn up. I'm really good to go if you see an opening, by the way."

"There's only a couple more on the street. Let's get ready to go."

"Right on." Mark stood up. An assortment of tools sat in a line on the ledge. Mark skipped over most of the ones with a motor and tossed a wrench my way. He held the hammer. "Like the old days."

"Like the old days," I agreed.

We tapped our blunt instruments together with a silent *cheers*. We watched the last of the crowd stroll off down side streets. Off in the distance, I heard a car engine. I immediately felt better about allowing Katy and Jackie to leave without us. Mark and I climbed down the fire escape, not making any noise. It wasn't until we climbed down the ladder that I remembered not talking or making noise was unnecessary. Still, we moved like burglars, ducking behind cars and into bus stops, not making a sound just in case. New Orleans held more than twice the number of screamers to dodge than either place we had stopped before. We snuck down four blocks of congested streets before we ran into any direct problems. A lone monster stood in the center of an intersection. I only describe him this way because the rest of the screamers looked indecipherable from normal people. I could tell this one was different as soon as it came into view. I held Mark back so I could process what I was seeing.

From behind a station wagon, I thought the metal shards sticking out of his skin were sweat reflecting the sun. He glimmered from head to toe in an unchanging pattern instead of all over his skin, so I put aside the idea that it was just sweat. I really homed in on what I was seeing. Blades stuck into him up and down his body—scissors, pocketknives, forks, even chunks of unmolded metal. The once-man standing in the street seemed to have been standing too close to the home-decor department when a Walmart exploded. His shoulders bowed, ready for a fight. He paced around the intersection, looking for someone to separate into pieces. His skin was red from either sunburn or dried blood, I never really found out. He wore only dirty jeans and tennis shoes. Everything else about him was normal. His chest had a little hair on it. His dark-brown hair was dirty, messy, and cut like the average guy's. He wasn't old or young. The way he paced back and forth made him look bigger than he was. Even I could tell that before the change he might have been a bank teller or paper pusher or semiprofessional chef—just an average guy looking to pay off his mortgage in a shitty economy. After the switch he could be compared to one of those loonies marching down a freeway swinging an axe at passing vehicles on a police show. The look on his face told the story of what was probably going through Lee's head the night before as he threw gas cans around a spreading fire. He was the very definition of deranged.

"We need to go around that guy," I said.

"Damn right we do. How though?" He had a curious look on his face.

"What?"

"Have you stopped to consider that yet?" He pointed to a manhole cover next to a brown Lincoln with its doors wide open. "What do you say? Drop down the hole and run toward the building, like Harriet Tubman and the Underground Railroad. Pop up, grab some 'za, and wait on Jack and Katy. Ninja Turtles style. It's possible."

"Wow. Just for clarification, you know that the Underground Railroad was not a literal subway system, right?"

"Jesus Man Christ." Mark snuck down the length of the car. When the coast was clear, he performed a mad crawl to the brown Lincoln. After brushing off debris from no telling what, Mark went to work on lifting the manhole cover, shoving his index fingers into two small holes in the cover's surface.

"Those things weigh almost two hundred pounds, man. You can't pick it up with just your fingers. You'll break them off."

"Then bring that ass over here and help me pull it up."

"I'm honestly more interested in the car," I said as I followed in his cartoonish footsteps to the Lincoln.

I put my fingers through the holes on the other end of the manhole cover and counted to three. The lift came slowly, but as soon as it did, sunlight filtered down into the sewer. Screams blared up at us. I looked down, and someone was climbing the ladder at an alarming rate. Anger burned in the woman's eyes. We dropped the plate back where we found it. No more than a second later, the female screamer banged on the cover from underneath, knocking it up and nearly out of its place.

"Shit, bitch," Mark said, jumping on the metal circle.

"I think she likes you, bro," I said.

"Come on, man. Do your magic on the car."

"You sure? I think you got this under control."

"Dude!" Mark shouted.

I went to work on the wires after kicking the paneling loose.

"For fuck's sake, bro."

A few sparks and magic moments later, the Lincoln sputtered to life. A much shorter person must have owned the car because my knees were right behind the steering wheel. As Mark ran around to the passenger side, I adjusted the seat. By then the manhole cover had been knocked out of the opening and into the street. A flock of them crawled out from the sewer. My theory of their object awareness was all but confirmed when the woman stood erect and walked away at a leisurely stroll in no particular direction.

I floored the pedal. The car backfired, lurched forward, backfired again, and finally spun the wheels. Screams filled the space around the car, but the first screamer that charged at the car was the man with the silverware and shrapnel sticking out of his skin. The different shining surfaces of the metal caught the sun and reflected it into my eyes in what seemed to be a deliberate attempt to hinder my vision. Although I doubt even that one had the wherewithal to put together something so complicated as to temporarily blind me. What I have come to realize is that he was just running at the car like a murderer.

I wanted to jerk the car out of his path and miss him completely. However, when the car crossed his path, it happened to be at the point where a fire truck and minivan blocked most of the road. I honestly didn't have a choice in the matter. Although I'd be lying if I said I was upset with whoever's choice it was. Now that I think of it, I suppose I could've just stopped the car or driven down a different street. Hindsight. Maybe it was because of the intersection in which he just happened to be standing. I didn't tag him hard enough to bring him completely down. I was only going about fifteen miles per hour to avoid a collision with the other vehicles around me. The thing jumped onto the hood. It landed on its hands and knees. I jerked the steering wheel to one side. The Lincoln banged into a Freezy Freezer's ice-cream truck. The thing on the hood lost its balance. The blood on its hands caused it to slip toward us and tumble over the side. A three-inch piece of glass caught on the edge of the hood as the thing rolled over the edge. The glass fell out of its shoulder onto the Lincoln's windshield. When the front of the car cleared the wreckage, I floored the accelerator again. The thing climbed to its feet and ran after the car. I took a turn down a random street in an effort to lose him. I turned the car in the direction of Shell Square.

"Do we need to discuss what the fuck that was?" Mark asked.

"I don't have a clue."

"Makes two of us, then."

I rolled our windows down when the coast was clear. I called their names and laid on the horn. We waited for a response. I could see the shine of the Mississippi River behind the building with the red smoke.

Chapter 60

"Why does it feel like he's still chasing us?" Mark nervously checked the rear window.

We hadn't seen it for blocks, but I felt the same way.

"Did you see all that shit coming out of him? That was sick."

"I thought he was just wet or something."

"Definitely not. I think you knocked a nail file and a letter opener out of him. They're still sitting on the wiper blade."

"That one seemed different, right?" I was trying to talk out the jitters.

"Different how?"

At this point I had grown used to driving in the city under the circumstances. When a group of screamers started toward the car, I would try my best to dodge them—if I couldn't I didn't think much else of it—and then turn down a street to lose them. As long as I was pointed toward the smoke, I couldn't get too lost. My eyes were more peeled for Jackie and Katy than for oncoming lunatics.

"Like he had an agenda of some kind," I said. "You see how he was waiting in the street like that? It was like he showed up early for a street fight. It made me nervous."

"Street fights are a little more spontaneous than that, but I agree. He was in a wrestling ring waiting for someone to challenge him for the hard-core championship. This is so fucked up."

"Surely you don't realize this just now, right?"

"Some of it, yeah."

"Why just some of it?"

"Well, I was just thinking..." He paused.

I could tell he was thinking very deliberately about what he was going to say.

"There's always been something to protect us, you know? A place to go, a number to call, something put in place to make us feel safe. Parents, police, military. It's always been there, no matter how big the problem got. We could always feel like someone's got our back. There's nothing now. Feels really shitty. I feel more alone because of that than because most people aren't people anymore. Shit, watch out."

I swerved to miss a group of about four. As we moved closer to the building with the red smoke, I noticed that their numbers were thinning out.

"Have you seen any sign of Katy or Jackie?" I asked.

"No."

"I didn't want to get there without them."

"That's OK. If they aren't there, we'll just circle back and find them."

"Yeah," I said. I could tell he knew I was uneasy. Anyone passing us on the street would've been able to look through the windshield and tell I was on edge.

"They're going to be fine. We haven't heard a pistol shot all day. They're not going to need it. Jackie is an awesome strategist. Katy's a bit on edge, but she works awesome under pressure. I don't know if you know this, but that shit with the flare was pretty smart. Everything she did at the theater was clutch. They'll be fine. Probably have more reason to worry about us than we do of them. We're the ones keep getting our asses kicked."

"I didn't think of it that way." Somehow, more than anything else Mark said that day, that put my mind at ease.

Chapter 61

Five or ten minutes later, it came into view—the Hampton Inn Sarah was using when everything changed. When I saw it, everything in me nearly fell to the floorboard. Waiting in front of the glass entrance, James stood waving us inside.

"Who's that?" Mark asked.

"That's the kid the people in the theater thought I murdered."

"That's not true," he said in disbelief. "How the hell did he get here? Do you think we should stop and pick him up?"

"Something tells me he's going to be fine without us."

I stopped anyway. James ran around to the back of the building, laughing. I watched him until he was gone. Then I waited for a moment and called his name. I put the car back into gear and looked up at the building.

"What's wrong?" Mark asked.

"That's where Sarah is."

"How do you know?"

"That's where she was staying when it happened."

"How do you know she's still there? She could be in the Square. Looks like it's only about two blocks. She could have made it. They could have come and got her."

"I just know."

"Yeah, but how? Anything to do with the pictures Jumpy McBlindguy was talking about?" He tried his best to look me in the eye. I wouldn't let him. "You already know that I'm not going to let this go without you telling me, don't you?"

I did. So reluctantly I told him about the flashes, pictures, whatever they can be called. I told him how they'd always been there, even before we met, and how they're always hazy or confusing but they're always close enough to reality that I never have to worry about her. Then I told him about the images of the hotel and how completely vivid they were. I told him I could see every detail of her skin, from freckles to scars. I told him about the running water in the sink and about the blue screen blinking 410 with different colors. I told him about the shadow in the corner and how I knew someone was with her.

"And she has them, too, apparently," Mark said after a long wait.

"I guess so. Never asked her."

"Do you want to stop now or come back after we find Jack and Katy?"

"I figure if she's made it in there this long, a few more minutes won't hurt. Jackie and Katy are a little more out in the open. They need more help than she does."

"I appreciate that."

The Hampton came and went. I noticed then how clear the street had been for the last few blocks. The car trudged forward another two blocks until the Square was the only thing in front of us. The street was wide. I could see all of the building through the intersection, everything but the top, that is. A reddish shadow weighed down on the street from the smoke.

The first time I saw the black boxes, I think I thought they were storage containers with supplies or food for everyone in the building. They were lining the front of the building, probably thirty or forty of them. The survivors in New Orleans had strategically staggered them so that each one could be seen from the street. I remember there being four rows about ten feet apart in front of the building. The police had made another two rows by the time I saw them used. It's hard to give them much more of a description than that. They looked like plastic black storage cases. Completely innocuous. I didn't think anything of them. As we pulled up to the building, a flood of police officers came to the car. We got out and put our hands up. Much to our surprise, they waved Mark and me into the building like third-base coaches—no issues, no confrontation.

Chapter 62

The Square was silent. I went to an interview for an internship in Dallas once right after college. The building was huge. All the walls that were not made out of glass were painted a brilliant white. The lobby was a wide, echoing room. A thin, large-chested, blond woman with red lipstick and a white smile sat behind a sleek and, no doubt, pricy desk, greeting the visitors as they walked into the building. The only real difference between the building in Dallas and the Square was that the woman behind the sleek desk in New Orleans was a brunette. The police officers guarding the front of the building stayed outside, which made the echoes of Mark's and my footsteps exponentially louder.

"Welcome," the woman said. She spoke as if we were at a funeral. "I'm sure y'all had a rough trip getting here. A lot of people lost family and friends. I'm sure y'all've had y'all's share of loss. We're going to get you set up here. You can stay as long as you like."

"Um, thank you," I said. "You wouldn't happen to have seen two women recently come here, would you? One looks like him without the beard. The other, red hair and feminine."

"No, sir, but I only started my shift ten minutes ago."

"You have no idea if anyone before you saw them?" Mark asked.

"No," she said. "But I can tell you that everyone showing up after about four or so will be placed in a room at Hilton down the street. Everything here is full. People feel safe with the police around. Luckily, a couple new cops came in today from Mississippi. We might be able to have a few guards over there while they build the walls."

"We are with that group," I said. "One of the women we are with is a cop, too."

"What walls?" Mark asked.

"We're blocking the city off. We don't want them getting in here, obviously."

"And by them," Mark said, "you mean the Atlanta Falcons?"

"What? No." The woman was taken aback. "I mean those things out there."

"Wow," Mark said, astonished. "I'm so sorry. My mistake."

"So do we need a room key or what?" I asked her.

"No, y'all just need to go down this hallway." She pointed to a door to her left. "There are some doctors in a room who will make sure you're OK. Then they'll send y'all to another room, and then you'll go where they give out the hotel keys."

"Well, I guess we better be off, then." I smiled and put up two fingers as Mark and I made our way across the lobby to a huge set of double doors. A red exit sign flickered a little. "Is there power here?" I asked the girl behind the counter.

"Sure!" She was suddenly a different person from the somber, melancholy sympathizer by whom we were welcomed. I was then aware that just like the blonde in Dallas, she was only here to do what she was told and nothing else. I imagined someone telling her to make sure the people are comforted and always be sympathetic. Try smiling, maybe even unbutton that top button. In the empty lobby, the word echoed into eternity. "Well, sort of. They are working to get it on for good. Something about a barn or a stable or something."

"Stabilized?" I asked.

"I bet that's it. It comes on and off for a minute or two. It doesn't stay on for very long. They said it could take a-whole-nother day or two before they can get it working right."

"A-whole-nother," Mark said under his breath.

"You're talking about the power plant, right?"

The cutesy girl nodded her head vigorously.

"How many people are here?"

"They said between thirty-five hundred and four thousand people were here yesterday."

"Wow," Mark said. "All locals?"

"About half." She smiled very big.

"Well, right through this door then?" I asked.

"Right through the door."

"That's a lot of people," Mark said as we entered the dark hallway. "Hope you don't run into Lee again."

"Yeah. That'd be interesting." I laughed even though thinking of Lee chasing after me rocking the Freddy Krueger complexion unnerved me. "It is strange to think of that many normal people. Don't the movies usually have like fifty or a hundred tops after the apocalypse?"

A number of black arrows drawn with a Sharpie on pieces of printer paper directed us around the building.

"That's sweet of them," Mark said. "They're helping us find where to go even though there is only one way to go. Sure hope it's not a setup."

"We'll get to the end, and there will be a sharpened stump with a hook sticking out of it in the center of a room."

Mark and I laughed, even though it kind of hurt to be joking about what was essentially the death of the one person who wanted to help us not be murdered.

"If I see a bunch of cages, I'm taking the fuck off."

There wasn't any of that, though.

Chapter 63

The waiting room to see the doctors was nothing more than a glorified bank line. The black posts with their nylon straps created a very simple labyrinth for all the new residents of New Orleans to navigate. When Mark and I showed up, we walked half the length of the maze before arriving at the back of the line. I could imagine with thousands of people flocking here over the past few days, this building was packed to capacity, probably until we arrived. The line moved quickly though, and that was a good thing. A couple, each about sixty years old, waited in front of us. I wondered how the hell they were able to make it from wherever they lived. They were holding hands and flirting like newlyweds. The man stood tall and portly with gray in his beard and around his bald spot. The petite woman had sandy-blond hair, but her gray roots were showing. The couple was dressed like they were on a trip to Hawaii.

"How you guys doing?" I asked them.

"So tired," the woman said.

"I like your accent," I told her. "Where are you guys from?"

"Des Moines," the man said.

"Iowa? No way," Mark replied. He was getting excited. "I love your accents. Hey, look, I know you're not from there, but could you say 'Da Bears' real quick."

They did it as if performing a party trick. The four of us laughed. The people ahead in the line turned toward us, not in annoyance but with tiny grins on their faces. It was like we were all in on the same joke. Behind us an Asian family finagled the maze. The youngest of the children ducked under the straps.

"How'd you guys get all the way down here from Des Moines?" Mark asked.

"We just took the camper, ya know," the man explained. "Pretty straight shot."

"I'm Derrick, by the way. This is Mark."

"Gladys," she held out her hand. "This is Barry. Where are you from?"

"Alabama," I said. "Not as far as you guys. Why'd you come here?"

"Honestly?" Barry said, and the two looked at each other. "I always told her I would take her as soon as the time was right. That was five years ago. She never did leave her husband. This just seemed like the perfect chance."

"What he doesn't tell you," Gladys said from around Barry's arm, "is that he didn't leave his wife either."

"Holy shit," Mark said over his own laughter.

"Wine isn't the only thing that gets better with age," Barry said and popped Gladys on the bottom. She giggled and playfully tapped his chest.

"So I assume you are enjoying yourselves in the South then?" I asked.

"When her husband came into the shop that night, kicking and screaming, I thought it was 'cause he found out about me and his wife. Have you tried reas'nin' with one of 'em? I swear. I could do nothin' right. I got in my car and took off. I called Gladys. She had no idea what was going on. Said her bridge club was just playin' cards, and boom!—they went and got the taste of shit in their mouths. I met 'er at the Chevron, and here we are. Best four nights of my life. My legs are sore."

"I'm sore everywhere," Gladys added.

"So to answer your question, yes. We are having a great time in the South."

"Well, I'm glad you guys finally get to nail each other openly," Mark said.

"What's your story?" Barry asked.

Mark began the story. Then when I came into the picture, I took over, abridging our time in Jackson to "and then we picked up his sister, and here we are."

"We're actually looking for the other two," I said. "We got separated. You wouldn't happen to have seen them, would you?"

"No," Barry said. "The two'a us have been in line for a while. Unless they came before, we wouldn'ta seen 'em."

"How long have you been here?"

"Only a couple hours."

By then a few more people had come in behind the family of Asians. Luckily, I only had one person and then Gladys and Barry to go before I moved on to the next room. I became nervous about Katy and Jackie again. The car I had heard earlier was not them after all. Or worse, it was and something had happened to them.

Inside the doctor plaza, dozens of gurneys and hospital beds were packed so tightly that there was enough room to walk and not much else. Doctors—about 70 percent of whom were totally bald—waited at every bed. One waved me over, and I sat on his gurney.

"How you doing there?" The doctor smiled at me.

"I got where I was going so much better than out there."

"Ha, I hear you. It has been a busy week for us. And not everyone was in a good mood, if you can believe it. What kind of damage are we looking at?" He peeked under the bandage on my head. Then he shined a flashlight in my eyes.

"Well, I bonked my noggin. I also caught one pretty good in the thigh."

"It all looks good up here. Drop your pants."

"You sure you don't want to date me first?"

"It's only to look around. At least it's not the backdoor treatment."

"That's true." I lowered Ted's pants so the doctor could see.

"Oo," he said. He applied pressure to my thigh. I winced at the pain that shot through me. "That looks fun. I'll be right back."

Then he went to a room that wasn't marked exit. I pulled up my pants and looked around the busy room for Jackie or Katy. Either one would've done, but neither was there. Mark entered and sat on a bed. A doctor looked him over, talked to him for a second, and that was that. The doctor put a red paper bracelet around his wrist. With a quick little handshake and a clap on the back, Mark was done.

"That was kind of a waste," he said after crossing the room. "He could have at least talked to me about football, done something to make the visit longer than the waiting time."

"What'd he say?"

"The usual: keep working out, everything gives you cancer. Also we have one more stop on our tour around the building, then they'll give us a key. The key will either be to a room at the Hilton or a *brand-new car!* Probably a room, though."

"Yeah, I would guess so."

"Where's your guy?"

"I don't know. He looked at my leg and took off."

"That can't be good."

"He said it looked fun, so it can't be all bad."

"Do you really want a doctor having fun with you? Especially one of these. It's like a Turtle Wax convention in here. We could light the city with their shiny heads."

"I actually got one with hair."

"No way."

The doctor came out of the dark room with a needle and a box.

"That him?"

"That's him."

"You got a needle. Bet it's an infection. That leg hole is fucked up."

"I don't feel infected. I'm just a little sore."

"That's how it starts. The next thing you know, you're dead."

"OK," the doctor said, laying the box on the gurney. "You just have a little bit of an infection. This should knock it right out."

"Bam, motherfucker," Mark said. "Nothing but net."

"Luckily, we haven't had too many of those," the doctor said. "We're starting to run out of things to give people. Take two of these every twelve hours for a week, and you'll be fine." The doctor handed the box to me. He gave me the shot before I was paying attention to him again. "You may feel woozy. I don't know. They didn't even tell us what this stuff does." The doctor laughed and clapped me on the back. We shook hands. Then he put a blue paper bracelet on me.

"Do the colors matter?" I asked.

"Not much. Red means fine. Blue means send someone later to check on me. The green ones are the only ones to worry about."

"Why is that?" Mark asked.

"Because we're almost out of them." The doctor laughed at himself. I couldn't help but laugh with him. "No, no. The green ones mean the patient needs assistance. So in the next room where you will just get directed to the hotel, they would get a volunteer."

"I think we got ripped off," Mark said.

"I don't think so," the doctor said. "Most of the people with the green bands aren't able to walk to their new residence on their remaining limbs."

"Got it," Mark said. "Count yourself lucky."

"Well, that's your call, really," said the doctor.

"I would think most of the people here would have the green ones," I said.

"I don't mean to get serious, but how many people have you seen who got away with only one injury?" The doctor raised his eyebrows.

"Oh, here are some bandages for your leg. Tell the folks at the desk to send someone to check out those stitches in your head. They look ready to come out."

"That can't be right. I only had them in for a day."

"I'm sure," the doctor said. "Now move along. I got more patients to attend to."

I stood from the gurney with a mob of thoughts, each one headed its own direction, bouncing around in my head. I knew that Mark's palm had healed at a staggering rate. I knew I didn't have whatever gene made that happen, though. Was it an adaptation in the people who survived? If that were the case though, no one would have green bracelets, and most of the blues would be red. I don't think my leg would have been infected if that was the case. I followed Mark into the next room where another maze led to a long line of tables. This maze was much shorter and moved much faster. We never stopped walking.

"You OK, bro?"

"Yeah, yeah, sorry. I just started thinking about something and zoned out."

"Was it Peggy? Nah, you'd be sporting a partial if that were the case. You're a Ken doll right now. Look alive, bro. We're coming up."

At the end of the line, two rows of tables went on and on and on. There were over a hundred volunteers sitting at the tables. A hand would go up somewhere along the line, and a representative at the end of the far row would say blue, and a person at the end of the closer row would say red. This continued for nearly a minute before Mark and I reached the tables. We went to our respective row of tables.

The line was thin by this point, so I greeted the first volunteer I saw who was no longer helping someone. She was a middle-aged black woman. She wore a bright smile lined with purple lipstick even though I could tell by her voice that today was not the day for jokes. She asked my name, I gave it to her, followed by age, where I was from, and what brought me to the blue line instead of the red line. I told her of the stitches in my head and the hole in my leg, sparing her the unnecessary details of how I came to acquire them. I saw her write the word *infection* on a piece of paper along with all the rest of the information I had given her. Finally, she looked up and told me in a very warm yet fake tone that once I got settled into a room down at the hotel, I could expect one of the little bald doctors to come by my room as soon as one became available. She said that half the staff of doctors was moving through the rounds, and now that the number of people showing up had tapered off, the process would be moving much quicker. Just outside the door, there would be an escort to the hotel if I wanted to wait, which most people did. She assured me that I was safe. Oh, and one last thing, everything was going to be fine, and now if I would just continue down through the double doors at the end of the row, I would be escorted to the hotel for placement. I thanked the middle-aged black woman with no name and continued toward the next phase of orientation.

On the way down the line of tables, a large woman, to be nice about it, slammed her meaty hands on a table and screamed, "But they took my son! *My son!*" The equally enormous woman on the opposite end of the exchange did her best to politely calm her down. By then multiple people were on their way toward the hysterical woman. Two men who also looked like linebackers flanked her. Instead of grabbing her by the arms and dragging her into a padded cell like I expected, they simply put a hand on her shoulders. They spoke to her calmly, eventually bringing the spectacle down to a scene, down to just something, and then down to nothing in particular to see.

Mark waited in what was probably a smoking area before this happened. Concrete benches and decorative plant structures circled a wide, open area. He was in midconversation with Gladys and Barry Hornygeezer when I walked out of the building. The sun was nearly out of site. We'd be in the dark soon. The creeping worry for Katy and Jackie began to boil up again.

"What are we waiting for?" I asked the three of them. "I figured you guys would be halfway to a bedroom by now."

"Just waiting for the escort." Barry slid his hand into the back pocket of Gladys's jeans. "A shuttle just left. They said there would be another one in a minute or two."

"Barry and Gladys say they're up for a switch when Jackie and Katy make it back." Mark couldn't contain the giddy rising up in him. Barry blushed a little. Gladys tried to protest around her giggles. "I call Gladys."

"This one's all mine," Barry said. He kissed Gladys on the top of the head.

"It's good to see that people can still be happy."

"There's no point in being unhappy," Gladys said. "If I'm killed within the next twenty minutes by whatever's out there, it's not going to be the sad parts of my life that flash in front of my eyes. It's the joyful ones. Why not make that flash last a little longer? Postpone the inevitable just a little bit longer."

"Why not indeed, sweetheart?" Barry pulled her closer.

"I'm learning a lot from you guys," Mark said. "I hope we have a room sort of close by. Not sharing walls, of course. But close."

An extended golf cart pulled up. Sheets of metal had been welded onto the sides and front of it. One entire side was fixed on a hinge to swing open for people to move in and out.

"Where are the spikes and machine guns?" Mark asked the driver.

"These are strictly for transportation purposes," the driver said. "The ones with artillery are on patrol, cleaning the area for the walls."

"Well, shut me up," Mark said.

The golf cart strained to start up with all the extra weight, but in a matter of minutes, we reached the hotel.

Chapter 64

Generators kept the lobby of the hotel out of darkness. Mark and I allowed Barry and Gladys to go ahead of us.

"I just don't want to be around when those blue balls burst," Mark insisted.

The wall behind the front desk was taped off into three different sections, using blue tape, red tape, and green tape. Papers were stacked against the wall on a counter. The stack in the green section was almost nonexistent. The blue had a little more. The red section was the obvious majority. A young man between twenty and twenty-five waved me over.

"Hi there," he said. "I'm Devon. Did you make it here OK?"

"Hey, Devon. I'm alive, so I'd say so." That earned me a courtesy laugh.

"What's your name, sir?"

"Derrick."

"And last name? Or however you told them at the original check-in."

I told him all the same information from before and included the injuries I had.

"So what happened to your head?"

"I slept under a shelf at the last place we stayed and forgot that when I woke up. It's just a nick, I think."

"Well, let's hope so."

"One of the doctors says I could probably stand to get the stitches out."

"Already? You're a fast healer."

"I like to think of it as efficient, but that's fine, too."

"So about the checkup. You have a blue wristband, so that means, after all the people with green wristbands have seen the doctor—and don't worry, there aren't many—you will be in line for a visitation."

"Right," I said.

"We'll let everyone know when the doctors arrive for the second round. You'll see 'em. They're a bunch of little bald guys."

"Right."

"And they're going to get some information from you—what kind of place you lived in, what you used to do, probably even ask about your family—but you don't have to say anything if you don't want to."

"Right, so why do they have the doctors do it?"

"Well, they have an assistant so you have someone to talk to when the doctor is feelin' you up." He giggled. Actually giggled.

"Why didn't they already do that back there?"

"Because we know that after they get here, people don't wanna wait in line forever, so we tried to make a system to get everyone in and out and to a place to lie down. We thought that would be for the best. Then when they get their visitation, people can take as much time as they need and feel more comfortable."

"You guys have shit together here."

He leaned in as if to tell me a secret. "Well, I wouldn't curse, but, yeah."

"Just curious, does anyone want to leave?"

"Oh, people leave all the time," Devon said. "Sometimes people stay just long enough to sleep and skedaddle. Also, we may still have a couple rooms on the ground floor if your leg is bothering you. We don't have the elevators working because the backup generators only power the door locks and a few lights."

"Do you have anything on the fourth floor?"

"Let me check." Devon walked to the back counter and picked up a box that had a blue four scribbled across the short side. He giggled again. "We do have some vacancies. Take your pick. Looks like you'll have the floor to yourself for now."

"So ten is available?"

"Sure is."

"I'll take ten, then."

"All righty. Is there anything else I can do for you?"

"Not specifically," I said. "I am curious. How did the street get so clear around this area?"

"Oh, there are a number of police officers on top of the buildings making sure we clear them out. They're putting the walls up soon. They don't want any getting trapped in when they do."

"Is that right?"

"Sure is," he said. "Is there anything else I can help you with?"

"Do you have a list of the people who have been rescued?"

"I do. Are you missing someone in your party?"

"Yes, actually I am." I gave him the three names of people I was missing.

He walked back to the counter and picked up a yellow note pad. He scanned the names for about a minute, flipping pages over. "I'm really sorry, sir. I don't—Oh wait! I have a Jacqueline Feltcher. Is that right?"

"No," I said, steadying my heart again. "I appreciate you looking, though. I think I'm actually done here. Thanks for your help."

"Well, if you need anything, security men are wearing the safety vests that glow when you shine a light on them." He pointed to a tall, well-built man a little older than he was. His gaze lingered a little too long.

"OK, thanks," I said, walking away.

"Hey, man, what room you get?" Mark asked me.

Behind him a stir brewed between a man and a woman behind the counter. The woman was one of the Latina nationalities, and I honestly couldn't tell what race the man was. He looked like someone a company would hire to cover as many minorities in one person as possible. And bless her heart. She was giving it her best to defuse the situation. Mark and I watched the build.

"I'm going to laugh if he does something stupid." Mark grinned from ear to ear.

"He's not going to hit her or anything, is he?"

"No," Mark said in that of-course-not way everyone somehow knows.

"Are you kidding me?" The man's voice rose to an outside voice.

A pair of security guards made their way to the desk.

"You're telling me I have to walk up two flights of stairs after what I just went through? I bet if I were some lazy spic, you'd power up the generator for me."

"Hey!" Mark shouted.

"No, Mark, no." I tried holding him back.

The security guards grabbed the man by the arms and started talking him down.

"Get the fuck off me," the walking minority said.

Mark ripped away from me and made a beeline for the man. He tripped the bigger of the guards, who fell like a pallet of bricks, and pushed the smaller guard enough to send him into the next room. Mark grabbed the man by the head and slammed his face into the counter. The man recoiled so violently that one of his feet came off the ground, and the other was on the tip of his shoe. Mark grabbed him by his blue button-up and yanked him to his feet. The look on his face was a confusion of terror and disbelief. There would be a bruise on his cheek in a few hours. It was already forming.

"Look at me, you ignorant *fuck*," Mark began, shaking the man inches from his face. "We have all been through some shit. I've nearly lost my sister. My whole family is gone. Who do you think hasn't seen their share of this mess? *Who?*"

The man started to talk. Mark shook him silent.

"Shut up! The world has ended, you pile of cat shit, and I don't know how all of us made it out of the loony pool, especially you. This is a new time. We have a glorious opportunity to start everything over, and you're going to say some ignorant, racist shit like that? Fuck you. There is no more race. Do you understand? We're all just different shades of brown. We are all the same thing. Survivors. Do you get that? Huh? Do you? The only way close-minded shit like that lives on is if we bring it with us, and after everything I left behind, I refuse to bring that." Mark dropped the man.

"I—I'm sorry," the man said from the floor.

"Don't fucking apologize to me."

The man turned to the woman behind the counter.

"Don't apologize to her either." Mark walked back to where he was standing next to me. "Apologize to all of us for spreading that disease."

The man, in tears now, said, "I'm sorry."

"Will that ever happen again?" Mark asked from his place at the counter.

"It won't. I'm sorry."

"Goddamned right, it won't." The lobby of the hotel was a vacuum. Everyone stared. Mark turned to me. "What room did you say you got?"

"Oh, uh, what?"

"What room?"

"Oh, four ten."

"Shit, that's a lot of stairs," Mark said. "Does this hotel have a room four hundred?"

"Yes," the fat man behind the counter said. He was wearing a Hawaiian shirt, and that made me think of Barry. Despite his size, he looked nervous. I'd be willing to bet everyone in shouting distance looked the same way. I kept my eyes forward.

"OK." Mark took a moment to think. "Zero is probably on the end, two and four are together, six and eight, ten and twelve. I'll take four twelve, then."

"I will be right back." The man behind the counter walked to the box with the four.

"You OK?"

"Yeah," I said. "I'm just worried about Katy and your sister."

"Just give them time. We were in a car, remember that."

"It's getting dark."

"Tell you what. We go upstairs to see if there's a minibar then go look for them."

"Here you go," the man in the bright-blue Hawaiian shirt said. "Room four twelve. If you need anything, the security guards have on reflective vests in case the power goes out completely and we just have the lanterns. You can find the lanterns in your room."

"*Mahalo.*" Mark swept the card-key envelope off the counter.

"Is there anything else you need?" the man asked.

"Is there any way I could get a typewriter?"

"Are your eyes OK, sir?"

"Yeah," Mark said.

I couldn't see them, but I knew what color they were.

The man behind the counter blinked. Unsatisfied with the results, he rubbed his own eyes. "OK," he said suspiciously. "I will see if anyone knows where we can get one and will send it right up."

"Tanks, brudda," Mark said. Then to me, "Fourth floor it is." His eyes were brown.

We walked up the stairwell to the fourth floor.

Chapter 65

We stayed in our room long enough to light the LED lanterns. Room 410 of the Hilton was nothing special. Two beds, a loveseat, and a dresser with a television on top, and in the corner stood a run-of-the-mill hotel table set. I tried the lights, but nothing happened. I walked to the window and separated the thick layer of drapes and then the transparent layer. Outside the room a cluster of buildings blocked the majority of my vision of the city. There was nothing to do, so I went back into the hallway.

Mark spent a minute in the bathroom, and then we met back in the corridor outside the rooms.

"Sorry, man." Mark adjusted his clothes. "It kind of got away from me in there."

"That's nice."

As we walked to the entrance of the stairwell, the light came on, flickered, and went out again.

"We haven't seen that in a few days," I said.

"Is that good news?" Mark asked.

"Can't be too bad. The heater will kick on soon if nothing else."

Mark and I walked down the stairway, which was very crowded. People were finally making their homes on the second floor. We met some of our new neighbors in passing, telling them we would be back shortly. Maneuvering the stairwell through a crowd of people who didn't know what floor they were on as well as people mourning the loss of their family, and some both, proved to be a stressful affair. Mark accidentally bumped into a woman who immediately started crying. After defusing the situation similar to the way the guards had, Mark helped the woman find her room.

Eventually, we returned to the hotel lobby. People only trickled in by that time. The room wasn't as loud as before, but people talked freely as they waited in line. A golf cart pulled away from the front of the building just as Mark and I walked outside.

After a minute of seeing neither a screamer nor a golf cart, we decided to walk the block back to the Square. A distant scream broke through the open air and around the buildings. Then a pop, and then nothing.

"Shit. You think that's them?"

"I don't know, bro."

"Come on. Let's get one of those carts and go look for them."

We sprinted toward the Square. More of the black boxes lay in the street. Their reach had expanded up the street in an arc around the entrance to the Square. I noticed something strange about them then. The side facing away from the street wasn't made of plastic but electrical tape, and it bulged slightly as if ball bearings were inside. The boxes didn't sit flat either. They were angled upward slightly, and now the police officers were running cables to them. I didn't have a reason not to yet, but I didn't like those boxes.

I recognized Officer Jacobson.

"What's going on here?" I asked.

"You're Officer Phillips's little brother, right?"

"No, he is. What's with the boxes?"

"They're called the flash defense."

"What do they do exactly?"

"They have an electric trigger in them. When we press the levers, the trigger engages a flash, like from a camera, and then the air compressors inside fire the marbles or ball bearings, whichever it has inside, at an amazing speed. I've never seen them in action, but I can't wait. They showed us a video of the first time they used them during our training. It is very entertaining."

"Is it for entertainment or safety?"

"Luckily, both." He walked to the detonator. "All we have to do is flip this lever, and *click*. We got a slew of dead screamers."

"Whose fuckin' idea was that?" Mark chimed in.

"No goddamned idea, but it's fuckin' brilliant. I've seen something like these in movies," Jacobson said.

"Watch a lot of action movies, do ya?"

"Fuckin' A."

"By the way, what happened with the bus?" Mark asked.

"Busted the radiator on the way down," Jacobson said. "Thought it'd be easier to wire a van than to fix it, so I made a decision."

"Must have been going pretty fast," Mark said. "We were pushing it pretty hard after we got back on the road. We probably should've caught up to you, right?"

"No, sir," Jacobson said. There was a noticeable swell of pride in his posture. "I deactivated the governor this morning. If they were going to run at the car, I might as well not make them suffer."

"But you put—"

A scream ripped through the streets. It wasn't the insane homicidal scream we had grown accustomed to over the past few days. This one was the same one from the apartment complex before Jackson. A flash of pale skin swinging from a second-story window forced its way into my mind. I made to run, but Jacobson grabbed me.

"Don't be fuckin' crazy," he said.

Katy's was no longer the only scream. Two more went up. I couldn't see them, but they were only a few blocks away. More shrieking. Not from Katy. Jackie came into the street. She turned back, aiming her pistol. She fired multiple shots down the street in the direction she'd come from. Katy rounded the corner toward the Square. The mixed emotions I felt at the sight of her were nauseating.

I was relieved that she was alive, but at the same time, terror shook me because I knew what was behind her. Jackie fired more shots, dropped the gun, and ran. Katy was ahead of her, but with her training and stamina, Jackie caught up quickly. I absentmindedly stepped toward the rushing crowd.

"Stay right there," Jacobson said. "These things will kill you."

At first I thought only two or three of them followed Katy and Jackie, but then more came around the corner. Looking at the herd stampeding down the street behind them, I estimated at least forty screaming psychopaths. They ran at breakneck speed. For Jackie I didn't worry for a second. She rocketed down the sidewalk. Katy slowly fell behind.

"OK, boys, get ready," a voice called from behind us.

I hadn't heard the voice before. I assumed it belonged to the officer in charge.

"The first two is Maxwell. Jacobson, you got the second two, and if we need it, I'll finish them off. On my count."

I didn't know what to do, so I jumped and waved my hands over my head. Looking back, that probably only drew more attention to their direction. I wanted Katy to know I was there. I thought if she heard my voice, she would know that the running for her life was almost over. "Come on!" I called. "You can make it. Just run."

Mark joined in. "Move your ass, Jack."

Katy and Jackie drew closer. They were only a few hundred feet from the building. They closed in on the black boxes. At their speed they devoured the space between them and the safe zone. Another pop sounded, and somewhere in the middle of the herd, a head opened up and fell. The body tripped a few screamers behind it. A few more pops from above ended those screamers also.

"Come on, Katy," Mark said. "Get here so we can find a bowling alley."

"On my count." The voice from behind us was confident and authoritative. The man who possessed it imposed confidence in him.

Demanded it. "Three, two, one, *fire!*" The first round went up just as Jackie and Katy passed. A brilliant flash dominated the darkening street, lighting it as if the sun was out. The air compressors released with a loud, quick *ppsshh*. Metal balls flew down the street, cutting the number of screamers down to about ten. Then a second flash and *ppsshh* as Jackie and Katy passed the second row. There were only two screamers then. One looked just like every other teenage girl throwing an epic tantrum. The other was covered in metal debris.

Jackie cleared the next row. Katy made a soft, nearly inaudible whimper sound. She was scared. As she cleared the next row, the flash filled the street, but this one caught her in the periphery of her vision. I knew that was what happened because there were three shadows projected onto the side of the building across the street. Katy stumbled but caught herself before she fell.

"Whoa," I screamed to the officers behind me.

Another pop took out one of the screamers. The last one, the one I hit with the Lincoln, reached for Katy. It was only a foot away from the ends of her hair. Then a flash went off. It reflected in the handle of a pair of scissors. I saw Katy's face in the bright light. I heard the sound and saw the marbles obliterate the screamer. The sound of metal *tinka tinka tinked* on the concrete. Katy stopped running. The whimper in her voice continued. She looked at me. Her trembling hands went to her stomach. They came away red and wet. She looked down at her fingers. When her eyes came back to me, tears spilled down her cheeks.

Katy fell.

My feet couldn't take me to her fast enough. I ran past Jackie and fell to the ground beside Katy. I rolled her over onto her back with her head in my lap. I was shaking. She was crying. Behind me Mark screamed. I couldn't make out his words, but they didn't come closer, so I assumed it was for one of the little bald doctors.

"It hurts, Derrick." She put her wet hand on my neck. Her blood ran down my chest.

"It's OK," I said. "Someone's coming."

"Don't leave. Please." She trembled.

"I'm not leaving."

"You have to put pressure on the wound," Jackie said. I didn't see her, but I saw the towel dangle into view. "Katy, sweetie, can you help us do that?"

"Don't look away, Katy." I grabbed the towel and glanced down as I laid it across her stomach. There were two holes there and a gash on her leg. "Just look at me."

Jackie dropped down to the other side of her and helped with the towel.

"It hurts," Katy said again.

"Hey, you're going to be fine," I said. "Just going to slap some duct tape on there, and you're going to be good as new."

Katy smiled. She was weak. Soon she would be asleep. Mark stood over us as the doctors and the gurney arrived. My heart had shattered. Sadness wore me like a glove. Tears welled in my eyes. As I stared down at Katy through the blur with Jackie and Mark around us, I thought, *At least we're back together.*

"That motherfucker is laughing," Mark said.

The crowd spent no less than twenty minutes pulling Mark away from Jacobson. Mark left with a busted nose, but Jacobson left with a green wristband.

Chapter 66

I had her blood on my clothes. The doctors wouldn't allow me to watch as they patched her up. They didn't want me anywhere near the room. Under the circumstances they were afraid I would bang on the door wanting an update. So Mark and I escorted Jackie through the Square's arrival procedures. Doctors poked and prodded her as they had with Mark and me. I fidgeted the whole time. They were constantly telling me not to worry. Even the doctor chimed in at one point and assured me she was in good hands.

"How long did you say you've had these in?" the doctor asked Jackie about the stitches in her stomach.

"Got them three days ago."

"Really?" The doctor sounded amazed. "That's rather odd."

"How so?" she asked.

"Normally, a gunshot wound would have you down for days. These stitches are ready to come out."

"That can't be right," Jackie said.

"That's what I'm saying," the doctor said. He wrapped a blue bracelet around her wrist. "I can take them out here if you like. There's no longer a line, so I'm in no rush."

Once he took Jackie's out, he took mine out as well. He sent us away, and Jackie was told at the next part of the orientation process that she would move on to the police training.

"I'm already a police officer," she said.

"Oh, I know," the man behind the table said. "They want to make sure you're on the same page as everyone else on the team."

"They actually have their shit together here," I said, still impressed.

"We do require that you leave that behind, though." The man pointed to the gun clipped onto Jackie's belt. "Just in case. You can leave it with one of these gentlemen if you would like. I'm sure they don't mind keeping it warm for you."

Jackie took it off and held it behind her. I took it from her. Instead of walking down the hallway to the courtyard, she continued to a door behind the line of tables.

"We'll meet you in the lobby of the hotel," Mark told her. Then to me, "So what do you want to do until then?"

"I have to get to the hotel."

"Which one?"

"The one where Sarah is."

"Do you need me to come with you?"

"If you want to risk it. I don't mind going alone."

"I obviously can't let you do that." He clapped me on the shoulder. "If I did that, you'd be gone before we picked up Katy."

"How's your leg?"

"Why? We going to race?"

We took a lantern that hung on the outside wall of the Square as we left.

Chapter 67

Mark checked the clip in the gun before we entered the hotel, something I never would have thought to do. He added that he had no idea how to make sure it was full without dumping the bullets out. Luckily, Katy's dislike for artillery saved us the trouble of an empty weapon. The building was locked, but the front doors were glass, so really it wasn't. Mark found a brick and used it to unlock the doors. After we stepped through the shattered remains, we were ushered into darkness. We stood very still. Mark powered the lantern on its lowest setting. The bulb was small, as was the lantern itself, but even on low, it illuminated the lobby enough to see every inch of the room. We followed the sign's lead to the stairs. The door to the stairway was locked. After a few kicks, we gained entrance. The door flew open. Behind it stood a screamer. The light from the lantern glittered in its eyes as it charged. The report from the pistol boomed all the way up to the top floor. It felt like a full minute had passed before the echoes stopped.

We waited at the foot of the stairs for a scream, or footsteps, or anything. It dawned on me that it was the first one I had to put down myself.

"So I guess that makes the score one to one," Mark said.

"That was one, right?" A rush of adrenaline surged through me. Tears came forward.

"Yeah," he said with a hint of *no duh*. He held the lantern over the once-person. "Got him good. Katy wasn't kidding. You are a real shot."

"Got a football? I wasn't kidding either. I'm freakin' Ray Guy."

"Settle down." He leaned in for a closer look. "You could pierce someone's ear with that thing. Maybe you could start a new business, farm boy."

"I don't know if that's my thing."

"This guy's name was Hector."

"How do you know?"

"Name tag. Jesus Man, where are you from?" he asked the body. "The twenties?"

"Come on. Be respectful."

"Yeah, 'cause you're dead now, Hector."

The stairs circled around the entire interior of the shaft. The space between each flight allowed a view up the stairwell. I found myself checking the gap constantly for someone peeking his or her head over the edge. We rounded another flight, and I saw one—a black shadow of a head lying on the handrail barrier. Completely motionless, the head pointed in our direction. It rested on the body's laced fingers as though posing for a family portrait. I couldn't see the cheesy grin, just the outline of a head and the eye flickering in the glow of the lantern. The entrance to the fourth floor stood in the thing's background. I grabbed Mark and gestured toward it.

"The fuck does it want?" Mark said.

"I can't tell if it's alive or not."

"You got the gun, Annie Oakley. It's up to you."

"Let's see if it blinks."

We waited. After a minute or two, nothing happened.

"You see anything?" Mark asked.

"No."

"Well, I've blinked twice just looking at him. I think we're good."

"OK," I said. "Guards up."

We stepped closer to the head. With each stair the tap of rubber sole on concrete went up like a smoke signal through the shaft. When we stood on the fourth-floor landing, the man hanging over the stairwell barrier came into view. They had beaten him to death. His shirt had been ripped open. His back was so solidly bruised that Mark asked if it was a tattoo. His arms had been yanked through the space between the barrier and handrail. The swelling in his joint kept him stuck, hanging from his elbow. One leg rested on the ground. The stump of his right leg hung above a dark-red puddle.

"Dammit," Mark said.

"I'm going to find out if I can see anything under the door," I said, still fixed on the carnage.

A loud boom filled the shaft. Mark and I both jumped. From behind us a screamer pounded on the door in a fierce rage. The metal door barely muffled the screams. Fists on the door echoed all around.

"He's going to beat the thing down," I said. "We better come up with something."

Mark kneeled next to the hanging man. He held the lantern a little higher than where his waist would have been. "Open it, and stand way clear."

"You sure?"

"We gotta get in there. Just do it."

I stood where the door wouldn't cover me when it swung open. I didn't want to fight it off if whatever Mark planned didn't work. I twisted the knob, and the door flew open. A screamer charged the lantern. As it drew close enough to reach, Mark stood up. He used the screamer's full-on momentum to flip it up and over the railing down four stories to where Hector lay.

Before I could join Mark to see if it stayed down, a second screamer charged through the door. It struck him in the jaw. Mark's hat teetered on the back of his head. The screamer grabbed him by the throat, and his hat fell off completely. I whipped it in the back of the head with the gun. It didn't go down like the movies led me to believe it would. It turned to me, grabbed me by the throat with one hand, and laid into my abdomen with the other. The air in me evacuated. My vision pinholed. Then the hand was released. I sucked in air and watched Mark topple the thing over the barrier. It hit something on the way down.

"I don't think that was enough to do him in." Mark looked over the railing. "He's not moving, but keep the gun ready."

"I'm just going to sit here a second, if that's cool with you." I slid the pistol to him.

"You got it in the blood." He picked up the gun and shook it dry as he placed the cap back on its perch.

After a few motionless seconds of peering over the ledge, Mark was satisfied that the thing wasn't going to get back up. He sat next to me by the fourth-floor door. My vision came back to me as I sucked air.

"That was intense," he said.

"Well said." I laughed with the little bit of air I had in me.

"How do you know she's up here?"

"Remember the pictures I told you about?"

"Yeah, weirdo."

"And the number four ten?"

"Yeah." His voice became serious.

"I've seen it everywhere: the address of the theater, the bowling alley. The kid they thought I killed, he did this card trick once with Katy and once with me. The number showed up there both times. The truck we took to get back to the police station, the license tag was H41 0JM. The number was blinking on the screen of the television in the vision I saw. I think it's telling me where Sarah is. I know she's in this hotel. I was with her when she booked the room. That has to be her room number. The only thing that worries me at all is that shadow in the vision. I'm worried if she's holed up with one of those. Now that we're here, all the possibilities are fighting for attention."

A shriek came from down the hall. It sounded like a woman. Her feet beat on the carpet as the sprinted toward us.

"Turn that off," I said.

Mark got up and hurried to the lantern. The screamer tackled him as the stairwell went black. The lantern tumbled to the floor.

"Shit, bro!" Mark hung from the railing.

"What happened? What happened?"

"I'm hanging! It's on me."

"Shit, where are you?"

The thing shrieked again. Its voice cracked.

"Follow the sound of this bitch's voice."

"Is she hurting you?" My hands felt desperately along the floor for the lantern.

"She's got my leg. *Fuck, my leg.*"

"I found it!"

"Shoot her!"

The lantern on its highest setting flooded up and down the shaft and into the hallway. Another scream behind me. I lifted the lantern and pointed the pistol over the barrier. I took the woman out with one shot. I heard her fall all the way down.

"Fuck that bitch!" Mark started his climb back onto the good side of the barrier. "Help me up, bro."

I reached out. Something stopped me. Hands reached around my neck. I dropped the lantern and pistol. I couldn't think or breathe or call for help. I learned that we've been strangling people all wrong for millions of years. The screamer's fingers closed my windpipe. The pressure from his thumbs on the back of my neck was excruciating. If the thing wanted to strangle me, I would've been gone. Instead, the thing stepped on my pant leg and yanked my neck upward. It was trying to pull off my head. If I had been facing it when it grabbed me, the thing would have had a foot to step on, keeping me tethered to the ground. If I were facing the wrong way, the thing would have killed me. It stomped again, getting my heel. When it yanked again, my foot came free, and I went into the air. This sent the screamer into an all-out fit. He slung me from side to side. I hit the wall hard. He lifted me and slammed me on the floor. The light from the lantern shone bright in my eyes. I was off the floor again. The thing yanked on my neck. He stepped on my heel again and yanked. The thing grunted in outrage. Suddenly, the light was off the floor, and a deafening bang filled the stairwell. The thing released me as it fell lifeless to the concrete.

"Goddamn it," Mark exclaimed. "Pull your pants up, and let's get the fuck out of here."

He tossed me the gun and brought the lantern back to its lowest setting. We stepped into the hallway. The room immediately to our left was 436.

"Don't suppose we could ask them to come to us," Mark asked.

"I doubt it."

I called for Sarah…No answer.

I chalked that up to being on the opposite side of the floor from her room. There was another boom on the door next to us. Something was trying to get out of room 436.

"Jesus," Mark said. "Should we turn it off?"

"I don't think they can get out. The doors open inward."

"Let's just hurry."

We made our way down the corridor, passing rooms 436 through 421. As we did, all but one door banged until the light subsided from the cracks around the doorway. The hallway then split two ways. The sign on the wall had an arrow to the left guiding us to the vending machines, office, and elevators. An arrow to the right set us in the direction of the remaining rooms. The banging became much wilder. The walls mocked thunder. I could feel the vibrations coming from the doors as we passed.

"That's getting to me, man," Mark said. "I'm going to turn this off. We can just feel around until we get there. There's no one else here."

"That's fine. It's getting to me, too." It wasn't, but it was the kind of thing that I would feel bad about asking for, and I could understand how the noise would make him uneasy. Under normal circumstances I would have felt the same way. I had more on my mind, though. The hallway fell into darkness. We stood at 416.

In a matter of seconds, the banging and screaming stopped completely. We followed my hands around two more sets of rooms until I felt the 410 just to the left of a doorknob. I knocked. Nothing happened. I called her name. Nothing again. Suddenly, realization washed over me. I knew Mark stood behind me, but in the pitch black of that powerless hotel, I had never felt more alone in my entire life. I knew my wife was gone. I banged on the door, calling her name. I became frantic. Begging her to come to the door. I fell to my knees, crying. The sound of my fist grew weaker and weaker against the wood until I simply rested my open palm against it.

"Come on, man," Mark said, standing in the black. "We did what we had to do. Now we know." His arm cradled me and helped me to my feet.

I stood facing the door.

"You coming?" He had walked a few rooms away.

I kicked the door as hard as I could.

"The fuck, man? Don't do this. Nothing good is gonna come from you getting in there."

"Get the lantern ready." I slammed into it with all my body weight.

"For what?"

"When I tell you to, turn it on." I kicked it again.

"And then what?"

"I have to see her again. Just give me that, Mark. I came all this way. I just have to see her again."

"No, Derrick. You don't *have* to; you *want* to. Now come on, man. You don't need to do this." He had made his way back to my side now.

"Just give this to me. Did you get your moment with Khakis?"

There was no answer.

"Well, I'm not going to kick it down for you. My leg is busted."

I slammed into it again. Only black and faint tinnitus came to me.

"You know what you're going to have to do?"

"I'm aware." I kicked the door again. It gave a little. Just enough to give me hope. The tears had stopped now. I wiped my eyes clear. "One more time, and I should be in. Get ready to turn on the light."

"You have the gun ready?"

"I got it." The door let go. I pushed it open, but the security latch halted my attempt. "Fucking thing." I kicked the door. It gave a little. "Now." I rammed my full weight into the door again. It flew open. As it did, Mark followed me into the room with the lantern held over our heads so I could see.

He was right. Nothing good came from what I saw in that room.

Chapter 68

The room was a regular meat-and-potatoes hotel room—bathroom to the right, closet area with a safe to the left leading to a small, carpeted room with a king-sized bed. The empty cushioned hanger dangled on a rod to my left. On the floor lay a disheveled arrangement of scrubs, women's clothes, and lingerie. The carpet, which was a similar pattern to that of the theater, was wet, although the water was not running. The room smelled moldy. The power was out, so the only light before Mark and I broke open the door came from whatever filtered between the thick curtains. A lamp had been knocked over and lay between the bed and the door. The same happened to a stack of the medical books I bought Sarah. Her wedding band lay on the table across from the bed. The candy-cane picture frame lay on the ground. The glass was shattered, and there was no way to tell who was in that picture.

Of course I saw none of these things. I only saw my wife sitting at the foot of the bed, naked under the open hotel robe, and a younger blond woman standing behind her wearing a black thong and the black-and-green teddy I hadn't seen Sarah wear in years. For a moment I mistakenly thought there was a specific look in Sarah's eyes. I thought she wore the curious face of recognition, almost like she saw who I was. I said her name one more time. Instead of turning to a face of shock at my discovery of her affair, her face scrunched into rage. The two screamers shrieked. It was the last thing they would ever do.

Chapter 69

"Hey, man, are you all right? I know that had to be tough." The doors rattled. The sounds of fists violently pounding wood and outrageous screams filled the corridors. Their maniacal rage was somehow worse than anything I had witnessed so far. The light from the lantern shook in rhythm with our paces, but we weren't running just yet.

"Let's just get back to the hotel. I'll deal with it better when there's less to worry about."

A door splintered at the hinges as we passed.

"I'm not feeling good about this." Mark started limping.

"We can turn the light off if we want to rest."

He powered down the lantern. "Shouldn't they be stopping? Maybe it's just me being a little bitch in the dark, but it feels like they only got worse."

"Let's keep moving. They may still know we're here, and if that doesn't go away, we don't want them to see us. Just follow me until we get back to the exit."

My fingers met the frame of the emergency exit. The hinges behind us gave in the hallway. We closed the gateway to the stairwell. I heard more cracking wood, felt more footsteps on the carpet.

The stairs were surprisingly easy to maneuver. With hands on the railing, the only thing to do was spiral downward until the stairs ran out. I counted three full flights of steps and five down the fourth, which meant we were somewhere between the second and third floors when I heard something stirring below us. Something had gotten back up from its four-story fall.

"Did you hear that?"

"Yeah," Mark said. "Do you think we should turn on the light?"

"It's probably that or risk bumping into something down here."

"Got your piece?" he asked.

I pointed the gun in the direction of the sound. White filled the stairwell. I jumped, not at the sight of the screamer but at the extreme closeness of it. If my arms had been four inches longer, I would have touched it with the gun. It opened its mouth to scream. My finger squeezed the trigger without me telling it to do so.

"I really think I shit on myself," Mark said.

The fourth-floor emergency exit ruptured so violently that the door banged down the stairway to the ground level. The choir blared again. Mark and I took the stairs two at a time. He tripped over one of the bodies piled at the foot of the stairs. The lantern hit the floor. He picked it back up in stride. We slammed the door to the stairwell. It would only keep them in until one of them accidentally bumped into the lever hard enough to release the lock.

The entrance came into view as we crossed the hotel lobby. The light from the lantern reflected in the broken glass. A flock of screamers saw this and infiltrated our path. After an about-face, we crossed the lobby again. The door to the stairs flew open. Mark tried to kick it closed again. It only slowed them enough to let us pass. We passed a collection of office rooms and the gym, all of which held moving bodies inside glass walls. The path narrowed as we ran through a kitchen and then opened to a large dining room. There were screamers everywhere.

"Goddamn it," Mark said.

Fear devoured me. I looked my fate in the eyes. They surrounded us on all fronts. The hysterical shouts from the kitchen grew closer and closer. The things in the dining room joined the ones behind us. They advanced toward us. The screams became deafening. I stopped running. Mark dropped the lantern on the ground. The sound was maddening, but the sight was even worse. In that moment, right before they reached us, I thought of Katy. I thought of her laugh, her voice. I thought of the plume of air in the moonlight as she slept on the table, and the tattoo on her shoulder. My heart went out to her. I wanted to tell her I was sorry for dragging her here. Tell her I was sorry I couldn't keep going. I wanted to hold her hand and tell her she was going to make it and that I'd take her anywhere. For a second, with her in mind, the screams went away. I waited for the cruel hands to grip me. I watched their eyes as they rushed us. I felt a single finger on Ted's shirt.

Then everything stopped.

The screams were stifled, cut off in midyell. The light from the LED bulbs died. Mark didn't say a word. There was nothing to absorb, no sensory input stimulated. The only thing remaining was the hum of my heart. Finally, I remembered to breathe.

"Mark?"

No answer.

"Mark, what's happening?"

For a moment I thought I was dead. I thought they had taken me fast, without pain, until my arm brushed against Mark's. And when it did, a single green circle appeared before me. I knew the color well by then. Then another materialized no more than an inch away from the first. Then more at different depths sparked to life two by two. All around me the little circles came to life. The darkness of the dining room was so absolute, so pure, that I was the center of a universe of green stars. I looked to where Mark stood before the lantern died. His eyes were glowing green. Not glowing so much as becoming visible. The shine was so dull that even the whites of their eyes couldn't be seen. Their eyes looked like those of a cartoon character when the lights turned out. Even if I hadn't seen the green coloring of his eyes before, I would have known where Mark stood. Not just because his eyes were nearly a foot above most of the rest, but also because those little idiosyncrasies of the past few days allowed me to know Mark. I knew how he held himself, the way his face looked, even in the pitch black of the dining room. If Katy or Sarah was in the room, I would be able to pick their eyes out of the group as well. It was because of this that I knew exactly where Mark was without a doubt. Even when the voice coming from the crowd around me was not his, I was certain that whoever was talking to me used Mark's mouth to do it.

"Derrick."

Chapter 70

I didn't answer him. Soaking in the beauty surrounding me, I stood silent. The little green circles swayed back and forth with the imperfect stillness of their bodies. I sensed him moving, a harmless gesture—a wave of the arm. Then it stopped. A flame sparked to life in the palm of his upturned hand, and in that moment I could see the whites of their eyes. The flame floated to the ceiling, folding in on itself and disappearing, leaving behind the bare light in the palm of Mark's hand. The light was orange and flickered like a candle's flame, but it didn't come from anywhere. There was no flame, no bulb, nothing. It just was. And it only lit my face and part of Mark's. The light reached to the shoulders or torsos of a couple nearby screamers, but for the most part, the only thing visible in the room was the little green circles.

"Hello, Derrick."

"Hi," I said. The confusion was utterly paralyzing.

"Is it safe to assume you know that Mark is not the person talking to you right now?"

"It's a little obvious. Who are you?"

"A friend," the voice that wasn't Mark's said. "You probably know by now that I've been keeping an eye on you. Pretty closely."

I looked around at the green stars surrounding me. "I've noticed something, I'll admit."

"I need your help."

"With what? Who are you?"

The voice sighed. Whether from irritation, loss for words, boredom—I couldn't tell. Mark's eyes looked away for a moment and came back. "You see, a lot has been made of who I am. Most of it is skewed. Not necessarily wrong, just off. Let me ask you—what do you think has happened here? What is your take on the situation?"

"I don't know. Everyone is scared. I'm scared. I had to kill—" I choked back a sob.

"I know. It's fine. But what is this? What is happening to the world right now?"

One word came to mind like a freight train. "Apocalypse."

"OK." He snapped enthusiastically. When he did, his fingers covered whatever made the light. "That's a great place to start. I was hoping you'd say that, honestly. Not exactly right, but let's go from there. And if you don't mind, I'll stick to the religious version, because you were raised Baptist, and that's the easiest way I can connect it to actuality. In Revelation the apocalypse, loosely speaking, is brought on by the four horsemen. The first represents worldwide conquest. I think you can tell that Semmes isn't the only place affected by this. It's obviously a little more widespread. Managed to get everyone in on it. Well, most people. The second represents war. I feel like that speaks for itself. The third represents famine. Let me ask you another thing: you saw the cow that first day on your way to find Katy. Have you seen any more? What about a bird chirping? Or even a spider? A few cats, yes, but who would that feed?"

I couldn't speak. I just stared, mouth agape, up at the eyes.

"I hate to be the one to say this, but you're a vegetarian now. I am so sorry." He laughed at his little joke. The joy didn't just vacate him. It was sucked from him. "All those things are things that I've *done*. The fourth..." I heard him swallow. "That's who I *am*. But not just the man wearing a cloak and holding a blade. I don't just bring death. I create the lives I am forced to take."

"What?" I finally managed to say.

"Should I start over?"

"No. You—You're the reaper?"

"That's a bit of a caricature of who I was. I don't wear that stuff anymore. Besides, the scythe is a bit outdated. But as you grew up learning, the living creature on the ashen horse was called Death, and Hades followed him. But no. That's just a bit too dramatic. Nothing comes after this. I'm much more interested in the story of Noah than the end of times, you know? The rebirth. The renaissance. Starting over. That's so much more optimistic than the complete annihilation of everything on the planet. I don't want everything gone."

"Then what is all of this for?"

"Everyone still here has something I need to start over. Something I want to bring with us into the new world."

"Lee? All those people? They had something you needed? Why are they gone?"

"They are gone," he began. His voice rose to stop me. "Because you deserved that. You gave up everything because a stranger ruined a massive portion of your life, and that is the opposite of what mankind is designed for. And those people had a reason to die the way they did. Those people caused what you had to go through."

"Why didn't *you* stop it from happening then?"

"I can't stop free will. I couldn't stop it with the first two, and I can't stop it now. People are going to do what they want to do. And more importantly, they do what they *have* to do. Tell anyone not to do something they don't want to do, and they'll do it twice."

"Why get rid of everyone in the first place?"

"I'm trying to create heaven."

I didn't know what to say to that. The idea that heaven was a work in progress never crossed my mind. "Heaven isn't real?"

"Yes, heaven is real. It's real in the minds of everyone who be-lieves in it. Since before mankind came to be. No matter what level of intellect or communication, the one thing across the board, from ants to humans—anything possessing thought—is that there is a place of perfection. Somewhere out there, be it on another planet, another plane of existence, or an island in the Pacific, there is always the idea that somewhere along the line of existence, there is a place where souls or bodies or minds go where there is only happiness and peace. Although no matter how hard I try, I haven't been able to do it yet. I'm getting closer, though. People pray to God or ask Santa for presents under the pretense of being a good person. Even now people pray for safety. The problem is, if one prayer gets answered, another one doesn't. So I have to let free will decide what happens. And when free will is in charge, everyone can't be happy all the time. But you. You and this guy and Katy and Jackie. You found some-thing together. A way to look the end of the world in the face and laugh—a way, despite everything going against you, to be happy. You found a way to *make it work*. That's what I *need* to create heaven. Not jealousy or rage. I need happiness to live on through you and everyone who still lives."

We stopped talking. It felt like I really was in space, where sound doesn't travel. I noticed the tears in my eyes then. "Why Sarah?"

"You know exactly why Sarah. There's a reason I let you get to the fourth floor of this hotel. There's a reason for everything that has happened. For the same reason the ones spilling out of the hotel during the fire didn't go the opposite way and run you down. You didn't have to make it out of the barn. You needed closure, and I al-lowed you to have it because I need you."

"You need me for what?"

"You have to tell them."

"Why can't you do it?"

"Would you believe me if I told you I was Buddha reincarnat-ed? Or that I was Sandman? Or would you need someone who was already convinced of it to convince you? I need you to be Noah. I need you to help me start over."

"Why? Why are we even here? If it's so hard to make heaven, then why do it?"

"The same reason I'm here. Because we can. Because if reality will let us, then why don't we? If we can find perfect happiness, then why don't we?"

"What about the screamers?"

"How long do you think they will last with no nourishment? Using the energy they do, maybe another day or two. They'll fall down and cease to live just like the ones in this room will as soon as you and Mark leave."

"Why me?"

"Because someone has to."

"But I can't possibly tell everyone's story."

"You're not the only one. God, don't be so conceited. There are people all over the world I'm asking to do the very same thing."

"What if I don't want to do it?"

"How about I tell you what will happen if you do? If you do help me, these people around you will fall to the ground without any problems. I'll see to it that Katy is delivered to room four ten of your hotel, and you will be able to watch over her while you write down your version of this story. And when you're finished, you can do whatever you want, and I'll make sure you get to. If you choose not to tell your story, you won't leave this room."

"But I don't even know all of my story. I can't tell everything that happened at the theater."

"Then I'll step in. Whatever you don't know, I will fill in the gaps."

I looked down to where the light originated. The cut on Mark's hand had vanished completely. I asked, "Are you healing us?"

"No, but I could. You are the one doing that."

"How am I doing it?"

"There was once a time when everyone could do it. Even sync up minds the way the blind man on the roof of the apartment building could. But they used it to hurt each other. *He* used to hurt people with it. So I took it away. There's more to it than that. You will learn, though. Soon enough." Mark's hand curled into a ball, extinguishing the flickering orange light. The eyes went black. The thump of bodies falling to the floor reverberated in the open dining room. "Your typewriter is ready for you. I'll be around. And when you're finished, you can do whatever you want."

"Why have you been coming to me through Mark?"

"Because he's fun." That was all he said. I had to agree.

"Will Katy live?"

"With you there, she will. You'll have to get to her soon. The day is fleeting."

The color in Mark's eyes dimmed and then disappeared completely.

"The fuck was that, bro? Is he still in me? Oh *God!*"

"Let's go find your sister. Maybe we can see Katy now."

PART 6
THE END

The anchor drops. Just as the soles of our shoes meet land, it begins to rain.

Chapter 71

The walls are up now. For what, I don't know. I haven't seen one of them moving in days. The power is restored to its former glory, currently heating the room in which I sit with a dwindling supply of paper and ink ribbons. The old typewriter waited for me when I returned to the room that night.

They moved Katy into the hotel. I refused to let her stay anywhere but room 410. There were no hospital rooms anyway, so they left me in charge of giving her something for the pain. The first day, I didn't leave her side. The little bald doctors and their assistants came to get any information I had for Katy—I had almost none whatsoever—and me. This time I didn't lie. I didn't feel the need to. They left her with an IV drip, a green bracelet, and a promise that they would be back soon.

Later that night, I held Katy's hand, wanting to be there when she woke up. She opened her eyes in a morphine-induced stupor.

"Where am I?"

"You're safe. You don't have to worry about a thing."

"I don't like it here. Let's go away."

I laughed. "Where do you want to go?"

"I wanted to go to the beach."

"Oh yeah? The Gulf is within walking distance."

"No-o-o." Her accent changed the one-syllable word into a drawn out *nawoo*. "I want a real beach. A California beach. Malibu, son." She giggled at herself. A little drool glazed her lip. She fell asleep as I used the sleeve of her hospital gown to wipe away the spittle. Then she was out for a while. I wanted to see the damage so I could gauge how quickly she healed if I didn't leave her side. She lay on her back. As if hearing my thoughts, she raised her arms, and the gown slid upward, revealing a white bandage with two tiny red circles in the center between a pair of plain white panties and the tail of her gown. The area around the bandage was a dark-purple bruise. It looked pretty bad.

My thoughts were cut off by a loud thump on the ceiling. No one had been placed on the fifth floor yet, but I knew who it was. Whoever, or whatever, had taken over Mark was telling me to get the lead out. I stood from the side of the bed and sat down at the table.

Chapter 72

The next day Katy told me about a weird dream she had where we planned to run away together to a place on the beach. She was able to sit up by herself. I asked her if she needed anything for pain or to eat. She was asleep before she could answer. She talked a lot during the brief time she was bedridden. Mostly she slept.

Jackie and Mark made time to visit, sometimes alone but mostly together. Mark even met a family he knew from a few years back, and he brought them by once. The little girl reminded me of Gabriela, sweet and bashful. I'd never felt more normal and like it was supposed to be this way than when they came together. Twice we explained to Katy that the wound was a simple through and through and that she lost a lot of blood. The pain-killers were still running the show the first day, but by the second day, we told her she was flying solo.

Two days ago Katy stood up, groggy from the medicine. Her legs threatened to give out with every step. She rolled her IV bag on its metal pole across the room to where I sat. She kissed me gently on the corner of my mouth. "Thank you," she said. She backed all the way to the bed so I wouldn't see through the opening in the gown.

Most of the days writing this I spent with Mark looking over my shoulder, helping when I needed it, correcting when I didn't capture his true essence. A lot of the time, we stared at the blank paper waving in the breeze of the air conditioner, daring us to make the wrong move, until a thump would come from overhead. More often than not, Mark would say something to the effect of "That's not very important. I wasn't there for that." I kept it in anyway. We recounted every possible moment together until we laughed so hard it made Katy stir in the bed, and then we laughed hysterically without making a sound. We always laugh the hardest when we can't laugh our loudest.

Jackie cooks for us most nights. That may be a glorified way of saying she bakes potatoes, but she's happy to do it. She works for the city—as a police officer, if that can be believed. I think regardless of what happens next, Jackie is going to stay in New Orleans. She's happy here. I think we all are now that the screamers are dying off, not that I ever thought of myself as an unhappy person. Since settling down here after everything that happened, I can't stop thinking of how lucky we are that we weren't broken along the way, and that we wound up together.

Chapter 73

This is the last piece of paper I have—last ink ribbon, too. What a coincidence, right? Now that this is done, I'm not sure what we'll do. I wonder what I looked like with green eyes. Katy is up and walking around with no problems. She removed the IV and stitches herself, making Jackie and me take out the ones from her back. She talks a lot about leaving, even now that she's sober. I like the idea of going out West. Mark will probably come. He's said on multiple occasions that once this is done, we can go anywhere we want. He has mentioned Phoenix nearly every day since settling down. Jackie will stay, though. I can't tell if that's our free will or if it is whatever entity took over Mark nudging us in the direction of leaving. Now that this is over, the desire to leave is incredibly powerful. I don't know where Katy and I will go. Maybe we will run away to that place on the beach. Somewhere quiet. Somewhere we could always hear the ocean. And a lot less screaming. It'd take a lot of hot-wiring. A lot of gas. But we have a lot of time. An actor once said that the best part of living is not knowing what's next. "Delicious ambiguity," I believe is how she put it. Seems like a good place to start to me. I don't know.

But we'll make it.